MIDNIGHT

A WALKING SHADOWS NOVEL

MIDNIGHT

BRENDEN CARLSON

DUNDURN
PRESS

Publisher: Scott Fraser | Acquiring editor: Rachel Spence | Editor: Catharine Chen
Cover design and illustration: Sophie Paas-Lang
Printer: Marquis Book Printing Inc.

Library and Archives Canada Cataloguing in Publication

Title: Midnight / Brenden Carlson.
Names: Carlson, Brenden, author.
Description: Series statement: A walking shadows novel ; 2
Identifiers: Canadiana (print) 20210155124 | Canadiana (ebook) 20210155205 | ISBN 9781459745827 (softcover) | ISBN 9781459745834 (PDF) | ISBN 9781459745841 (EPUB)
Classification: LCC PS8605.A7547 M53 2021 | DDC C813/.6—dc23

We acknowledge the support of the Canada Council for the Arts and the Ontario Arts Council for our publishing program. We also acknowledge the financial support of the Government of Ontario, through the Ontario Book Publishing Tax Credit and Ontario Creates, and the Government of Canada.

Dundurn Press
1382 Queen Street East
Toronto, Ontario, Canada M4L 1C9
dundurn.com, @dundurnpress 𝕏 f ⬚

For Cindy and Brian:
I'm sorry you two didn't get to read this.

We are what we pretend to be,
so we must be careful about what
we pretend to be.
— Kurt Vonnegut, *Mother Night*

CHAPTER 1

GODDAMN IT. NOT AGAIN.

I was outside the warehouse in the Meatpacking District. A bunch of boys in blue were stacked up beside the main entrance. Paddy Sinclair, my first partner, my old war buddy, the closest thing I've got to a best friend, led the pack with rifle in hand. Even before a raid he had to side-sweep his hair.

"Ready, El?"

I groaned. "No."

"All right, moving in on your go."

I shut my eyes, trying with all my might to melt the scene, willing something else to appear instead.

Opening the metal double doors onto the warehouse floor revealed a battlefield of mud and blood and shit. Hell on earth, eliciting whistles from NCOs and artillery alike.

No. Something else, anything else. A change for once.

Then I saw my old police cruiser and the Lower East Side Diner behind me.

Yeah, this one will do. Better times. Well, as good as they'll get.

I had just popped into the diner to grab a Stuffed Pig: a breakfast sausage wrapped in a pancake, a new favourite snack of mine after seeing Commissioner Robins order one a few weeks back. An hour after the six o'clock shut-off, the Plate above me was calm, with the last rays of daylight gleaming off its eastern towers. The diner was just at the edge of the Plate, which granted some of the buildings here a few hundred yards of sunlight and fresh air without the monolithic turd looming over them. A penny slammed against the hood of my cruiser, leaving a dent as large as my thumb and reminding me of the assholes living up top. Goddamn Upper City folk.

As I got behind the wheel of my police cruiser, the motion shook a glob of syrup loose from my treat, flinging it onto the seat.

"Ah, shit." I grabbed a napkin out of my glovebox, moving the spare .38 in there, to clean the stain.

"Really?" the rusty Automatic next to me remarked. Glowing blue eyes, a gutted, wire-filled left arm, and shaggy plain clothes. My last partner.

"Hey, if you were human, you'd love eating these." I bit into the Stuffed Pig, looking at the machine as it groaned.

"If I were human, I would enjoy much better things than eating one of those."

"Oh yeah?" I swallowed the mouthful of dough and pork, feeling my energy shoot through the roof. "What would you rather do?"

"Honestly?" My partner looked out the window and smirked, at least as much as a machine could. "I'd want to ride around in a Manual. Give me a big ol' robot, some 20mm ammunition, and let me have a day of it. The Lower City would be clean in a few hours."

I laughed as I bit into the snack again. "You sound like a friend of mine."

"A pretty sensible friend, sounds like. Who is he?"

"Paddy's brother, Eddy. He's not around anymore."

"What was he like?"

"He was a man who liked his cars and his giant fucking robots."

"No wonder me and Paddy get along so well. And me and you. I must be a half-decent replacement."

Finished my snack, I got the car started up. "Don't tell him that, he might get upset."

"And why aren't you upset?"

"Because, like you said, you're a half-decent replacement." I smirked. "It's like I get to ride with Paddy's brother every day."

"Har har. Let's get a move on. Don't want to be late for the car show. I heard they've got some of those European models" — the Blue-eye raised its rudimentary eyebrows suggestively — "if you get what I'm saying."

"You don't even know what you're insinuating," I responded, pulling the car out of the parking spot. "You just like giving the eyebrows because Paddy taught you that."

"Yeah, fair, I got no idea what it means." My partner laughed and shrugged. "Anyway, get a move on, Roche! I'll kill you if I miss this."

I turned the car over and did as he said. "No problem, James. Fucking Blue-eyes ..."

———

Back to the land of the living. I woke up in a city that can't sleep. On a Tuesday.

It was definitely past shut-off time; the regular lamp-based Platelight had been replaced by blinking warning lights, indicating that the turbines above were open, revealing starlight and the full moon through their semicircular openings. A warm draft drifted down into the Lower City, and the lights reflected off my window, alerting me to my own tardiness. My watch told me it was nine at night. Staying under the Plate mixed up night and day too much. A Rotorbird screamed past my apartment, the noise rattling the walls and windows enough to fully shake the sleep off of me. Sleep was a commodity I enjoyed in short bursts, so I'd forced the habit of taking every moment I could in my bed.

As I sat up, my body went through its automatic motions: I grasped a cigarette and clenched it between my lips. I looked at the lighter in my hands as I lit the dart. My last one had broken, but thankfully my "employer" had gotten me a new one, no charge. The engraved eye on the base of the lighter looked right through me. I placed it face down on the table. I didn't need to be more creeped out than I already was.

Outside my bedroom window the Plate was hanging low, the snow that drifted through the turbines caressing the buildings and street below. My building creaked, bearing the weight of the world on its shoulders as one of the Control Points leading right up to the Upper City above. Down below, traffic was congested all over, judging by the horns and sirens, but otherwise it was a night like any other in the Lower City. I stood, put on some slacks, and walked to the bathroom to begin my ritual: I shaved as best I could, splashed water on my face, then went to the kitchen for coffee.

The calendar on the wall said December 6, 1933. A month before my birthday. And nearly a month after the Cop Killer case, with nothing to show for it besides the Lower City precincts being hounded daily for any information on the person responsible for cracking FBI Agent Edgar Masters's head in. Who knows whether they were actually in the dark or if they were trying to give off false ignorance. If it was the latter, they must have been as pissed as they were scared after Masters showed up as a bloody smear. That was what you got for trying to muscle in on the Iron Hands.

With the coffee done, I got the rest of my outfit on, along with my coat, and went downstairs to get some breakfast. The elevator, I was surprised to see, was manned by a Blue-eye liftbot in a red bellboy outfit. I snickered, leaned against the back wall, and called for the ground floor. The machine unenthusiastically depressed the bottom-left button.

I cleared my throat. "So, they're hiring Blue-eyes again, huh? I thought with Second Prohibition ..."

"Last Greenie kept breaking the buttons. After all, not like they can think for themselves," it said in a flanging voice, shifting uncomfortably in its restrictive and, quite frankly, ridiculous clothing. "Seems people are starting to remember that there's a reason Blue-eyes are Blue-eyed: they can actually do their jobs."

"Ah, you must be happy, then." I gave a stiff smile. "More job opportunities than just GE or garbage collection, eh? Do you get to press the buttons in the executive elevator to the Upper City?"

The machine gave a deadpan stare, as only a mouthless, seemingly emotionless machine could. "Any more questions?"

"'Sir'?" I finished for it.

"Don't push me."

I exited the elevator and went through the lobby. Outside, the old Cossack Yuri was at his cart plopping new hot dogs on the grill for the nightshift crews as they came by for their hand-held dinners. He broke into a little dance when he saw me approach.

"Detective!" he said, getting a dog ready for me. "Another late night?"

"Yeah, I run best at this time."

"Ah, and you need fuel for adventures!" He handed me the dog, and I dropped him a tip.

"Do you have anywhere warm to go to, Yuri? I hope you're not out here all night." He was a short, chubby man, but I thought maybe his cheeks looked a little less full than usual.

"*Nyet*, I stay in lobby of building at night. Security guard is nice, let me rest on couches. Good people. Like you!"

"I'm not good people," I chuckled. "You ever need a place to stay, let me know. I owe you that much."

"You give me business. I owe you much more! Good evening, Mr. Roche!"

I concluded our interaction with a wave and was soon leaning against the black Packard, a rental from a friend of mine who was looking after my car. I didn't want to be spotted driving a vehicle with a broken window and dozens of bullet holes in it. Plus, I still needed to lie low after my last endeavour, and my Talbot wasn't exactly subtle.

I lit a fresh cigarette and gazed up at the Plate, the enormous steel slab separating the elites of the Upper City from the rest of us down below. It blocked out natural light twenty-two hours a day and literally sat on the Lower City — on top of the all-powerful and well-protected Control Point buildings, of which my apartment building was one — a constant reminder that we were the have-nots. For now the plate's borders ended at the edge of Midtown, but expansion plans would have it stretch from Battery Park to Yorkville. That was the plan, anyway. The prospect of covering Central Park would probably ruffle too many feathers.

I spotted an Automatic clad in black approaching, looking quite chipper despite the horrible temperature. I couldn't believe it still walked here every night from Stuyvesant, crazy bastard. I needed to get it a car.

"Detective," my partner, Allen Erzly, greeted me.

"Constable." I grinned saying that. "Looking sharp, as always."

"I do try, Detective."

Hard to believe it had caught on so quickly to idioms and metaphors and slang. A month ago, when we'd first met, it had been serious as hell and had a head as thick as concrete. Now it'd smartened up. I still got goosebumps sometimes, seeing its realistic facial movements.

"You haven't come by the precinct in a while," Allen noted.

"No, I have not." *Oh boy, it's started.*

"I suspect that is because you've been busy screening the many calls you've been receiving. You screen them every night we're together. And you always hang up unless it's Sergeant Sinclair or Commissioner Robins."

Perceptive as ever, Al. "Well, some of the cops who can't be bothered to do their jobs have been giving away my phone number to civilians, expecting me to be their magic cure-all."

"Have they done this before?"

"It happens every few months, until I tell them to cut it out. Then it starts back up again."

"That does explain your terse tone when answering the phone …" It was getting more observant, and snarkier. "Nevertheless, the 5th Precinct hasn't asked for your assistance with anything for the past month or so now, yes?"

"Yes …"

"Therefore, you should be free tonight to fulfill a civilian Night Call. Seeing as the other precincts currently have no need for you."

I groaned. "Allen …"

"I believe you need to work on your people skills."

I tried to keep my focus on the Plate above me. "Is that a fact?"

"And it might help you feel you're making a difference in this city."

"I *am* making a difference," I snapped back. "And saving a kitten out of a tree isn't going to help save this city."

"But it could instill hope."

"People don't need hope, people need a solution."

Allen paused for a moment before responding. "People need hope to inspire them to find solutions of their own. And they won't feel hopeful if the only thing they get from your end of the line is a dial tone."

Dealing with this machine would be the end of me. How many nights had I been parading around with Allen, zooming to different bars under the guise of doing work? No doubt it had caught on by now … which left me in a bind. What other work could I do that didn't relate to making bodies? The Eye had been uncharacteristically quiet recently. Then again, that might have something to do with my not returning her calls.

"Fine." Hearing me say this, Allen perked up, no doubt thinking it had broken through my tough exterior. "One."

"One call, and then another if you're feeling it."

"One call. I choose which."

It looked at me doubtfully. "I hope this isn't an excuse for you to screen calls and run out my clock. You know I don't tire easily."

Smart bastard. Too smart for its own good. That would get it killed one day. Or me. Or the both of us.

I snickered. "You said it yourself, you ain't a regular Automatic. You'll get tired eventually."

"Don't call me that!"

I slammed the phone down. I was sitting in my favourite chair next to the phone, and Allen sat on the couch across from me like a therapist. It gave me a look that had a near-permanent home on its face: disappointment.

"What?" I spat out.

"That is the sixth call you've declined, Detective. If I didn't know any better, I would say you were trying to avoid holding up your end of the bargain."

"It isn't like that. These folks call for every reason: cat in a tree, son out too late, husband won't stop hanging with his buddies at the speakeasy. I'm not here to be an errand boy, I'm here to solve issues. City-sized issues. If you want to be an errand boy, go out and be my guest. Until I get a call worth my time, I'm staying here."

Allen stood up and paced around my apartment, looking out the window at the street below. The floodlights on the Plate had begun to shine, making up for the extreme loss of visibility thanks to the heavy snowfall coming in. Hell, I might end up celebrating New Year's holed up in this place, stuck under ten feet of snow by January.

"What do they call you that you dislike so much?" Allen asked.

"Something stupid. 'Nightcaller' or something." The last five people had called me that.

"Fitting name, you must admit."

But the Eye, leader of the Iron Hands, had already given me a nickname. I was no Nightcaller — I was *the* Iron Hand, though that wasn't something I'd call myself in public. Given the stories they spread about themselves, I wasn't sure how many people outside the 5th Precinct and the other crime families considered the Iron Hands a real organization, as opposed to the bogeyman.

"Do you dislike people so much?" Allen asked, when I didn't respond.

"No, no, I want to help protect people," I said, and Allen's face relaxed. "But it's best if the things I do stay under the radar, and if only cops hire me to deal with Night Calls. I don't want every Tom, Dick, and Harry begging me for help."

"But if our previous case was any indication, you're already quite well known — not just to the police, but to all the criminal cartels, as well. Wouldn't you say?"

I got worried for a second that he was getting at something, but it was an innocent question. Allen was smart, but it didn't know about me and the Iron Hands. Not yet.

"It's different with civilians, Allen. It would cramp my style if everyone knew about me and what I do. Plus, people stress me out."

I almost fell out of my chair when the phone rang, bouncing its way to the edge of the glass table before I grasped it and held the receiver to my ear. The laboured breathing of the person on the other end came through. From just that, I guessed that whoever was calling me was elderly, smoked, and didn't have much time left.

"Hello?" A woman's voice. She sounded distraught, but calm, like she'd just smoked a pack in order to get herself down to a conversable level. "Is ... is this the man who takes jobs the police don't?"

"Maybe," I stated. Allen narrowed its eyes. I put my hand over the receiver and pulled it away from my mouth. "What, Allen?"

"Answer her properly."

The woman was still struggling to say something, making noises of hesitation. I interrupted her before she short-circuited on the other end.

"What's the issue?"

"My … my son, he disappeared. He was visiting me for a quick moment — he comes over once a month to check up on me, bring me scratch cards and food. He left to grab something from his car, but he never returned. I looked outside, and his car was gone. And he would never run out on me."

"Well, ma'am, there's a first time for everything. I'm sure you'll see him next month, as usual —"

"Please, I know he's in trouble. Call it a … a mother's intuition, but my son needs help, and if the police won't look, I need someone who will."

The police won't look — meaning they'd been paid off by the Mob in the area. The Iron Hands? No, they didn't do that, not anymore. Last I'd checked, the only people who pulled poor saps off the street were junkies needing a ransom to get high, but they'd never steal a car. I had to admit, I was intrigued. That, combined with the look Allen was giving me, made me decide to accept the call.

"Where?"

"Where he could be, I don't even — oh, you mean … The apartment building on the corner of Park Avenue and East 31st Street."

Kips Bay. "Ten minutes." I slammed the phone down, stood, and grabbed my coat. Allen jogged after me, no doubt curious as to why I'd accepted it so quickly, so I filled it in.

"It's in Kips Bay. Kips fucking Bay is a shithole and a breeding ground for fights. I forgot they've been pulling people off the streets in Kips to use as meat shields during raids, which means that lady's son is in a bad position. Lord knows they wouldn't kidnap people from any other neighbourhood."

"If I didn't know you any better, Detective Roche, I might think that you cared about this young man's life."

"No one deserves to get manhandled by the Maranzano Mob, Allen, and I'll be the one to hammer that in. Grab your gun."

I pulled my Diamondback from its holster and popped it open to check the cylinder. Fully loaded with seven rounds, and more in my pockets. Allen pulled out its 1911, the one it was borrowing from Commissioner Robins. I turned, swung the door open, and began walking down the hall. When I glanced back, I realized that Allen wasn't following me. It was still standing in the doorway, looking at its gun as if it had just been pulled off a corpse. It must be stuck in a bad memory; it had used that gun to take its first life.

I walked back and grabbed the 1911 to ensure Allen didn't jerk the trigger back in surprise as it was shaken from its daydreams.

"Allen, we good?"

"Yes, I apologize, Detective. Let's go." It holstered the gun, following behind me as my apartment door slammed shut.

A lot had happened in the past month. Maranzano was getting greedy; he'd started moving more of his forces into Gramercy from Kips. The Iron Hands were quiet, which was always a bad thing, and the distinct lack of legitimate Night Calls had been eating at me. Whatever I was about to find saving this kid's life, I doubted it would be good.

I'd told the old woman we'd be there in ten minutes, which meant I had a schedule to keep, for once.

═══

Allen drove, getting us to the building in seven minutes flat. We rolled up to the apartment complex and parked in front of the entrance. The streets were dead quiet for a change. It was an odd time, just after dusk; the city had an uneasiness, like the calm before a storm.

The view out the window gave me all the insight needed about the area: it was cramped, dingy, looked far older than it actually was, and had too many crevices and cracks to count. The alleys could be hiding Brunos, junkies, or victims — three very good reasons to stick to the main road. The snow on the street was untouched, pristine, retaining everything that pressed into it like a fingerprint.

The few yards of snowy street in front of me held a pair of tire tracks, confirming that a car — possibly Jeremy's — had indeed been here, but was now gone.

There was also a single set of footprints leading to and from the front of the apartment building.

"Ready to roll?" I asked Allen.

The machine was fiddling with its gun, making sure everything was in working order. "Yes."

"Good, let's get the info we need and move quick. I don't want to wait around for this kid's corpse to show up in the newspaper."

We stepped out and headed to the apartment entrance. The lobby was illuminated by a single dangling lightbulb. Behind the glass doors stood a small old woman biting her nails, tapping her foot sporadically — a nervous wreck. She was short with a bent back, puffy grey hair, and eyes that I could tell would burn a hole in your heart if you even thought about disrespecting her. In contrast, the building she stood in looked like the place where hoodlums lived, not defenceless old women.

"Oh, Mr. Nightcaller, thank you for coming," she said as I opened the door. I rolled my eyes, but Allen cleared its throat, snapping me back to attention. "My son, Jeremy, he's done nothing wrong in his life. He's an accountant and he visits me often, brings me a meal each time he visits. Speaking of which, would you two like something to eat? You must be famished at this time of night."

I peered over at Allen, who took the lead. "We would love that, ma'am."

Minutes later, we were in her rinky-dink apartment on the second floor. Allen and the woman sat at a tiny table fit for a single occupant while I leaned against a nearby door frame, inspecting the place. The wallpaper was intact behind hanging pictures of her now adult kids. It was also surprisingly clean. Her son must come over to help her with that. *Good kid, better than I ever was.*

I peered through the window adjacent to the small table. From here, she had a clear view of the street below, but given her age, she could be excused from missing a scuffle, if one had taken place.

Allen was busy stuffing itself with beef stew. I had decided to forego the meal; she'd need the food if her boy was going to be out of commission for a while. She didn't seem to notice Allen was eating, preoccupied as she was.

"Could you tell us what happened, ma'am?" Allen asked.

"Oh, it was terrible. He brought me the stew and told me he had a present for me, something he had been working on for a while. He's such a talented painter, I wonder why he never pursued it. Anyway, I waited for what seemed like forever, and when I looked down, he was gone. The tire tracks were all I saw. I called the police, and they said he must have run off. I pleaded and I begged them for any kind of help, and finally they gave me your phone number."

And here I thought the 5th was trying to be careful when giving my number out. It seemed like almost every precinct in the Lower City was pointing people in my direction. *Come on, people.*

"How long ago was this?" Allen inquired.

"Maybe two hours ago? Took forever to speak to the police."

"What kind of car does he have?" I piped up. The old woman turned around in her seat to face me.

"Oh, an old one, that's for sure. A Model T, I believe. He did love that car so very much. He wanted to buy me one, but I refused, told him to save his money. I wouldn't be able to drive it, anyhow."

They hadn't been after the car. Her son must have had something valuable inside it. But if it had been something for this old dame, it couldn't have been anything terribly expensive. That led me back to my initial assumption: they'd needed *him*. To what end was the question.

"You have a picture?" I asked. "Of Jeremy, I mean."

The old woman stood, went over to a nearby frame, and handed me a picture of her son. It was his graduation, class of 1922, Cornell University. That would have been my alma mater, had I stayed. Jeremy was lean, smart-looking, with a head of black hair and a square face. We'd need this photo to identify the guy. Or the body.

"Please bring him back safe. Please find him," she begged.

I nodded. "I'll do my damnedest."

I signalled to Allen to follow me out. We needed a better look at the scene. It spoke some encouraging words to the old woman, and then we departed through the decrepit apartment back downstairs.

The tire tracks in the snow were interesting. Judging by how prominent they were, the vehicle must have been carrying something heavy. The tracks led eastward. The car could have been dumped at the docks. Perhaps driven away by someone extra weighty? Jeremy's location was much harder to predict.

Allen kneeled beside me to inspect the tracks, breaking my train of thought. "Heavy-set. Must have been carrying something big."

"I thought the same thing."

"Then we have a lead. Eastward it is."

It got up and started off in the direction the car had gone, but I stopped it.

"No, Allen. The car is useless to them. We need to track the person. The car they would have just dumped in the bay. But since there are no footprints ... Wait a minute."

"What?"

"The only footprints on this street are ours and the kid's, and his are obvious here. The street is clean, as well. So where did the people who kidnapped him come from?"

Allen was perplexed. "I'm ... not sure."

"I don't think this is Maranzano's doing," I stated.

"I concur, Detective. In studying the rise in Mafia activity detailed in the 5th's reports, I've noticed the Maranzano Mob seems to be focusing its efforts outside of direct confrontation, on the south and west sides of Manhattan, away from their main areas of operation. You know from previous experience with them that kidnapping is one of their methods. But given the lack of, well, evidence that anyone was here, we must be careful assuming who is responsible."

"Right. That leaves us with street junkies who could've mugged and killed him, but it makes no sense that they took his car, since they can barely drive hopped up on the shit they get from their dealers. Plus, no footprints. No regular human could just appear out of thin air … which means it was most likely an Automatic that took him."

"Do you know any Automatics that leave no trace?"

"I know of one, but I sincerely doubt it's the same machine …"

I looked at the old woman's building. The walls were made of crumbling brick, plenty of holes for little critters to hide in, and plenty of handholds for something to climb up and leap at the car from. I hoped it wasn't the machine I thought it was.

"Since Maranzano doesn't like using Automatics outside of straight-up hits, that leaves the Iron Hands," I finished.

"And what do they do to people they kidnap from the streets?"

"Leave them in halfway houses. They call them the 'less than dead,' because people search for corpses, but not for junkies. There's a house a few blocks east of here that keeps getting raided for druggies." I snapped my fingers and Allen threw my keys. "Let's narrow down this search, Officer Erzly."

"Of course, Detective." Allen smiled as it jumped into the passenger seat.

I turned the key in the ignition, but the engine failed to catch. I turned it again. Still nothing.

The hairs at the back of my neck spiked. I turned swiftly to Allen, who was still climbing in, and gave it a kick across the central console, forcing it out of the car before diving out of my side. Hands covering my head to protect my eardrums, I waited for the explosion.

Moments passed, and nothing.

The car was intact, I was alive, and it was still freezing.

Allen stood up from where it had landed and rounded the car to help me up, brushing snow off my jacket.

"Detective, are you quite all right?" it asked, concerned about me and my sudden change in demeanour.

"Allen, sorry, holy. I've heard stories from bystanders of car engines that don't catch, and moments later they explode. The Mob sometimes hooks up a bomb under the hood to deal with people too dangerous to face in person. I just thought …"

No. No, they wouldn't do that, not without pissing her off.

"Perhaps the cold caused the Fuel Gel to stick, and we just need additional time to warm up the engine before it can properly turn over," Allen suggested.

"Yeah. Older cars do have issues in the cold." I tried to shake off the adrenalin. *No one would dare fuck with me, not even in Kips.* "Pop the hood and give it a manual crank."

I got in the driver's seat, and Allen manually turned the engine over. It climbed back inside the car and stared at me for a while in silence.

"Detective."

"Yes?"

"You kicked me out. You tried to save me before saving yourself."

"Not a word, Allen."

It nodded. I knew it was smiling when I looked away. The damn thing was making me go soft. I couldn't let that happen.

═══

The halfway house looked like a place right out of Harlem: boarded-up windows, rats running around outside, and moans echoing through the shattered windows. Yup, this was definitely the place we were looking for. A halfway house usually denoted a place where people went to sober up, so it would have been more accurate to call this an opium den, like the kind that had dotted England in the 1800s.

There was an empty door frame where there had once been a legitimate entrance. Allen walked in unarmed, but I kept my hand on the handle of my Diamondback in case any junkies got bright ideas. The floor creaked under the machine's heavy frame, but the moans within continued despite our intrusion.

The hallway was cramped, bordering a stairway to our right and several doors to the left. Inside each room, bodies were curled up in blankets and newspapers around firepits dug into the wood flooring. Used syringes and empty bottles covered the floor.

I elected to go up the rickety stairs alone while Allen searched the lower rooms for our boy. I still had the picture frame in my jacket pocket, bouncing against my hip as I walked. After this call I could get back to scanning the police chatter to see if Robins needed some muscle. The faster I got away from this hell, the better.

The upstairs hallway was even narrower, bordered by more rooms and a shattered bannister. The first room looked and smelled like a bathroom — no porcelain, just darkness. No movement inside, though I doubted anything in this house moved much, anyway. I was beginning to wonder if the smell from the dark room was shit or a corpse.

Walking toward the next room, I didn't have a chance to react when someone came running out. The barely human creature collided with me, but quick footwork kept me from going down and breaking my back on the stairs. The man was tiny, his skin tight against his frail arms, scraggly hair pouring off his head. His hollow eyes were filled with a single emotion: desperation.

He made a gasping noise, trying to speak, but lacking the energy or words to do so. Pushing him back was easy enough, but he came at me again, so I had no reservations about letting him tumble over the bannister and down onto the stairs, putting a dent in the rotten wood below. The crash was much louder than I had anticipated. I moved to the next room to put distance between myself and the scene.

The room at the far end of the hall was desolate, more worn down than the ones downstairs. It contained several ruined mattresses, blankets, and some piles of black and brown material. I pulled my shirt up to my nose, trying to filter out the smell as I got to work identifying the five bodies inside.

They were all much the same as the guy now taking a dirt nap on the stairs: somewhat awake and somewhat alive, with dinner-plate-sized pupils and wasted muscles. The first was a man with little to no hair left on his body, the next a woman with vacant eyes, missing patches of hair, and flea bites covering her hands and feet. At least one of the bodies was definitely dead, with rigor mortis setting in.

The last body in the room seemed fresher, still writhing underneath a blanket. I pulled the blanket off the junkie to see he was restrained; duck tape was wrapped around his limbs and over his mouth. He was tweaking out hard, thrashing so violently that the restraints were actually preventing him from hurting himself. I had a feeling our search was over.

"Allen, up here," I shouted.

I turned the body over and recognized the guy from the photo. He was balding and less malnourished than the junkies in here. But there wasn't much need for accountants in the Depression, and he must have been bringing his mother most of his own food, because he was still far too thin for his own good. A good son. It hurt to see him like this. He was only a few years younger than me.

Allen arrived and snapped off the duct tape restraints. To our surprise, the guy was spry, jumping up and backing against the wall, his hands groping the solid surface, searching for something to use as a weapon, I guessed. He was wild, looking at me like I was a carcass ready to eat.

"Easy, easy. Jeremy, yeah?" I spoke as softly as I could. "Your mother sent us to look for you."

He tore the tape off his mouth. There was blood on his lips, either from ripping off the tape or from being struck earlier.

"Get ... th-the fuck!"

"Jeremy, relax ..." I placed my gun back in its holster. "Who did this to you?"

I didn't get a verbal response. He leaped at me like a chimp, grappling, striking. I curled up, my shoulders and back shaking from the pain, unsuccessfully trying to fend him off. Allen grasped the kid and pulled him off, delivering a few quick jabs with its metal fist to get Jeremy to release his grip. The metal man took some abuse, but the kid only hurt himself struggling against the machine. He was frantic, mad even, his fingernails bending and chipping as he clawed against Allen's grip.

I went over to the small mattress he'd been lying on and found a syringe and a small glass bottle, empty. Morphine? There was no blood in the syringe; it wasn't even wet. The bottle was clean, too, nothing inside, no bitter smell. I tried to check the guy's pockets, but his legs flung up to kick me. I pulled out my Diamondback, and with a quick backhanded hit to the temple, knocked him out cold.

"Perhaps we should avoid damaging the victim any further," Allen suggested.

"Agreed, partner."

I found something in the kid's pocket and pulled it out. It looked like a small cigarette box, about half the size of my palm.

"What is it?"

"Looks like a dart box, though I don't see any cig-arettes." I made sure by opening it up. Nope, nothing there. Smelling it, I was hit by a fishy scent that prompted me to close the box again and shove it into my pocket. "Well, once again, Allen, you were correct."

"It seems to be a running theme," it said smugly, still holding up the unconscious Jeremy.

"And it seems I need to get better at my job." I smiled. "Let's get him somewhere safe. Then we're square."

"For now."

Sure, metal man. Whatever helps you sleep.

CHAPTER 2

FOUR TARGETS, NO MORE, NO LESS.

I'd been waiting a long time for my targets to gather together like this. In the end, they made the fatal mistake of being predictable.

Standing on a roof opposite the hotel, facing almost dead centre, I counted them:

First one on the sixth floor, the far left room. Hard to see from this height. I'd kill him first.

Second on the eighth floor. Near the centre line, a smidge to the left. He was preparing to play with his new toy. A slippery one, always careful. He'd closed the blinds. But I could see his silhouette, and that was enough.

Third on the twenty-second floor, right side. He clearly liked being near windows. He pushed his girl obnoxiously against the glass, already half-finished. Easy pickings.

Fourth was in the penthouse. Bit of an angle, but I didn't need to be precise with the last shot. The prime target was up there, enjoying his night of luxury.

Stupid men, all of them.

My tripod was up and the iron sights set. I despised scopes; they were too finicky, and the light could give you away, especially under the Plate. The rifle had built-in iron sights — might as well use them.

Three barrels. I'd start with the centre barrel first. I just needed to wait for the perfect timing, for the city to cover my sound. The hardest shot would be the first one.

Police Rotorbird, 7th Precinct, heading back to the station from routine patrol, right on schedule at 11:38 p.m. The boys in blue were always punctual. The vehicle would fly between the building I was standing on and the hotel. Its rotors were powerful enough to drown out other sounds without causing too much shot interference.

The sixth-floor target moved to the window to close the blinds. The Rotorbird approached. Loud enough now. Centre trigger. Glass shattering. One down.

Finger on the front trigger, I rotated the barrel assembly clockwise.

Eighth-floor target on the bed, silhouetted against the blinds. Body shot. Shattered glass, an audible scream, now that the Rotorbird had passed. Two down.

I turned the rifle counter-clockwise, finger on the back trigger.

Twenty-second-floor target was still pressed against the glass. His hands on the girl's hips, his body behind hers. No clear shot.

Sorry, love.

The window shattered, the girl screamed. She had a hole in her thigh, but she'd live. He wouldn't. Three down.

Releasing the lever, I turned the barrel assembly 180 degrees. Penthouse target, entwined with his girl, was none the wiser, despite the screaming below.

The girl wouldn't have made it out, anyway.

I pulled the centre trigger. Explosion.

The last three rounds had only made holes, but this round destroyed all of the windows of the penthouse. The detonation showered the street in wood and plaster. Cars screeched to a halt. The screaming of the three surviving girls was audible.

Four down.

Tripod up, rifle snapped, I easily stored the two pieces of the weapon and gathered the shells.

And now, to wait.

CHAPTER 3

WE HELPED THE POOR KID TO A hospital and dropped a few bills beside him. The nurses swore to me they'd have him shipshape in no time. I was just relieved that I had fulfilled my end of the bargain and completed a civilian call so the metal man wouldn't make a fuss for a while. As we drove back to my apartment, the installed police radio installed in my "rental" car began to chatter away under the dash.

"*10-33, get someone on the horn at the 7th or 11th. Explosion at the Edison Hotel. Five dead, I repeat, five dead at the Edison.*"

I looked over at Allen, whose eyebrows were raised inquisitively. "Should we check it out?" it asked.

"The hell is a 10-33?" I said.

"Explosive device present. The NYPD has been experimenting with brevity codes. It started after your time. This sounds like something up your alley, given the body count."

"But it's not a Night Call. I'm off the hook."

Almost as soon as I had finished speaking, the radio crackled again.

"*The 5th called in, get R on the horn,*" the scanner announced.

That was my cue.

"Shit."

I spun the Packard around in the middle of the street. Cars swerved to avoid me, and Allen yelped in panic. We headed northwest toward yet another crime.

And I had almost been glad that things were slow.

———

The scene was like something out of a movie: broken glass and debris all over the street, half a dozen police vehicles cordoning off the building, and even a few police chiefs on site. Rotating red beacon lights stabbed at my eyes, making the streetlights and Platelights seem dim in comparison.

The Edison Hotel was not one of the Control Points that supported the Plate and kept it from toppling over from its own weight, but it was a masterful work of architecture. No doubt its reputation would now be shattered after this incident.

Two ambulances — glorified hearses, in actuality — sat with their back doors open and three covered corpses loaded inside. Nearby, emergency workers looked after three women draped with blankets. One woman had a moderately sized chunk missing from the back of her thigh, though she seemed calm, probably thanks to a generous application of morphine, Syneal, and bandages. The other girls' wounds appeared to be more psychological than physical.

Commissioner Jeffrey Robins, head of the 5th Precinct, was standing by, his look grim and his posture impatient. One of the few Black veterans of the Great War, he was a tough boss who wanted his men to be the best. He'd lost most of his hair stressing over his job and had sacrificed his marriage trying to make this city a better place. No one wanted to tell him how fruitless an endeavour that was.

Beside him were the heads of the 7th and 11th: Yevgeny Viessman and Tony Shen, respectively. The former was a Russian man, bearded and scarred from his days riding horses in the Cossack Division for the Czar. Whereas everyone else was wearing a parka or something similar, Yevgeny wore only a thin shirt, his cheeks rosy and skin peachy. Tony was given a odd look by a lot of onlookers. Most Chinese Americans were, seeing as we were in a cold war with the Republic over the Automatics industry. But I knew Shen, and no one would have been more willing to take a bullet for Lady Liberty than him.

They all seemed to relax a degree as soon as I walked up with Allen.

"Sinclair is calling for you now," Robins told me, nodding toward a nearby phone booth as he lit a cigar. "How'd you know?"

"I have my ways. They said five dead, but I only see three bodies. Is there a surprise waiting for me upstairs?"

"*Da*," spat Yevgeny, as the five of us walked to the lobby. He rarely spoke, but when he did, his Russian accent contrasted starkly with everyone else's.

"You're more talkative than usual, Yev. Things got you spooked?" He scowled as we entered the revolving doors, making me grin. "Shen, were you first on the scene?"

"Unfortunately." Shen lit a cigarette. "Took until Viessman got here before they'd listen and set up a perimeter."

"Pricks, eh?" I said. Shen just laughed.

The lobby we walked into was decorated with fantastic woodwork and ornate stone pillars. The ceiling was bevelled and adorned with chains, from which golden chandeliers hung. Dozens of wealthy members of the Lower City were walking out in nightgowns and whatever else they could throw on. They peered at us like we were Automatics walking around up on the Plate. I ignored them as best I could. We entered the closest elevator, and Shen hit the button to the penthouse. He waited for the doors to close before speaking again.

"The shot that got our attention was fired at about eleven thirty-nine p.m. It shook this place to the bone. People got all stirred up and ran outside. We were able to deal with three of the bodies. They all had these stuck in them." He handed me a small envelope.

Inside were some mangled rifle rounds. They were bent and crushed from slamming into muscle and bone, but still identifiable.

"Who are they, Mafia?" I asked.

"No, actually," Shen replied, "they're Upper City officials who worked underneath the dead VIP in the penthouse. They came down here for some rough and tumble fun, and now they're all dead. The women are dimes from the streets. We did thorough background checks, and trust me, they have no motivation for murdering their clients at the exact same time. The bullets came in through the windows, so we think there were multiple gunmen involved."

"Multiple?" Allen took the opportunity to butt in. "I know several people and Automatics who can fire quickly and accurately enough to take out four people from a single vantage point."

"The first three bullets aren't evidence against that — it's the fourth one."

The elevator opened, and the three chiefs fell back, allowing me and Allen to walk out first. We entered a large foyer with two arches on either side of the central wall before us, both leading into a larger room on the opposite side. The effect of the ornate wallpaper and lavish decoration was diminished by the sound of wind passing through the broken windows. I was wary of what I might find as I passed through one of the arches.

Now I understood why there were only three bodies downstairs.

The fourth and fifth were splattered all over the walls.

Allen stared at the thick smear of blood on a nearby armchair and immediately doubled over, puking. I relieved it so it could go pull itself together. Its acidic spew was already burning through the rug … ugh. The chiefs were standing far back, looking to me to deal with their problems.

"Well, a rag would be helpful!" I yelled over. Robins picked up a cloth napkin from a small table and threw it to me. I tied it over my mouth to keep the smell from hitting me too hard.

The windows had blown out onto the street, and the walls were coated in blood, gore, and chunks of bone. The chandelier hanging overtop the room was newly adorned with a rag-covered limb balancing on one of its arms. The explosion had jolted several pieces of furniture out of place, but it hadn't been strong enough to knock down the walls, which meant that it had been contained. Dynamite charge? No, that would have involved shaping the charge and carefully placing it. And a grenade wouldn't have done this kind of damage.

Robins approached, holding a handkerchief to his nose. "Theory, Elias?"

"Von Whisper?" I suggested.

"Looks that way, don't it?"

"Tell me more about the victim."

"Desmond Hartley, big name in GE's Automatics Division. Another shill in a suit. Good riddance, I say."

"And the other body?"

"Another prostitute. Poor girl."

"They couldn't have shot from the street." I looked down through the broken picture window and saw the roof of the building opposite in plain view. "The perfect vantage point is the top of the Barrymore Theatre. It wasn't a hard shot for an experienced shooter. What kind of bullets are these?"

"They're 8x50 Lebel, used by the French in the War," Robins answered. "Odd, huh? How many people do you know who use French rifles with outdated bullets?"

"Might be a good time to start asking. Lock down the scene. Me and Allen will do some work down there. Say it was … fuck it, the Iron Hands."

"Don't you think that's dangerous, pinning this on them?" Robins kicked a piece of glass underfoot, trying to keep his shoes off the bloody carpet. "We've put in enough marketing effort for them as is. We need to stop saying that every mysterious murder is their work, else she might get upset. Pick someone else, please."

Robins was nervous. I would have been, too, if I were him, with so many suspects for this crime. If only crime families weren't running both cities.

"Maranzano?"

"Better."

═══════

I collected Allen and headed for the theatre. On our way in I asked a security guard if anyone had come through the stairwell to the roof. She said that she'd been nowhere near the stairwell when the shootings happened. Figured.

The concrete rooftop was empty. Up here the horns and engines and other noises of the city came through undiluted. The end farthest from the hotel was teeming with evidence, though it wasn't immediately obvious — you just had to know where to look. The rooftop access door came out in an enclosure that resembled a small brick shack. On the back of it I found two divots and some streaks of black, indicating that something heavy had been placed down there and dragged across.

"Someone set up a rifle here." I pointed to the divots. "Got it assembled, moved to the perch, and took aim. Jesus, those are some difficult shots, even from this angle. He must be one hell of a shot."

"A tripod would have helped," Allen noted, its fingers drifting over the parapet. "They set up here, got into a better angle, and went to work. The recoil was absorbed by the concrete, as evident by the depressions. But using two different cartridges ... that's where things get tricky."

"Multiple shooters?" I asked. Allen shrugged in response. "Go and do your thing, see what you can find."

Allen scoured the area a quarter of an hour or so. I looked down over the parapet, watching a crowd coalesce around the scene. It was a mix of onlookers and reporters. Journalists both glamorous and stoic tried to get the scoop while their audio-jockeys followed, carrying recording equipment on their backs.

Allen finally returned with a displeased expression.

"No evidence of more than one shooter," it said. "An 1886 Lebel is quite a collector's item, but seeing as there are thousands of Great War veterans, that rifle is not exactly scarce. The last round came from a much larger rifle."

"A Von Whisper."

Allen scrunched up its face at me. "I don't know that weapon."

"Oh, you don't know the slang. A G30 Von-Nernst."

"Ah, the 15mm rifle. It was billed as an 'anti-Automatic platform,' as I recall."

"Doesn't stop people from using it on humans. Still, there's no way someone could walk up here with a Von Whisper, even disassembled, and get out fast." I was missing something, as usual. But there was nothing else here. "What do we even have to go off? Hair? Shoeprints?"

"Nothing. Whoever took the shot was good, cleaned up almost everything. Perhaps they thought the tripod marks were inconsequential," Allen said.

"Robins won't like this. Shit, we're dry up here." I pulled out a dart and bit on it. I was getting nervous again.

———

Back on street level, the police were wrapping up the scene and covering any last avenues that might have served as an escape route for the shooter. The cordoned-off area was being assailed by the wave of journalists I had spotted. On the Cop Killer case, I'd been being hounded by cops and by the Eye, but thankfully, no press. When the news got involved, things always got messy. Especially when I was around.

One particular reporter was especially eager; she ran through the bustling crowd and slipped around a dim-witted cop from the 7th, her audio-jockey running just behind, holding the cord attached to her microphone. She was respectable-looking in tapered slacks, black flats, a grey blouse, and a thick white wool coat. She had shoulder-length blond hair and her emerald eyes drilled through me as she approached. What did she want with me?

"There he is, come on!" she said to the audio-jockey behind her. "Detective Roche!" Her voice pierced through the noise. Hers wasn't a New York accent. And how did she know my name?

"What in the hell …" I turned to my partner. "Allen, car, now."

"But —"

"Allen!" It listened that time. We hurried toward my vehicle, but I wasn't fast enough to escape the woman. She ran around to block me. Behind her, the audio-jockey was spooling up his recorder.

"Shit," I said, as she held the microphone to my mouth.

"Detective Roche, can you comment on the crime that occurred here? Who were the perpetrators? Are you hot on their trail?" She pushed the microphone even closer. I swatted it away in annoyance. "Anything for the listeners of 980 AM?"

I dug my nails into my palms to keep myself from breaking the equipment and wasting money on damage compensation. "Who the hell are you and how the hell do you know who I am?"

"Simone Morane of WAR Radio, and this is my audio-jockey —"

"I don't care." She didn't seem offended by my interruption. "You didn't answer my other question."

"The police pass out your phone number like they're giving out parking tickets. I'm surprised they never let your real name slip. But I managed to figure it out, Mr. Nightcaller."

"Are you the one responsible for that ridiculous nickname?"

"Oh, no, you can thank the officers with no imagination for that."

I clenched my jaw. I wasn't going to play these games. "Regarding the crime scene here, all you need to know is that the Maranzano Mafia is overstepping its bounds, and I need to reel them in."

"Are you talking about the 5th Precinct, or just yourself?"

"Audio off," I said. I glared at her until she signalled her jockey to cut the feed and stowed the microphone in her coat pocket. "Expensive coat you're wearing. Didn't think radio reporters made enough for something this nice. What brand? Lanvin?"

"I could ask the same of you, with that Talbot I've heard so much about, though I don't see it with you. Trying to stay under the radar? Must have cost a fortune to get something that cutting edge." I clammed up. "I've been waiting months to see you in action. You're a slippery one."

"I try my damnedest."

"You're the biggest thing on the news now, you know that, right? Well, the Nightcaller is, anyway. RCA has made you into a radio show — the marketing is everywhere — and there are rumours MGM is already interested in adapting it for film. You're a star!"

I'm a what? "Hold the phone … How am *I* the biggest thing on the news?"

I was halfway to reaching for my Diamondback. I felt like I was being pushed into a corner.

"You don't listen to the radio?"

"Can't really listen when I'm always on the move."

"Stories of the Nightcaller have been coming in since mid-'30, and you've only gotten busier since then," she said. "An old lady called a news station an hour ago saying you'd gone to save her son. I knew if you were going to turn up anywhere after that, it would be here. You're at the forefront of every major investigation. I mean, for three years, this mysterious hero has been popping in and cleaning up the streets of Lower Manhattan, and now … here you are!"

I'd always known that taking these jobs on the side was going to bite me in the ass. But a radio series? A movie deal? They had to be fucking with me.

"You're saying there have been advertisements for this?"

"They're all over the radio. There's even a TV commercial! You sure you haven't heard any?"

"Like I said, I don't care for the media."

"What about the billboards in Times Square?"

"I don't like looking up."

She frowned. "None of your friends told you about it? How about that Automatic sitting in your car?"

I turned to look at Allen, who looked back at me, perplexed. "It doesn't listen to the radio, either. At least, I don't think it does."

"You'd better start catching up on things, huh, Nightcaller?" She smirked. "Debut episode is in a few days. Don't miss it."

That dumb name again.

"Let me make something clear, Miss …"

"Morane."

"I'm not the Nightcaller, I'm not a hero, and I'm not a star. I'm just doing my job to protect the people of New York, as all cops should be doing —"

"But instead, they relegate such issues to you," she interjected with a grin.

"If you want an official statement, Maranzano was behind the attack. His enforcers took out some Mafia bigwigs belonging to Gould's gang of spooks, end of story."

"Gould, the CEO of GE? Owner of the Plate?"

"Yes, of course *that* Gould, who else would I be talking about?"

Simone nodded. "We can work with that."

"Get that show off the air. I don't condone my likeness being used in a radio show."

"But you just said you weren't the Nightcaller." *Goddamn it.* "If you are, I could tell that to RCA, and they might pull the plug. But if you aren't, you shouldn't mind the show airing one bit."

I sniffed. The cold was freezing my nose, the air stinging my throat. "You're just the most insufferable of all reporters, aren't you? I know the Upper City gets its kicks hearing about the crazy shit we do down here in the mud, and I'm sure you get enough time up there as it is, but this crime is far more important than a radio show or one of your goddamn stories. So do me a favour, because I know for a fact you didn't turn this off" — I grabbed the microphone out of her coat pocket — "and tell RCA to fuck off."

She was grinning the entire time, seeing how easily she'd pushed my buttons. I sucked in air to calm myself before things got messy.

"Well, if you have any more complaints, please call me." She slipped me a card with the radio station's number on it. "I'm open for an interview whenever you are. Be seeing you, Nightcaller."

"Don't call me that!"

She strutted off back into her milieu, proud to have gotten a comment about the freshest corpses in the Lower City. The moment the other reporters saw her victorious expression, they began clamouring for my attention, too. I tuned them out easily and headed to my car.

When I got in, I noticed Allen peering over at me, but trying to be subtle about it.

"Yes?" I asked.

"Simone Morane? I can read lips. That name sounds familiar. Perhaps she has relatives in law enforcement?"

"Hopefully no one important. I've already pissed off too many people in the city."

"What was it she called you?"

"The Nightcaller," I said with a grimace. "The same stupid name the civilians have been calling me on the phone. I suppose it's more poetic than making an R call. She said she's been following stories about me for years, waiting for me to 'appear.' And now there's a damn radio show about me."

Allen's eyebrows went up in surprise. "That's fantastic!"

"No, it isn't, Allen. I don't like being noticed. Having a stupid radio show attached to me means regular people talking about me. If some camera-happy kid gets a picture of me, next thing you know people start bugging me where I work, live, relax. I'd rather keep a low profile. We have a job to do. We don't need to be bogged down by this bullshit. That was the reason I stopped doing civvy Night Calls for a while — I didn't want something like this to happen. Too late now."

Allen nodded and reached into its pocket. "So, shall we pursue this, Detective?"

"I don't know. There's no real evidence we can use to track down the killer. No way to tell which rifles were used, no way to tell who he is, nothing we can go off. Maybe we can muscle some of the local goons for information, but I doubt it was any of the Mobs that pulled this. It feels too sloppy to be a Mafia hit."

"No, I meant this." Allen handed me a folded slip of paper smaller than a business card. "It was under one of your windshield wipers. I thought one of the commissioners might have left it for you."

I unfolded it and read the neat cursive letters: *Kips Bay shipments. Deal with it.*

The Eye was calling on me again. This was either an olive branch or a gun against my head. Or, knowing her, both.

"Yeah, Allen. Just a side job I need to clear up. It shouldn't take more than an hour. Maybe we can kill two birds with one stone this way."

≡≡≡

We arrived at Maranzano's footprint in Lower Manhattan, the Kips Kompound, as he called it, a string of warehouses refurbished and gutted to create a veritable barracks in the heart of New York, much to the chagrin of the city's higher-ups. The front entrance was built to look like the front of a prison, with watchtowers and barbed wire running along the walls, and the only way in or out a large sliding gate on wheels. A half-dozen mobsters stood out front, eyeing us the moment we drove up. Two spotlights came down from the watchtowers and centred on my car, leaving us nowhere to hide.

No one could touch Maranzano in here. No one but me.

Allen was rubbing its hands together nervously. *You'll get used to this in time, partner.*

I stepped out first, not bothering to lock the door after me. Allen followed close behind, babbling.

"Detective Roche, this place feels … I believe it's inappropriate for officers to be here alone."

"Relax, Allen. These are my people. I'll do the talking."

Allen stayed back as I continued walking forward. The first Bruno at the gate held up a hand and told me to stop. His other hand was holding a Thompson. I got in his personal space before he could react. A sharp jab in the gut made him double over, and I quickly pressed my weapon against his crown. The other five mobsters trained their weapons on me, and still more standing on the wall above pointed barrels in my direction. The clicks and slams of bolts placing bullets in chambers echoed through the air for a few seconds. Allen stumbled back, putting more distance between itself and the killing floor.

"I got a message for 'Zano. You going to open up, or should I knock?" I asked.

The show of force was enough. Seconds later, the gates were opened, the guns were all pointed down, and the fellow balancing on my Diamondback's barrel was on the ground, clutching his stomach. Eyes wide with fascination and fear, Allen chased after me, too afraid to ask questions. The mobsters at the gate backed away, allowing us into the Kompound, though their faces curled into sneers and snarls.

The interior of Maranzano's headquarters was a mess of alcohol and Automatic parts, the two most valuable materials for a bootlegger. Wheelbarrows, car trunks, and crates were filled to the brim with both types of paraphernalia. Passing through this space was like walking through a graveyard for robots, and unsurprisingly, Allen looked terrified. It stayed right on my heels, perhaps afraid that if it strayed too far, a Bruno might nab it and strip it down to its circuits.

The conversations around us were disturbing, to say the least. These punks were more animals than men.

"'Ey, Roche! How's the life of a lapdog treatin' ya?" screamed one.

"Got a few shipments from up north. Damn, the Grotto boys know how to strip Autos efficiently ..."

"Hey, I bet ten bucks Roche won't notice if we nab his fancy new Blue-eye."

That last comment almost made me stop. *No, don't take it personally, they're just assholes.*

Pale theatre footlights lit up the face of an impressive stone building ahead of us, as if it was some red carpet deal. The sliding barn doors on the front were parted by two guards as we approached. Walking through them was like stepping into another world. The welding and grinding and sawing was replaced by pleasant music, gold chandeliers, and marble pillars. Mobsters in dirty garb replaced by people in lavish dresses and fitted suits. Everyone stared at us, the guards warily, the partygoers with disgust.

Maranzano loved hosting his fellow public enemies. While they waited for the heat to die down elsewhere in the States, they'd come to the Lower City, since most of it was controlled by 'Zano himself. I spotted faces that had been featured on posters dotting the walls of the 5th. There was "The Owl" Banghart, fresh off an armed robbery in Detroit. Lord, he was an ugly bastard, especially when he sneered. The Barker-Karpis gang, in all their glory, leaned on the western wall of the place, though they were one member short, thanks to me.

The band performing at the far end of the hall didn't miss a beat upon our entrance. Above us was a second floor with stone railings where the even richer criminals stood looking down at the stage. Bonnie and Clyde were hiding out up there, the former with a fat cigar between her teeth, the latter eyeing me up for a fight. Noticeably absent was the Dillinger gang, though from what I'd heard, 'Zano wasn't stupid enough to let a group with a bounty that high into his inner sanctum. I guessed that those I didn't recognize were former members of the Five Families, or something similar.

I nabbed a shrimp and a bottle from the buffet table and implored Allen to grab a glass of alcohol to calm his nerves. We walked over toward the stage and sat down in some large red cushioned chairs in the front row. No one was stupid enough to stop us, luckily for them.

Then the man himself appeared, blocking my view of the stage. Leaning on a cane, he was flanked by guards who served to make him look bigger. With bulldog cheeks and a pointed hairline, Salvatore Maranzano was built like a brick shithouse. No one of sound mind would have willingly gone toe-to-toe against him, limp or no limp. On his right was man with a flat-top and a handlebar moustache: Santoni, which meant "Uncle Tony" in Italian. I had yet to meet a man more unpleasant, though I did try. So far, no one matched him for sheer bitterness and rudeness.

"You disrespect me by walking into my house with that *thing* in tow." Maranzano jabbed a finger at Allen, who was wide-eyed, gripping its champagne glass in panic. He sounded like he smoked two packs a day, and a faint Italian accent was noticeable, as well.

"I don't decide when the conversations need to happen." I bit into the shrimp and threw the tail on the carpet. "I just get told to show up."

"You are a villain, an absolute villain!"

"That's rich coming from you, Sal." I reclined in my seat, propping one knee against a chair arm and sinking into the cushions. People started moving away from us.

"What happened to honour among thieves?"

"It died a while ago. I think I might have killed it." I winked and sipped at my drink.

"Luciano, Gagliano, Mangano, Profaci — those men, they were men of honour and respect, as am I. They should be here tonight. Instead, I host the mad lapdog that killed them and his metal chew toy. I should have you shot and that thing stripped apart, its parts sold to the highest bidder!"

His intimidation tactics didn't work on me anymore. He was scary to the common street thug, but he only ever spoke like this when he couldn't touch whoever was offending him.

"Look," I said, "she wants you to pull out of Chelsea Piers completely. She staked a claim a few weeks back in a few warehouses, and she just wants them to herself. She's offering you a place in North Jersey as recompense."

The warehouses she wanted were the ones I'd nearly died in. She'd gone in and picked up the parts I'd offered her, and now she wanted the whole damn building, too. Why did Masters have to set up shop in Maranzano territory?

Maranzano's hands shook, and his face went red. The band kept playing, but the wavering voice of the lead singer reflected how heated things were getting. "You walk in here and demand one of the greatest avenues of our business in exchange for a box off-island?"

"It's not like you were using those warehouses, anyway. Don't shoot the messenger."

"I've done so before, and I will again! Your harlot does not scare me, nor do her advances upon what is mine. She and I made a deal, Roche! We made a deal, and you spit on it with this request. Gramercy to Midtown is mine, anything south is hers. She has the gall to walk into the centre of our territory and demand we give it to her? Tell that bitch that I will kill, maim, and dismantle any man or machine that walks into Chelsea, and send them back in pieces. I'd rather burn the docks down than let her have them under these circumstances!"

I rubbed the bridge of my nose and then stood to face Maranzano, stopping within inches of him. The crowd held their breath, and the music stopped.

I spoke as calmly as I could, almost in a whisper. "You have two options. The first is to refuse and do what you said. Kill them, maim them, dismantle them. Next thing you know, there will be a trail of blood and gore running from Jersey to Chelsea, with your men feeding it. Your ships burned, your cars wrecked, and your lieutenants dead. I know it'll happen that way, because I'll be the one to do it. I'll kill every single one with my bare hands, then send them and a cinderblock down to the bottom of the Hudson, or splatter their innards onto the streets. Or, you can take the second option: give up the docks, head to Jersey, and make up for lost profits with some land shipping, using vehicles she will provide. I know which option I would take, and which one you're going to take, too. You want to know why?"

The short man didn't answer, but he did listen. I leaned in closer.

"Because Luciano, Gagliano, Mangano, Profaci, even Morello — they *were* men of honour. Best remember why they ain't here tonight."

I grabbed Allen's champagne and gulped it down, then placed the glass in Maranzano's hand before backing up. He was hesitant, not wanting to be humiliated in front of his guests, but not willing to push it, either.

"You have three days. Get packing," I said.

"This isn't your turf, boy. Mind your tongue," he snarled.

I nodded. "I'll consider that for the next time I drop in."

We departed. The moment we were through the barn doors, the music started up again. We could let Maranzano have his fun. He needed the chance to relax. He was getting old, after all.

———

The car doors slammed shut, and Allen and I settled in. I heaved out a heavy breath, my heart rate slowing. Allen was tense as a board and didn't make a peep. A few miles away from the Kompound, it finally spoke.

"I didn't think ..." It stopped to organize its thoughts. "I didn't think you were playing both sides of the law."

Shit. I hadn't warned it beforehand. And I hadn't intended to let it know like this.

"I have to keep the peace, no matter the method."

"Who is 'she,' Detective? Another mobster to take orders from?"

"No. A dangerous woman with her claws in everything in this city except the Plate."

"And you carry messages to the other crime families?"

"You could say that, yeah." Morello had been the first to get a "message," but that had been the result of rage. The other four had taken patience and planning, organization. I'd sent a message, all right. "I'm a courier of sorts. It pays the bills."

"Who were you working for during our previous case, with Masters?"

"I …" Shit, it had me in a bind. "Myself. No one else. Maybe Robins. Yeah."

Allen could see right through me. It had just wanted to know whether I would lie.

I would and I could. If not for my own safety, then definitely for Allen's.

CHAPTER 4

A FEW DAYS AFTER MY BUSINESS at Maranzano's, I decided to pay Jeremy a visit. Alone.

The hospital we'd dropped him at was a pricy one, but you got what you paid for in the medical system. The receptionist sent me to his room. I could see he looked much better than when we'd first met him. He squinted, as if trying to place where he had seen me before.

"I'm sorry, can I help you?" He also sounded less jittery.

"I'm Elias Roche. Your mother sent me to find you a few days back."

"Oh, you're the one who brought me here!" His face lit up as he shuffled to give me space to sit on his bed. "I can't thank you enough for what you did. I have no idea how to repay you. Saving my life, paying for my stay, it's too much!"

"You can repay me by telling me what you remember from the night you got nabbed. I was hoping you could help me figure out what happened."

He smiled. "I don't really know what happened, I'm afraid. I was bringing food for my ma, brought it up, then I went back to grab a present for her. She's a big fan of the old country — came here from Denmark, of all places, and met my father here — and I got her this painting from a Danish artist she loves. I went down, and next thing I knew, someone was holding me down. I remember having this terrible taste in my mouth, and then … I was here."

"You didn't see anyone approach you? Even from the street?"

"No, there was no one around for miles, not even cars. People don't like Kips Bay, which is why the rent is cheap."

I rubbed my temple. "So, you're an accountant?"

"I'm trying to be. I don't work much — not many businesses left around to need me — but I do volunteer my time at the local shelter."

"Shelter for what?"

"Addicts. I try to bring them in, help them detox, get them on their feet. It's hard keeping them from relapsing, but it's our duty to help people, no matter what."

I pulled out the strange tin box I'd found in his pocket and placed it in his hands. "You have any idea what this is?"

"I sure do. Junkies call it a Huffbox, the newest way to take drugs. Why put a needle in your arm when you can aerosolize the stuff and suck it down?" He chuckled a bit, but he didn't smile. "A lot of the older junkies who come in sound like they have TB. Often, they don't make it more than a month without numbing the pain, and even then, they die from their lungs just giving out. It's terrible."

"How does it work?" I asked.

"You put whatever you want to take inside, add a cartridge on the underside of the thing, and suck and click and swallow. Automatics have started using even stronger cartridges to get the stuff into the same funnel alcohol goes into, so it's like a universal applicator."

"Huh." I took the Huffbox back and turned it over in my hand. "Seems someone tested it out on you against your will. You have any idea what they gave you?"

"I can barely remember the last few days. I'm sorry, Mr. Roche, I'm not too sure."

"Figures." I pocketed the box and got up from the bed. "You have any idea why someone would target you?"

"Maybe because I work at the shelter. I mean, I can confiscate any drugs the addicts have on them."

"And do you?"

He clammed up for a moment and bit on his lip. "Well … I need to pay the bills somehow."

"Mm-hmm … You take care now. Oh, and, uh …" I opened my wallet, grabbed a few bills, and threw them on the bed. "Stop peddling that shit and get yourself something to eat. Your mother would be mortified if she knew you were giving her all your food."

He looked shocked by the generosity. I made my way out before he could thank me again. Poor bastard must have been nabbed by the Iron Hands because he volunteered at that shelter. Maybe they thought he stole product and resold it, or maybe they thought he was a narc. No doubt they'd fed him their own cocktail to bury the trail, and it seemed to have worked.

But the fact that he had no idea who took him … that was concerning. No footprints, fast as hell, weighed a ton, quiet enough that the old woman hadn't heard or seen the kidnapping happen. Like I'd said to Allen, I knew an Automatic who could do something like this. I just didn't want to be right.

━━━━━

I made my way to the 5th Precinct, intending to catch up with everyone while Allen was away. It got dark early this time of year, and it was only going to get worse. My temporary car, a black Packard, would have blended completely into the night, had the little lights on the Plate not reflected off its shiny exterior.

Walking into the precinct, I heard my name called out several times as the cops on duty spotted me. They were half-hearted greetings, given that Sundays were slow days and no one wanted to be here. Patrick Sinclair was nearly asleep at his desk, trying to figure out how to play a card game on his green-and-black desk terminal. Even half-awake, he'd had enough time to style his hair before — and during — the workday. I leaned on his desk as he jabbed at the keyboard and gave me a lazy acknowledgement.

"Paddy," I said.

"El, good to see ya." He leaned back, thankful for the distraction. "Busy few weeks?"

"I'm not at liberty to discuss that," I said jokingly.

"Prick. Anyway, somethin' the matter?"

"Yeah, you listen to the radio at all?"

He gave me the side eye. "Yeah."

"Heard about this Nightcaller shit?"

"Oh yeah! They've been advertising it like mad for a few weeks now. I hear that damn advert at least five times a day."

"You know that's about me, right?" He turned, making the same face he made whenever he had a bad hand in poker. "Don't start," I said.

"You think it's authentic?"

"What do you mean?"

He put on a shit-eating grin. "You think I'm in it?"

"Pray that you're not. I'm not exactly happy about being turned into some kind of folk hero."

"Speaking of, how'd you manage to get a radio show?"

"Can it, Paddy." I changed the subject. "I solved a kidnapping a few days ago. Just talked to the guy whose ass I saved. He had a strange encounter when he was visiting his mom in Kips —"

"Ugh, Kips," he interrupted.

"And he was taken by someone. But the kicker is, there weren't any tire tracks, no footprints, nothing to show someone strolled up and grabbed him and his car. You know any people that can float?"

"I don't know any person or machine that can do that." He turned back to the flickering cards on his screen. "But I'm guessin' Allen has a hunch?"

"No, I do."

"Oh, so you're doin' your job for once."

A slap to the back of his head made him yelp in surprise. I grabbed a nearby chair and pulled it close, straddling it and resting my arms on the back. "This is serious, Pat."

"Well, excuse me for being a bit skeptical, but ain't ya the same guy who thought your dead partner was killin' cops in some backwater speakeasy?"

"That was paranoia. This is grounded in reality."

"Next thing you know you'll be seeing my dead brother around the city."

"Paddy." Sinclair looked away from his screen to give me the time of day. "I'll be more direct: do you know of any machines that don't touch the ground?"

The colour drained from his face as he processed what I said. Now we were both on the same page, and this time he knew I wasn't chasing ghosts.

"I thought she got rid of that thing," he said.

"Well, she does what she can to get ahead, no matter what. She probably had to track it down, which would have been hard in and of itself. I need you to keep an eye out for me. Just report any strange murders or kidnappings or even break-ins, anything that could confirm she's bringing old friends back into the fold."

"I'll let Robins know when he's back."

"Back? He left the 5th? For more than a lunch break? Where the hell is he?"

"He's headed up to the Plate for a 'constructive safety seminar.'"

Classic FBI intimidation techniques. "All right, let him know when he gets back." I stood up to leave.

"Oh, Roche, by the way ..." Sinclair leaned back on his chair. "How's that Edison Hotel case?"

"Why?"

"Our end has been quiet. Whoever did it is smart to stay off the radar. It's just strange that nothing else has come up, no evidence or eyewitnesses or anything. Does *she* know anything?"

I hated relying on the Eye for information. "I haven't really been in contact with her. Trying to put some distance between us because of Allen."

"Ah." Sinclair nodded, turning back to his terminal. "There's the reason."

"For what?"

"The reason that thing is back."

I shook the words from my head and walked toward the station's glass doors.

As I approached and looked outside, I spotted something standing across the road, under the streetlight near my car. It was tall, lanky, with red eyes. I found myself hoping it was just some unhinged Red-eyed murder-bot roaming the city, and not who I thought it was spying on me. My body went cold and I kept staring, peering harder and harder to try and figure out if it was real. I traced the lines of the figure with my eyes, expecting it to lunge toward me.

A streetcar drove in front of the thing, stopped for a moment, then departed, leaving a tall mechanical body with blue eyes where the apparition had been. The machine entered the precinct and took off its coat to reveal a police uniform underneath.

"Roche, good to see you."

"Toby," I greeted it. Weird seeing Toby back in a police uniform with Second Prohibition still active. Even weirder because box-chested, utilitarian Grifter models were most often connected to the Mafia, not the police. Robins had never been a fan of Green-eyes; something that blindly followed orders seemed like a liability to him. There was a joke in there somewhere …

I looked back outside, wondering if whatever I'd seen was still there. Nothing. Maybe I'd imagined it. Maybe it was just a tree branch and some reflections from … something.

"Robins bring you back in?" I asked Toby, still peering out.

"Yeah, funnily enough, he did. He's recently developed a 'fuck it' attitude for most things, which makes the station much easier to deal with," it said, chuckling.

"Other than the murders and the patrols and the looming threat of the Mafia," I mentioned.

"Like the derms say, grain of salt, Roche, grain of salt."

There was still nothing out there. I was getting paranoid.

With that, I left, making haste to get inside my temporary car. Once there, I scanned the interior for a note, a signal, any signs of tampering. Needless to say, I had the door open and half my body outside the car when I turned the engine over. When no explosion followed the key turn, I drove back home as quickly as I could.

I needed a break from the streets. I was starting to see things.

CHAPTER 5

IT WAS DECEMBER 16, a few days after my visit to the station, and my car was ready for pickup. Seeing as I was "on duty" with Allen, I had to bring the metal bastard with me when I went to get it.

We were watching a building in the Meatpacking District like hawks, and in turn, all of 'Zano's men watched us. They were everywhere here: on street corners, on rooftops, near the entrance to every major warehouse. I'd bet half the kids in this neighbourhood were on his payroll, seeing as kids made for good spies. But after nothing happening and no unpredictable movements for a solid hour and a half, I turned the Packard over and began our drive north. I knew Allen wanted to ask why we were moving, so I quickly explained.

"I need to get my Talbot back from a friend of mine. She's all fixed and juiced up, so I can swap out this old hunk of shit for my pride and joy."

"She?" It didn't understand the personification. Guess it believed I was talking about a woman.

"Yeah, the car. She. Just a term I use for the old box."

"I understand your use of personification when referring to your vehicle, Detective. It's your sporadic use of it that confuses me."

"Sporadic?"

"Yes." I waited for it to continue. "You see, I've noticed many people refer to inanimate objects with personal pronouns, giving them a more human feeling to express emotional attachment to them. However, I have not witnessed many people refer to Automatics or Synthians with personal pronouns. It seems humans prefer us as objects, rather than beings that can elicit emotional attachment."

It must have been chomping at the bit to talk during our little stint watching the warehouse. "Can't we go one day without some pseudo-philosophy?" I said. It stared at me blankly. "And about your fellow Synthian friends — I haven't seen many around. Not many reports of machines that can eat and seem to be almost alive."

"They must be very good at blending in," Allen retorted. "And don't try to evade my questions."

"Ugh." I rubbed my temple. "The fact you're still referred to as 'it' bothers you a great deal, I presume?"

"I suppose it does bother me, though I don't suppose it surprises me completely. However, I have heard that Automatics had much higher standing earlier in the twentieth century, with many seeking public office or even civil rights, as humans do."

"Best thank GE's lawyers and their case back in the early '20s for that. Legally, Blue-eyes are considered human."

"How did Automatics go from mindless drones to thinking machines in the first place?"

"How would I know? Ask a GE bigwig."

Allen sighed. "Regardless, in the Prohibition era, most machines were reduced to the level of objects yet again. It doesn't feel right."

I kept my eyes on the road. I couldn't look at Allen and say what I felt. I knew I shouldn't ignore its plea for attention or its desire to belong, but what could I do? Lie and say it was just a phase? Who knew if it would ever be different — who knew if the Depression would ever end?

"That's just how the world is."

"But why is it this way? You never elaborate."

"I don't know. I'm not an analyst, I don't know everything about social convention. The world wants Automatics to be below humans. That's how it is. We're afraid of what's different."

"But we aren't different. If anything, we're very similar to humans."

"I think that's why people are afraid."

―――――

We headed north to the abandoned Morningside Heights area. Though most of the neighbourhoods north of 90th were devoid of permanent residents, many "entrepreneurs" had moved their businesses there, out of the public eye. One of those many shops belonged to a good friend.

We pulled up through 100th West, approaching a small abode that had used to be an apartment complex. Most of the upper floors had been left to rot; only the first floor was intact, with the section facing the street adorned with two large metal garage doors. As I approached the building, someone in the window recognized the car and pulled the chains inside to lift the leftmost door.

I brought the car inside, killed the engine, and stepped out. A mess of steel and electrical equipment covered the western wall, and a monstrous jury-rigged crane hung above us like a monolith. Against the eastern wall, which had a wooden door at the top of a small set of concrete steps, stood a man — my mechanic friend, Crate. He released the chain in his hand, and the gate slid down hard and hit the concrete, filling the room with the sound of vibrating metal. His dark skin and bald head contrasted against his blue-and-white outfit, which was covered in so much grease that it was hard to believe it had ever been clean.

"El! Good to see you, my man. You've been absent from my happy little neighbourhood. Work been getting you down?" He had a deep, jolly voice that rattled my bones.

"Something like that. You know how the Eye can be."

"Amen to that, brother." He shook my hand and turned to give a nod to Allen, who was standing motionless. "Who's the new guy?"

"Allen Erzly, my new partner. Don't give me that look."

"Pleasure to meet you, sir," Allen said, extending a hand.

Its hand was accepted and shaken quite vigorously. Allen looked down and saw that Crate's arm was cut off from the elbow down; the missing limb had been replaced by the metal framework and fingers of an Automatic's arm. Allen froze like a deer in headlights.

"Call me Crate. Good to see El is still a softie, getting another partner and all."

"We don't need any of that," I said. "Can we skip the pleasantries and get my car?" I put an arm on Allen, jolting it from its thoughts as Crate laughed in response. He walked around us toward the Talbot, which was taking up the right side of the garage.

"But man, the pleasantries are what rustle you the most. Who would I be if I didn't poke the bear now and then?" He winked at me and gave Allen a pat on the back before unlatching the hood of the Talbot and swinging it open.

I liked Crate for two reasons: he was discreet and he was good. He'd built that arm himself, after all. I made sure he was the only one who ever got to touch my car. The Talbot looked brand new. Most of the parts had been repainted and replaced, no doubt a job Crate had had to do by hand for a concept car. He turned the engine over. It sounded like all ten cylinders were pumping away without cause for concern. Yup, worth every penny.

"The thing sounded like it was dying when you brought it in. The hell did you do to it?" Crate asked.

"Uh …"

"Let me rephrase that: how many recharge packs did you slot in before you brought her to me?"

"You won't like the answer."

"Yeah, your baby here already told me that."

"Twelve packs, for three months." I leaned against a wall of rims and tires, bracing for impact.

"Three months! El, Christ almighty. *One* pack for a *week*, that's the max before you need a full cell change. If you want to buy a new concept car, be my guest, but I can't fix this engine time and time again if you keep doing this."

"But I'll pay you to try. How much do I owe you, outside of favours?"

"Well, to clean out the dirty Fuel Gel, replace the cell itself … And, I mean, you broke a window, put holes in some parts, the frame was warped, and the drive shaft needed serious maintenance … and the parts! A concept car doesn't have replacement parts. I had to make them myself."

Called it. "Will this cover it?" I reached into my coat pocket.

Crate's eyes went wide upon seeing the gold brick in my hand. Allen's, too. I'd kept a few lying around the apartment after the Cop Killer case. I was sure Crate knew a few people who could give him a good dollar for this.

"Yeah, that'll more than cover it." He held out his mechanical arm and grabbed the bar out of the air after I tossed it. He inspected it for a good moment, then nodded. "Grab a seat inside and help yourself to whatever you'd like. I'll finish up the paperwork in a jiff and get you on your way."

═══════

We spent about a quarter of an hour waiting, Allen motionless on the same chair the entire time, myself wandering the "waiting room" — otherwise known as Crate's living room. *In a jiff, my ass.* I was bored out of my mind and unwilling to turn on the TV or radio to hear mindless programming or how shitty the world was.

The room had two couches, three wooden chairs, some taped-up windows, a large desk where Crate did his finances, and a fridge filled with everything from soda to water to liquor. He'd only started stocking alcohol in there after I started coming regularly. I forewent the eggnog I spotted in there and grabbed a cream soda. The place was a shambles. I doubted the electrical systems had worked for the past five years, which meant the single battery bolted to the back of the fridge ran everything in this room, or maybe every room other than the garage.

Allen had been sitting still, like it was in detention, but watching me grab something to drink, it broke the silence.

"Detective Roche, may I ask you something?" it finally said.

"Yes, Allen?"

"Why is your friend called Crate? It's not a common name."

"He lifted it off of some engineer a few centuries ago who supposedly worked on machines for Alexander the Great's army. He sees himself as some sort of catalyst in that regard, I guess."

"Does he have an Alexander the Great to build for?"

"Good question."

I cracked the top off the bottle and took a swig. Good stuff, quite tasty. Almost better than alcohol. Almost.

Allen remained rigid and erect. It had another question, and it was counting down the seconds to the moment when it would be acceptable to ask.

"Yes? You always look like that when you have a question."

"Am I that predictable?" It looked around as though trying to find a mirror to see itself in. "I apologize, Detective. My other inquiry is as to Crate's … arm."

"He lost it in the Great War. Got it caught in an artillery piece, sent the shell flying at the Krauts and his hand the other way. He built the new one himself, and it's been working ever since."

"Don't you shun people who augment themselves with mechanical devices like that?"

"That's quite a low level of modification. He ain't an Auger until there are tubes running in and out of him, feeding his organs chemical cocktails. Nah, he's just an amputee. Crate is a good guy." I took another sip, and Allen slumped back, satisfied with the answer.

Our conversations these days were quick and brief. Allen was thinking up fewer questions to throw at me.

Finally, Crate walked into his little office looking darker than ever, grease caking his hands and face like glazing. He put the pristine gold bar on his desk and sat down behind it in an old executive chair. "All righty, things are in place, everything is good to go. But before I let you out of this room, regarding your engine: *one* week, *one* pack. I'm charging you double if you go over that."

"Yeah, but you'll still fix it."

I got up and shook his hand, the two of us grinning like idiots. I was lucky to have people like him and Sinclair around to keep my morale up enough and prevent me from falling into depression. Allen stared at us, still trying to wrap its head around human friendship, or companionship in general.

Back in the garage, Allen and I entered the Talbot and pulled out. Crate waved goodbye and dropped the garage door down. Soon his home was another silhouette in the distance.

"Detective," Allen began. "What was the War like?"

I looked at the machine. "Wasn't very fun."

"And dealing with the ... nature of war?"

"You mean the constant presence of death?"

"Yes. It's been almost a month and I feel ... like a coiled spring all the time. It's hard to go to sleep or do anything. I always feel like there's a crushing weight on my chest or my head or my stomach. It never really stops. Will it ever?"

I didn't answer, because in all honesty, it never would. The best you could do was numb yourself to it, but I knew that would be traumatizing for Allen to hear. I hadn't realized it was this affected by killing someone. Had I been the same way back then, right after the War?

I couldn't even remember. It felt like I'd always been an apathetic mess.

I should help Allen find someone to talk to so it could get its mind off of this stuff, lest it end up like me. God help this city if there were two of me in it …

CHAPTER 6

ANOTHER WEEK PASSED. Another week of snooping, prying, searching, and attempting to find the Edison Hotel killer. And we came up with nothing.

Sure, Maranzano pulled out of Chelsea Piers, and the Eye now owned everything there. And sure, recent skirmishes between her Automatic battalions and his guerilla mobsters were now as frequent as the nightly news. But given the rivalries there and the bad blood they'd had between them since '30, nothing surprises me, not even the fresh bodies. In the meantime, Allen, with its infinite patience and intelligence, hadn't been able to find out anything more about this killer. How did someone kill four Upper City officials and walk away free? No hair, no discernable footprints, nothing but some dust and tripod divots. He was good. Then again, I was slacking, and Allen was doing all the real detective work this time. At least I'd gotten my Talbot back.

With the frequent civilian Night Calls, I'd made some side cash, and I decided to splurge tonight at the Brass and Pass. It was December 20, and the cold was beginning to catch up with the time of year. Man and machine alike wanted to be behind warm walls, which was why Allen and I were huddled against the metal door of the entrance as I knocked. Well, Allen was up at the entrance, I was a few feet to the side.

The Red-eye Titan on the other side opened the slot and looked Allen up and down. When it opened the door, I pushed my hand out so I could walk in first. The big guy on the other side slammed me back so hard I almost fell over. A massive chunk of its cranium was missing. Only scrap metal kept its Neural-Interface from falling out of its head.

"No derms allowed." Its heavy mechanical grumbling rattled my bones when it spoke.

"Let me talk to Tiny," I responded.

"No ... derms."

"Tiny! Get this big asshole out of my way and let me inside!"

The customers of the machine-filled speakeasy all turned to look at me. Unlike the people at the Maranzano Kompound, these people — machines, whatever — were unconcerned, unsurprised that I was trying to get in. Many returned to their drinks and talk.

A loud, high-pitched voice rang out. "Oi, Dallas, out of the way, let 'em in!"

The bouncer moved aside, and Allen followed me inside. The warmth hit me in the face like a slap. A Tapper bot with six legs and only about a foot in height crawled toward the nearest booth and beckoned us in. It had one cracked glass eye, but both bulbs were red and functioning.

"Roche, ya bastard, how ye been holdin'?" Its flanging voice melded with the programmed Irish accent, making its English sound almost alien to the untrained ear.

"I've been holding as best I can, Tiny." I nudged Allen. "Meet the new partner, Allen."

"Allen, good to meet ya." The tiny machine scuttled over a table and extended a pointed leg. Allen shook it gingerly. "Keepin' ol' Roche in line?"

"As best I can, sir."

"Ah, fantastic! What'll it be, gentlemen?"

Allen started. "Sugar —"

"No, not sugar water," I interrupted. "Two pints, imported, Canadian. Heard they make some good brews up there."

"Aye, damn good brews. Back in a jiff!"

Tiny jumped to the floor and ran off. I heaved a long sigh, returning to some semblance of calm and feeling my jitters cease. We'd had nothing but typical jobs lately, finding lost things or solving minor murders. I was starting to prefer these civilian Night Calls, though it was best not tell that to Allen; it would never let me live it down. But having gotten so many easy jobs under my belt did make this whole Edison Hotel thing feel more manageable.

Allen didn't feel the same way, apparently; it was still the most rigid robot in the room. And that was saying something, considering where we were.

"You're quieter than usual, Al. Nothing some beer won't fix," I said, melting into the booth.

"I'm exhausted. Things have been rough at the 5th lately."

"You've all had to start doing your jobs, eh?" I smirked.

"Yes, actually," Allen retorted. "Ever since your jaunt to Kips Bay, Mafia-driven violence has skyrocketed across the Lower West Side and Chelsea. It's been worse in the last couple weeks than the past half year. I can't imagine why."

"Jeez, Sinclair's sarcasm sure is rubbing off on you."

"You do have to admit it is warranted," Allen said offhandedly. "Besides that, I've spent many late nights pursuing information on these murders."

"The usual ones, or the serious ones?"

The waitress came by and slid us two mugs of beer before departing.

"All murders are serious, Detective," Allen responded gravely.

"You know what I mean."

"Yes, I unfortunately do." Allen practically rolled its eyes. "I used whatever leverage I had in the precinct to do more digging into our prime victim, Desmond Hartley. On the record, people are up in arms about his death, and they want his killer found as soon as possible. The assassin is wanted on four counts of first-degree murder and one count of manslaughter, as well as a variety of other unrelated crimes they want to pin on him."

I took a swig of the beer and slid farther down. "And off the record?"

"Robins says he's heard that GE doesn't want anyone to investigate further. The state is pushing a bill that will be a precedent for the rest of the country, called the America First Bill. It will prevent the import or purchase of any Chinese or French Automatic parts, reducing the number of bootleg items that can be brought in and distributed. This will impact the entire bootleg industry, from the Mafia to small shopkeepers like Jaeger."

"How does our vic play into that?"

"He was fighting against it."

My eyebrow popped up. "So he wasn't just any official?"

"No. He was no doubt tied to one of the cartels in the city. I believe Maranzano was the one who purchased his vote to put the bill down, seeing as he had some very fresh parts that have only seen circulation in the Upper City. At least, that's what my research has told me. But with Hartley dead and the money now drained away from campaigns against the bill, it will no doubt pass, and decimate Maranzano's business in the Automatics sector."

"Who are our possible perps for this kind of operation? Not many people have access to hardware like a Von Whisper rifle. We're looking at paramilitary, or a deeply rooted Mafia running heavy weapons. Maybe the Iron Hands, or maybe Gould's group."

Allen shook its head. "Perhaps not Gould. While he has motive as an active supporter of the bill and the resources, his people would have left a trace. I should know. Gould's people came down to the precinct a few days ago. They clearly spare no expense on personnel. If Gould wanted Hartley dead, he would have sent a team, not a lone gunman, and there would have been much more evidence. The Iron Hands are a possible suspect, too. But let's not rule out the possibility of this being an inside job. Agent Masters's previous actions have made me wary of the government's actions. It's possible that someone within GE itself, or part of the New York legislature, wanted him dead in order to push the bill."

"That leaves us with an awful lot of suspects, then. All of GE must have hated this guy, and the number of people with the money to hire a well-equipped assassin isn't exactly small." I rubbed my chin. The clinking of glasses and the small talk of the machines around me pulled at my brain, distracting me. "We need help. Someone to walk where we can't and ask questions we shouldn't. You're too suspicious, and I ... I have a reputation."

"Surely we can't add another person to our investigation? The last thing we need is for our hunches and evidence to become public."

"First off, don't call me Shirley." I grinned. Allen didn't. "Never mind. Second, trust me, this is already just about as public as it gets. The front of a ritzy hotel was just blown apart. There was glass raining down on civilians. The Prince and Greene thing was easy to hide, but this crime is of a magnitude that not even the 5th could contain, if they tried."

"So you want to find someone to assist us?"

"Maybe ... maybe. I don't know, we're stuck. Our only angle now is to wait for another attack and then hope for more evidence. Not the best plan, but it's the one we got."

Allen took a moment to let this sink in. "It's a much sloppier plan than I'd hoped for."

"I don't know what to tell you, bud, but you said yourself no one wants this thing solved. Half of me wants to let this whole thing slide, since they didn't kill anyone too important. But at the same time, I don't like how high-profile this is for GE and for the Mobs. The way it was done, either he's professional enough that this was a cakewalk, or he's been doing hits like this for a while leading up to something this big."

"We don't have much to go off," Allen remarked.

"We can try to guess. There were five dead, but four targets. Focus on that. Try to dig up cases or files regarding four-person murders. Specifically, try to find connections to hits on the Mob or possible Mafia contacts."

Allen rolled its eyes again. "Do you know how many coincidental matches could come up where four people got killed during a hit or a raid or something else?"

"You'd best be patient and thorough."

"Four targets in a hit isn't a signature, Detective … but I will try."

I sipped down more beer with a smile. "Good man."

"Any developments from that kidnapping case we solved two weeks ago?"

"Oh!" I almost choked on my beer as I began to speak. "I went to see the kid in the hospital. He was pretty shaken up, but otherwise seemed fine. He told me about what happened, and it was odd."

"Odd how?" Allen perked up, seeming to forget its annoyance with my request.

"He said something jumped him, but remember, there were no footprints. Not sure who could have managed that. Actually, it's more like I have a semblance of an idea, but I don't want to be right."

"You did mention you might know who —"

"Anyway," I interrupted, "other than that, nothing much else to talk about. Violence as usual, but that's the Lower City."

There was a short silence. Allen kept glancing at me, while I continued to drink. I sighed and broke the tension.

"You look like you want to ask me something."

Allen was surprised. It had no idea I was picking up on its mannerisms. "The Tapper ..."

"Tiny."

"He has red eyes, but he hasn't tried to ... kill us ..."

"Oh, you must think all Red-eyes are psychopaths after the last case, eh?" I enjoyed more of the beer. Allen grimaced as it watched me suck it down. "Being a Red-eye doesn't mean you're a monster, despite the fact that most of them are little else. Some, like Tiny, just want to run businesses without being hampered with the linear thinking ability of a toddler. No clue who Red-eyed it, but what the process does — though I'm no engineer, mind — is turn off certain inhibitors that keep Blue-eyes from thinking like us. Not a perfect explanation, but close enough."

"But couldn't he replace his red bulbs with blue ones?"

I shrugged. "If it could be done, it would've done it."

"And if only some Red-eyes are dangerous, why are they so feared and persecuted?"

"Most people Red-eye Automatics in one of two ways. The first is to just unhook them from their hard coding and let them run amok. The other way is to basically enslave them to a direct set of programming or to certain orders, making them like violent Green-eyes. Both methods are barbaric, but the former kind of Red-eye gets a bad rap from the latter. Tiny is as much of a threat to humans as a rat would be."

"But if he wished to, Tiny *could* be violent, even kill."

"You could, too, Allen. Don't be judging too hard."

My last comment struck a chord, and Allen froze, obviously hurt by it. I played it off and went back to drinking, but the divide had been made. Recovering from it would be difficult.

The familiar tipping and tapping of Tiny's legs resonated once more above the speakeasy's noise. It hopped onto the table. "Talkin' business again, eh?"

"Do you have to eavesdrop?"

"Aye, I need to know what's happenin' in me bar at all times. Can't let ya be sayin' shite that'll get folks riled up. What's this about a bill?"

"Congress is pushing a law to keep French and Chinese parts out, and its main opponent is little more than chunks now."

"That might be a problem."

"For bootleggers, sure."

"Aye, and for the people they sell the parts to."

I lowered my beer and noticed half the speakeasy was watching me. Not with anger — I was used to seeing people look like they wanted to flay me alive — but with concern, or as much concern as an Automatic could show. I might be looking at this politically, but these poor bastards had to look at it practically. The passing of this bill would result in hundreds of dead or dying — I mean, hundreds of broken or breaking machines throughout the States. But, of course, it wasn't like humans to give a shit about their own kind, let alone another species.

"Let's roll, Allen."

"But —"

"You didn't pay, Roche!" Tiny yelled after me.

"Put it on my tab." I got up and went to the front door, which was blocked by the Titan. "Move it, lard ass." The Titan moved aside as I stepped out, and Allen was right on my heels.

It was starting to feel like everything I had to deal with was world-shaking. Why couldn't things be quiet for once? Always the fate of the world on my shoulders — our shoulders now, it seemed.

═══

I had parked a few blocks away from the speakeasy so as to not draw attention. The entire walk back to the car, I was fraught with nerves, the hairs on the back of my neck sticking up. I could have sworn something was watching us the entire time, but I had no idea from where. Allen could tell I was agitated and did its best to not speak until we got to the car.

Even driving home was a chore, as I had to try not to crash while constantly looking out all around us for something following us. No matter how far I drove — and I drove around all of south Manhattan to try and put distance between myself and my imagined pursuer — I never lost the feeling.

Arriving home, we walked past Yuri and gave him a nod. He'd known me long enough to tell when I was unable to talk. I felt some measure of comfort once we reached the elevator. The liftbot in the bellboy uniform grumbled something under its breath on seeing Allen and pressed the button for my floor.

"I think I know what's watching us," I said, finally breaking an almost hour-long silence.

Allen turned to me. "Someone's watching us?"

"Maybe. I don't really know." There was a clicking sound coming from the little gearbox just above the elevator. That was new, and unwelcome. "You got Robins's gun?"

"Yes."

I pulled out my Diamondback, keeping it close to my chest. "Best load it, because whatever it is, it ain't human. Don't use it unless I get in trouble."

Allen retrieved the handgun and loaded a round, then held the weapon near its side, with its finger off the trigger.

"Excuse me!" the Blue-eye liftbot exclaimed. "Put those away!"

The clicking was getting louder. And it was slowing down.

"Have you ever gotten stuck in an elevator, Detective?" Allen asked.

"Once. I was by myself, though. I wasn't stuck inside with three other people."

Allen scrunched up its face. "Three?"

The liftbot looked between the two of us. "What in the hell are you two on?"

The clicking stopped, as did the elevator. It rattled as inertia carried us up a few more inches, then it dropped down to settle on its cables. The fluorescent light in the ceiling was still on, and the bell announcing each floor had been functioning before we stopped, which meant it wasn't a power issue.

"I'll call it in," the liftbot said.

"Don't." I put my hand out and raised my revolver. "It ain't a mechanical issue." I turned to my partner. "Don't look up."

"Don't you fire that in —"

I released four rounds into the ceiling of the elevator, cutting the liftbot short. Each shot made Allen flinch from the sound bouncing around in our steel prison. Even I groaned at the pressure on my eardrums. The liftbot, less affected by the sound, was still reaming me out in its muffled mechanical voice. Several seconds later came some loud scrapes and the scurrying of limbs. That shut it up. The elevator started moving again.

I looked up at the four holes I had made next to the elevator service hatch, which was open. A thick black liquid dripped from one of the holes. Disregarding my order, Allen looked up, too, and touched the strange liquid with one of its fingers. The doors of the elevator opened on my floor, and we proceeded to get out.

"What —"

"It ain't oil," I answered. "Don't ask."

Allen decided not to question me. It put its weapon away. I exited the elevator first after making sure the coast was clear.

"You're paying for these damages!" the liftbot screamed after us.

We ran down the hall to my apartment. I threw my partner the keys, and it began to unlock the door, its hands trembling. My hand was still tight on my revolver, though I'd need more than three rounds to ward off this thing, let alone kill it. I peered down the hall, desperately trying not to blink.

But eventually I did, and in that fleeting moment, something appeared near the still-open elevator door. It was wrapped in black cloth, and its head was inches from scraping the high ceiling, which was peppered with holes made by its metal fingers. It was well over thirty feet away, but I knew how quickly it could move when it wanted to. It could have crossed the distance between us like a footstep. Allen glanced at it and dropped the keys in panic, then crouched down to grab them again.

"You're getting predictable," I said to the figure, levelling the barrel of my revolver at it.

"AM I?" Its voice was more grating to the ear than that of any regular Automatic. It sounded unnatural — more unnatural than machines usually did — each syllable like it was speaking through a metal tube, making my skin crawl. Its red eyes looked back at me from under the cloth.

"I was hoping you'd been scrapped for parts by now."

"IS THAT ANY WAY TO GREET AN OLD FRIEND?" it asked.

"You stay away from us, you hear? I don't know where you were or why you're here now, but you stay back. I won't hesitate to kill you, you metal fuck."

"I'M SORRY I'VE BEEN GONE FOR SO LONG, BUT I PROMISE WE'LL BE WORKING CLOSELY FROM NOW ON. SERENDIPITY HAS BROUGHT US BACK TOGETHER."

"Detective ..." Allen hammered out.

"The door, Allen!" I called over my shoulder. "I'm guessing you were responsible for kidnapping that guy two weeks ago?"

"PERHAPS. YOU'VE MISSED PLENTY OF OTHER THINGS." There was a silence between us for a moment or two. I faced it for what felt like an eternity. Then it spoke again. "BE CAREFUL, DO YOU HEAR? YOU'VE BEEN IGNORING HER, AND YOU KNOW HOW SHE FEELS ABOUT BEING IGNORED."

Allen finally got the door open, and we got inside. I slammed the door shut and secured it with every lock I had. If Allen'd had skin, it would have been as pale as I was.

"Detective, what on earth was that?"

"An old partner of mine." *Shit, I shouldn't have used that word.* "No, more like a co-worker, sorry."

"Another henchman of your mysterious employer, I presume?"

"Sure," I grumbled.

"Who do you really work for, Detective?" Allen stood and assumed a commanding presence. "Because this is pretty damning proof that you haven't been completely honest with me."

You're not wrong. "It's complicated."

"So you better start explaining."

"Goddamn it, Allen, what do you want me to tell you? That I'm some mindless gun for hire, or that I work for someone who's dangerous enough to have you killed if I even step out of line once? Which would put your mind at ease?"

It paused to think about this. "The truth."

"Well, the truth is both, sorry to say."

"Detective!"

"Fine. Fine! I work for a particular group of people ... the Iron Hands."

Its jaw practically dropped. "Supposedly the largest cartel in America, whose exploits are so exaggerated that some civilians consider them a bogeyman myth — you're working for *them*? For actual hardened, organized criminals?"

"On the side, mostly. Sort of. Yes."

"In what capacity? As an informant?"

"As ... an enforcer."

"An enforcer!" I hadn't realized Allen could yell. "You are an enforcer for the Iron Hands?"

"Well, *the* enforcer, but —"

"Elias!"

"Technicalities aside, I'm a peacekeeper, Allen. I settle disputes, whether with words or with bullets. She roots out the small fish for Robins and me, and I deal with the sharks myself."

"You are actively working for one of the most dangerous organizations in the history of the human race and you lied to me about it?"

Our roles had been reversed: for once I was calm and Allen was losing its mind.

"Yeah, I lied, because I didn't know how you'd take it."

"I'm taking it pretty darn hard, Roche!" Oh man, it was getting serious … it had used the word *darn*. "I can't believe that you would go behind my back to serve these murderers and degenerates! Police officers are meant to uphold the law, not help people break it!"

"I ain't a cop, Al."

"Even so, I'm connected to this by association with you! I never thought … Oh my, I'm an unwitting accomplice to I can't even imagine what!" It threw its arms up in exasperation, obviously struggling with all the questions running through its head. Eventually, it posed the simplest one. "Why?"

"Why? Because I was in an emotionally compromised state when she found me, and I let her use me for her own ends."

"Being emotionally compromised is not an excuse for throwing out your morals and becoming a glorified murderer!"

I approached Allen, and it backed up. I challenged it the same way I had Maranzano weeks before. "I've done some terribly stupid shit and I'm still paying for it. Don't talk to me about excuses and what you would or wouldn't do until you've lost almost everything, like I did!"

Allen tightened its lips and gave me a few moments to control myself. "Have they helped your investigations?" it asked calmly.

"Plenty, but regarding *our* first case, I answered to Robins first, them second. They just sped things along."

Allen nodded. "Andrew Stern, one of the suspects from the case — finding his apartment was their doing, I suspect."

"It was." I backed away, letting it relax.

"And that thing out there was … who you answer to?"

"No, I answer to the Eye, their leader. She's … difficult to read, negotiate with, or even contact. Dealing with her can be dangerous. We're both in danger now because of my recent truancy. And you aren't helping things. She thinks I've gone soft because of you. That's the only reason she would send the Rabbit after me."

"The Rabbit?"

"That thing we saw tonight. It was her old enforcer, before me."

Allen nodded. It looked like it was trying to keep itself from screaming in panic or disapproval, or both. "And why was the Rabbit not an issue in the previous case? Were you doing your job admirably?"

"Maybe … I don't know. With the Rabbit, you never know. She sent it on 'vacation' a year or so back, after that massacre it caused."

Allen frowned, but otherwise did its best to ignore the last part of that sentence. "How are things different with me here? I'm your partner, nothing more."

"You're much more, Allen. I, um … I'm not good with partners. But you knew that. My last partner …"

"I know about James. Commissioner Robins briefed me so I wouldn't pester you about your attitude toward me or say the wrong thing. I didn't want to mention him — it, sorry — until you were ready."

I nodded. "Police reports will tell you that I killed Morello and Luciano for the good of the city or whatever bullshit they put down, but trust me, they were not the only ones I killed that day. Or since. There's a lot of blood on my hands, and I'm not proud of it. The Eye picked me up while I was investigating who set up the 5th to get whacked, and she offered me a deal I couldn't refuse: she gave me the seven men responsible for killing my partner and threatening the 5th in exchange for the heads of whomever she pointed at."

Allen was quiet, rubbing its hands, a nervous habit it seemed to have picked up. "How long have you worked for them? Or for her, more accurately."

"Four years. More than four years I've been killing for her. The first two were chaos, utter havoc, destruction … It was sickening, even to me. Things are better now, but not much. But your being here, a new partner, means the wounds are healing, and she doesn't want a hardened and matured man. She wants an animal, an impulsive, violent animal to do her work."

Allen sat down on the couch. Its metal brow was furrowed, doubtless spinning countless scenarios and thoughts through its head as it tried to calm itself. I went to the fridge and poured myself a glass of Scotch. I returned and sat beside Allen, placing the glass on the table in the centre of the room. I looked over at my phone. The small square recorder beside it was blinking its red light to show that I had messages.

"The Rabbit. Is it a threat to us? To me?"

"God, I hope not. But if it is, I'll kill it. At least I'll try to." I had let loose with my trigger finger tonight. Allen knew I was nervous, and now the Rabbit knew, as well. I had to keep my cool, for both our sakes. "I'm still her enforcer, and unless I really screw up, we're safe."

"I hope as much."

We sat there awkwardly. I could tell Allen was repressing the rest of his questions. I admired its willpower.

"It's for the greater good."

"I understand that. While this isn't the best situation to be privy to … I understand."

I thought I'd try and defuse the tension by playing my phone messages. It was at Allen's behest that I'd bought the new recording machine a few weeks back. And my new TV, too, which stood on four oak legs, its screen grey and lifeless. Just like most machines, only less colourful.

"You mind, Allen?" I asked, pointing to the machine.

"Not at all, Detect— er, Roche." Looked like it was going to start crushing that habit. "If there are any civilian calls, will you be taking them?"

"One step at a time, Al."

Overall, that had actually gone better than expected. Good thing we'd gotten the worst of it out of the way a month ago. I pressed the button, and the tape spooled up and began to play, the audio popping a bit.

"*Hey, Detective Roche? This is Curio. Reginald Curio. This is the third time I've called, and I really wanted to know about your story. I've heard about the Nightcaller from the broadcasts, and I just have to know more about the real —*"

"Nope." I pressed the fast-forward button, followed by delete.

"Who was —"

"Don't," I snapped. The answering machine spooled up again and played the second message.

"*A message for Mr. Elias Roche. This is Elise Schafer calling for the Radio Corporation of America. It is with great honour that we invite the supposed inspiration behind our newest, and so far, most anticipated radio series to the annual RCA Gala this Sunday, December twenty-first. You will be on the guest list with a plus one, should you wish to bring a date. Do call ahead of time to confirm your presence. Thank you.*"

The voice ceased, the tape stopped, and the light went out. Turning to Allen, I found its wide blue bulbs mere inches from my face, making me back away in surprise.

"A gala tomorrow?" it began. "This must be at least a few days old. She must have called while you were out on a civilian Night Call."

"Yeah, plus I'm bad at remembering to check these messages."

"An event like that would be extremely helpful for our investigation."

"How do you figure that?" I asked.

"You said it yourself, any number of GE higher-ups could have hired the man who killed Hartley. I suspect many of them will be there, seeing as RCA is a subsidiary of GE. Wouldn't it be proactive to attend this gala and narrow down a possible suspect?"

Not a bad idea, metal man. "Yeah, just what I was thinking."

"No, you weren't."

I laughed, but it didn't. Jeez, it didn't even get its own jokes. "You comfortable letting me lead the investigation, knowing who I'm connected with?"

"Well, as they say, keep your friends close," Allen said. "I'm not saying I condone your allegiances, but you are still doing your best to *act* like an officer, even going so far as to protect this city in ways an officer cannot. It's admirable, if irresponsible."

"You didn't answer the question."

"No, I'm not comfortable with this revelation, but I don't have much of a choice, do I?"

Poor bastard was right, it didn't have much of a choice. Either it was stuck with me and was protected by my name, or it went on desk duty and some Black Hat tried to Green-eye it next inspection. No doubt FBI Director Greaves had been trying to have it shredded ever since she'd set eyes on it.

"Just … can you leave the gun in the car when we go?"

"Well, if we do go, I'll need a suit. And it's already" — I checked my watch — "eleven at night."

"No tailor shop will be able to get a suit ready for you in less than a day. Where will you get a tailored suit at this hour, on such short notice?"

"Trust me, Allen. If there's one thing I've shown you, it's that I know people."

CHAPTER 7

TEN AT NIGHT THE FOLLOWING DAY, we pulled up to the GE building for the gala. We were directed to the main entrance. Not the entrance I had walked through a month ago — no, *that* was the employee entrance. The executive entrance was nice and secluded and harder to get into than the Upper City. It was hidden behind a semicircular driveway that went into the footprint of the building itself. The twin entranceways into this crescent drive were protected by titanium poles that prevented cars from ramming into the entrance. At the moment, the poles were retracted down into the concrete, allowing me to creep the car into the building. The lights of the Plate were replaced by the light of silver chandeliers. Around us, humans in their best attire filtered toward the large double doors of the Exhibition Hall.

To say it all felt weird was an understatement. I was used to driving this car through garbage, Automatics, even humans. Rolling up beside a fenced-off red carpet with a waiting valet — that was something I had never done before. It made my skin crawl. Allen, on the other hand, was loving it. Face pressed to the windows, it was absorbing everything it could, taking in the people, the lights, the hubris of the entire endeavour. I could have sworn I saw a smile as it whipped its head to and fro.

I stopped the Talbot, and we got out. Allen was wearing its usual suit, and I was decked in my all-red outfit, as I called it: black blazer, pants, and shoes, with a red shirt and tie. It was a style of clothing I'd gotten used to wearing while under the thumb of the Eye. It felt tight, constraining, and uncomfortable, which was the reason I'd since switched to regular street clothes. But wearing this suit made me feel put together for the first time in a long while. I almost felt like I'd fall apart if I took it off.

"Sir, your keys?"

The valet's voice shook me from my stupor. He smiled at me. I didn't reciprocate.

"You won't scratch her, will you?" I asked.

"No, sir."

"You damage this car in any way, and I will find you." I dropped the keys into his shaking hand. "Do not."

He nodded and got into my vehicle, carefully pulling out of the drive and leaving me and Allen stranded in the midst of the wealthy and powerful.

The guards at the security checkpoint just inside the double doors were decked out in heavy body armour and held Frag Rifles — not the kind of people you'd want to tussle with. They noticed the holster under my blazer and were happy to confirm it was empty. They raised hell upon seeing Allen, but one look at its badge made them back down. They might raise a stink about machines any other time, but seeing the number 5 on the badge was enough for them to shut their mouths and move aside, even for just this evening. And with that, we entered the beating heart of both Manhattans.

Think Maranzano's Kompound, but bigger. Much bigger. Looking up through the empty space in the centre of the hall, I spotted five floors above us. Each of the higher floors had a glass balcony surrounding a tremendous space that was filled by a brass statue rooted on the floor below ours. I couldn't tell who the statue was of, but I doubted anyone here cared who it depicted.

Thanks to the open design of GE's Exhibition Hall, I could see who and what was on each of the floors: small five-piece bands, waiters and waitresses — all human — carrying hors d'oeuvres and drinks, and ritzy people of all ages, all of them with more money and time than sense. The designs of their outfits were strange; most of the suits and dresses were composed of triangular or rhomboidal interlocking shapes. On first glance, the fabric appeared metallic and rigid, but when disturbed, it distorted and flowed like cloth, only to return to its previous shape moments later. Fashion mixed well with stupidity; the eye-catching designs did well to camouflage the dull, unremarkable-looking people.

It was overcrowded and overstimulating in every way. I was sweating bullets in my suit. I hated being in any place I wasn't in control of. I felt like I was an insect to these people, something to be swept out of the way or crushed, if need be. I had no idea who wanted me to be here, but Allen had a point: we had to be here for the sake of the investigation, whether I liked it or not. Still, I could feel eyes all over me and my partner. They weren't used to seeing an Automatic in an environment like this. And I was shocked at the lack of machines here. No flanging voices, no squeaky motors and servos, no blue and green lights … just people. Horrible, unpredictable people. They chirped, gossiped, and narrowed their eyes in our direction. Hopefully, Allen's presence shielded mine.

A woman in a navy-blue dress moved through the crowd and approached. My paranoia sent me groping for my gun's handle, but my common sense forced my hand away from the empty holster. The woman wore a cape-let that draped over her right arm, and she was wearing elbow-length white gloves. It made her look like she was investigating a crime scene, or like she didn't want to leave any evidence behind. A purse dangled in the crook of her elbow. Given its weight, it must have been holding a gun.

"Elias Roche?" she asked, coming within a few inches of me, her eyes level with my own. She was as tall as me, which was rare, given my height. Her raspy smoker's voice was familiar, though, despite having previously been distorted by the phone lines.

"What?"

"As blunt in person as you are on paper." She smiled, more out of pity than amusement. "Elise Schafer, head of finance for GE. Happy to meet you."

"Why?"

Allen turned, translating my curt dialogue. "We're thankful for the invitation, truly. My companion here isn't well acquainted with social situations like this one."

Schafer turned to face Allen, her prim and proper black hair frozen in place by chemicals. She looked it up and down, conceit radiating from her. "When I said you could bring a plus one, I meant a human date, not one of these … things."

Allen and I looked at each other before I spoke. "If you want me to go, I have no problems with that. I don't need any snide remarks about me or my partner from you and your self-righteous, silver-spoon-fed —"

"Relax, Roche. Have a drink." Unfazed, she handed me a glass of something clear and illegal. "The investors want to see their new poster boy, even without a muzzle. Shut up, smile, take a few photos with the bigwigs, then get out. And make sure that thing isn't in any of the shots."

"If I'm your poster boy, where's my paycheque? No sane lawyer will turn down my case once I tell them you're using my likeness without consent."

Schafer smirked. "One of our reporters sent us a transcript of your most recent interview. We paid top dollar for it." She opened the purse on her elbow and pulled out a small pad, her eyes dancing over the page. "Ah, yes, and I quote: 'So, do me a favour and tell RCA to fuck off.' How many lawyers would take the case with that on the record?"

I finished the drink she had given me and placed it on a nearby table. "You don't know many Lower City lawyers. A case like this, they'd start making corpses to get it done. Trust me, I've seen some bad shit in courtrooms. No Upper City prick could ever stop a dirty Lower Manhattan lawyer."

Her smugness came clean off. "We'll consider sending a paycheque now and then, Detective. Do enjoy the festivities."

"Not so fast. You may be done with us, but not the other way around." I took a dart out of my coat pocket and put it between my lips. I needed to get the nerves out.

"There's no smoking in here."

"Assholes over there can have a cigar or a pipe, I'll do what I want." I lit the tip and felt a rush of nicotine giving me a mental cushion. "Heard about the Edison Hotel?"

"The murder? Yes, of course."

"Murders. With an *S*."

"Hartley was a stain on the company that needed to be cleaned. His cronies were even less important. No one is sad to see him or them go. I doubt Hartley's wife and kids are upset, either. They left for a reason."

"No doubt. His reputation for infidelity is noted, along with his illicit activities — smuggling alcohol," Allen piped up.

Looked like it had done more research.

"He wasn't a smuggler. He was just a corporate asshole," Schafer retorted.

But Allen doubled down, and I stood back to watch the show.

"On the contrary, he was a good businessman, so good that he kept a paper trail, which was almost too easy to find. Police seizure of his home and assets allowed me to track down the shipments he referred to as 'shoeshine.' His own shoes at home were filthy, I might add — a dirty man in practice and at home. Needless to say, seizing those assets uncovered his involvement in the Maranzano crime family. You must be a little upset, seeing as Hartley embezzled funds from GE in order to fund these operations. He spent your fortune to make his."

Schafer's expression turned into a snarl, in response to Allen or the victim, I couldn't say. Seemed that this was a tidbit she hadn't uncovered.

Allen continued: "Finding his paper trail uncovered some interesting things about General Electrics. He worked to put down several projects besides the America First Bill, such as the Cellular Project, and another called Ferrodermis. And there was talk about him trying to pull funding from a high-risk project, something called the U—"

Schafer took a quick step forward. I pushed myself between them. Her eyes were on fire, hot rage building inside. "You'll shut your mouth if you don't want to go into the shredder, capek."

The standoff between the three of us was quelled by the arrival of a pompous man who smelled of smoke and alcohol. He inserted himself between me and Schafer, forcing her to pull back, her eyes still fixed on Allen. He had a group with him. Our trio suddenly grew into a group of nine.

"Ah, welcome! You must be our Nightcaller, welcome again. David Sarnoff, head of RCA. A pleasure!" He grabbed my hand and shook. "No smoking in the building, by the way."

"I'll put mine out when you get rid of yours."

Sarnoff puffed on his pipe and chuckled, his entourage laughing, too. "I like this one. And one of our metal friends, too? We don't often use them for intimate events like this, seeing as, well, a machine can only do so much compared to a human. Must have been hell to get through the door, hmm?" Allen offered a firm handshake but no greeting. "It lets everyone breathe a little easier to know they pop out of the factory pre-Greened these days. Speaking of which, when were you built?"

"Don't," I said. It was getting crowded. Too many people with too much power.

"Oh fine, can't be rude to the Nightcaller, our star, it seems!" Sarnoff signalled to a waiter and asked him to bring over something stronger. At least he was enjoying the party. "So, Mr. Roche, how are you enjoying the party? Networking?"

"Trying to find the person who killed Hartley."

"Oh, move past that! He's long gone, just a bump in the road to success. Another Farnsworth." He turned to his entourage. "Remember that little spat in '31? Tried to beat us out of a television patent. Didn't last long against the might of General Electrics. Hartley might have had some political protection, but that doesn't stop a bomb, does it?"

A bomb. This idiot had no idea what had killed Hartley, which meant he hadn't ordered him dead. Sarnoff was too fat and happy to care about Hartley. He could've crushed the man with just paperwork, if he'd wanted to. Maybe I was barking up the wrong tree here; no one seemed to care about Hartley.

"At least Maranzano helped us with that one," Sarnoff continued, more to his sycophants than to me.

"The only thing that tax dodger has ever done for us. Perhaps next time we can get the Iron Hands to help us with cleaning up the streets of America, hmm?" His group erupted into laughter. Hard to believe the Eye had managed to keep the wool over everyone's eyes for this long.

Any other possible suspects? Maybe Schafer. She seemed like the murdering type, but how would she have avoided leaving a paper trail? The Eye was still on the table, seeing as the Rabbit was around again — no idea how long it had been back, but certainly long enough to pull off something like the Edison.

My eyes wandered from the fat man and drifted through the crowd. Like a magnet, I was drawn to the glare of a man, not much shorter than I, who was smartly dressed, with dark hair and a firm stare. A lot of folks here were probably curious who I was, but that wasn't the type of look he was giving me.

"Mr. Roche?" Sarnoff asked, snapping me out of my trance.

"Who's that?" I pointed, and the fat man followed my gesture. The space I was indicating was now empty.

"Who was who?" he asked.

I groaned. "Never mind."

"Well, maybe not the talking type, but a damn good listener! Heard the show?"

"No."

"Oh … too bad." He seemed sullen and upset at that fact. "So, no praise or criticism of accuracy? Nothing to tell us about what we did right or wrong?"

"No."

"No matter, we have someone under our employ who helps us out with that kind of information." He turned to Schafer. "Is she here?"

"I would hope so. We sent her an invitation," Schafer confirmed. "There she is."

She beckoned with her finger to bring the person in question into the already crowded group. I had a hunch as to who it was, and confirmation came when she made her way through. Blond hair, green dress, confidence in her walk, and a smug smile — not smug like Schafer, but smug like she knew what I was thinking. Simone Morane, the reporter.

"Roche," Simone said, nodding to me with a grin.

I stared, not sure how to respond. Allen appeared pleased to see her, though, and offered its hand to shake. Feeling my heart in my throat, I threw my cigarette to the ground and stormed off.

My head was ringing, and my body was shaking, switching from ice-cold to on fire every other second. People called to me, but I ignored them. My hand grabbed a glass of something and drank it. The alcohol was soothing, but not healing.

I pushed past people to get to the safety of a smaller room I could calm down in. My shoes squeaked against the marble floor as I walked into a washroom. The mirror reflected my panicked expression. I would have felt less afraid walking into Maranzano's without a gun. Why was I like this? These people were rich, but they weren't anything special. Schafer was frightening, Sarnoff complacent, and Simone was too curious for her good or mine. I splashed water on my face, trying to rid my head of this swirling panic. I needed to get out of here.

"Goddamn it, focus!"

Without thinking, I punched the nearest thing, which happened to be the mirror in front of me. My right hand was bleeding, and there was a crack in the glass, splitting the reflection of my hazel eyes. I hoped there weren't any shards in my skin. I should clean it, make sure I didn't get blood on the floor. I didn't want to go out there again. I'd make any excuse to stay in here.

"Losing it, huh, Roche?"

The man who'd spoken was emerging from one of the toilet stalls. He left without washing his hands. It was the same man I'd noticed a few minutes ago. As badly as I wanted to run after him, it wasn't worth it. Not with everything else that was out there.

CHAPTER 8

"IS HE OKAY?"

Allen was sitting in a small booth opposite Simone. Both had drinks in hand. He wasn't one for partaking while on the job, but since it was customary here, he didn't mind wetting his throat.

"He's ... yes, I hope he is. I've never seen him like this." Allen scrunched up his face, the taste of the alcohol and concern for Roche making his thoughts fuzzy. "I would have thought, given his past, that he was accustomed to large crowds. Just the other day I saw ..." He stopped.

"Saw what?"

Simone leaned forward, spinning the large ice cube in her drink with a stir stick. Allen's eyes locked onto the glass, then glanced up at her. If he were capable of sweating, he would have been now. There was something comforting, but at the same time, terrifying, about looking at her.

She smiled and repeated herself. "What did you see?"

"Oh, he was speaking to Maranzano and —"

"Salvatore Maranzano, the crime lord? Are you kidding me?"

"Not a bit."

Simone leaned back, laughing. "Who is this guy? Helping old ladies and talking to crime bosses? Is he a cop, is he a vigilante? And you! You must see all sorts of things with him. Have you been to the Plate?"

Allen was entranced by her voice and everything about her. He kept staring and forgetting to respond. "Y-yes, once. Indeed, Roche is … unique. I believe he prefers to work only loosely with the police because he likes dealing with criminals himself. I'm not sure about his relationship with the Mafia, however."

"Aren't you a cop? I never got your name, by the way. You know mine?"

"Yes, Miss Morane. I'm 41-EN. Allen. Allen Erzly." He shot out his hand again, which she shook gently. "I work for the 5th Precinct."

"The 5th! I shouldn't say anything too risqué around you, then. I could let slip a crime I may have committed."

"We — they aren't like that. Roche used to be part of the 5th. They're good cops."

"Haven't heard a cop called 'good' in a while. 'Rough' and 'opinionated,' yes."

"Rough, but effective. You need to be rough down here to survive. The Lower City will chew you up and spit you out if you aren't careful."

"For a second there, I thought I was talking to Roche." Simone smiled again, laughing to herself.

"He does have a way of talking. I guess it rubs off on people."

"I'll say. He's strange ... charming, almost, in a dark and dangerous sort of way."

"I beg your pardon?"

"I mean, some of our listeners, and our executives, too, have said that just the thought of a man prowling the streets in search of justice and retribution is ... attractive! You know, dominance over the city, not letting anyone tell you what to do — it's a sort of wish fulfillment for people too poor or weak to do anything themselves. And the way he talks is all part of that. He doesn't let anyone push him around, and people enjoy that. Could you imagine if they saw a picture of him? I mean, he's not half-bad, even if he is rough around the edges."

"They smooth out if you spend enough time around him," Allen joked.

"An Automatic that gets figures of speech? I've misjudged you."

Her eyebrows gave a suggestive flair to the end of her sentence as she took a sip from her drink. Allen was frozen, his synthetic heart palpitating from her mere presence, let alone what she said.

"We don't really want to let people see pictures of him, though — it would ruin the whole allure. The anonymity, how anyone could be the Nightcaller, all that jazz."

"Of course." Allen nodded.

"So why are you here, Allen? Care to explain why Roche would drag a Blue-eye to an almost exclusively Upper City gala?"

"Uh … that's confidential." Allen tried winking, which prompted a laugh from Simone. "But, well, you already know Detective Roche and I are following the Edison Hotel case, seeing as you cornered us at the crime scene. In fact, it would help us to get a political lay of the land in terms of GE executives. Would you mind?"

"Oh sure, I know them all a bit too well. And I'm very willing to help our boys in blue." Simone grinned and turned to survey her surroundings. "Well, you already know David Sarnoff, head of RCA, golden boy for GE, and one of the main investors on the Board of Directors. He's one of the most powerful people in the company, and he's only climbing higher. RCA is just a stepping stone. If he could burn it all for cash, he would."

"Who else?" Allen asked, leaning in. His attention was more on her than on who she pointed out.

"We have Owen Young over there, founder of RCA and current president of GE. Little guy knows how to handle his liquor and fame, unlike Sarnoff over there. And over there are Sanford Moss and Harold Black. The former heads GE's avionics and aeronautics division, and the latter is responsible for the Tesla Grid on the Eastern Seaboard. Funny how even with free energy for one and all, we're still surrounded by greedy assholes, eh?"

"Inequality is the root of greed, unfortunately," Allen agreed.

"Yeah, but even with significant equality, people will find something to pick apart and have more of," Simone said. "Anyway, they're both on the Board of Directors, too. Tesla used to be on the board until the mid-'20s, but we have no idea where he went. He sort of just up and disappeared. You know all about him, though, right?"

Allen gave Simone a quizzical look. "No, should I?"

She almost choked on her drink. "How do you not know?"

"No one's ever told me about the man the battery is named for."

"Jesus, Allen, Tesla is the man who saved the world, so to speak. His little accident at the Wardenclyffe joint on Long Island is what made the first Tesla Battery. It's funny — it almost never happened, which means you almost never happened."

"Oh?" Allen raised an eyebrow.

"Yeah, see, he was deep into debt making that tower thing and pleading for money. The guy who financed him, JP Morgan, was about to pull out, but at the last second, he decided to give Tesla the funds he needed to complete his experiment. When it all went up in smoke, people were quick to disregard him, until he found the core of his tower intact, and producing a ton of energy. He was able to reproduce the results with the money he gained selling the thing. Made towers all over Long Island, and things went from there. He revolutionized the world, yet hardly anyone wants to remember him. Disgusting, isn't it?"

"Yes ..." Allen pulled back from the conversation. Why had no one ever told him this history? He really should have known all this, or at least read about it somewhere. Something to research further when he had the time. "Do you also know how the first Blue-eyes came about?"

"Ah, that's history no one likes to acknowledge. Many consider it a mistake." The corners of Simone's mouth pulled down. "Automatics were sold as cheap labour, and the one company that needed cheap labour the most was the one that made them, GE. You know how Green-eyes are, right?"

"They can be single-minded," Allen said.

Simone nodded. "They can miss things a human wouldn't, which cost the company thousands of dollars in damages, because they'd tell a machine to do something and it did it ... even as the room was burning. So, a little tweaking led to Blue-eyes: it gave them some self-preservation instincts and broader perception, and developmental experience led to their gaining personalities. Of course, free will led to other headaches, like how they didn't want to work 24-7, and even bigger ones when they started demanding paycheques. Even with all that, they still consider Blue-eyes more valuable than Greens."

Allen scratched his neck. "And they just ... started paying them, just because the machines asked?"

"Oh, no, that was a case headed by Franklin Deist. Getting Blue-eyes a decent paycheque was the only case he took pro bono."

"I know that name."

Simone smirked. "I should think so. He was the lawyer that got GE their extraterritoriality; they're exempt from the jurisdiction of state law. Only GE and a few other companies can legally employ Blue-eyes. You know, for the benefit and sustainability of modern civilization."

"Hmm …" Allen took a moment to process everything. "Are Blue-eyed Automatics still being made?"

"Not since the Prohibition. Now they come pre-Greened, and they don't get the same freedoms the Blue-eyes have. That's a lawsuit waiting to happen, especially if they start spilling over into critical infrastructure sectors. Too bad Deist is dead, else he'd jump on that." Simone turned back to the crowd, looking for more important figures. "Dr. Vannevar Bush should be here, but he's not one for formal events. He heads GE's Automatics Division, and he's one hell of a brainiac."

"I've met him. He was quite cold … direct."

"Sounds like Vannevar." She grinned.

"He probably isn't the only one who tends to avoid these gatherings," Allen prompted.

"Yeah, Gould doesn't come, either. But as the man who owns the Plate and GE, he has that privilege. Last but not least, the newest appointee to a directorial position, Elise Schafer, head of finance. She's an absolute corporate monster. She'd tear out throats if it would adjust her bottom line."

"Is that bad?"

"No, it just means she knows what she's doing and what she wants. But I do wonder what kind of damage she could do, now that she has all this power." Simone put down her drink and looked over her shoulder to see Schafer approaching. "Speak of the devil, boss woman coming in."

Allen sat up straighter. Schafer was snarling in his direction. She reached the table and addressed Simone. "Where's our poster boy? Sarnoff wants to show him off to investors."

Simone looked at Allen. "He's in the washroom."

"For an hour?"

Allen shrugged.

Schafer rolled her eyes. "Move away, capek."

Allen took his leave, sliding out of the booth and walking a few feet away. Even through the noise of orchestral music, glasses clinking, talk, and laughter, he was quite adept at eavesdropping. His first encounter with Roche had been to listen to him from the other side of a door.

Schafer began, "You're stepping on toes, Morane, and people are taking notice."

"Excuse me?"

"I don't give a shit who you know on the Plate, you are not getting out of the reporting business down here. This stunt with the robot — seriously? It's here because of a radio show. Don't give it the dignity of being acknowledged like a person. This Nightcaller business will not help your career. Remember who sits on top and gives you your paycheque."

"Yeah, a bunch of assholes with no sense of decency. I saved RCA by finding Roche and giving you the idea for this radio show, and you're reading me the riot act?"

"I've looked into your paperwork and your calls. Transfer to the Upper City? What the hell are you going to report on in the Upper City? Oil prices? Clothing sales? Get over yourself, you're not the breed of person who lives up there. You're a Lower City girl, and you'll be one until the day you die."

"And how would you know what a Lower City girl is or isn't? You come down from your ivory tower once, maybe twice a year, make your appearance, get some votes for reapplication to the Board, and fuck off back up top. You're more out of touch than I thought."

"I could kick you out of this building and destroy your reputation in seconds."

"But you won't. My father would blow a fuse. You can stop me from going up top, but if you want to keep your promotion, you'll leave my career alone."

Schafer seethed with rage, gripping the glass in her hand so hard that her knuckles went white. "Entertain the capek, I don't care. But you won't last much longer here. Just look at Hartley."

"Is that a threat?"

"It might be."

Schafer stormed off, and Allen saw Simone flush with tension. He went back to her, noticing her loosen up when she saw him approaching.

"Enjoying the party?" Her voice wavered, and she cleared her throat, trying to shift gears.

"As much as I can, considering Detective Roche has disappeared. I can see now why he's uncomfortable in this setting."

"Do tell."

"He's a man who deals with things using a gun. Maranzano, the Iron Hands, common crooks — if you threaten them, things move. But here ..."

Simone chuckled, causing Allen to trail off.

"What's funny?" he asked, genuinely confused.

"Oh, it's just that you mentioned the Iron Hands so seriously. Given all the crazy stories we hear about them ..."

Allen continued. "Here, pulling a gun out would put him in hot water or prison or worse. It's one thing to put your gun against a don's head. It's another to put it up to society's."

"That makes sense." Simone put her fingers back on the stir stick, spinning the melting ice cube. "But I admire his tenacity. He doesn't let anything get him down. We could all learn something from him."

"I hope not," Allen remarked.

―――――

Midnight came, and people began to leave. Drunk off fun or alcohol, they were sure to have a good night in their million-dollar estates on the Plate or outside the city. Allen had coaxed Roche out of the bathroom long enough to get a few pictures with Sarnoff and other big names at RCA and GE. Even Vannevar Bush eventually made an appearance for the GE holiday photo, though he stayed far away from Roche.

Schafer departed soon after the photos were taken, and Simone left around the same time Allen and Roche did. Roche insisted on Allen driving them out. The valet was nervous handing the keys to the machine. After a quick inspection, Roche declared himself happy that the Talbot wasn't scratched. The tip he gave the valet made up for his previous outburst.

The drive back to Roche's apartment was quiet, but not tense. Roche gazed out the window at the passing buildings, while Allen focused on the road.

"Thanks for not prying, Al," Roche said, in passing.

Allen nodded. "I'm getting better at reading situations."

"You're a quick learner."

He was hesitant to ask, but he was curious. "You noticed something, didn't you? When we were talking to Schafer and Sarnoff?"

"Just some guy. Tallish, black hair, weathered. Looked like a soldier. It was odd …"

"Odd how?"

"He was looking at me, with … I'm not sure. Something wasn't right about it. Can you look into him for me?"

"It'll be hard without a name, but sure, I'll see if anyone recognizes the description." Allen smiled to himself. "So, I can drop you and the car off?"

"Keep the car," Roche said. Allen's eyes went wide in surprise. "I'm going to be lying low for a few days. You might need it. I trust you." Roche let the silence simmer for a time before speaking again. "Tell me about those GE projects in the future sometime. They sound interesting."

"Can do."

They arrived at the apartments of Bowery and Bayard, and Roche stepped out. He gave Allen a final nod before departing.

Allen made haste back to his own residence, making sure to park the Talbot somewhere it wouldn't get broken into. Though, given Roche's reputation, people likely recognized whose car it was.

Allen's tiny apartment on Madison Street had been given to him as a gift during his "integration," and it was well maintained, inside and out. The rooms were spartan; Allen wasn't the kind of person who needed much in the way of amenities. There was a couch, a small radio on a table, and a fireplace in the living room. The tiny kitchen was dusty and forgotten, the stove and oven untouched. The fridge was the only appliance he used.

Down the hall was his bedroom, which contained a chair, a small bed, and a closet. Allen took off his suit jacket and shirt, placing them on his bed. He could feel things, both psychologically and haptically, but he found no comfort in his bed. Not since he'd taken a life a little over a month ago. He found no respite in soft sheets or a comfortable mattress and had started sleeping in the chair, perhaps to punish himself, or perhaps because it was less constraining than lying under thick blankets.

He walked to the bathroom, flipping on the light in the tiny room to reveal a toilet, a sink, and a bathtub. In the mirror, he inspected himself. Though metal on the outside, he was alive inside, his electrically oriented cells moving and growing within. At the moment, though, he was more interested in his exterior: his almost human face, concave funnel chest, thin frame, and broad shoulders. He widened his stance and stood at different angles, trying to look at himself the way a human might.

This newfound self-consciousness wasn't welcome in his head. But Simone was lodged in his brain. Something about her made him lose focus, lose his logical edge. What might a human woman see in another human, but not in him? It was stupid, maybe, but if human men could use feminine Automatics for their own needs, wasn't it possible for a human woman to perhaps feel some sort of attraction to a male Synthian like him? Or even to an Automatic?

"Focus on the murder," Allen reminded himself, trying to move his thoughts off of Simone and onto Hartley. He pointed at himself in the mirror. "Stick to the case. The murder first, then deal with everything else. If it becomes an issue again. Only if it persists."

He turned off the bathroom light and went to the chair in the bedroom, reclining as his blue bulbs shut and his body went rigid. He never usually rested well in the chair, taking hours to find some semblance of sleep. But tonight it took only seconds to close his eyes and drift away. Tonight, the images of his past sin were blocked out by a smile and the stirring of an ice cube.

CHAPTER 9

I HATED MADE MEN. They talked too much and did too little. This one was no exception.

The truck behind me full of alcohol, drugs, other expensive toys, and three fresh bodies was burning in the alleyway. No one would come investigating. Commissioner Tony Shen wasn't a man to blab about anything, especially not after his men had been threatened.

"Goddamn, my arm!"

The made man cradled his dislocated shoulder. The arm drooped dramatically lower than the functioning one. I was covered in a mix of oil and blood, the former from the truck, the latter from the dead boys burning inside.

"You knew this would happen," I told him.

"You crazy fuck! Do you know who you're messing with? We will find you, gut you, tear your throat out!"

I cracked my rifle open, extracting the three empty cartridges and placing them in my pocket before reloading the three barrels. "I know who you are, and I know you can't do anything. You and your boss are too brash, too hasty. You don't think."

"You're dead, you hear me? Dead!"

His voice slurred as he slumped and groaned in pain. The blood loss and shock must be getting to him.

"You're not dying that fast. Get up," I said.

He moved his legs, struggling to stand, hindered by delirium. Finally he turned and faced eastward. I put the end of my rifle in his back.

"Get walking. I have a nice place to string you up from." He stayed where he was, so I jabbed the rifle forward. "Move! You want two busted arms?"

I wasn't expecting him to have the balls to try and struggle out of this. But without warning, he twisted around and grabbed the barrel assembly with his working arm, pushing it down to keep me from firing at his chest. He was helpless without two working arms, though. He'd have to rip the gun from my hands to get away. Good luck with that.

I shoved him up against the nearby wall. His arm was weak, as was his willpower. He pushed the rifle down to his stomach, and the end of the barrel assembly lodged itself just above his belt. He was red, sweaty, panic in his eyes. He knew he wouldn't make it out of here alive.

A shove and a kick from his leg pushed me backward. I lost my balance, landing with my back against the opposite wall, dazed. He pulled out a knife and threw it in my general direction.

Instinct took over, and I yanked on the centre trigger. The other two got pulled back, as well, dropping all three hammers.

The bullets hit his chest and stuck into the wall behind him. The smoking holes in his sternum were almost cauterized. He slid down the wall, his face slack. The knife I soon found between two bricks in the wall behind me. It had carried some blood with it after cutting my right bicep.

Shit.

I kicked the fresh corpse, angry I'd let that happen. *Goddamn it, never again. Don't be stupid. Be quick and clean. There's no use sending a message to these assholes.*

I used dirty rags to close the wound, then broke the rifle in two and hid it in my briefcase nearby. My pocket felt lighter than before. I might have lost a shell or two during the struggle, but I had to get moving. The 11th might be dissuaded from coming here, but Elias Roche wouldn't be.

CHAPTER 10

ALLEN'S WAKE-UP RITUAL WAS VERY different to Roche's. His day began at seven in the morning: inspecting his suit, getting dressed, polishing his badge and shoes, and getting breakfast ready. His morning meal consisted of oatmeal and bacon, meant to balance the proteins and carbs necessary to keep his synthetic organs operating and his body active. He was technically alive under the layers of interlocking metal, which meant he needed food, as well as a powder mixed into water that made up for the lack of silicon in his system. The tiny table in his kitchen was set with utensils and a napkin, and there was a single chair. He didn't have anything to read over breakfast; he'd been considering buying a few books to read before and after work each day.

Allen chowed down and quickly cleaned up afterward. Then he stared at the loaned pistol in his possession for about five minutes. The contemplation wasn't necessary, but the weapon was hard to look at.

He pulled the magazine out, unloaded the bullet in the chamber, placed it back in the magazine, and loaded it without pulling the slide back. Even though he had the safety on, he wanted to be sure he couldn't discharge a bullet unless he meant to.

He nearly forgot the keys to Roche's car but grabbed them before exiting into the cold morning. A thin layer of snow had coated the car and the street overnight. The sun had yet to reach the horizon. He got inside and revved the engine. The distance to the 5th Precinct was short, but he was much happier in the loaned vehicle than he would have been walking. After all, he could still feel the cold, despite his metallic exterior.

In front of the station, Paddy Sinclair was already outside smoking, getting some fresh air, or at least making an excuse to get out of the stifling office space. He saw Allen approach and waved him over.

"How's it goin', metal man?" he said, sucking in the tobacco. Allen noted that Sinclair had relapsed from quitting yet again.

"I'm fine, thank you, Detective Sinclair. Has Roche come by today?"

"Nah, he's lyin' low, so he says. Must be real low since he gave you the ol' girl there. Might play into our favour — Robins wants us to run some patrols around Kips and the Lower East Side. You okay drivin' an unmarked cruiser?"

Allen nodded. "I just need to get some files first, Sinclair."

"Good, because I'm seriously hung over." Sinclair finished the stub of his cigarette and threw it into the snow. "And that's Sergeant Sinclair to you!"

Allen parked the Talbot a block away from the entrance to the Kips Kompound. The searchlights and watchtowers of Maranzano's base of operations were visible even from down the street. The first rays of sunlight had peeked out from the east and blasted the side of the Kompound with yellow. Inside the car, next to the groaning sergeant, Allen watched the day begin. He swore he could feel the eyes of a dozen henchmen all over them, perhaps curious whether Roche was inside the vehicle or someone else. Sinclair reclined in the passenger seat, a hat over his face and a heavy coat around his shoulders.

After two hours of waiting and even after driving around the block twice, there was nothing to report. He'd tried to read through the police reports he'd brought from the precinct, but his mind kept wandering for one reason or another. Half his brain was overridden by self-preservation, the other half distracted by lingering images of the reporter with the kind smile.

What he did manage to get from the reports was that the violence in Chelsea between the Hands and 'Zano's gang was tapering off. Turned out everyone at the 5th referred to anything south of Chelsea as the Iron Hands'. Roche talked about them like they were a force of nature. It was hard to make sense of. Many believed them a group of ragtag bootleggers; others thought them a veritable underground army. It seemed no one had the straight story when it came to who the Iron Hands really were. Besides Roche and the Rabbit, he had yet to meet anyone who truly worked for them, whereas he had seen Maranzano's base of operations.

"Sergeant Sinclair." Allen's voice pierced the silence, and his companion groaned in acknowledgement. "Do you think the Mafia observes the holidays as a time for peace and compassion, despite their morally questionable stance?"

"Huh." Sinclair laughed under his hat. "I've worked plenty of Christmases and busted plenty of crooks on the twenty-fifth." He sat up, spurred by his own interest. Allen noted that he recovered quickly from his hangovers when he chose to. "I got a story for you about that: the Silver Gun of '27, one of the finest pieces of detective work I've ever been a part of, if I do say so myself."

"Oh, that's not necessary …"

"It's no trouble, really. I've told this to Roche and Toby a few dozen times each." Sinclair rolled down the window and put a dart between his lips, lighting it. "Okay, so it started in December of '27. Picture it: the rich were rich, the poor weren't too bad, and Roche was still running with the 5th. Well, he isn't the star of this story, but he's in it. Anyway …"

Allen yearned to know what Roche was like in his younger years, but Sinclair's introduction had left him disinterested. His eyes moved around the vehicle, looking for anything to distract him while Sinclair prattled on. Adjusting the rear-view mirror, he spotted someone walking around outside, the only moving thing on this desolate street. His flight or fight instinct kicked into overdrive, and adrenalin made him reach for his gun, alerting Sinclair that something was wrong.

"What's going on?" Sinclair peered behind them. "Oh, he came. Relax, Al, it's Toby."

Allen allowed himself to breathe and relax his grip. The familiar Grifter frame and blue eyes came up to the passenger-side door, urging Sinclair to get out and push the seat forward to allow Toby to enter.

"How goes it, pretty boy?" Toby said, patting Allen's shoulder as he climbed inside and settled into the cramped back seat. "And you, too, Paddy, you ugly fuck. Three musketeers without our Athos to lead us to victory. We have the new guy, though, and he was a main character last time I checked."

"You read?" Allen was genuinely surprised.

"What is that supposed to mean?" Toby didn't have eyebrows, but if he did, his expression would have been one of offence. "You think because I'm some lowlife Blue-eye that I'm not literate?"

"No, no, I didn't mean anything by it —"

"I'm just fucking with ya, Allen. Roche called himself that a while ago. I never let him live it down." Toby cackled, making Sinclair put his palms over his ears to block out the flanged laughter. "Take it easy, all right? You're as stiff as a board and half as useful."

"Can do," Allen responded. "I'd heard that Commissioner Robins allowed you back on the Force."

"I guess Robins has a soft spot for me after I helped with that raid in Chelsea. It's all under the table of course, but I still couldn't say no. I missed running with the boys."

"Amen to that, Toby," Sinclair agreed. "See anything on your way here?"

"Nothin'. Not even the Hands are out to play. Too busy keeping Chelsea from exploding. Jesus, that's a ticking time bomb. What jackasses gave them Chelsea on a silver platter?" Toby leaned forward, looking at Allen as he spoke. Allen stayed quiet, keeping his hands on the wheel and his eyes forward. "Relax, metal man. Whatever we did still ain't as bad as the 4th Precinct."

"Yeah, now *that* is ancient history we don't talk about." Sinclair stretched his legs in his seat and reclined once again. "Well, I say we give it another hour, then take a break at the Funhouse."

"Funhouse?" Allen said curiously.

Toby tried to roll his eyes. "Man, don't tell the new guy that, he'll rat us out."

"What's the Funhouse?" Allen asked.

"It's a place Paddy and Roche set up for long patrols and stakeouts, a little hidey-hole to pass the time with drinks and cards. Seems you're in on it, too, now, since Paddy can't keep his trap shut."

"Fuck off, capek," Sinclair groaned.

Toby snickered. "You won't be ratting us out, will you, Al?"

While Allen was indeed uneasy about doing something behind his supervisor's back, he knew that getting in the good graces of his fellow officers would be beneficial. He didn't want to be the one to rock the boat.

"Of course not. My lips are sealed," he said.

"I like this guy, Paddy. Better than you, even." Toby patted Allen's shoulder again. "All right, let's get the fuck outta here. Kips creeps me out. Makes me feel like they'll pull me off the street and tear me apart if I close my eyes for a second."

———

The aptly named Funhouse was a shanty tugboat at the end of the old East 34th Street docks and marina on the East River's edge. It had been abandoned since midway through the '20s, and it showed: mould on the wood, rust on the metal, and seaweed on everything else. Inside the boat's central structure were three rooms: a bathroom, a room with rotting tables and chairs, and the now abandoned driver's quarters, where the wheel had been removed, leaving the boat unsteerable.

The three officers faced eastward as the sun crawled up through the sky. The Plate was several dozen metres behind them, leaving open sky above. The sight enchanted Allen; he didn't want to look back down. Seagulls called while flying across the water, and the lapping waves elicited a tranquil calm in him as he listened.

Toby skipped a stone. It slapped the surface of the water three times before sinking. Paddy sat against the nearest wall, drinking an old expired beer to help with the hangover. Allen sat beside Toby on the edge of the anchored, tied-down tugboat, taking in the view.

"Sorry to burst your bubble, Allen, but police work isn't all paperwork and action," Toby said, sending another stone across the water to hit three times again before sinking. "Ninety percent is boredom. Well, usually ninety-nine percent, but things have been rough recently, huh?"

"Yeah, haven't seen violence and kerfuffles like these since before the Purge of '30," Sinclair commented. "Remember before then, when the Five Families were tryin' to gut each other for territory and cash?"

"Man, plenty of roughhousing then. Then things got boring. Still can't believe the precincts actually had to lay off cops because of the 'peace.'" Toby snickered. "Peace, my ass. They've just had too many guns and not enough targets since then. I miss the raids. Remember the stakeouts we used to have?"

"Yeah, those were great." Sinclair chuckled and turned to Allen. "How was your first stakeout with Roche?"

"Uh, it was fine, I guess." Allen shrugged. "It was entertaining. We played darts."

"Ah, world champion he is," Toby commented, Paddy laughing in response. "Robins doesn't need us back from Kips for a few hours, and seeing as we're parked in the middle of Maranzano's territory with 'The Nightcaller's' own Talbot, I envision a boring day ahead of us. So, any topics of conversation? You're usually talkative."

Watching the sunrise and the stones skipping, Allen felt a peace that he hadn't thought he ever would again. He didn't remember his dreams, but he did remember his last thoughts before sleeping last night. Now, with nothing but bliss surrounding him, his mind drifted again to her face.

"I … I think I need advice. About a woman."

Toby, midswing with another stone, released the rock early. It plummeted straight down into the water. Sinclair fumbled with his beer as it almost escaped his grasp and peered at Allen. The Synthian felt violated by their gazes. He tried to defuse the situation, but all that came out was a series of mumbles and gibberish.

"Are you fucking with us?" Toby asked.

"No, no, no. I don't joke. Well, you know that."

"A woman? Oh boy." Sinclair laughed and drank from his bottle. "Allen, my boy, a woman is much more complicated to deal with than a case. I would suggest giving up. You don't have the body to do anything about it."

"How in the fresh hell does a machine even think about a human that way?" Toby seemed almost disgusted.

"You don't?" Allen responded.

"No, *we* don't. We ain't programmed like that, not even Red-eyes, I don't think. It just ain't in the code! What makes you so special?"

"Well, Allen ain't an Automatic," Sinclair said. "Don't you remember? I thought you saw inside that cranium of his. His brain."

"Right, yeah. The rest of us Blue-eyes ain't blessed with great memories." Toby slapped the side of his head.

"Shit, yeah, you're gettin' old. What's your capacity limit, again? Like six years? You probably forgot an entire war. When're you gettin' the ol' hard drives swapped?"

"When I damn well please, Paddy," Toby snapped back.

"Can we get back to the topic at hand?" Allen asked, feeling forgotten.

"I just needed a jostling is all, keep your pants on. Cells and electricity, a brain, lungs, and a stomach, et cetera, you're special. I always wondered if you had anything down in yonder parts." Toby laughed and threw another rock. "I guess we know now."

"Who's the girl?" Sinclair asked, grabbing a fresh beer and cracking the top, then offering it to Allen. The machine accepted the drink and leaned against the same wall as the senior officer. "Some pretty face down by Times? Or a big name?"

"We met at the RCA gala that Roche and I went to as part of our investigation into the Edison Hotel murders."

"No shit, eh?" Sinclair said.

"Simone Morane. She's … well, from a distance she's beautiful. But up close, she's stunning. Just talking to her, her voice and her mannerisms, all of it is impossible not to be taken by," Allen said with a smile. "The more we talked, the more it felt as if she could really hear me. The others at the party were less than pleased about my presence, but she treated me, as one woman said, like a person."

Toby made a groaning sound. Sinclair clinked the neck of his bottle against Allen's and finished his drink. "Morane, the girl from the radio, huh?" he asked.

"Exactly."

"Yeah, she has one hell of a voice." He grabbed another beer. "Must be good lookin' in person, too. You gotta be to make it in that business."

"Can we acknowledge how fucking weird it is that we're talking about this with *Allen*?" Toby butted in. "Christ …"

"At least it's something positive to talk about, ca- pek," Sinclair snapped back. "Now, her name, that's an important bit. You know who her father is?"

"No," Allen said, guessing that he should.

"Colonel Sebastian Morane of the U.S. military. Or, sorry, General Morane now. He's one step away from be- ing the secretary of defense in D.C., lives in the Upper City. Her word must be law down here with a name like that behind her."

"Maybe down here, yes, but from what I heard, it doesn't seem to matter much up there." Allen sipped the beer, grimacing at the taste, but fighting through it.

"You overhear somethin'?"

"Just a big name at the company telling her to watch herself. The Upper City must not like her too much, but for what reason I can't say."

"That's politics. It's everywhere you don't want it to be. Makes life shitty and complicated. Even those pricks up top aren't immune to it," Sinclair noted. "Makes me feel better to know that they're as trapped under some- one's thumb as we are. But back to the woman — what are you gonna do about her? Woo her with your magical powers of observation?"

"I don't know. That's why I wanted to talk to you. You seem to have experience with women, much more than Roche, I think."

Toby laughed. "If only you knew, Al."

"I'm not a lady's man, not like I used to be," Sinclair said. "I mean, plenty of men can tell you what they *think* a woman wants, but I'll tell you what they really want."

"What?"

"For you to leave them the hell alone. They got enough to worry about without someone trying to rope them into a relationship, or worse. Leave it be for now. If she's into you, you'll know. But if there's any advice I can give you, it's to be confident. Everyone likes confidence."

Allen sipped at the beer, his mind wandering back to the gala. The way she'd described Roche as both feared and respected — was that what Allen had to be like? Until now, Allen and Roche had mostly interacted with the people of the underworld. It was eye-opening to meet someone who wasn't trying to kill them and to learn what she thought about the now famous Nightcaller.

The crackle of the police scanner in Roche's car was loud enough for Allen to hear. He stepped off the tugboat and walked across the dock back to the car. Leaning through the window, he adjusted the volume and frequency of the radio to hear the broadcast that was going out.

"This is Reynolds. Skirmish at Chelsea Piers. Requesting backup. Looks like the Italians are pushing against the Hands again."

Allen ran back to his companions to relay the message. Toby skipped his last stone, watching it bounce six times before being swallowed by the rising sun. Sinclair chugged Allen's beer and threw the bottle in the water, then stretched. With everyone back in the cramped cab of the Talbot, Allen took off from Kips due west.

He couldn't help but smile as they drove away. Sinclair and Toby were good people, even if they weren't the best cops. It had felt good to get everything off his chest. Maybe one day he could feel the same way talking to Roche.

CHAPTER 11

IT WAS NOON WHEN I WALKED UP to the barber shop. I wasn't getting my hair cut today.

Eight Stuyvesant Street, otherwise known as the Angel's Share. Back in the 1920s, this had been *the* place to be. Women, drinks, famous faces, connections, money — everything had passed through that secret door in the barber shop down to the basement. Douglas Fairbanks, John Barrymore, even Gloria Swanson were said to have gone down those very steps to have a drink.

I stood before the dilapidated shop. The barber had left long ago, and the speakeasy had been forgotten by many. Not by all, but by most.

I wasn't alone. The Eye's actual lapdog stood behind me, looming in its overcoat, which hid its rusted skin and red bulbs from any people who might see us. The Rabbit was only back in the fold because she thought I was being irresponsible, because she thought I was going soft. For my sake, for the 5th's, for Allen's, I couldn't let her think that.

"I KNOW IT'S BEEN A WHILE," the Rabbit began, coming up from behind. I could hear the servos inside it buzzing and creaking as it moved. "SHE WANTS YOU TO TAKE CARE OF BUSINESS THE OLD-FASHIONED WAY, TO PROVE YOUR LOYALTY. YOU KNOW HOW IT IS."

It slid a weapon into my right hand. It was an old wooden hammer. The head was bent and dented, the wood stripped of varnish, and the carved M at the bottom almost worn away. I grasped the handle, turning it over to see a hole in the head of the tool. The perfect circumference for a .46 calibre bullet. The machine's other hand held a dozen or so of the aforementioned bullets.

"No," I said.

"YOU DON'T GET TO CALL SHOTS, ROACH. THERE ARE NO MORE NOES UNTIL YOU MAKE UP FOR THINGS."

"Not with this. I told her I wouldn't touch this again." Yet here I was, holding it tight. "I don't work like that anymore."

"YOU DO AND YOU WILL, ROACH. SHE'S PAYING GOOD MONEY FOR AN ENFORCER, AND AN ENFORCER NEEDS SOMETHING TO *ENFORCE* WITH, YOU SEE? GO IN THERE, DEAL WITH HIM, AND GO HOME. BUT IF YOU LEAVE THIS HERE WITH ME, SHE WILL TAKE IT AS A FORMAL RESIGNATION. YOU UNDERSTAND WHAT THAT MEANS IN HER WORLD."

I spat on the ground, half of me wanting to turn this weapon on the Rabbit, the other half wanting to use my gun. Neither half would act. When the Eye had first seen this weapon, she'd said I should give it a name, something stupid and contrived like Justice or Mercy. I never had given it one, and I never would.

"WE APPRECIATE YOU DOING THIS FOR US," the Rabbit said smugly.

"I ain't doing it for you." I ground my teeth. "And it's *Roche*, capek."

"SHOULDN'T YOU BE WEARING A COAT? YOU HUMANS GET COLD, AFTER ALL."

"I ain't cold. You should warm up, though. Your servos might freeze on the job. You're getting old, Rabbit."

"NOT AS OLD AS YOU," it snickered, disappearing into the cold air.

I gripped the hammer hard and fit the butt of a bullet into the hole. The magnetic ring caught the round without striking the primer. I sheathed the tool under my right arm and drew my revolver from under my left as I approached the barber shop. The chairs were gutted, the mirrors cracked, and the moveable wall that had hidden the stairs leading to the basement was cracked and strewn on the ground. I descended to the metal door and knocked. The first two knocks made the slider open so the guard on the other side could see my eyes. The second two knocks made him unlatch the door and run past me, up the stairs and to another city, if he knew what was good for him.

The scene I wandered into was like something out of an old Western. Everyone turned to face me, and the bartender hid under the countertop, which was on the left wall. There was also a hallway on my right leading to restrooms, and the central area in front of me was filled with bar tables. A total of twelve people were in that rotting old husk of a speakeasy: two at the barstools near the countertop to my left, one coming out of the bathroom, six at a table ahead, and two more at the far end of the speakeasy. And, of course, the hiding bartender.

The two at the far end of the speakeasy pulled revolvers from their waistbands. The six at the table dropped their drinks and cards, scrambling to grab their irons. The two at the barstools reached for unravelled Foldguns that had been sitting on the counter.

None of them fired, possibly wanting to confirm my knocks hadn't been a mistake. Stupid of them. They shouldn't have hesitated.

My left hand pulled my Diamondback's barrel parallel to the floor, and my right hand fanned the hammer. The first round slammed into the barstool fellow farthest away. He took a round to the chest. The closer one was faster to grab his Foldgun, but a second bullet from my revolver flew into his head and launched his body over the counter. The bartender's screams confirmed the kill. Bullets three, four, and five hit three unlucky bastards at the table; I'd aimed for the closest ones so their corpses would fall on the three behind them. Bullets six and seven blasted into the guys at the far wall — one in the shoulder, the other in the stomach.

I holstered my still-smoking gun and took out the hammer. The three unharmed men at the poker table pushed their dead friends aside, leaving their guns down and grabbing objects more appropriate for close-quarters combat; after all, a loaded gun could easily be taken and used against them. One had a knife, another held a broken bottle, and the last slipped on a set of brass knuckles with barbs on the ends.

The one with the knife took a swing at me, leaping forward to go for my neck. Moving left out of the way of the blade allowed me to send the hammer in my right hand upward, swinging to hit his jaw. The compression of the bullet against his skin and, consequently, the pin firing inside the hammer's head sprayed most of his skull on the speakeasy's ceiling. The recoil fired my arm back, resetting my shoulders for a second swing.

Both lackeys behind the fresh corpse were running at me, the one with the bottle going for my stomach, the one with the knuckles for my face. The body lying between us provided the perfect trip hazard for the guy with the knuckles. I moved to the left again and waited for his feet to catch on the fresh corpse. The brass-knuckled bastard stumbled and fell to the ground behind me.

As the two bodies tumbled, I focused on the guy with the broken bottle. My left hand grabbed the weapon, pushing it away, my hammer's claw going for his head. It snapped into his temple, and I ripped it back out in one fluid motion. Both he and the bottle crashed onto the floor, the latter shattering.

I'd underestimated the guy with the knuckles. I was shocked when I felt the barbs and brass slam into my right side, cutting up my shirt and skin. I spat out a short scream and curled my back, swinging the hammer out of reflex, going too low to hit his stomach and instead bringing it down onto one of his knees. He fell to the ground in pain, the fall pulling the barbed wire out of me, along with a chunk of flesh. A large spot of blood seeped through my ripped shirt. I slammed the hammer into his other knee after he fell, hearing it crack and the kneecap shatter. He screamed bloody murder, but he would learn his lesson better if he couldn't walk again.

A bullet whizzed past my head, and I turned to find the source: the guy at the far wall with the busted shoulder was alive and held a gun in his functioning hand, trying to stay lucid as blood pooled underneath him. I reached for one of the .38s on the poker table and unloaded the magazine into him. Overkill, yes, but I had to be sure he was done for.

I turned to the man who had just come out of the bathroom. He wasn't there anymore. There was a flash of his black shoes at the top of the stairs beyond the open door.

"Shit," I spat.

I grabbed a second loaded pistol from the bar table and stopped just before running out the door when I saw the bartender peeking out. He looked at me as one might a ghost.

"Sorry for the ruckus," I said, and dropped a wad of bills onto the counter, making sure to keep it out of the blood. "Fix it up nice again. Keep it on the down low, you hear?"

The bartender nodded, took the money, and made his way far from the blood and bodies. I took my own leave from the speakeasy, ascending the stairs and jogging after my target.

He was making a break across the street of the scarcely populated neighbourhood. I put a few bullets downrange. One clipped his thigh and sent him tumbling onto the opposite sidewalk. Another bullet must have hit his heel, because he was crawling, unable to stand on the wounded leg. I dropped the gun and followed him, a thin trail of his blood leading me to an alleyway.

Poor bastard ... that's last place you want to crawl to.

Reaching him, I grabbed his collar and hoisted him up against a wall with one hand. He was pale, and it smelled like he had evacuated his bowels. The only sounds were his breathing and the faint screaming of the poor bastard with two fucked-up knees back in the Angel's Share. I gripped his chin and cheeks with my left hand. With my right, I grabbed a fresh .46 bullet from my pocket, loaded it in the sweet spot of the hammer, and held the weapon at the centre of his noggin.

He'd made one mistake: he wanted out, but not on her terms. Stupid mistake to make. One I'd nearly made, too. I supposed this wasn't just a job, but also a lesson for me.

"Vito Genovese," I said.

"You can't do this to me! You know what an asset I am! Let me go, *bastardo!*"

"You were helpful with some of the Five Families' stragglers, but you made a mistake. You forgot that you don't call the shots. I'm here to remind you of that. You have a debt to pay."

"Wait, wait! Let me talk to her, parley with her, you owe me that!"

"She ain't Masseria or Luciano. You don't get to fix what's broken. I'm here to punch your ticket."

The hammer and the bullet slammed into his skull, blowing the back of it against the stone wall and splattering some of it onto my face and my shirt. He slid down and slumped in his own blood, and the tool went back into the holster under my right arm.

Having dispensed my justice, I turned around to find my mechanical peer standing too close for comfort. The Rabbit loomed high enough to cast a shadow that swallowed me whole. It looked pleased, seeing me like this. *Fucking abomination.*

"QUICK AND DIRTY, LIKE YOU ALWAYS ARE." It held out an envelope full of cash. I walked past it. "IT'S PAYMENT FOR SERVICES RENDERED."

"I don't need the cash, freak." I lit a dart and sucked in the nicotine, my stress levels dropping like a rock. "Get back and tell her Vito's ticket was punched. I want a meeting soon. I got things to discuss."

"SHE ISN'T IN THE TALKING MOOD, ROACH. DO SOME MORE JOBS, AND HER FAITH IN YOU MIGHT BE RESTORED."

"If that's all, you can fuck off."

I didn't hear it go. Turning back, I saw that it had left behind the envelope of money. I looked around before reaching down to grab it with my right hand, clutching my bloody side with my left. Walking around the city like this would draw attention. Good thing I knew someone who could help me.

———

"I usually require patients to book an appointment."

The doctor looking me over was called Nightingale, and she was good. Too good, in fact. She was the kind of woman who could stuff a corpse full of fluff and make it look like it was still living and breathing. She'd used to be on the Eye's payroll until she got out. The right way.

Her office was a hearse, with medical supplies adorning the blackened windows and a small table where she treated her patients. The ride was smooth thanks to the car's powerful suspension, and her sewing was clean and precise. It didn't even feel like she was stitching me up. Then again, I also had a few milligrams of morphine running through my veins.

I should have studied chemistry. I should have been making this chemical, not having it pumped into me.

"Not talkative today? That's odd for you, Elias." She finished the stitches and placed some gauze on the wound. "The old Iron Hand himself with nothing to say. Is it the drugs?"

"No, I'm fine."

"I know how temperamental you are with morphine, but I had to give it to you. You weren't looking good, and hydrocodone is in short supply."

"I know."

"You don't like working for her, that's obvious." She put a bandage on me, reinforcing it with some medical tape. "I know you won't take bedrest, so hopefully this keeps the bandage on. Please, change this dressing tomorrow. Don't put it off like you do with your car."

I laughed. They all knew my habits. "I'll try."

"I know you wouldn't have gotten into this scuffle unless you had to. I've known you long enough to know you're a good person, Elias."

"I ain't a good person, Doc. I just ain't. I try to help, but things get worse. I'm fighting a losing battle. How the hell did you get out?" I turned to look at her. She had short brown hair and emerald eyes that had seen more of my veins than of my face. "How the hell did any of you get out?"

"Jaeger got lucky, because he never kept a paper trail. Crate hired someone better than him — shocking to think, I know. Moses disappeared, but he made sure to screw with any guns sent to Maranzano or Gould. Me ... Something bad happened to a favourite of hers, took a bullet to the head — frontal lobe, you know how those go. I pulled it out, and he made a full recovery. She gave me a favour. I cashed it in. But you're different, Roche. You can't get out like we did. You're too valuable."

"She has the Rabbit. It's more of an animal than I am."

"She doesn't want an animal, she wants a knife, and your name still carries weight in the circles she deals in. Something to slide in and cut out the affliction with minimal collateral damage. The Rabbit is more akin to a sledgehammer."

We chuckled together. I pulled myself up and rested my back against one of the walls of the hearse.

"I'm tired of this," I said. "I thought I was doing good work, skirting the line and helping out both parties. I really thought I was making a difference. But stepping back after everything, I can see that I've just been making things worse. I mean, this whole 'peace' I've helped set up ... It's not really peace if it can come undone because of some rogue FBI agent. I've wanted to get out for years, but with things the way they are now, that desire is … exacerbated. What the hell happened to me?"

"You're not the man you were before. We grow, all of us. I'm sorry about James, but she can't milk that rage forever. And neither can you." Our eyes met. "Everyone can see you're getting sloppy. If you were really as brutal as people expect you to be, you wouldn't have gotten cut up today. Or the last time. I've seen the mighty Iron Hand fall from grace over the past two years, and if it's obvious to me … If you're serious about getting out, you'll find that opportunity and take it."

The hearse stopped outside my building. I crawled out the back. Nightingale whistled to me, handing me a small wrap of canvas with glass rattling around inside.

"Take some if the pain gets bad. I trust you not to abuse it."

"Much appreciated. I'll pay you back soon," I said.

"On the house, Roche. Stay safe."

She closed the doors, her associate got back into the driver's seat, and the black vehicle disappeared. Turning around to face the door of my building, I saw Yuri sitting there with a dog in his hands, his eyes wide with worry. My clothes were caked in blood from my wound, and the bandage was visible through the hole in my shirt. Thankfully, she'd cleaned my face before letting me out.

I smiled to Yuri and walked over, putting some change on the cart and taking said dog from his hands.

"You die, Mr. Roche?" The thick Russian accent was almost comical, in my state.

"No more than usual."

"Ah, good. If you die, I must raise prices to make up for lost money."

We laughed, enjoying each other's company in the cold. The Plate's turbines were open. Unable to keep up with the cold, it was letting the snow fall through down to us. Some of it fell on the street meat, but it was no matter.

"Sorry about the blood."

"Nah," Yuri said. "I see more blood in War. You get paper cut?"

"Okay, don't be an ass." I laughed again, and he gave me a hearty chuckle back. "Do you have anywhere to go for Christmas, Yuri?"

"Christmas? No. Family is all in Russia. Maybe I go back one day, but no one here to celebrate with. No one out to eat dogs, either. I go to bar some days, see boxing fights, pay good money for seats one time. Save all year for it."

Poor bastard. He had no one here. No one but me. Well, if I was turning soft, I might as well make sure everyone benefitted. "I, uh, don't do anything for Christmas, either. I usually work for the police, you know? Recent years, I take it easy, get some brandy, and just read a good book. Nothing special."

"*Da.*"

"If you need a place to stay, I wasn't kidding about that. In any case, if I do anything for Christmas, you should come with me. Just get out of the cold for a while, put the cart in the lobby, and live a little."

I saw a tear well up in his eye. He quickly blinked it away. "I consider it, Mr. Roche."

My touching moment had to be ruined, of course. I'd almost expected it.

I heard tires screech as a car pulled up in front of my building. My car. The horn sounded as I grabbed a second dog and threw down some more bills. Yuri tried to object, but I left to keep him from returning the money. Allen leaped out of the car.

"What happened?" I asked.

"I could ask you the same thing," Allen said, staring at my bloody shirt.

"Cut myself again. Shaving accident."

"Mm-hmm ..." It pursed its metal lips, but didn't dwell on it. "We might have something on the Edison Hotel murders. We called, but you didn't answer, so we came to get you ourselves." It seemed almost excited. "Time to get back to work."

"You hungry?" I asked.

Allen grinned, taking the second dog from me. We got in the car, Allen slammed on the gas, and we rocketed northward.

─────

Deep into Maranzano territory, in an alley near 72nd and 3rd, was a burning truck. From it came the smells of toasted flesh, melted steel, and boiled alcohol. I hadn't made this fire — that alone narrowed down possible suspects. Aside from the crispy transport filled with bodies and illicit substances, another body was slumped against a brick wall with three bullet holes in his chest. The guy was underdressed for a funeral and overdressed for being a stiff.

"Why the hell are the 7th's boys here? I thought the 11th ran the Upper East Side," I commented.

"Why the hell are you looking like that?" Sinclair countered.

"Business as usual. Now your turn."

"The usual boys in blue weren't around," Sinclair explained, still looking at the carnage across my clothing. "Someone called in the smoke, but when some boys from the 7th rolled by and didn't see any tape, they cordoned off the area. That was at … four in the morning? We're the only ones who know about the particulars, seeing as Viessman wants it kept on the DL. After all, we wouldn't want the ritzy folks in the Upper East Side worried that their city might be gettin' dangerous." He snickered.

"Yeah, all the high-profilers live around here," I groaned. "Trying to make this their own little slice of the Upper City."

"Fat chance that'll happen with Maranzano hanging around."

"Anyone make any other radio calls besides the ones to Viessman and Robins?"

"Besides the original report that didn't get anyone's attention, just the call out for you. Allen picked that one up," Sinclair explained. "Other than that, nothin.'"

"All right, good, they plugged any possible leaks." I moved closer to the slumped-over man with the holes in his chest. "So who's the stiff?"

"Davin McIntyre, an enforcer for Maranzano. He ain't no Santoni, but he was gettin' there," Sinclair said, handing me a wallet and licence. "A dead Maranzano boy on their own turf — it seems like the noose is tighten-in' around their throats more and more these days. Everyone wants a piece of 'em. Whose dog did they kick to get this much hate recently?"

"No clue. This ain't the Eye's style, though." I inspected the corpse. The holes through the chest matched the almost triangular pattern in the brick behind him. "Nor Gould's. He's a long-range head shot sort of guy. Four corpses, Allen."

"I see that," the machine responded. "You were correct, it seems. I'll redouble my efforts."

"They complained about the smoke and the smell, not about the noise. Bullets are basically the ambient background for this city. But no explosion means no Von Whisper," I noted. "Paddy, got any solid evidence other than dead bodies and burnt stock?"

Sinclair snapped his fingers at the head officer from the 7th and beckoned him over, then retrieved a small paper bag from the man. He passed it to me, and I dumped three crumpled bullets into my hand, along with a casing. They had been found nearby. Whereas the bullets were mangled and shredded from slamming into the brick wall behind the dead enforcer, the back of the casing was intact. I couldn't read French, but I recognized the numbers 8 and *50*, as well as the word *Lebel*.

"We also retrieved this," Sinclair said, handing me an intact shell much larger than the ones in the bag. Long, black, about 15 millimetres in diameter. A Von Whisper round. "Need any more evidence?"

"Nope. Shit, this was our man. He didn't get the chance to use this, though."

I put the Von Whisper shell into the bag and pocketed it. *Fuck!* My stitches ripped and itched with my movements. I shouldn't move too fast until I'd healed more.

"How much did he burn?" I asked.

"A few tons of guns, hooch, drugs, some bodies, Automatic parts — the standard Maranzano affair," Sinclair noted. "This doesn't tell us anythin' other than that this guy has one hell of a grudge against 'Zano."

"Not just that," Allen said, inspecting the wall opposite the corpse. "We have a few things. The killer's height, for one. And the fact that they have blood. Seems McIntyre had one last try at escaping and gave us some credible evidence."

The machine pried a switchblade from the wall. Its edge was coated in dried blood. I doubted that it was McIntyre's.

"Hell of a throw for a man with a dislocated arm. What can this tell us?" I asked.

"Well, the murderer isn't a Red-eye," Allen noted.

"A nice change for once," I said, grinning.

"The bullet holes give us a height estimate," Allen continued. "If we assume they fired their weapon from the hip, the murderer should be between five-eight and five-ten. If they fired from their shoulder, I'd say they were around four and a half feet."

"We ain't chasing a little guy, so I'll take the former assumption," I said.

"This knife and the blood it produced will coincide with a wound on their arm. Without a blood trail, I can't determine any more about them, but the wound could be useful in identifying them if we're able to round up several suspects. There's also the bullet pattern, which will be critical in finding them."

"Yeah, triangular, with three bullets. Don't you think it's just him having one hell of a trigger finger under pressure?"

Allen moved closer to the holes that the mangled lead had been pulled out of. It inspected the entrance holes, measuring the depth with its fingers. "Would you be able to replicate this pattern with your Diamondback?"

"I could try."

Allen directed me a few feet away from the corpse and pointed at a spot in the wall to fire at. I switched the Diamondback to double-action and made the shots as accurate as I could. The pattern I made was similar, but not perfect. Allen inspected my bullet holes — their depth, angles, and everything else.

Several officers from the 7th came by to find out what was happening, not used to the lack of discipline I displayed in my work. One of the cops caught my eye. He was tallish and looked at me with a knowing scowl. Was it the same guy from the gala? I couldn't be sure, but something about him didn't fit with the other cronies from the 7th.

"Allen."

"Hmm?"

"That man." I kept my gaze on him.

"What man?"

I turned to Allen, flabbergasted, and when I turned back, just like that, he was gone again. I ran over to where he had been standing and looked around for any alleys or avenues he might have disappeared into, but saw nothing. I asked the damned cops, but they knew even less. They'd been transfixed by what I was doing. I went back to Allen.

"Just as I suspected, it wasn't a fast trigger finger. These bullets were fired perfectly parallel to one another, at the same time, from three different barrels. Your attempt did not have the precision the other pattern did, and small changes in your angle are evident in the entrance holes, along with bullet depths being dramatically different."

"Couldn't the —"

"No, McIntyre's sternum could not have deviated the rounds to have a perfectly parallel and triangular pattern."

"Any clue how many guns out there have three parallel barrels that can fire 8x50 Lebel?"

"No idea," Allen said.

"Paddy?"

"Not a clue, El," Sinclair said, lighting a dart. "We need someone with some serious knowledge of firearms to figure this out. You got a guy for that?"

I nodded. "I just might. Might have a girl for it, too. That reporter might know her way around the city, and she might know which people want to dismantle Maranzano's operation. Plus, the Iron Hands are still on the table as suspects." And there was that man I kept seeing. But I felt like I should worry about that one myself. Another assassin in the Eye's pocket? A professional from GE?

Then, looking at the body nearby, something hit me. I wasn't sure why. Maybe it was the smell, maybe it was the burnt truck and the fact the fire had died out quite some time ago.

"Paddy, Shen has jurisdiction over the Upper East Side."

"Yeah, and?"

"The 7th's boys came to cordon the area, not the 11th's. And if my memory serves, Shen runs a tight ship. Nothing gets by him or his men."

"Your point?"

"That body is old, that truck fire ain't exactly going, and this is one of the only crime-free neighbourhoods in the Lower City. I know Tony Shen, and I know for a fact he ain't ever tardy when it comes to crimes. Remember the Edison Hotel? He was first on the scene, and that wasn't even in his area of operations. His cops would have seen this fire hours ago. He should have been here by now."

"Civilians would have seen it, as well, and called it in," Allen noted.

"Yeah, but how many people in this city would want to involve themselves in something like this? Especially in the Upper East Side. They leave near-certain death to the cops."

"You think Shen had something to do with it?" Sinclair asked.

I shrugged. "We should ask, because I see no reason gunshots wouldn't draw in at least a few curious cops. I don't care how empty the Upper East Side was last night — there are always cops on the street." I turned to Allen.

"We're heading to the precinct. Paddy, get them to put this place on lockdown, then you're coming with us."

This might be a blessing in disguise. We could release an official statement about the murder, make it as vague as possible, and wait for someone to reveal too much detail. But that was a tactic for the long term. For now, I had a friend to question. I wasn't happy with the implications surrounding him.

After Sinclair had locked down the scene, we climbed into the car, him in the back, Allen driving, and me riding shotgun.

"Detective, is there a reason you have a hammer in your holster?" Allen asked.

My blood ran cold, feeling Sinclair's eyes on me.

"You said you didn't work like that anymore, El," he said, his tone dead serious.

"I know." I took the hammer out and put it inside the glove compartment, out of sight and out of mind. "Let's go, Allen, drive!"

CHAPTER 12

THE TRIO WALKED UP TO THE Upper East Side's precinct situated on the southwest corner of 81st and 2nd. The 11th Precinct had always been the nicest of the precincts in the Lower City; much more modernized than the 5th, and much cleaner than the 7th. According to Sinclair, Viessman said he kept the latter filthy to spook the perps, but most cops in the city knew it was because no one wanted to clean it after it had gotten *that* dirty.

Shen, however, wasn't one for cutting corners. Approaching the precinct, Allen could see the 11th's interior was all drywall and glass, making it feel larger, with more ambient sunlight. He could see from one end of the station to the other without even walking through the front door on the eastern side.

Shen's head snapped up and his eyes met theirs as they walked into his building. The place was half-empty; most of the officers were out on duty, keeping the streets clean and free from Maranzano's hijinks. Not that there would be any hijinks. Maranzano was reported to live in this area, but he operated strictly out of the Kips Kompound. As Roche had said, if the old Italian crime lord knew one thing, it was not to shit in his own backyard.

The glass office Shen was sitting in was on the west side of the building, with a solid wall to his back and a window looking out onto 81st Street on his left. His desk faced east, out across the station. He had opened the blinds on the window looking north, as well as on the windows beside the door to his office that looked into the station.

Entering the room, Roche stood in front of the desk, and Allen and Sinclair sat down in the cushioned chairs before the commissioner.

"Detective Roche ..." Shen began with a hint of worry, "are you perchance here to report a crime or ... are you in need of an ambulance?"

"Nah, I'm good," Roche groaned.

"I see ..." Shen's tone was agitated. Allen had previously deduced the subtle difference between fear and annoyance. Shen was feeling the former. "Perhaps you should make your way home, looking like this —"

"Allen, how long was that fire burning, would you say?" Roche interrupted, still staring at Shen.

"About four hours. It burned out around seven in the morning."

"Four hours. So that means it was started around three. Is my math correct, Shen?"

"What are you two on about?"

Roche checked that the door was closed before continuing more quietly. "There was a murder in your neighbourhood at that time. Yet somehow you failed to hear the shots and go investigate. Why didn't you?"

Shen started to speak, but Elias ploughed on.

"I always thought you were credible and committed, but I can see now you're as dirty as the rest. How much was the bribe, huh? Maranzano weighing down too heavy? You had to let someone walk in and take out a favourite of his? Or did your cops pull the sting and you covered up for them?"

Allen could tell that Roche didn't like saying these things, but they all needed answers.

"They told me not to go looking, no matter what I heard! They threatened my officers. I could not in good conscience sacrifice their lives out of principle. You would have done the same!" Shen blurted out.

"This isn't the first time the 11th has been in the crosshairs," Roche said. "You got a reason this time is special?"

Shen was silent, looking at Roche first, then at Allen. Suddenly Allen understood. Shen wasn't talking, not because he didn't have an excuse, but because he was being watched. His pale face and tight lips confirmed it. Roche turned to look at Allen, his own face reflecting controlled dread.

"Commissioner Shen, where are they?" Allen said.

"If I answer that, the moment you leave this station and go after them, I'm a dead man. I leave this office, I'm a dead man. You even look in their direction, we're all dead men."

"Looks like they can't hear you, so that's something," Roche said. "Look in their general direction. Their view can't be good enough to spot something as subtle as a glance."

Shen carefully darted his eyes at the rooftops outside his north window three times. Roche kept staring at Allen, who hadn't moved a muscle.

"You know where he's looking?" Roche asked.

Allen thought he could make out a figure on the rooftop in his peripheral vision. "Yes. Northeast corner of 81st and 2nd," Allen responded. "I think."

"You think? Okay, I'll stay here and pretend to grill Shen to keep up appearances. Allen, you go to the washroom, find an open window, and move your way around the block to get to the gunman without being seen. Paddy, the moment it leaves, close the blinds. The ones looking into the precinct."

Allen stood, excusing himself out of habit, and walked out into the hall, knowing the assailant could see him. He walked through the frosted glass door back into the station, hanging back for a moment to see and hear what happened.

Roche leaned forward toward Shen. "I'm going to have to rough up your desk. I'm real sorry. But this will keep you alive."

Shen nodded. "You're a good man, Roche."

"No, I ain't."

Roche yelled, grabbed a tray holding a stack of papers, and threw it against the east window, leaving a small scrape in the pane. Sinclair pulled the blinds on the office door, looking nervous.

Allen made his way to the bathroom and found a window with a latch above one of the toilets. It wasn't very dignified, pushing himself through and landing in a snowbank, but at least it was out of sight and quiet. He came out in an alley on the south side of the building and looked up to see clear sky — no Plate. He moved out to the street and peeked around the left corner, looking northward onto 2nd Avenue.

He spotted an almost unnoticeable black figure atop the northeastern building. Not many people could have seen them, but he was no ordinary person. The precinct was on the southwest corner of 81st and 2nd, and the assailant was at the northeast corner. Crossing 2nd Avenue would be the hardest part of this flanking manoeuvre due to lack of concealment.

Across the street a line of parked cars gave him something to run to, once he had moving cover, as well. He waited until a large GE supply truck carrying fresh Automatics from the downtown factory started moving southward down 2nd Avenue, blocking the shooter's view of the precinct and of Allen. The machine sucked in air, breathing shallowly as he calculated his chance to cross, and began sprinting in front of the truck.

A heavy horn sounded just as he jumped out of its way, his back slamming into the rear tire of a parked black Packard. Thankfully, there weren't many civilians nearby to see an Automatic making a run that might have killed a normal man. The mad dash left him shaking and paranoid. After a solid minute waiting behind the parked car and listening for gunshots, he considered it safe to emerge and continue his journey north.

Allen spotted an alleyway leading east and made a dash for the narrow path. He soon turned north and reached 81st Street several dozen feet east of the intersection the shooter was surveilling. Now out of the shooter's line of sight, he moved toward the apartment building he believed the shooter was perched on. The door was unlocked, and the concrete stairs were safe enough. He ran up as quickly as he could, indifferent to the cusses and complaints of the Automatic-hating residents of the building who saw him go by.

His synthetic lungs were hyperventilating when he reached the top, his hands shaking. He held his breath, pushed his anxiety down, and took out his 1911. He loaded a round into the chamber, held it in one hand with his finger far from the trigger, unlatched the safety, and counted to five. He would try to take them alive, but if a bullet went wild, it wasn't his fault. It wasn't.

He slammed his shoulder into the roof access door and pointed his gun forward.

"NYPD! You're under ..."

The figure in black was atop the adjacent snow-covered rooftop, well over twenty yards away. Their gaze moved from the sights of a rustic-looking rifle onto Allen. Both of them were frozen in place. The shooter was crouched behind the edge of the roof, rifle resting against the parapet, a black briefcase lying nearby. Their clothing was black and baggy and covered by a heavy coat that obscured their features beyond recognition. A black trilby, a bandana, and a set of welding goggles further hid their identity. It wasn't elegant, but it was effective. Allen wouldn't know much about this killer until he got them into custody.

The rifle swung in Allen's direction. He ran forward and tumbled as a Lebel round flew inches above him, almost scraping his metal body. He rose out of the roll and continued running, hopping down to the same rooftop that the gunman was on. The shooter kicked the briefcase toward Allen to trip him up, but he jumped over it easily and sprinted after them.

Far away, the gunshot of a Diamondback revolver confirmed that Roche was on the move, having heard the shooter's weapon go off. Allen snapped his head right to see what Roche was doing. His partner had blown out the north window of Shen's office, allowing him to jump out and run across the intersection toward the building Allen was on.

The shooter leaped from the rooftop over to the next, urging Allen to follow, though the shooter had a significant lead. They threw themself at a fire escape ladder, flying over the iron railing, releasing their grip, and using gravity to their advantage. Seconds later, they arrived at the concrete ground. Roche had just reached the entrance to the alleyway, and he signalled for Allen to cut off the target farther down. The detective was huffing loud enough that Allen could hear him from the rooftop.

The metal man looked ahead to see that the buildings and, therefore, the alleyway ended at 82nd Street. He ran along the roofs, the thrill of the chase filling his heart with adrenalin, his movements a feat of gymnastics as he hopped from air conditioning units to adjacent surfaces, slid under water tanks, and dodged garbage and other debris littering the rooftops. Below,

Roche was falling behind, using whatever oxygen he had to scream for the shooter to stop.

Allen made his way to the edge of the roof at the northern mouth of the alleyway, momentarily forgetting his fear of heights as he leaped down. He dug his shoes into the brick wall of the opposite building to slow his fall before hitting the concrete ground. His inhuman speed had given him a small lead on the shooter, and now that he was steady on two feet and standing in the path of his target, he levelled his weapon and fired a round at the ground to deter them from running past. The shooter stopped, skidding to a halt as they pulled their rifle around their shoulder and aimed it at Allen. Whether it was the adrenalin or his sense of duty, Allen remained as steadfast and resolute as a machine could be. Even as all four barrels stared him down.

Allen's brow furrowed. *Four* barrels?

Roche caught up, winded and coughing, his hand clutching his wounded right side. Fresh red began to spread across the already stained white shirt.

"New York ... Police ..." he spat and heaved, sucking in air while aiming his Diamondback at the shooter. "Do not test me, asshole, I've killed too many people today. Put the gun down and come with us. Jesus, both of you jump a few stories, and you're both fine. I do it, and my back ... fuck ..."

Allen looked at the shooter beyond the sights of his pistol. They were about the height he had predicted, though it looked like their strange platform shoes increased their height artificially. The shoes must also help in traversing rooftops by absorbing the shock of landing large jumps. Their quarry had to be in fantastic shape to be running and manoeuvring like this in such baggy clothing.

The four barrels were still pointed at Allen, and it looked like the shooter had no intention of lying down and putting cuffs on themself. Allen knew the rifle was down one round, but of the three that were left, only two of them were Lebel cartridges. Given the sheer diameter of the bottom barrel, there was no doubt it could fire a 15mm shell, enough to cut him in half.

During this standoff, Allen's greatest strength and weakness was Roche. A second gun outnumbered the shooter's, but Roche was still a source of human error, given his limited patience. Which, unfortunately, reared its ugly head.

"Okay, asshole, let's tango," Roche said, pumping himself up by beating his chest with his fist before running straight for the enemy. As he ran, he fired the Diamondback. The bullet skipped off the concrete between the shooter's feet. They jumped and turned in the air, their body twisting like a gymnast's to point the rifle at Roche. The rifle spewed out a Lebel round — the shot meant to dissuade, not kill — forcing the detective to flinch as he twisted his body and threw himself onto the floor, screaming, no doubt in pain from ripping his stitches.

Allen dodged the Diamondback's wild round, feeling the heated bullet sear the air as it flew near his legs. He rushed to save Roche, switching the pistol from his right hand to his left, wielding it like a club and swinging it. The bottom of the grip connected with the shooter's left shoulder, making them grunt in pain, their voice distorted by the synthetic vibrations of something hidden under the bandana. They turned to strike him with their rifle's butt. They were fast but couldn't compete with his fibre optic nerves. Allen dodged the combat manoeuvres easily. The shooter was using the kind of close-quarters combat techniques that were taught to military and police personnel, both of which Allen had trained with.

Muscle memory took over, allowing him to grab the rifle with his right hand, his foot kicking the shooter's knee to get them onto the ground. His left hand flipped the pistol into the air, grabbing it the proper way and pushing it against the shooter's head. He flipped off their trilby to see what was underneath and found black fabric wound around their head to hide their hair. He could try and yank it off, but his hands were currently full. Roche, on the other hand …

"NYPD … You're under arrest for the murder of … I think at least eight people, including Desmond Hartley, Davin McIntyre … among others," Allen said, sucking in air to come down from his adrenalin rush, his grip unwavering as he pushed the gun harder against the shooter's head. He could feel them trying to pull the rifle from his grip, but not trying anything too hasty yet. Allen felt his finger half pulling the trigger, his senses blinded in the moment.

"Fuck … ow …" Roche grabbed his side and pushed himself up, his gun level with the captive. "Tag 'im and bag 'im."

"We can bring them to the 11th for processing."

"No, not again … pull the trigger," Roche said, putting his own gun against the shooter's head. "Or I'll do it."

"Roche, we can't just throw reason to the wind and kill a suspect!"

"This asshole has caused enough damage. He threatened a cop."

"Threatened, but didn't kill. I won't allow you to jeopardize another investigation with rampant murder!"

"Excuse me, Allen? Hardly the time to argue about this." Roche pulled the hammer back on the Diamondback.

The shooter had other ideas. Their elbow came up the moment the hammer clicked, smacking into Roche's side and making him fire the gun into the air. He clutched his wound. Allen pulled his gun away in a panic, allowing the shooter to push the rifle's front against the ground to rotate the barrel assembly 180 degrees. Allen froze, and the shooter charged past him, destabilizing him with their elbow. With the large barrel now sitting up top, they sprinted off as they turned to pull the trigger, the weapon aimed above him and Roche.

The scene played out in slow motion. Allen's eyes tracked the bullet as it fired off. Roche, seeing the trigger pulled, put his arms up over his head. The Von Whisper round, Allen soon leaned, was aptly named. The noise it made as the projectile exited the barrel was as loud as a potato gun — basically silent, compared to any other rifle. When the explosive tip hit the brick wall above him, Allen was blown backward by the shockwave. His head slammed into the ground, dazing him.

The world spun as bricks from both buildings fell on either side of him.

He lay on his back for several minutes. All he could hear was a shrill, piercing scream, and he had double vision. Everything was melding and solidifying as his brain gradually recovered.

He turned onto all fours, pushed himself up, and wandered over to where Roche had been, grabbing a garbage bin to steady himself. His centre of balance was askew from the explosion. He made out his partner trapped under a small pile of bricks and garbage, only his top half visible, and leaped forward, digging into the rubble to pull him out. Blood was pooling under the detective from his aggravated wound.

The rest of the precinct seemed to have gotten the picture. Sirens grew louder as patrol cars and ambulances converged on the area. Roche groaned. Allen pulled his partner up and helped him walk to the south end of the alley. Cops from the 11th ran over to see what had happened, and the sight of blood sent one of them running back to call for a medic.

———

Twenty minutes later, Roche was sitting in the back of an ambulance, hooked up to a blood bag, replacing what he'd lost. He was visibly in pain. A paramedic attempted to stitch up his wounds. Roche grunted with each stab of the needle. The paramedic told him to stay still, though Allen knew very well it wasn't Roche's fault the stitches hurt going in. Sinclair and Shen came to the scene to question civilians about what they'd witnessed before coming over to see him.

"Are you okay, Detective?" Allen asked.

"Peachy, Allen. Fuck!" Roche slapped the paramedic's hand away. "Just patch it, I'll get someone better to do the stitches."

"You need to rest," Allen said. "You don't have very much blood left in you, and that wound —"

"I recommend you shut your mouth. If you'd just let me do my job, this would be over, and I wouldn't be lying here with a pint of blood missing! Do we need to have that discussion again, the same one we had when you chained me to my goddamn fridge?"

"No, but maybe if you'd thought ahead and stopped acting like an animal for once, we wouldn't be in this goddamn mess!"

Roche shut up. Sinclair's head turned sharply. Allen realized they were both shocked that he had sworn. He cleared his throat before speaking again.

"I'm sorry. I don't know what came over me."

"No, you're right. As always." Roche sighed irritably. "Paddy, make a call to Nightingale. Tell her I need stitches. *Proper* stitches. Shen, do you want to make a statement about what happened?"

The commissioner nodded. "I already did."

"You didn't tell me," Roche grumbled.

"I received an anonymous letter in the early hours of the morning. It said that if I or any of my officers investigated any crimes occurring at approximately three in the morning, they and I would be killed. You were around for the rest."

"You were in your office for four hours waiting for us?" Roche asked. Shen grunted in affirmation. "How long was he on that rooftop watching you?"

"He showed up thirty minutes before you got to the precinct."

"Odd. I wonder how he knew we were coming," Roche said. Shen shrugged before walking off. Roche turned back to Allen. "Shen really was in a bind. Robins would have done the same. I'm sure he'll be fine, but I'm not too sure about us."

"Should I remain here and —"

"No, Allen, go home and get some rest. I'll catch up with you later."

"I don't think leaving you would be a wise decision."

"Just listen to me for once, okay? I need you to … Aw, hell …"

Allen turned to see what Roche was staring at: Simone, wearing a fur coat, followed by several men carrying newfangled cameras and numerous microphones on their backs. She had sweat on her brow, probably overheated by the coat despite the cold weather. Allen got between the reporters and Roche, providing a half-decent buffer for both parties. He didn't mind Simone's close proximity as she tried to speak to Roche, but he felt stripped by the thought of the powerful camera lenses capturing his likeness.

"Detectives Roche and Erzly, any comment on what happened in this usually crime-free area? I'm sure many of our listeners recognized the sound of an explosion and are curious as to whether the New York Police Department is capable of maintaining peace, what with this incident."

Roche groaned again, and Allen stayed steadfast. "I'm sorry, but Detective Roche is in no shape to be answering questions. I would be happy to —"

"A comment for WAR Radio, Detective?"

Allen felt a stab in his heart. He remained rigidly protective of Roche, but his insides twisted at having been ignored. Roche grabbed his side and stood, leaning on Allen.

"What the hell do you want from me, lady?"

"Language!" one of the men warned, indicating the recording equipment.

"This is not the best time," Roche continued. "I have a hole the size of the fucking Grotto in my side …"

"Language!"

"Can you just give me a few hours before you bombard me?"

"Gladly." Simone pulled a card out of her pocket and stabbed it into Roche's hand. "I'll be waiting for you to call. Don't try to avoid me, either. We know where you live, and we've had long stakeouts before. The first card was a courtesy, this one is not. Good day, Detective."

She smiled and backed away from Allen, leaving with her crew to interview anyone else willing to give an official statement. Roche looked at the card, turning it over, and put it inside his blood-free pocket.

"Are you going to call her?" Allen asked with a feeling he realized was envy.

"I'd rather not drag this out longer than necessary." Roche looked into traffic as though waiting for someone. As if on cue, a black hearse pulled up. A woman exited the back and leaned against the car. She regarded

Roche with an expression of utter disappointment. "I'm going to get cleaned up and then try to fix this PR nightmare," Roche said. "I need you to do something much more important."

"Yes?"

"Find out what kind of weapon that was. I need to know, because it sure ain't military issue."

"But their skills were," Allen interjected. "They are military trained, or at least police trained. They used the same techniques I was trained with. This fact alone will narrow down the possible suspects, and we can refine that even further by finding out which weapon they used."

"Agreed."

"The shooter also left a briefcase up on the rooftop when I began chasing them. I should go get that. It might help us narrow down our search."

"Yeah, you do that. Now, if you'll excuse me ..."

Roche stood up, eyeing the crowd warily as another person made a rush for him. While Simone's very presence had parted the sea of people, the man clamouring for Roche's attention was more frantic. He was intercepted by two officers guarding the scene.

"Is that the man you saw at the gala?" Allen asked.

"Can't tell. Get him away from me before I shoot him." Roche pulled the blood bag from the ambulance, holding it above his head as he walked to the hearse and away from the growing crowd. "I swear, Allen, I ain't dying."

"You'd better not be," Allen said.

CHAPTER 13

THE ONE GOOD THING THAT came out of this wound was that it made me sit down and read a book. After showering and suffering through the discomfort of hot water on my fresh stitches, I was able to get on some half-decent clothes, lie in bed, and catch up on some of the reading I'd been putting off. It was preferable to listening to the radio. Turning that on might blast my radio program at me and send me spiralling into anger. I don't even want to think about how badly they butchered it.

The business card Simone had given me drilled a hole in my pocket the entire time I was reading, though. I'd have to call sooner or later. Sooner was better, if I wanted to avoid being pestered by the press. She might be bluffing about knowing where I lived. But was I willing to take that chance? I wasn't a gambling man; I'd learned my lesson from casinos.

I made the call and set up something for tomorrow afternoon. I needed a meal, a quiet night, and sleep. It was rare for me to get to bed at a decent time, so I might as well take advantage.

The next day, December 23, I awoke late in the morning feeling ... not terrible. I had been so high-strung chasing this killer that I'd had a constant throbbing tension in my neck, setting me off whenever some inconvenience crossed my path. When my feet hit the floor, I was strangely lucid, like I had been living in the clouds for the past few months, the gas tank never really topped up. But standing and getting ready now, I felt more complete than I had in a while.

Slacks, a fancy polo, and my old leather jacket. It was roughed up and patched from dozens of fights, but it worked well to offset the white shirt. Slinging my holster on before the jacket, I was prepared for anything the day could throw at me. The interview with Simone wasn't until one, and I needed a police tool to help me collect information on the persistent journalist. This time, my gun wouldn't cut it.

Stepping into the 5th without hearing anyone greet me was odd. Usually Sinclair was at his desk when I wandered in here, so seeing his chair empty — along with most of the chairs in the station — was a strange sight. I went to his desk and found what I was looking for in one of the drawers: a pen and a notepad for taking notes.

"Never a break, huh, Roche?"

Robins leaned against an adjacent desk, sipping coffee. I was surprised. He'd been much quieter than usual in his approach. I closed Sinclair's desk drawer and prepared to take my leave.

"Do *you* ever take a day off?" I asked.

"I do. Sundays. I go water the plants outside my window overlooking Central Park, I listen to the radio, I write in my journal."

"You have a journal?"

"Yes, I do. It helps me deal with things. I can't talk to my wife anymore, so I have to make do."

Poor bastard. It wasn't just me who had problems. It was always so much easier to imagine that everyone's life was better than mine. But it was getting harder to believe that anymore. Had I missed this realization because I'd been so sleep-deprived and withdrawn?

Robins pointed with his mug at the notepad in my hands. "You never write anything down."

"I know, but this is a special case. I need to get down all the information about her that I can."

"Oh, a date?"

I groaned. "No, Robins. Business. It isn't a date."

"Is it Morane, the reporter? You know, for the past two weeks she's been climbing all over this place trying to find you. I've been married long enough to know when a woman is going above and beyond her job to see someone."

I stared at him. "And you didn't tell me?"

"It would have pissed you off. Just like the radio thing." He smirked. "Let her down easy, champ. Vinny's, right?"

"It's not a date," I repeated. "And yes."

"Well, get a nice bottle on me, will ya?" He pulled a wad of bills out of his pocket and slapped it on Sinclair's desk. "You need the buzz. You've been under quite some stress."

"And how do you know that?"

"Because you only stay away from the station when you're stressed. Same thing when you smoke — only when you're nervous."

I picked up the cash. "How much is in here?"

"You gave me a literal ton of gold. I sort of owe you."

I chuckled and pocketed the money, along with the pen and notepad. "I can't have too much. I'm nursing a fresh wound."

"Just enjoy yourself, okay? I miss the Elias who could have a pint after work. Loosen up."

"Is that an order?"

He laughed and walked back to his office, leaving me alone.

I supposed it was.

———

Vincenzo's, or Vinny's, was the one decent restaurant in the Lower City. It sported an open bar that everyone patronized: cops, crooks, and common people looking for a buzz. Sure, the Upper City complained, but they'd have had to wade through hell itself to shut it down. The servers were professional and quick, the food immaculate, and the owner one hell of a character.

Adamo was a classic mobster from back in the day. He'd used the money he made bootlegging to open the restaurant. The Mafia had been pissed when it first opened, since it sat at the corner of Kenmare Street and Bowery, the four-way point of the Mangano, Gagliano, Profaci, and Adonis territories. But after the four bosses sat down, had a parley, shared a bottle of wine, and sampled the Italian cuisine, they made it hallowed ground. There were very few agreements in the Lower City between the remaining cartels, but even the Iron Hands followed the statute cemented by the Five Families: don't fuck with Vinny's.

Adamo had knocked down the walls between three or four storefronts to create one massive entity. Two stories were needed to accommodate the volume of people they hosted on a daily basis. Mob money had helped to furnish a second level after they'd sold out the ground floor day in and day out in the '20s. Even this deep into the Depression, this place had only one quiet day — Thursdays — and that was only because Adamo needed a break now and then, lest he keel over from a heart attack. Two sets of spiral stairs connected the floors, and each held scores of tables. Candlelit ambience, live bands playing, and drinks in droves. Here, it was as if the previous decade had never ended.

As I walked in through the canopied double doors, a well-dressed woman with grey hair and reading glasses looked up at me. She smiled as soon as she saw my face and came out from behind her stand.

"Elias, it has been too long!"

"Good to see you, Maria." I kissed her on both cheeks, and she reciprocated.

"What's kept you from us? You know you always have a table."

"Business, unfortunately." I smiled. "I'm meeting someone for a late lunch and an interview. I'll need some wine." I handed her the wad Robins had given me, and she slipped it between her fingers. "I'll pay the difference. Get me something classic."

"Of course. Head on over, Adamo will be right with you. And who might you be having an interview with?"

"A woman. You'll recognize her when you see her."

"Hmm, an interview, ah?" She smiled and sauntered away.

"It's not a date," I said to myself, walking to my seat.

The booth — *my* booth — was on the second floor facing the street, in the centre of a small walkway with a line of booths on one side, and a railing looking down on the rest of the restaurant on the other. I slid in and looked out the window, watching the snow whip by, leaving crystals on the glass. The ambience was welcome: heat, laughter, and the band playing loud enough to drown out my pumping heart as my wound nagged at me.

The band was down on the ground floor, in a corner of the restaurant dedicated to various live performances. The ten or so restaurant tables that ordinarily went in that corner were replaced by small circular bar tables filled with people drinking and watching the band. The music was strange: blueswing, a grating electronic version of swing music. The lead singer had some pipes on her, though. The strange thing was seeing the Blue-eyes behind her playing electrical and mechanical instruments. The devices were either held in the machines' hands or built into their bodies, mimicking the sounds of trumpets and drums, but with a synthetic, flanging aftersound that was hard to ignore. It wasn't my preferred kind of music, but the people below were loving it, and even I found the beat quite catchy.

My attention on the band, I was somewhat taken by surprise when I heard clacking heels behind me. I turned my head as far as I could without threatening the integrity of my new stitches.

Simone was mere inches from the booth. She smiled, looking down at me, one hand on the cushion I was leaning against. She wore a green dress whose long hem hid her feet, though her arms were exposed, and she carried a small purse. Her blond hair was curled and pinned up off her shoulders and neck to show her earrings. The pattern on the dress seemed familiar. It took a moment to decipher; it was an ornate art deco rendition of the Empire Building, but upside down.

I realized then how underdressed I was. I must have looked like a jackass next to her.

"Detective Elias Roche, I thank you for this opportunity." She slid into the booth opposite me, placing her elbows on the table and her chin in her hands. "What a moment, seeing the Nightcaller in his natural habitat."

"Please don't call me that." It was already starting.

"Fine. For now, away from the public eye, I suppose we can stick with names, not monikers, Elias." She smirked at me. I didn't reciprocate. "Nice place. Very nice place. Very busy for the afternoon."

"You've never been here? Never heard of it?"

"Oh, I've heard of it. I try to stay away from public places, but I've heard all about who comes here and why. It's much nicer than I thought it would be for a

Mafia-run establishment. And serving alcohol here without repercussions? There's got to be a story there."

"There is."

"One that involves you?"

I scratched my head. "No, it happened before my tenure. As a cop, I did come here quite often with the precinct on Saturdays. Those were better times. Simpler times."

"And times are complicated now because of people, politics? I've heard you really get around."

"How so?"

"Your partner, Allen, said that you've met with Maranzano personally." *Goddamn it, Allen.* "I've tried to get him in public for years, and nothing. You must be pretty important to be in his good graces."

"Ha! Not his good graces. I know people who can get me in to see him, but if he could get rid of me, he would."

"And why can't he?"

I coughed, trying to think how to change the subject, but thankfully Adamo did that for me. He came barrelling in, louder than an ox, carrying a tray with a bottle of wine on it. He put it down, pulled me out of my seat, and wrapped his arms around me in a bear hug. *Please, God, don't let me bleed out from this.*

"Elias, *il mio scemo*, it has been too long!" He was tall, built like a truck, with a bald head and hairy arms. I couldn't help but smile. He let me sit down again. "You've lost weight! We need to fatten you up. Maria!" he screamed across the restaurant. No one batted an eye at us. "Get them cooking in there! *Piccolino* is hungry!"

"I'm not that hungry, Adamo. We'll be fine."

"And who is this?" He extended his hand to Simone, and she shook it, both of them smiling at each other. "Ah, *il mio scemo*, she is a thing of beauty! No wonder you wanted wine. I got some of our good stuff out, for old times' sake. Calabrese, from the old country."

I shrugged and let him show it off before running off to speak to some other customers. For the life of me, I couldn't get the smile off my face, and Simone noticed.

"I wish I had a camera," she remarked. "A good friend of yours, I guess?"

"Italians stick together." I sat back down "My parents were friends of his for years, and after they went to the Upper City, it was just me down here to keep him and Maria company. They're like my godparents, and in the old country, that basically means they're my parents."

"Funny," she said, pulling out a cigarette, "Roche isn't a very Italian-sounding name."

"Curious, ain't it?" I pulled out my lighter and helped her out, catching sight of the engraved eye before putting it back.

"Adds to the mystery. Nothing about you seems to add up," she began. "A cop for almost a decade who quit to become a vigilante? That's not a spur-of-the-moment decision. Or maybe it depends on the circumstances."

My brow went back to furrowing. "Yeah, best we leave the past alone."

"But people want to know! We can only peddle pulp characters for so long before the audience needs the backstory. Where did he come from? Who is he really? Does he have anyone to care for, or to care for him? People are on the edge of their seats, waiting for the next installment of the drama. What harrowing adventures or dastardly escapades will the Nightcaller get himself into next?"

"Why?" I slumped back in my seat. "Why any of it? Why are my adventures such a big deal?"

She smiled. With the hand holding her cigarette, she tapped the wine bottle. I poured some for her and a little for myself. She'd be more willing to let loose information if she were liquored up.

"Tell me, do you follow *any* radio programs, Elias?"

"No."

"Watch TV?"

"No."

"Read?"

"I don't have much time, but here and there."

"And why do you read?"

"What do you mean?"

She sipped the red wine, making sure not to stain her lips. Her eyes never left me, and it made me feel stripped of my defences. I hated it.

"The people out there working for a few cents an hour and holed up in apartments they can barely afford to feed kids whose circumstances they can't improve — they read and listen and watch for an escape. They've been under the boot of these Mafias since the '20s, and while before it might have been a good thing, now the Mob is a stain, more likely to leave you a corpse than to pay you your share. Hearing the stories of the

Nightcaller gives these people a semblance of hope that not everything in this country turned to shit after '29. It's their escape from their own personal hell, because beauty is a luxury they cannot afford."

I'd been wrong. It wasn't just me and my friends' lives that were shit, it was everyone in the city's. I was so caught up in my own world, I'd forgotten that the real one existed. I'd been depriving myself of sleep, compromising my health, and for what? The Eye? Pretending that I was doing the right thing? I doubted anyone would have considered what I'd just pulled at the Angel's Share a public service. Maybe I shouldn't be getting more sleep after all; being this aware of everything around me just made me depressed.

＝＝＝＝

Our appetizers came, and the conversation continued.

"So, Elias, where did it all start?" Her cigarette had run out, but her glass was only half-empty.

"After the War ended in '17, I took a year off to work in the navy for a spell. I started in law enforcement after that, in 1919."

"No, before all that. I know from public information that you were born in 1898. Now you're thirty-five and you've been toting a gun since '16, when the U.S. officially joined the War. Fill me in."

"And how much of this will be on the air?"

"Only what you're comfortable with. Swear on my life."

Careful what you say, Morane.

"I grew up in Manhattan. My parents owned an apartment up on 44th. When I was sixteen, I earned a scholarship to Cornell."

"For what?"

"Chemistry."

She seemed stunned. "Chemistry? I never imagined —"

"What? That I'm not just some dumb oaf with a piece?" She stayed silent, surely aware that she'd offended me. Finally, her confidence cracked. "Like you said, we joined the War in '16," I continued, "two years into my academic career. I was seventeen when I signed up for boot camp, along with most of the university. I don't know what made me join, but I did it. The day I told my parents … oh boy."

"Rough?"

"My mother hasn't seen me the same way since. My father sort of understood, but he felt betrayed, seeing his son throw away an opportunity at a prestigious school. I shipped out, and that was that. Came back and, walking into Cornell, I felt so out of place that I left. So, I signed up with my old squad mates to do some work with the navy, and after that, we all joined the 5th Precinct."

"But why didn't you want to go back to your studies at Cornell?"

"I was nineteen when I got home. I had spent almost a year in foxholes, my hands covered in grease or shit or blood. The first time I killed someone … I remember it like I'm still there now. The smell, the feeling of the rifle, the rain. Could you do this job you're doing every day, remembering the terrified, dying face of a man whose chest you just put a bullet in?"

Her expression faltered strangely. Was it sympathy? Empathy? Sadness?

I continued, "One look at a classroom and I felt trapped, like I was back in the trenches, surrounded by corpses. Before, I'd felt like I was part of a different world, a better world, at Cornell. But going to Europe and fighting, it pulled me down to a part of the human condition most people would rather not acknowledge."

Simone nodded, her overbearing demeanour gone. She seemed to understand. Without the smarmy attitude, I could sense real empathy, a rare thing for me to see. I had a feeling I'd struck a chord.

"My father was in the War," she finally said.

"I know, I served under him at Strasbourg."

"My mother was from Verdun." Goddamn … that wasn't a good place to be back then. "She wanted to go back in '14, said she missed the country and wanted to see some friends, had heard about brewing tensions. She went back, and then … everything started. My father was there, too, commanding forces against the Germans. He searched for her everywhere. I don't even know if she has a gravestone, or if she's lumped in with the rest of the faceless dead. He was never the same after that. Just a shell of his former self."

"I can't imagine what he went through." My gut wrenched seeing her like this. "I lost friends, too, but not someone that close. My heart goes out to you, truly."

"Do you know why I got into journalism? Because of my mother. Because where there once was her beauty, her love, her laughter, there's now just bones and dirt. She was another body in a mass grave, another forgotten name. Maybe one day my father will forget her name and her face. And when he's passed on, I'll just be me. I'll be the only person to have known her smile, her voice, her touch … It hurts to think about. All we have now are memories, and those fade far too quickly. At least as a journalist I can document and broadcast the lives of people whom otherwise no one would remember. Their names, their hopes and dreams, their struggles. And though I can't record the story of every man, woman, and child, I can *give* them stories. Your story gives people hope, and if that's all we can give, at least it's something."

That was moving. Beautiful, really. I only wished I had the same conviction for something, anything.

"You're a man of violence, Roche, but you aren't the kind of man to glorify it," she continued. "I know what you do on the streets isn't good, I know you kill. But I can't imagine you'd ever want to go back to how you used to be. Can you?"

I could. Yesterday I'd had the blood of ten bodies on my hands. I was a monster, a rabid animal meant to hunt and rip and tear. A wolf. I'd hidden it until '28, but since then, it had been out and wreaking havoc. But I couldn't be honest with her.

"No. I don't think I can."

"You kill because you have to, right?" she asked.

"Yes. Only if necessary."

First Allen, now her. And last, myself. How many people would I lie to?

A silence arose during the main course and remained for some time. Halfway through, I looked up to see her smiling at me.

"You're not as dark and brooding as I thought you'd be," she said, her lighthearted attitude returning. It was good to see she'd pulled back from her earlier dejection.

"What makes you say that?"

"I was expecting you to be all sullen and sad, but hearing you talk, even casually — it's refreshing. You're not wrapped up in all the bad that's happening around us."

"Trust me, I am. I just hide it when I need to. And I need to be positive for those around me, to keep them from getting dragged down by all that terrible shit."

"Then why were you all rude and distant whenever I wanted an interview?" Her confident smirk was back.

"I'm just an asshole," I laughed. "I'd rather keep people at a distance. It's easier to deal with them when they're well out of arm's reach."

"Then why do you keep Detective Erzly so close?"

I froze. I wasn't sure what to say.

"*Constable* Erzly. And it doesn't count," I retorted.

"He's a person, no?"

"*It* is a machine, nothing more. A good partner, but nothing close to human."

"I see."

Another silence, another pause. I had questions, but not the energy to ask them. Though there was one nagging query I had to put to rest.

"This radio show …"

"Oh? You're interested now?" She smiled, resting her chin on her knuckles and looking at me matter-of-factly. "What about it?"

"When did it come to fruition? To me it came out of the blue."

"RCA wanted to keep it under the radar until it was ready. The higher-ups thought it was a risky project, but they wanted something fresh, original, authentic. Overall, it was an experiment to try out a new style of radio show. I think it's going splendidly."

"They could afford not to advertise until weeks before release?"

She shrugged. "Well, they do own Times Square, so yeah, I think they can afford it."

"When did you come up with the idea for this … show?" I hoped she didn't know about my past, before I'd started taking real Night Calls. Before I'd stopped my rampage.

"Some stories about Night Calls trickled in for a few months in late '30, but we had no idea who you were. Then, about two years ago, civilians started calling the news desk to report your random acts of justice. It took some doing to get my hands on official reports — the police are very tight-lipped about the existence of a man who doles out justice to the Mob — but the stories passed along by civilians were enough to make you something of an urban legend."

"Uh-huh."

"We also have a source outside the city who told us about some of your past antics. Andrew Stern. He said he'd had a few run-ins with you in the past, even worked in the precinct with you."

Stern. What a bastard. "Should have killed him when I had the chance," I muttered.

"What was that?"

"Nothing ... He's just a prick, is all. A nuisance." At least he'd listened to me and gotten out.

"Well, those tales passed around, along with the police reports, were enough material to build the idea of the show, which I pitched to RCA. When the writers came up with a pilot, test audiences loved it, but RCA kept it on the down low until they felt it was 'ripe' enough. They had me keep providing them with research on you. Then I discovered Andrew Stern, who's living in San Francisco now. I contacted him and he gave me a lot of little details that make the show feel that much more authentic.

"I know you're not keen on your privacy being invaded, but I can assure you that RCA isn't eager to plaster your image all over. It would ruin the mystery and allure of the Nightcaller character. You're more attractive as a hero when you're anonymous."

"Ironic, ain't it? The reality isn't much compared to the fantasy on the radio."

"I wouldn't say that. I have a suspicion that the way you work is even more exciting than what they make up for the listeners."

She went back to her meal, and I to mine. The band changed, and now a man and a woman were singing a melancholy tune. No, not a man and a woman, a machine and a woman. His — or, rather, its — flanging voice resonated throughout the restaurant. The music was good, enough to get my foot tapping along. Simone smiled to herself.

My gaze drifted into the crowd around the stage. A firm, square-jawed face looked back up at me. Salvatore Maranzano, Caesar himself, was sitting with his cronies down below, all of them drinking and laughing. He gave me a nod and turned back to the music. At least he followed his own rule.

It felt good to get away from the underworld for a while, to take a walk on the outside. I wished I could stay here forever.

———

The meal ended, I bid Adamo and Maria goodbye, and then I walked Simone out of the restaurant. I might as well act civilized as long as I was in civilization. She put on the same long fur coat as before. It completely hid her dress, save for the hem at her ankles, and it made her shoulders look twice as wide as my own. I drove her home in the Talbot; I wasn't about to let the woman ride in a taxi twice. Plus, if I'd let a lady go unescorted, Adamo or Maria would have slapped me the next time I walked into the restaurant.

Her apartment was in Lincoln Square, one of the better districts of the Lower City, which wasn't saying much. Still, this was one ritzy place, especially given the salary most reporters got. I helped her out of the car and walked her to the door of her complex, the cold wind piercing my skin. The snowfall had ceased for today.

While the roads were clear, having been salted, the grass and bare trees in the small park behind us were coated in several days' worth of white. It must have been nice living somewhere that wasn't covered by the Plate. At least the vegetation didn't wither from lack of sunlight, even in the summer. I revelled in the feeling of the sun's searing rays on my face and neck.

"How can you afford a place in Lincoln Square?"

She smirked. "A girl knows people. I don't make all my money from reporting."

"That explains the coat, too. Mind telling me where that other money comes from?"

"And give away my secrets? Never." She climbed the four concrete steps to the front door. She was happy. This must have made her whole year. "Thank you for the interesting lunch. I can't imagine how busy that place must get at night."

"Oh, it's hell."

"But you can still get a table, right?"

I grinned. "Of course."

"Pays to know people, huh? Well, the interview was eye-opening. Good to know the man behind the name better. If there's anything I can do for you in return, please let me know."

"There is, actually." She raised an eyebrow. "We're tracking down the perp in a crime scene or two, and we'd appreciate your assistance if we need to get any-where … less accessible to the public. Can you do that?"

Simone leaned against a railing, excited. "Of course! I'm a journalist, I have keys to almost everywhere in the city. You call whenever you need me, and I'll be ready."

"Thank you. Enjoy your evening."

"And you, as well, Elias. Don't work yourself too hard."

I walked back to my car. On the way, I felt the notepad and pen in my jacket pocket slapping against my hip.

Damn it, forgot to take notes.

———

The drive home felt too short, and parking in front of my building felt like jumping back into the rut I had just left. I was disappointed not to see Yuri at his usual post. He must have been down the street selling dogs on another corner. Missing the relief of chatting to him, I went in through the lobby and rode the elevator to my floor. When the doors parted, I noticed that the hallway was unusually quiet. But the silence was soon interrupted by the buzzing of the flickering wall lamp above my door. *I should get someone to fix that.*

Stepping inside, I went over to the coffee machine and plugged it into the Tesla Battery in the wall. It spooled up to prepare the hot liquid for me. Suddenly, I heard something heavy drop behind me, in the middle of my living room.

"Jesus!" I screamed.

I looked around to see that something had indeed landed on the ground, right beside my new TV. An eight-foot-tall something. It was creepy how the Rabbit could crawl around like that, its every move smooth and silent. We locked eyes. We were both waiting to see who would flinch first.

"YOU'RE GETTING SLOPPY," it said.

"And you're still creepy as hell. How did you get in here? Actually, never mind," I said, looking at the fresh finger holes in my ceiling. The black liquid began to leak out into the cup under the coffee maker, and I reached for it when it was full. "Been waiting long?"

"LONG ENOUGH."

It didn't have eyes or a mouth, but judging by its tone of voice, it would have given me a shit-eating grin if it could have. Did it know about my meeting with Simone? *No, don't let it get into your head.*

"ONE LAST JOB, AND THE MEETING WITH THE EYE IS YOURS. THINK YOU CAN HANDLE IT?" It spoke slowly, trying to set me off.

"I shouldn't be treated like this, I'm her goddamn enforcer," I said under my breath.

"YOU HAVE BEEN SLIPPING. THESE LULLS IN COMMUNICATION ARE MEANT TO TEACH YOU A LESSON, ROACH."

"Did she tell you to say that to me? Or is that your own opinion, capek?"

The Rabbit didn't respond to my question. "SHE WANTS YOU TO STOP LOOKING INTO THE EDISON HOTEL MURDER."

"Why?"

It marched to my front door, its eyes never leaving me. "THE KILLER IS CHIPPING AWAY AT MARANZANO AND GIVING HER SOME BREATHING ROOM. SHE KNOWS YOU WANT TO FIND THEM, BUT SHE DOESN'T WANT THEM FOUND. LEAVE THEM BE. UNDERSTOOD?" I didn't respond. "I'LL TAKE THAT AS A YES."

The machine disappeared through my door, leaving me alone in my apartment.

This was too strange. Why? Why all of a sudden keep me away? Was I getting close? I wanted to find out if the Eye was up to something, but this visit had answered my question. There was no doubt the killer was working for the Iron Hands. I was so goddamn tired of grey areas and wavering loyalties. Next, that capek would be putting a gun to Allen's head to keep me away.

But not yet. The Eye's words had less and less power over me every day. She shouldn't have sent the Rabbit with this message. She'd just guaranteed that I'd get to the bottom of it all.

CHAPTER 14

IT WAS THE EVENING OF DECEMBER 23, two days before Christmas.

Allen had never celebrated this holiday before, so although he was on a mission to find out what kind of weapon had almost killed him and his partner, he also made sure to peer through every shop window on the way to the New York Public Library. Streamers, presents, electronics — all of them were dirt cheap, with sales everywhere. It was an overload of the senses, flooding his eyes and ears as he explored the frivolities of the season.

Meanwhile, Toby was not enthralled by anything. He was the anchor dragging Allen back from complete absorption in the show of capitalism. Allen had hoped that bringing Toby along would give them a better chance of being admitted to the library. After all, two officers were more legit than just one, even if they were both Automatics.

"I ain't no reading machine, Al," Toby said, taking out a half-full bottle of something from under his coat. "You going to entertain me while we search?"

"Didn't you quote Dumas a few days ago?"

Toby let out a grunt. "Shut up, you know what I mean."

"Please, be patient. And you can't drink on the job."

"I'll do whatever the badge lets me do, square."

"Well, hopefully that badge will be getting us inside."

"Yeah, here's hoping the derms don't try to stop us."

"I could have very well gone with Sergeant Sinclair ..."

"Nah," Toby dismissed the thought, "I gotta keep you out of trouble, especially after our little conversation at the Funhouse."

"I don't need to be kept out of trouble?"

"You surely do after the shit I've seen. "Toby snickered. "Watch out, Al, you're turning more human every day."

The two machines approached the library doors, and just as he'd predicted, Allen had to explain their intentions up and down, even after they'd both flashed their badges. The guard at the front of the library said he would have their police numbers looked up. A quick call to Robins cleared things up, granting them access and leaving the guard with an aching ear and a severe dislike of the two machines.

The interior of the library was magnificent, spectacular even by Upper City standards. The murals and painted ceilings were well-maintained, chandeliers illuminated the scores of desks, and to the left and the right off the central hall there were thousands of books. It was a bookworm's dream, and Allen desperately wished he could stay here and read every book they had.

Toby looked around rather lazily. "Fuck. You wouldn't catch me in here without you." Someone shushed him, making him twitch in annoyance.

"Try to be low-key," Allen said. "We don't want to cause any incidents. Not without a human present."

"Fair point, chrome dome. Lead the way."

═══════

Perched behind a small hill of books about the Great War, Allen was absorbed by the text, transported to a time neither he nor his ancestors had ever seen. He wrote down everything he could, copying texts and lists by hand, the reproductions almost perfect carbon copies of the originals. He was learning everything he could about the War, since he hadn't been given that opportunity while in Camp Theta, his "birthplace" out in the Midwest, where he had been stuck until about a year ago. The Balkan powder keg, the old Austro-Hungarian Empire, the Central and Allied nations, the chaos caused by Serbia that lead to the massive mobilizations, and each country jumping to aid another, followed by the trenches being dug and the machine guns taking root.

Everything had changed when the Americans approached Marshal Joffre in 1915 and the first Manuals were sent behind the backs of the general public. It all escalated from there, and the massive orders Russia placed had guaranteed co-operation between the two nations ever since. He read that the Czar's own Manual, called "The Hand of God," was cemented in the centre of Petrograd, immortalizing the Russian Empire's victory and survival in the War.

And then there was the German Debacle. Their need and want for expansion and their summary punishment by the Manual Corps of America and Russia led to their losing morale. That, plus their country being the central battleground after the Diesel Initiative was green-lit, made them want the War to end, no matter the cost. They'd wanted to surrender, but the Allies wouldn't accept a simple surrender. Even now, there was great resentment throughout Europe toward Germany due to their treason in sharing plans for the war machine they'd helped create.

Allen was distracted by the sound of someone hissing. His eyes darted to a clock, and he discovered that it was almost four in the afternoon. They'd entered at eleven in the morning. The hissing came once more, and he scanned his immediate surroundings, trying to find the source.

Sitting a few desks away, a man in a thick winter coat with small rimmed glasses and thin hair was staring at him, beckoning him over. Curious, Allen walked over. The man studiously pretended to be reading a book, even when Allen was within inches of him.

"Can I help you, sir?"

"Shh, not so loud! They're watching us all the time."

Allen looked around in confusion and embarrassment. "Okay …"

"Reginald Edwin Curio, writer and journalist." The man shoved his hand into Allen's before retracting it and hiding behind his dainty book once more. "I've been trying to contact you and your partner for some time. But I don't like meeting in the open — too many ears."

"Curio ... You left a phone message for Roche, correct?" Allen spoke in a whisper to appease Curio's paranoia.

"Yes! Now, this is of extreme importance, it is urgent I speak to you, or him, or both of you."

"About what?"

"I've heard the radio show. To be brief, it's garbage, absolute pandering trash! I can't believe that a man like Roche would condone something like that. I've tracked down information about him from people far and wide, all the way to the Grotto! I almost got clipped by the Gould Mob for snooping near the Plate. That should tell you how dedicated I am." He gasped to take a breath before rambling on. "I'm asking you and Roche to collaborate with me to put out the truth. The total, unabridged truth of the Nightcaller. I want people to see what it's like on the streets fighting the Mob — none of this cat-in-a-tree shit they're peddling on the tuner!"

Allen was stunned by the request, but he kept composed. "I should inform you that he doesn't actually like that name. But I will be sure to pass on your request."

"Good. Now get out of here before they spot us!"

Still confused, Allen wandered back to his desk to continue reading. As soon as he'd planted himself in his chair, Toby piped up behind him, making him jump.

"Hey, Al, Paddy wants you to check out the 11th, make sure Shen is holding up all right."

Allen grabbed his coat and joined Toby, a needle of annoyance piercing his brain. "Where is Sergeant Sinclair?"

"He's on patrol near Chelsea, making sure the Hands and 'Zano's boys keep the peace."

"Will you be coming with me to the 11th?"

"Nah, got to meet my dealer," Toby said.

"Dealer? For what?"

"For parts, scrub! Not all of us are brand-fucking-new."

With a sigh and silent resentment, Allen headed out, already planning to return later to get the information he needed. If only he had the time to continue reading what he wanted. Then again, if Roche didn't have the time, neither did he.

━━━━━

Allen dropped far too much money into the slot for the cab driver, running out before he heard a thank you. Even in the early evening, as the bulbs of the Plate wound down to be turned off, the 11th was a prism you could look straight through. The window in Tony Shen's office that Roche had shot out was temporarily covered with a large wooden board. Inside his office was the commissioner and several people wearing black. One of them had long, curled hair, brown with grey streaks.

"Darn," Allen said to himself, running through the door and to the office.

The moment he placed his hand on the commissioner's door, two G-Men turned and pointed guns in his direction. Allen's hands shot up as the barrels lined up with his chest. The spooks ordered him inside. Eva Greaves, director of the FBI, former spouse of Commissioner Jeffrey Robins, and no-nonsense hard-ass, paid no attention to Allen, continuing her speech without missing a beat.

"And given the gross, rampant destruction seen in this relatively quiet neighbourhood, I would be hard pressed to ignore it. People have complained — very high-profile people. The general might be senile, but he still understands what gunshots are. I don't know if this is some kind of publicity stunt to get your precinct more funding, but do I need to point out it's inadvisable to allow the public to think you're incapable of doing your job?"

"You're wrong!" Shen jumped up from his desk, nearly flipping it over. The G-Men didn't flinch, more concerned with Allen than the commissioner. "You think I would pay for a gun to be pointed at my head just to get more funding? I was almost killed! Had the officers of the 5th not been here to help me, I might be dead!"

"And this crime that the other precincts cleaned up — were you told anything about it?"

"No. I would rather not be implicated in the matters of animals. My life and the lives of my officers were threatened, so I wish to stay as far from it as possible."

Greaves sighed and looked at one of her lackeys, who shrugged. "Regardless, we will need to take you to the Upper City for further questioning. I want to make sure that —"

"That you can make me disappear and replace me with someone more complacent?" Shen glared. "I am proud of my heritage. I don't care what this country thinks of us. I thought, as a nation, we were above such petty oppression and profiling."

"This is business, not profiling."

"If so, why aren't you at the 5th asking Robins what happened at that crime scene? Or at the 7th, pulling Viessman's teeth?"

Greaves huffed again, grabbing a cigarette from her pack and waiting for one of her lackeys to light it. She turned, finally eyeing Allen.

"Erzly, I believe? The 5th's boy, working with Roche."

"Yes, ma'am," Allen responded.

"You had some lip on you last time. Will I be getting that again?"

"No, ma'am."

"Where's your little handler?"

"Detective Roche is investigating the murder of Desmond Hartley and his subordinates. He has yet to inform me of any developments. But in regard to this argument, I concur with Commissioner Shen."

"Is that so?"

Shen shook his head subtly, but Allen knew what he was doing. Shen was innocent, and if Greaves was going to be suspicious of anyone, it should be him and Roche. They were the kind of people who could handle stress and find a way out of dire situations. They had done it once; surely, they could do it a second time.

"You should be questioning someone else, not Shen, nor any of the other commissioners. The only person who fully investigated the crime scene by 72nd and 3rd was Elias Roche. If you want details, you should contact him directly."

Greaves coughed, her eyebrows rising and lowering as she took in a drag. "And do you have any knowledge of that crime scene? You seem attached to his hip."

"Perhaps."

"You said you wouldn't give me any lip."

"I did. And you took an oath to uphold the law to the standards set by this country, not to be influenced by a personal agenda or social stigma. It seems both of us were fibbing."

Greaves's face went red. "You'd better watch your mouth, capek. Did you or did you not see the crime scene?"

"I did, but not so thoroughly that I could answer questions about it. Your best bet is to speak to Roche."

"I'll be speaking to both of you soon enough." Greaves extinguished the cigarette under her shoe before moving her men out of the office. She walked over to Allen, standing well within his personal space, making him cower. "Do not take that tone with me again, or I will feed you to the shredder myself."

"This is a country built of freedoms: freedom of religion, of speech, of the pursuit of happiness. Every man and woman is entitled to that."

"That's true. There's just one problem." She leaned in close enough that he could smell her smoke-ridden breath and feel the heat of her anger. "You're neither."

After she left, Allen turned to Shen, who was slumped in his chair, exasperated and already pouring himself something strong to drink. Allen pointed to the bottle, and the commissioner poured a second glass.

"You've got balls, standing up to Director Greaves like that. That's the easiest way to get a target on your head."

"We can handle it." Allen sipped the drink. Much more bitter than the kind Robins drank, but it was quick to calm his nerves. "Roche will be angry when he hears about this."

"Roche will be livid," Tony laughed.

"He has the utmost respect for you, Commissioner. When I tell him why I did it, he'll understand."

"That's true." Shen nodded, cradling his drink. "As much as I warn my officers not to turn into Roche, he does have some good qualities. Lying to the director of the FBI to save me? Allen, I feel like I owe you."

"It's no trouble, Commissioner. Though if I am in a bind in the future, perhaps I could cash it in then?"

"I'll drink to that!" Shen smacked his glass against Allen's, downing the alcohol before leaning back in his chair. "Why is it still like this? My cousin has been working construction for years, and he's about to be booted out and replaced by a Blue-eye. I can't get my brother here from the Republic without causing a bureaucratic incident. I can't even catch a break from some of my snarkier recruits. I thought with you things around, the world might be different. I mean, I've done my time taking lip and kissing ass to get where I am ... I'm sorry, I don't mean to make you a pariah, but that's how the world works."

"It is." Allen nodded, still nursing his drink as Shen poured another.

"You should have seen China before the Great War. Utter chaos since the turn of the century," Shen began, lowering his voice. "Things have only just started settling down there, but I don't know if the country will ever recover from the Boxer Rebellion debts. They are putting a dent in them with the Automatics business, though. God ... I never get to speak about this to anyone. I just always have it sitting on my chest. It's good you're here, Allen. I doubt you'll run off and rat on me to Greaves, huh?"

"I won't," Allen responded. "I'm sorry you have to deal with all this animosity."

"It is what it is. At least I haven't been disappeared yet."

"Is the hostility that intense? Someone should do something."

"Like who? Greaves?" Allen shrugged. "It's bad, but it's nothing like it used to be. Maybe I should be thankful people treat me as well as they do, all things considered. I mean, used to be when America hated something ... well, you can ask Robins about what America did to him. His people got the worst of it. Enslaved, beaten, murdered in cold blood, not to mention the systemic discrimination after all that."

"I wasn't aware of that," Allen said, struggling to conceive of people's capacity for hate.

"They don't teach you that shit where you come from, huh? Yeah, America has always been one big poster for equality held up by its most oppressed people."

"Do all Americans possess this particular brand of hate?"

"No, not all of them, though it feels that way at times. And it isn't just here. Go anywhere else in the world and there will be a long, shameful history of people enslaving, killing, beating, torturing, and marginalizing others. People are shitty, it's human nature for us to be. We're animals, there's no two ways about it. I hesitate to call you things better, but maybe you *are*, since you're made in our image, but without some of the crucial human components."

Allen looked at the glass in his hands, not sure whether to keep drinking or not. "Like?"

"Well, you're quite tight as a collective. I don't see you or that coppertop from the 5th discriminating against other model types. You all just generally dislike people, and people generally dislike all of you. The perfect duality. The perfect storm to get us all to co-operate and coexist."

"It doesn't feel like it's working."

"Yeah, you're right about that. Anyone here will tell you I'm probably the biggest prick of a commissioner in the city. Look at Robins and how irritable he is. And Greaves is, well, Greaves. The only bigwig in the Lower City who isn't on edge all the time is that French bastard cruising with the 3rd Precinct. And you want to know why? Because we don't believe in this charade, not for a second. How easily people like me went from unequal to equal as soon as the machines showed up. We know that if anything happens to change that, it's straight back to the Dark Ages. Even now, it seems we'll find any excuse to regress."

Allen nodded as Shen finished. The commissioner downed his glass and refilled it once more, apparently trying to staunch his rage with alcohol.

"Commissioner," Allen began hesitantly, "surely things aren't all that bleak."

"No, maybe not. Some people are better than others. Benevolence is a rare trait in a human, something you might learn the hard way. But some people are good. People like Roche. He treats me like everyone else. He treats *you* like everyone else, too."

"Roche, yes, but Robins is also good, as is Patrick Sinclair. The reporter at RCA was kind to me, as well ..." Allen's thoughts drifted, thinking about her again. "Not so much Elise Schafer. She hates me."

"I'm glad I've never had to deal with her. She's almost at the level of director for GE, and their word is law in this town. That company gives us more orders than the FBI does, and if she ever gets to the top, I can't imagine what she might do to all of you." Shen checked his watch and downed his glass, his face flushed red.

"Are you ... okay, Commissioner?"

"I'm fine, Allen. Get out of here. Lord knows Greaves won't be barking up my tree again anytime soon, thanks to you."

"Please keep safe, sir."

"I'll be fine, Constable. Sorry you had to witness all that."

Allen nodded and took his leave from the empty station. The bulbs on the Plate southward had shut off, the streetlights were coming on, and the setting sun peeked over the western horizon, shimmering against the skyscraper windows. He called a cab and rode it southbound to the library again. Thankfully, Toby would have found his dealer by now, meaning there was one less distraction to worry about once he got there.

Resting his head against the window, Allen looked up at the behemoth above. It was easy to see and feel its oppression. Part of him did feel noble, giving humanity an excuse to coexist. Humans might be destructive and impulsive, but he wouldn't be. He would be better. Or, at the very least, he would try to be.

CHAPTER 15

I'D ALWAYS BEEN A FAN OF Dickens's work. It reminded me of days at home when my mother used to read to me. The first book I remember was *A Christmas Carol*. It had given me comfort to see the snow fall outside my bedroom window when my mother read to me and the world was quiet, peaceful. The smell of soup and of my father's suits, crisp from dry cleaning. Before the Plate, before the chaos of this new world had taken over. The book brought me back to a different time, a better time.

Allen let itself in around nine at night, its blazer covered in a thin layer of snow, which it shook off moments later. I peered over the top of my book and noticed it had a folder under its arm.

"Enjoy your time at the local library?" I asked.

"I did. It was a fascinating place. I wish I could spend all my days there. I've copied everything I found relevant to our search and organized it for you, since you have a short attention span."

I frowned.

"I also contacted Commissioner Shen," it continued.

"Shen?" I propped myself up on the couch, putting the book down. "He okay?"

"Yes. Sinclair just wanted me to check up on him, is all."

"Ah, good. So, what do you have for me?"

The table was soon covered with everything Allen had found relevant at the library: maps, shipment orders, and names for the exchange of something. Goods? Money? Maybe both. There were also a bunch of reports from the 5th, definitely new files, given the kind of paper used. One of the most prominent items on the table was a reproduction of a black-and-white photo of a Frenchman in a workshop.

"I also dug into the police records from a few months ago, and you were correct: there seems to have been a string of four-person hits perpetrated against the Maranzano Mob. No one paid much attention because they thought it was business as usual."

"Figures, with 'Zano. He's picky with who he cares about in his organization," I said. "Any connection other than the number of bodies?"

"They thought these were Mob hits, so no one felt it prudent to gather any evidence. A terrible nearsighted mistake, no doubt, but I'd bet money all the bullets were Lebels."

I turned my attention to the picture. The man's hair was slicked back, and he wore wide glasses. He had a smile on his face, a thick moustache, and a patch on his chin.

"Who's the Frenchie?"

"That's André Mercier, the designer of one of the most coveted firearm lines in the world, the Mercier Vierling. More importantly, the designer of the only *three* Mercier Vierlings in existence. Recognize this?"

Another black-and-white photo of the same workshop showed three identical rifles, each with three barrels on top and one at the bottom. The ornate metalwork on the barrels and stocks seemed to glimmer even in the crude reproduction.

"Beautiful work. This is it. It has to be."

"I concur, this is the weapon our assailant was using. The recorded measurements of the weapon match the dimensions of the briefcase's foam filling."

"Briefcase?" I asked.

"The container our killer used to transport their weapon discreetly. They left it at the scene when I gave chase during our encounter in the Upper East Side."

"Right."

"The top barrels are capable of firing breech-loaded Lebel cartridges, while the lower barrel is capable of firing a variety of 12-gauge shotgun shells."

"I don't remember the French using shotguns in the war."

"Well, the Americans did bring over shotguns in 1915, when the first Manuals arrived. It seems Mercier was infatuated with them."

"Regardless, he couldn't fire a Von Whisper cartridge from this ... not unless he had something to fill and rifle the breech so it could fire Von Whisper shells."

"Precisely," Allen agreed.

"Jesus, that's still impressive. That ain't a long barrel. He'd have to be a crack shot." I sat back on the couch, putting my hand on Allen's shoulder. "Nice work, really. This is amazing."

"Thank you."

"So, where are they? There are only three of them, so that narrows down our possible suspects to people who have access to one of these."

"Agreed. I've tracked the sale of the Vierlings between hands, even overseas. The first one made, called Richardet, is at the French War Museum. The other two are in the United States. The first of these two, Allard, is at the Metropolitan Museum. The second, Guichard, is owned by a private collector here in New York."

"How did you get records of private sales?" I asked.

"Don't ask." It winked.

Looked like it had some tricks up its sleeves.

Allen handed me the form detailing the history of the weapons' movements. The list was extensive, reaching all the way to San Francisco and back to the East Coast. The dollar values went up with each entry, and the numbers made my wallet and heart hurt equally. The final listing was dated September 1932 — the weapon had been sold for $125,000 to one Elise Schafer of the General Electrics Corporation of America.

"Holy shit," I whispered.

"There are rumours that a fourth Vierling was in development but Mercier died before he could finish it. It was to have been his masterpiece, named Renaud, completing the set of four all named after the Four Sons of Aymon, a medieval tale."

"And where might this fourth one be?"

Allen handed me a crude photo of a shelled field from France, dated 1917. The skeleton of a house remained, smoke billowing, with soot-covered soldiers nearby, raiding the area for food or supplies, one such soldier carting a barely intact ammunition crate from the smouldering ruins.

"The Mercier home … and workshop," Allen explained. "Supposedly it was hit by several stray shells that overshot their target. The fourth Vierling was inside, and it was presumed destroyed, never having been finished."

"I see." I handed back the photo and focused back on our current troubles. "If Schafer has one of the three surviving weapons, and she's in with the Iron Hands, there's a proverbial smoking gun right there."

"Roche, we need to think rationally. We can't go storming into her house without some solid evidence on that latter point."

Yeah, that would be the fastest way to get a bullet in the face. "Fair."

"Now, think: we have something to go off as to who this Vierling Killer might be. At the scene with McIntyre, the killer was wounded. Where, specifically, I'm not sure, but maybe the arm. Definitely upper body. There wasn't enough blood to indicate anything vital was hit, so a limb is likely. Our suspect will have severe bruising on their left shoulder, as well as a knife wound that probably hasn't healed yet."

This narrowed down our suspects, but not as much as I'd hoped. "So, who are our possible Vierling Killers?"

"Elise Schafer — or someone working for her — or perhaps someone working for the Iron Hands. Not that Rabbit fellow, but someone else. Maybe that fellow you keep seeing."

"Yeah, I need to find out who the hell that is …"

Allen nodded. "And perhaps Simone Morane."

I chuckled. "Well, I wouldn't put all our eggs in one basket, there …"

It raised an eyebrow, its suspicion now shifting to me. "Is there a reason you might want to exonerate her?"

"Well, I went to lunch with her, talked about life and days gone by. I don't see much in the way of a connection between her and this killer."

"She is quite snoopy, and seeing her appear wherever we go has been making me nervous," Allen explained. "Was there anything from your luncheon that you believe noteworthy?"

"Her mother was from Verdun."

"André Mercier lived in the city of Reims, several kilometres west of Verdun. Perhaps there was some connection?" It looked at me, hopeful, wanting to believe it could convince me.

"No clue. But probably not, seeing as her mother never came back after returning there in 1914."

Allen thought about this for a moment. "Did you check whether she had any wounds on her body when you met her?"

"No."

"As in there weren't any, or you didn't check?"

"The latter."

Allen's eyebrow popped up. I couldn't tell whether I preferred when it was more expressive, or less. "Well, we should find some way to do so. And we could pry into what happened to her mother during the War, in case there is a connection."

"Allen …" I almost slapped myself. "You can't ask something like that. But we'll see her again, I'm sure, and then you can ask all the questions you want … all the *appropriate* questions you want."

"Understood." It nodded and returned to the documents.

It seemed to drop the subject faster than usual. Was it avoiding talking about Simone? Could have been my imagination.

"Actually, she kind of owes me a favour." I reached for the phone and began dialing. "We might as well make use of the resources we've got. If she can get me into the Met tonight, I can check out that Vierling. She says she has access to a lot of places."

"I'd be happy to lead that part of the investigation."

"Slow down there, partner," I chuckled. "I need you to do something else."

It looked at me with hesitation and a tinge of disappointment. "Yes?"

"Go see Elise Schafer. Check out her Vierling."

"Uh … Can do. Shall I take your car?"

"Please do, Allen. Borrow Robins's Plate Card and ask around for her up there. If she lives off the island, you'll have to go for a little drive."

Simone picked up. I stood and picked up the phone base.

"Simone," I began.

"Elias. To what do I owe the pleasure?"

"I need to call in that favour."

"Of course." She was unperturbed by my brusqueness.

"The Metropolitan — can you get me in?"

"When?"

I turned to see Allen peering hard at a document, but obviously listening in on my conversation. What the hell was going on with that metal man?

"Now," I said.

There was silence for a brief moment, then she spoke again. "I'll need some time to prep. Meet there, or are you picking me up?"

"I'll meet you there, outside the doors, ten o'clock."

I put the phone down and put my hand on Allen's shoulder. It peered up at me. I knew its mannerisms by this point. It always had that awkward expression when it wanted to pester me with questions.

"You good, Al?"

"Yes, Detec— Roche."

"Do you want to switch jobs? I can go rough up Schafer instead."

Allen smiled and stood, looking more comfortable in its own skin. "After the ruckus you caused on the Plate a month ago, I think it would be best if I go."

"Good man. And be thorough: even if she never pulled the trigger, make note of anyone who seems capable of doing it. A used firearm will at least give us headway into the right line of questioning."

Allen chuckled. "You're starting to sound like me."

I grinned and walked out of the apartment with Allen, locking my door and throwing my coat over my shoulder.

"I'll put in a good word about you with Simone," I said. Allen stared at me, panicked, and I laughed. "You make it too easy to push your buttons, Al. Meet you back here at midnight."

━━━━━━━

I was no stranger to breaking into places, but standing outside one of the most famous museums in the world while a dainty woman jiggled a lock scraper into one of the front doors was not my idea of subtlety. She'd been waiting for me when I arrived. She'd done her best to dress unremarkably, but even in grey slacks and a loose brown coat, her blond hair was like a flare in the darkness. How many people might have spotted her here?

"When you said you had keys to anywhere in the city …" I muttered.

"I never said what kind of keys they were," she said with a smirk, raking the tumblers in the lock a third time. "I swear, they make these trickier every time."

"Not your first time popping these doors open?"

"I've covered stories about artifacts from Germany that came here after the War, so no."

"And when did you learn how to pick locks?"

"I thought it might be a useful skill to have. Damn it, these locks are just" — a loud click, and the door creaked open — "a pain in the ass sometimes."

We entered, closing the door after us and keeping away from the windows.

Simone had brought along a flashlight, something I hadn't thought far enough ahead to consider bringing. The light moved over art pieces from Greece, Germany, China, Japan, almost every corner of the globe. Passing through the medieval section, I glimpsed suits of armour, ancient weaponry, and paintings from the period depicting great warriors and noble deeds done for the king.

"So what exactly are we here for?" she asked.

"I need to examine a weapon. The Mercier Vierling."

She nodded, showing no reaction.

We headed on to the new section called the New York Wing. The Museum of New York on 106th had been abandoned during Red August, and everything meant to go there had been relocated here. It was small, with few artifacts, but it was a stepping stone to our objective. There was a hodgepodge of newspaper clippings about the founding of the city and pictures of the construction of the Empire Building and the Plate, and even of the first legislature to bring in Automatics.

That last exhibit led into the newest and most ignored section of the American Wing that was devoted to the "Art of the Machine." Old Automatic designs were on display; intricate mechanical arms and legs lined the wall, examples of metalwork and painting to give the standard chrome exterior some flare. Of course, no machine would have worn something that stupid; it would have cost an arm and a leg to maintain. They called such things the burgeoning "Technossance." A fat lot of good that had done for any of us besides drive us deeper into debt.

The southmost part of the American Wing had been converted into a housing for the finest artifacts of the Great War. Here lay designs for the original Manuals, weapons used by the Allied forces, and photos from some of the battlefields. Much of it was displayed with artistic flair, so as to keep it distinct from the natural history museum on the Plate. Regardless, you could only polish a turd so much.

I stopped to look at some retouched and enhanced photographs of the carnage. There was the victory of Gallipoli, with the Manuals guarding the canal and putting down the Ottomans from reinforcing the Centrals. There were also photos of some of America's biggest battles, namely Luxemburg and Strasbourg. I had been at the latter, and the photos brought me back. I could smell diesel fumes and iron from all the spilled blood.

"Roche." Simone shook my arm. "Let's go. I'll bring you here after the holidays."

I regained my composure and went deeper into the wing. Next to the Lugers and Mausers, the Lebels and the Springfields, was the centrepiece of the Great War weaponry: the Vierling. It was immaculate, the metalwork on top of the barrel assembly sturdy and carved to a degree of detail most sculptors would have envied. Horses and knights rode along the base of the weapon, their spears slamming through competitors in a great tournament. Along the barrel, a knight battled an unseen foe, his sword drawn and pointing in the direction the bullet would fly through the barrel. A horse was carved into the varnished stock, and *Allard* was inscribed beneath it in a beautiful cursive. I hadn't noticed any such details when I'd been fighting for my life. Remembering the encounter made my stitches itch.

Simone used the key rake to enter the backroom behind the display and retrieve the weapon. It was funny … all this felt far too easy. Someone — anyone — should have tried to stop us by now.

"I'm scared to ask, but there won't be any security guards knocking me out and dragging me up to the Plate, will there?" I asked as she returned.

"Don't worry, it's Christmas," she said, unconcerned.

"Why isn't there anyone here? We could take half this stuff and pawn it in a matter of days, walk away with a fortune."

"Everything in here can be tracked without much effort. It would be hard to actually sell anything. The moment something goes missing, it gets called in. People from the Plate would be swarming in to find out who took it."

It seemed like a poor explanation for the apparent lack of security. I looked around but didn't spot any obvious cameras. I was on edge the entire time, expecting that any moment there would be sirens blaring outside.

She deposited the weapon in my hands. The top was covered in a thin layer of dust. I cracked open the barrel and looked inside. Gleaming steel looked back, the light from the flashlight reflecting against the interior of the weapon.

"It's clean. Too clean." I closed the breech and examined the stock, looking for any marks that might show it had been used as a club.

"They clean regularly to make sure artifacts don't rust or tarnish. They're very diligent about it."

The stock was free of chips or scratches or stresses. It wasn't the weapon the Vierling Killer had used to fight us. The rifling, upon closer inspection, was tarnished. The largest barrel was tarnished, as well, but it was free of rifling, seeing as it was designed to fire pellets, not bullets. Underneath, there was one trigger, which I pulled to dry fire and reset the mechanism. I handed the weapon back to Simone, who put it back in the case and locked everything back up.

"Goddamn it." I pulled out a cigarette and placed it between my lips, but refrained from lighting the tip. "I was sure we had it. That asshole definitely used a Vierling. I saw it with my own eyes."

"Well, there are four of them," she noted, as we walked toward the front of the museum.

"Three. They're named after the Sons of Aymon." I wasn't well versed in the legends, but I regurgitated the tidbit, nonetheless.

"Where's the third rifle? I know one is in France."

"Owned by prolific gun collector Elise Schafer."

"You don't say. Looks like the case is closed, then, huh?"

"Not necessarily. Schafer may be ruthless, but I don't know if she's capable of murder. Maybe someone took it from her collection. Maybe she gave it to someone to use. I don't know, I just don't. Hopefully Allen has more luck."

"Do you have any other suspects?"

I squinted at her. "You going to keep your mouth shut?"

"I won't tell anyone. I haven't told anyone about your past. I swore, and I swear again."

I sighed, lit my dart and sucked in, feeling my stress come down a level. "Besides Schafer, we're looking at the Iron Hands … and you."

"Me?"

"You're always keeping close to me and Allen. Also, your father is a general, and the perp has military training. And the fact you can get in here so easily doesn't help your case. Allen's convinced, but …"

"I appreciate the compliment, but I wasn't trained by my father, nor by anyone in America. Women can't serve as GIs, as you well know. War is a man's game, and my father is very old school. He thinks the military is far too dangerous a place for women."

"Overprotective, huh?"

"In a way." She didn't look angry, but I wondered whether I'd offended her with the implication. "Anyway, I thought you just confirmed that this Vierling wasn't the one the killer used," she said.

"Nonetheless …" I puffed on my cigarette, not caring about any smoke detectors there might be. If the cops were going to show up at all, they'd have been here by now. "There is one other thing. The killer would have a wound."

"Where?"

"On the arm somewhere. They sustained some injuries at the last crime scene. I'm sorry, but just to put my mind at ease, please — your arms?"

Simone sighed, undoing her coat. Underneath, she wore a black blouse with cap sleeves. Her bare skin was as pristine as the rifle. Under the light of the flashlight, her arms looked normal, untouched, uncut. I didn't want to test my luck by touching them. She put the coat back on, and I handed her the flashlight.

"I'm sorry about that. I'll cross you off the list."

"I'm not offended. I mean, I am a little, but it is your job to be paranoid. I suppose you would have done this to anyone else if they had access to the weapon and a general for a father?" She smirked.

"That's right. Schafer will probably be getting it worse from Allen. It's so good at picking up the little details, it makes me feel inadequate some days."

Simone chuckled and resumed walking. "Aren't most machines good at that sort of thing?"

"No, just this one. Allen is weird, but it does come in handy."

≡≡≡≡≡

We went out into the dark city. The lamps above us weren't enough to illuminate the street under the shroud of night. It had started to snow, and with no Plate above us on 82nd Street, we had no buffer from the storm. It was difficult to see even five feet in front of me. That was going to make getting home difficult.

Descending the steps, we didn't even hear the platoon of Brunos approaching until they jumped us. Someone put a gun to my back and kicked my knee, pushing me to the ground. My side was on fire from the quick jerk. Simone was down on all fours, two Foldguns pointed at her head.

My only thought was how fast I could draw my Diamondback from its holster. Who would be shot first? The guy sticking me up, one of the two guys near Simone, or Simone herself? I knew I'd get off the first shot, but would I be able to save both of us if I caused that chaos?

From out of the haze of snow came Maranzano, his bulky frame wrapped up in black wool, with more men behind. He looked down at me, putting the end of his cane against my head to show that he was in control. Santoni held a Thompson in his hands. The barrel tip was frosted and felt extra cold when he placed it on my temple.

"Care to let us know what you were up to in there?" Maranzano asked.

"Following a lead on a case you have nothing to do with."

"Oh, I have everything to do with it." He pushed my head back with the cane so our eyes met. Then he withdrew it and hobbled over to Simone. "And so does she. Is it you, or her?"

"What are you on about?"

"Someone is killing my men, my friends, my people. Disregarding my control and influence over this city. You work for that bitch, so maybe killing you would solve my problem nice and quick."

"The Eye wants me to look the other way. She wants me to ignore the killer, because they're doing such a good job fucking with you," I said with a smile.

That comment earned me a strike across the face. Maranzano had a limp, but it didn't impede his arms any. My head snapped around, and my jaw felt like it might be dislocated. The rings on his fingers had probably left marks on my cheek, too. Blood dripped from my lips onto the concrete.

"Do not mock me! My men are dying, along with my business! The one person with motive is that bitch, working through you! You may take my land and my influence scot-free, but I'll repay you for it, don't you worry, Roche."

He pulled out his own pistol and put it to my crown. Blood continued to run from my mouth. Unable to look up with my sore neck, I stared at the concrete, feeling the barrel.

"I should make the both of you suffer for all you've put me through, but this will be much cleaner," he said.

"WILL IT?"

Maranzano flinched, pulling the gun away from me and pointing it elsewhere. Mustering all my strength, I craned up to see a lanky eight-foot figure standing mere inches from the Mob boss.

The Rabbit, in all its glory.

It seemed the Eye was keeping tabs on me. Eight more Red-eyes appeared, training their weapons on Maranzano and his men to keep them from doing anything stupid.

"HOW ARE YOU DOING DOWN THERE, ROACH?" the Rabbit asked me mockingly.

"I was fine." I spit out a glob of blood, feeling my mouth fill again.

"YES, I'M SURE." It turned back to Maranzano. "I BELIEVE IT WOULD BE BEST FOR YOU TO LEAVE."

"You don't rule me, capek," Maranzano said. "You're a machine. Not even a man can scare me off."

The Rabbit moved back, allowing another figure to approach in the darkness.

Holy shit. She actually came.

The Eye wore only black, her hair whipping around in the wind. She always had her face covered. A black veil obscured her appearance.

She must be really pissed to have actually come.

"Only a *human*, Sal. Hu-man," she said, enunciating carefully. "Remember, we live in a different world than the one you grew up in."

"You are both abominations, you and the capek! Your lapdog is at fault, and I deserve payback for this betrayal of our agreement! You swore no direct aggression between us, I have it in writing. And yet you own Chelsea and are pushing into my territory! My men will steamroll you if you continue to violate these terms."

"And mine you, Sal. You are not the only victim here. I doubt Gould would appreciate learning about your trafficking rings throughout his stores. I hope you can still afford their silence." She looked down at me. "Elias is not the killer. I did instruct him to forget this investigation, but he seems … persistent." She sounded aggravated. "Something I want to remedy."

Though not happy, Maranzano put his gun back into its holster and moved away from me. The Bruno behind me pulled his gun out of my back, and the two surrounding Simone retreated, as well. The uneasy truce gave me chills. The tension was palpable. Anything could have set one of them off, even the drop of a pin.

"Remember whose turf you're on," Maranzano said.

"Remember whose man you're threatening," she replied.

Maranzano took his leave, his men regrouping and glaring at us before disappearing into the snow, no doubt headed back to the Kompound. I got off my knees, wiping blood from my mouth and flicking it into the fresh snow. Simone stood up and crept over beside me to put someone else between her and one of the most dangerous women in America.

"The reporter?" the Eye asked me.

"A guide, nothing more. She knows nothing," I said, not looking up.

"Good. Do not disobey me again, Elias. There will be no more warnings."

I nodded, but before I could ask about her involvement in the killings, she was gone, the Red-eyes had vanished, and the Rabbit's red bulbs were visible in the haze for only a fleeting moment before it disappeared, as well.

"SEE YOU AROUND, ROACH ..."

Simone retrieved a handkerchief from her purse and handed it to me. I stuffed it against my lip to clot up the fresh wound and sat down on the concrete steps. Simone sat behind me, almost cradling my head as I tried to regain my sense of balance.

"I'll get you a new handkerchief," I said.

"No need."

"You okay?"

"Yeah." She didn't seem it. "It's been a while ... Haven't had a gun put to my head in a long time.

Jesus, was that Maranzano? I thought he was more of a passive don, not one who does the dirty work himself."

"Yeah, well, you learn something new every day."

"And her. The Iron Hands ..." She stopped, like her brain was still processing things. "They're real? I've never seen them in action, only heard stories."

"Mm-hmm." I looked at the blood-soaked cloth and cursed under my breath. "I'm sorry for dragging you into this."

"It was more of an adventure than I was expecting." She laughed nervously and coughed from the cold weather. "What if they hadn't shown up?"

"What?" I asked.

"What if the Eye or that big Red-eye hadn't shown up? How would you have gotten us out of that?"

"I would have pulled my gun, punched Maranzano, put bullets in everyone there."

"But would you have been able to save both of us?"

I paused. She knew the answer already. "I haven't worked with anyone else in a long time. A long, long time. I'm not used to worrying about other people in tough situations, but I would have done all I could ..."

"Would you have taken that bullet if it meant I'd have gotten out of there alive?"

No hesitation. "Yes. Yes, I would have."

She smiled. The tension dissipated, and it felt like we were back at the restaurant.

"Thank you, Detective."

"Just Roche. Or Elias. I'm not a detective anymore. Allen just calls me that as a formality."

Once I'd recovered enough to walk, Simone helped me up, and we walked a few blocks south back to the bustling Upper East Side. I hailed a cab and put Simone in it after I'd made sure the driver wasn't one of the Eye's goons.

"You can come back with me. I feel safe with you nearby," she said.

"I got some errands to run. I'll catch you later. Stay safe."

Simone nodded and closed the door, the cab heading back south to bring her home. It felt better to be alone up here. I didn't need people relying on me. That was the easiest way to get them killed. Besides, I had a feeling Maranzano and the Eye weren't the only people who knew about that break-in. I'd rather Simone not be prosecuted along with me if it came to that.

I stuffed the handkerchief into my mouth, laughing lightly as I remembered what that Black Hat Masters had said before I caved in his chest.

"At least James ain't around to see this." I chuckled again and walked off.

CHAPTER 16

ALLEN'S INVESTIGATION IN ONE of the lobbies of the Plate yielded the information that Elise Schafer was not a resident of the floating city. Whereas Roche would have cracked some skulls and gotten that information in seconds flat, Allen had had to wait until the 5th's Plate Card had almost run out of time before he got to speak to someone. He did his best to ignore the condescending comments and get the answer he needed, and by the time he did, the Card had seconds left on it. There was some comfort in knowing that the badge he carried could get him what he wanted, despite the lengths he had to go to.

He made his way out of the city for the first time since he'd arrived almost a year ago and went east to Long Island. It was surreal to come out from under the Plate and see the stars shimmer, without the Upper City's pollution choking the night sky. More than once, he caught himself staring upward, then having to swerve out of the way of an oncoming car, having drifted into the wrong lane. Still, the uncongested highways posed less of a threat than the busy arteries of Manhattan.

Queens opened up before him as he drove: suburban homes dotted the landscape, and highways and bridges under construction gave some lucky people work. Still, cheap housing and poverty were rampant here, since living in the city was just too expensive. Residents had to drive into the city for work; there were only so many construction jobs in the area. Ironic how even the abandoned Automatic neighbourhoods in downtown Manhattan were still too expensive for most. Speaking of Automatics, plenty of Blue-eyes roamed the streets, transient or perhaps looking for work. The people outnumbered them vastly, a stark contrast to inner Manhattan. Times Square was often completely populated by chrome and steel. There didn't seem to be many Green-eyes out and about, hopefully because they were working.

After Queens, it was nothing but trees and vegetation, urban development not having reached the northwestern edge of Long Island yet. The smell of fresh air and living things gave the area an unseen colour, even under the white frost. In the darkness, with the wind blowing through the shrubs and the coniferous trees shooting their green spines through the white blanket of snow, Allen felt an unfamiliar sense of ease. He turned north through Hempstead, where the roads were cleaner and well constructed, the trees tall and trimmed, and almost every exit led to a mansion or a golf club. There weren't any cars on the road besides the

Talbot. No police cruised the area, keeping an eye on everything.

Manorhaven, still in development, was visible even from several miles away. The tops of the manors were visible from the opposing peninsula, and the private marinas were full of yachts and sailing boats. Allen deduced that the farther east one went, the fewer machines there were. In fact, he hadn't seen another Automatic since Queens.

Schafer's manor matched all the rest in grandeur and aesthetic. It had two floors, white marble pillars, and a metal gate that was most likely electrified. She had her own marina and a pool, as well — who needed a pool when their property sat on the edge of a lake? He thought he could he see a green glow from a buoy bouncing about in the dark water that must be for directing yachts.

He exited the car and went up to the locked gate. There was an intercom attached to the brick base of the metal fence. He pushed the button.

"State your business," a staticky male voice demanded.

He leaned in to the microphone. "NYPD."

"This is Long Island, not Manhattan."

"This is still the state of New York, sir."

A groan followed as the gates spread back into the property, allowing Allen to drive through and cross the gargantuan drive that ended in a horseshoe in front of the manor. The large wooden doors were already open when he parked near the steps. He made his way up to meet a youngish man with slick jet-black hair and a thin beard. He was dressed in a clean suit and wore an exposed holster.

"State your business, capek. Miss Schafer isn't a fan of house calls," he said.

"I'm investigating the murder of eight people connected to General Electrics, and Elise Schafer is a prime suspect. I believe she would want this matter settled quickly and quietly, so it would be shame if she refused entry and this information was leaked to the public."

"It *would* be a shame. Is that a threat?"

"Not from me, but I believe she knows there are more than a few journalists in the city who are all too eager to find a big story."

The man nodded and opened the door wide. Allen got ready to display his badge just in case, but the man turned away from him before he could flash the symbol.

The interior was stunning: two curved staircases led to an upper landing. A chandelier hung above the foyer, firing light in every direction. From the massive entryway Allen could see a kitchen, a recreation room, a library, and a living room. This man was unlikely to be her only security personnel; Allen could feel eyes on him from every direction, as though every step he took was being measured and recorded.

Schafer came down from the stairs, the clacking of her shoes echoing in the foyer. She wore a smart grey suit and a black glove on her right hand. Her arms were covered by a jacket, and her black hair was pulled back into a ponytail. Allen couldn't help being intimidated, assaulted by her mere stare. She looked up at him, several inches shorter than his own gaunt metallic frame.

"Can I help you?" Her tone was harsh.

"Miss Schafer, I have documents showing you purchased one of the three known Mercier Vierling rifles. It has been in your possession for well over two years. Is this correct?"

"It is."

"May I see this rifle?"

"Why would I let you see it?"

"Because we believe that a Mercier Vierling was used in the murder of Desmond Hartley, along with prominent figures in the Maranzano Mafia. I'll require a look at the weapon to check whether it has been fired or cleaned recently."

Schafer gave off an aura of impatience, but not a sense of guilt. Given her haughty attitude, though, she might find it easy to hide such emotions. She led Allen deeper into the house. The security guard followed behind, the holster under his arm slapping against his side with each step. A staircase led down into the basement, most of which was a converted wine cellar for keeping expensive bottles chilled and suitable for drinking. A sliding door revealed a second room, this one catering to something very different from wine.

Weapons of ancient origin were displayed in glass cases and on racks, everything from spears to swords to pepperboxes and Colts from the Wild West. An old naval cannon resided in the corner, the stamp on it indicating that it was of British origin and older than New York. A glass case on the back wall held one singular rifle sitting on red cushions, and it was protected by both combination and padlocks. Schafer stood between

Allen and the case to make sure he couldn't see the combination as she opened it. The silence was crushing. If he'd had the ability to sweat, Allen's clothing would have been soaked through by now. The security guard's measured breathing behind suggested that one of his hands was on his gun, ready to shoot Allen if anything surprising happened.

Schafer retrieved the rifle carefully, cracked open the barrel, and rested it under her armpit and over her forearm, as a hunter might. Allen looked it up and down and held out his hand to take it. He couldn't help looking Schafer up and down, as well. Simone might have unlocked a part of him he wasn't sure he wanted to deal with.

"You think I'm just going to hand this over? This weapon costs half as much as this house. I'm not about to let anyone touch it."

"We can't complete our investigation without examining it."

Schafer raised her eyebrows, then turned to wander through her collection, signalling Allen to follow. He was unsure what she was doing, but he felt uneasy.

"What was the name they gave you, again? I can't remember whether Roche mentioned it at that useless gala."

"Erzly. Allen Erzly."

"Built off some combination of letters and numbers, no doubt."

"My original designation is Forty-One Echo-November."

"41-EN. That sounds more like a name for a machine. Tell me, if this rifle could speak, what would it say to us?

Would it tell us if it really did kill those people? Would it feel remorse or empathy? Would it acknowledge anything that it did at all?"

Allen drew a blank as he followed her around the room. "I'm not sure, Miss Schafer."

"And you, Dante?" she said, calling over to the guard. "What do you think it would say?"

"No clue, ma'am," he said, monotonous and emotionless.

"See, with Dante, I expect him not to know. He's human, same as me. You, on the other hand, Erzly, should know what it thinks. You and it aren't very different. Both of you are inanimate objects, originally weapons. Now, *it* is an artifact, and you … well, we're not sure what all of you are now."

"I'm not a weapon, Miss Schafer. Not mindless and violent like one, at the very least."

"You couldn't be, because a weapon is neither mindless nor violent. A weapon is a weapon; it does nothing its wielder does not. You couldn't blame a gun for taking a life, since the gun didn't load itself and shoot someone — the person who carried it did. A weapon is a tool to make real a violent intention. Does that make sense?"

"It does." Allen nodded.

"And yet you things are … confusing. An autonomous weapon — such a terrifying combination of words. Who's in control, do you think? Surely, if a machine takes orders, the responsibility falls on whoever gave it an order, as in Red-eye Law, when we prosecute whoever rewires the Automatic. The rules and laws are built around the concept that no Automatic can be at fault for a crime, because it's believed that they aren't capable of making decisions like that. You discard a weapon but prosecute a person, and the way we prosecute machines is to destroy them. That defines how we think of them. Do you see what I'm saying?"

"I think I follow, to a degree. Though I do believe it was GE that helped establish Blue-eyes as people in the eyes of the law."

"I thought you might have heard about that. Yes, we did our best there. But while Blue-eyes can be considered autonomous beings in regard to the development of a personality through experience and mostly free will, they aren't really people." She pursed her lips. "We did have to make some concessions on that case."

"If they are considered to have free will, surely they can be tried as people."

"In a perfect world, they would be. But if you were to turn that gun on me and Dante, you know who they would prosecute? Elias Roche and Jeffrey Robins, and then they would feed you to a shredder. You aren't at fault simply because you are just a weapon, a meaningless tool for violence. So long as society classifies you as such, you will be nothing more. Of course, without police programming, no doubt you couldn't even point a loaded weapon in my general direction. Nevertheless, no Automatic's actions are its own."

"I am capable of choosing my own actions, Miss Schafer. I am not a slave. Not like every other Automatic."

"As this conversation has indicated, yes, it seems you're correct. Project Lutum was one of GE's pet projects, green-lit by Gould. Tell me, if you're so offended by my grouping you with every other Blue-eye walking the streets, then why don't you make your presence known in the world? Why not stand up and shout that you are different, you can think, you aren't a mindless machine?"

Allen did not have a response to this, so Schafer supplied it.

"Because that would be suicide. Because we both know that you aren't the problem, and neither are Red-eyes or Green-eyes, nor the War, nor anything else related to you. As with weapons, the problem is people. They'd rather you remained weapons, both socially and legally, because it sets their minds at ease not to have to compete with you; you are all mindless things, and they will always be on top. The moment they realize their weapons can decide for themselves what to do and what not to do, that's when the pitchforks will come out. That's when people will get scared, and scared people do very stupid things."

She closed the weapon and held it out before her. Allen reached out and grasped the Vierling firmly in his hands. Schafer turned to leave the room.

"Dante, keep an eye on it. Get it anything it needs," she said as she left.

"Yes, ma'am."

———

Allen spent about fifteen minutes examining the weapon in its entirety. He cracked the breech back open and inspected the mechanisms in action. The bottom barrel was pristine, never fired before, with no scrapes indicating a barrel shroud had been used to fit a Von Whisper round inside it. The Lebel barrels, too, were clean. The weapon was dusty from disuse, and the rifling was polished. Not a single round had ever been fired from it. He moved the weapon around, feeling the four barrels rotate in their socket and testing the hammer and trigger mechanism. Each barrel fired its own individual bullet when aligned with the firing mechanism in the base of the breech. After several dry fires, he concluded that there was no way all three barrels could fire simultaneously.

Indeed, the pictures he had seen of the other Mercier Vierlings proved that this was a feature in all three of them; the three Lebel barrels could not fire at the same time. Even if Schafer had used this weapon, scrubbed it clean, polished the rifling, and disposed of the rest of the evidence, there was no way she could have produced the firing pattern he had seen at the scene with McIntyre. He even asked the security guard if there was a possible way for all three barrels to fire at the same time, but the man confirmed what Allen now knew: they had the right weapon *type*, but not the right weapon.

He laid the rifle back in its case and closed it, hearing it lock automatically. The guard escorted him back upstairs, where Schafer was waiting by the door, her gloved hand already on the handle as he approached.

"Regarding our conversation downstairs," Allen began, "I do feel regret for what I've done. I made a decision to save the lives of my friends, but it cost someone else's. Every day, I think about that, and how I don't want to be in a position like that again."

Schafer nodded, her hostility seeming to diminish upon hearing this. "And would you do it again if you had to?"

"I don't know. In that moment, I knew I had to, but if I'd had time to think and find another way … I just don't know. The entire experience was … disturbing."

"Then you're more like people than we'd care to admit. People are indecisive, impatient, temperamental, instinctual, everything we shouldn't be to survive as a society. We wear sheep's clothing — we're born into it — though all of us are wolves underneath. But things like you and your people — what are you? Are you born sheep or wolves? Do you feel the same desires that humans do? For sex, for violence, for anything at all? I hope not. I'd rather deal with someone who doesn't lie to themself about their true nature."

"But you yourself are human." Allen almost laughed at the irony. "How can you say that? Are you willing to admit that you are like that, too?"

Schafer tilted her head to one side, not in annoyance, but interest. "As I've climbed the ranks of GE, I've realized one thing. Call it humanity's number one rule: everyone's a hypocrite, and if they say they aren't, that proves the point. This has been and always will be true, no matter who or what you speak to. No doubt your Nightcaller friend has some ironic attitudes about the things he has done?"

"He does, as do most people."

"Point made, it seems."

Allen nodded and took his leave, walking out of the double doors back into the cold. He turned back before she closed the door. "By the way, one more thing, Miss Schafer."

"Yes?" She didn't seem impatient this time.

"Nightcaller — Roche doesn't like that name. I'd suggest not calling him that."

She smirked and closed the door, leaving him alone on the lit steps. She wouldn't follow his advice, but he felt better for saying it.

───────

The drive back to Manhattan was bittersweet. Allen could see the Plate shining all the way from Manorhaven, and seeing it grow closer and larger reminded him once again about the Depression the city lived in. Watching the foliage and vegetation fade into concrete and steel made him feel like the city was digging its claws back into him as he drove west. Reaching Queens, he could see details on the underside of the Plate, the bright lights on top blocking out the stars and turning the black night grey. The hour's drive went by in a blink, and before he knew it, the Talbot was crossing the 59th Street Bridge. Once again, the wind in the trees was replaced by car horns and old drunks yelling at rusted machines. The crunch of snow replaced by gunshots, and the entrances to golf clubs replaced by dark alleyways and overused lanes.

He parked the Talbot in front of Roche's apartment building and made sure it was stable and locked. As he approached the hot dog vendor, Yuri, Allen felt his stomach churn with hunger. Looking at his watch, he saw it was eleven at night, too late for anywhere else to be open. He put some change on Yuri's cart.

"Cond-i-ments?" the man asked in his thick accent.

"Please. Everything you've got," Allen responded, resting his arms and head on the trolley. "Thank you."

"You okay?" Yuri handed him his meal.

"I'm not okay. I'm tired, I'm stressed, and I might get killed if I'm not careful. Everything is a mess." Allen bit into the hot dog and his eyes lit up. "Holy moly, this is good."

"I make best dogs in city, no one but Elias believe me!" the Russian said, almost jumping up in triumph. "Other machines not eat, why you?"

"It's a long story."

"Ah. Why you drive Elias's car?"

"He wanted me to check on something, and … ugh. I'm going up to wait for him. If you see him, tell him I'm here. My name is Allen, by the way." He shot out his free hand.

"Yuri Semetsky," the man responded, shaking Allen's hand. "Some people before ask about Elias, say they need to meet him."

"Who?"

"Not sure. Girl. Tall, look mean."

Allen had a feeling he knew who was looking for Elias. He made his way to the lobby to get up to the apartment. He almost ran, but he needed to eat first; even with fear clenching his stomach, his hunger was immense.

The elevator ride to Roche's floor took forever. Running to the apartment door, Allen could see it was ajar. He reached for his gun, hesitated, then put his arm down by his side . Easing the door open, he saw five un-invited guests sitting inside Roche's apartment, none of which he was happy to see.

"Erzly, sit. We need to talk to you and Roche."

CHAPTER 17

THIS WOULD BE THE FIRST TIME IN recent memory that I'd gone to the Brass and Pass without the intention of drinking. The cab driver who brought me to SoHo mentioned that I looked like a guy who needed a drink. Still, it didn't matter too much what he thought. I knocked three times on the metal door, leaned back against the brick wall, and spat out another glob of blood. My face was on fire, and the cold weather didn't help things.

The Red-eye Titan named Dallas opened the slide, saw me leaning there, and muttered the sentence I had heard too often: "No derms allowed."

"Dallas, I ain't in the mood." I coughed from the dry air. "Just open it. Get Tiny, I don't care."

"No ... derms."

"Dallas, you open this goddamn door right now, I ain't in the mood to knock!"

The stupid machine closed the slide on me. I had no more patience. So I knocked.

Two times, twice.

The door swung open, and every Red-eye in the joint was holding on to a weapon: pistols were drawn, bottles smashed, knives sharpened. Dallas clenched its fists, its non-blinking eye shimmering red. The Blue-eye bartender at the far end had a mean-looking shotgun. The rest of the armaments were comprised of standard .38s and .45s.

One of the closest machines was a Boomer with a 1911, the gun looking like a toy in its oversized hand. It towered over me, the hydraulic pistons in its back meant to make it look larger than it really was. The damn thing could bench-press a building, and I was several inches into its personal space, with its pistol pointed at my forehead.

The Boomer began to speak. "Don't do anything stupid, or —"

"Or what? You'll what?" I interrupted. It didn't respond. "Just because you got some back-alley police programming, you think you're hot shit? You think that's enough to deal with any derm with a grudge?"

I grabbed its hand with both of mine, my thumbs pressing down on the metal finger that was wrapped around the trigger. I pushed my forehead into the barrel and pressed my thumbs down harder. Its finger resisted my force. It was like pressing against a steel girder. No matter how hard I pressed, the trigger remained where it was.

"I thought as much," I whispered. "Let go."

I grabbed the gun from its hand — the machine allowed me to take it — and let it dangle by my side. Every other firearm in the room was pointed to my chest. My finger slipped against the trigger, and the Automatics turned their aim onto my arms and legs.

"Some advice for you all: don't pretend to be something you ain't. You'll live longer that way," I said, pulling the slide off the gun and letting the stripped parts fall to the floor, save for the frame. "The only thing I *should* be afraid of is Dallas over here, but I ain't, because it's too stupid to do anything."

The tension lifted when Tiny scuttled over, yapping. It leaped onto the bartender's rifle and pushed it down. "Oi, relax, people! Jesus, Roche, yer gonna get yourself shot doing that."

"Your Titan is about as stupid as a gorilla," I remarked.

"He got 'alf his fuckin' Interface blown off in a fight a few months back, be patient with him!"

I gave the Boomer back its pistol by tossing the frame at its head. It didn't react to the impact, but I could feel its eyes on my back. I grinned as I sauntered up to the bar. Dallas closed the front door and resumed its lazy post while the rest of the Automatic patrons put down their weapons.

"What can I do fer ya, Roche?" Tiny asked, as if nothing had happened.

"I need to meet with Moses. He likes to work here, if I remember correctly."

"Aye, he's here. Might'a spooked him with that knock of yers, but let's hope not."

Tiny chattered in Bitwise to the bartender, who led me around the speakeasy to a hidden door in the wall, just beside the bar. While the place was nice — wood-panelled and buffed to shine — the backroom I was brought to matched the rest of SoHo, with decrepit concrete walls, burst pipes, chipped paint, and something or other leaking. The bartender closed the door after me.

The man I was here to see was packing up when I came in, but he stopped once he saw me. He had a bald head, pale skin, and a prim and proper moustache of the sort an Old West sheriff might wear. His tense body loosened a bit, and he slid the loaded gun on the table beside him out of view. He replaced his small suitcases and containers back on the folding wooden tables he had set up. There were several reclaimed wooden chairs nearby for customers to sit in.

"Elias, thank goodness." He opened his wares once more, revealing multitudes of weaponry and ammunition. His voice was quiet but solid, unmistakeable in its fluid delivery. "I thought the Eye might have come for me. Can't be too careful here."

"Why not get out of the city, Moses? I'm sure you could find paying customers out there."

"You have no idea how much money I make here. It's almost worth the death threats and paranoia … almost."

I smirked and sat in one of the chairs, feeling my side itch, and now my mouth, as well. I pulled out a small wad of bills and pushed it onto the table, then leaned back to try and staunch the blood flow. "Hopefully this covers it."

"Covers what, exactly?"

"I'm looking for a present. A friend of mine saved my life and has continued to be helpful ever since. I want to get him something nice, something practical."

"Ah, you've come to the right place." Moses moved over the many containers, looking over his stock. "Any idea what his preference is? What's his dominant hand? Is he a fan of German or American designs?"

"He's not a fan of weapons, in general, though he uses them reluctantly. He seems capable when firing at Automatics. Got anything good for that?"

"Well, you do have your Diamondback," he said, smiling.

"I ain't lending it to him. And I doubt you have another."

"Fair enough." Moses searched through his cases, considering his stock. "You need something with some punch. I recommend the Browning Hi-Power. It's a new prototype I wanted to test out before purchasing a few crates, and it might fit the bill. The ammo can be hard to come by, but that's not an issue for me."

"Show me."

He brought over the weapon, placing it on the table. My left hand was holding the handkerchief against my jaw. With my other hand, I lifted the pistol and felt it out. It was lighter and shorter than the 1911, but it felt much more versatile, if less lethal. The trigger felt heavy to pull, but that wouldn't matter much to Allen.

"It's chambered in .40 Luger, seeing as the Germans and French are having fun making Frankensteins out of each other's technology," Moses scoffed, something he did often when referring to the Germans. "While your standard .38s are fitted with heated rounds, I'm sure tungsten-tipped bullets will suffice for getting past either flesh or metal."

This seemed perfect for the metal man. I nodded and placed the pistol back on the table. "Will my cash cover it?"

He took the money I had already put down, flipped through it, and set it down. "No, but I'll cover the rest."

"You're not one for letting things slide, Moses."

"You've done me a great service. That fiasco you solved a month ago spooked the Feds and kept them up on their cloud. The less they look down here, the easier it is for me to sell my wares. One less thing I have to worry about. The extra money you've made me will cover your purchase."

"How did you know that was me?"

"Word gets around between the Eye's old compatriots."

That was one good thing that had come out of that last case. "Great. Excellent. It is a gift, so, you got any boxes to wrap it up in?"

"I'm a dealer, Elias, not a Sears. Can't you get this wrapped anywhere else?"

"It's almost Christmas Eve, Moses. Come on."

He sighed and took the gun from me. "Cretin."

═══

It was midnight, the morning of Christmas Eve, only twenty-four hours before society felt obliged to be complacent and kind, but I sure didn't feel any different as I took a cab back to my place. I held the small wrapped box on my lap, the green bow on top bouncing as the cab's wheels smacked against each bump and pothole in the road. Seeing my car parked in once piece in front of my building was comforting; it meant that Allen was safe upstairs. Yuri was just bringing his cart into the lobby, an apartment attendant helping him to push it up the steps through the double doors. They'd finished the job by the time I paid the cabbie and got out.

Yuri looked tired, but happy to see me. He was curling up on a bench in the lobby with some patched-up red cushions, his cart resting nearby.

"Elias, good man, back before tomorrow!" he said with a smile.

"Nah, it's tomorrow, Yuri. I'm right on time."

"Friend of yours came here, went upstairs. Also, other people looking for you, just so you know."

I groaned and thanked him and went to the elevator. Why did everyone know where I lived? Simone, the Rabbit, and who knew who else? Maybe some people knew, but never showed up because of my reputation. Or they were just being courteous. I wished they'd keep it up, because seeing a new person in or around my apartment every night was really starting to piss me off.

Entering my apartment, I noticed how quiet it was, but then again, I hadn't expected Allen to be making a ruckus on its own.

"I'm back. Any luck with Schafer? The museum was a dead end, and Morane is clean, I think."

I found Allen in the living room with several more people. Not the ones I'd expected to see, either.

"Roche. Sit." Eva Greaves, punctual as ever.

I'd had a feeling she'd be back on my tail before long. Judging by its expression, Allen was more surprised than I was. Really, I was more bothered than shocked. I knew the museum had been too easy to slip in and out of. First placing the wrapped package on my kitchen counter, I obeyed Greaves's command and sat down on the couch beside Allen.

Greaves was sitting in my favourite chair beside the TV. Two Upper City spooks nearby kept the room under her thumb.

"Productive night?" she asked.

"Not particularly." I wiped my lip with the handkerchief. It was still bleeding. Maranzano had better not have dislodged a tooth.

"I'd say otherwise. Breaking and entering a city-owned property — not your smartest move. Find what you were looking for?"

"No."

"We did. Plenty of security footage showing you, and you alone, sneaking around that museum. I'm shocked that your bumbling didn't set off the Automatic Security."

I hadn't realized there were Automatic guards.

"Roche?"

"Sorry, lost in thought," I said. "Just trying to think what a state-owned Green-eye could do to me, seeing as they can't roughhouse."

"Did I say the Automatic Security was composed of Green-eyes? We spotted you looking at some peculiar weapons." She snapped her fingers, and one of her

lackeys passed her a folder from a briefcase. "Let's see ...
Mercier's Vierling, same calibre weapon as the bullets
found at the Edison Hotel murder. Coincidence?"

"No, but —"

"I'm not finished. I know about your current employ-
ment. It may scare officers down here, but not us at the
Bureau. We take criminals and terrorists very seriously."

"Terrorists? Are you out of your gourd, lady?"

She pointed at me sharply. "Don't interrupt again.
As I was saying, plausible motive for committing the
murders, ability to procure weapons matching the ammunition found at the scene, record of violent acts in
the Lower City for well over four years, and clear camera
footage depicting you as the sole trespasser at the Met
earlier tonight. The evidence doesn't lie."

"About what?" She stared at me, waiting for me to
figure it out. What she was doing finally clicked in my
head, and I almost laughed out loud. "Are you kidding?
Me, the killer? Did you not see her?"

"Who?"

"The —" I abruptly choked down what I'd almost
said.

Simone had said that she'd done this before. Perhaps
she'd known where the cameras were and taken care to
walk in the blind spots. Maybe she'd let me be captured by
the cameras ... to cover her own trail. Then again, I hadn't
noticed her taking any odd paths through the museum.

"The who, Roche?"

"The ... man I thought I saw in there, stealing some
medieval artifacts to bring up to your house on the
Plate." I grinned, and Allen cowered lower.

"You said 'her.'"

"I'm a bit thick-headed."

"If we're done here, I'm placing you —"

"No." I stopped her, standing up. The agents put their hands at their hips, and I held out my own hand to tell them to relax. "No, I am not the killer. That's stupid. Why would I threaten Tony Shen?"

"To make sure no one but you and your metal friend here investigated that crime scene. I asked Jeffrey about it, and he said there was no formal report about the crime in the Upper East Side. He says the only two people who investigated that scene were you and the machine here. That gives us even more probable cause."

Robins must be covering for Viessman's people and for Sinclair. No doubt they'd copy their boss and be tight-lipped about the whole thing. "From plausible to probable. Ain't that convenient?" I remarked.

"Your newfound fame on the radio will not save you from prison, Roche. I assure you, you cannot run from this one. Killing thugs on a street corner is one thing, but pissing off people from GE is another."

"How many times do I have to tell you, I didn't do it!" I stepped forward, and her goons pointed their pistols at me. "I was at a gala with Allen when the Upper East Side murder occurred." That wasn't quite true, but I needed an alibi. "I was saving some old lady's kid when they shot up the Edison. I'm not the killer!"

"Sure," Greaves said. She motioned for the agents to relax, but one of them took out a pair of cuffs.

Nope, that ain't happening.

"I can prove it," I snapped.

"Oh, you can prove it? You can counter all this incriminating evidence and exonerate yourself, just like that?"

"I'll bring you the real killer." Greaves laughed at me. "I'll bring him, dead or alive, to this apartment, and show you that it wasn't me. You can follow me for the next few days, I don't care, but I am not going to prison because of your inability to think!"

"Why would I allow that, Roche? You've said nothing to convince me of your innocence, why should I believe you?"

Fuck, I had no idea what to give her. But there was no way I was walking out of this apartment without cuffs on my wrists or blood on the walls. I needed to be smart about this. What did she want more than me? Even more than the Vierling Killer?

Now that I thought about it, the only person she'd want more than me ... was me.

"Give me the chance to prove my innocence, and I can find you the man who killed Masters," I finished.

The room went dead silent. Greaves narrowed her eyes. She was interested, and she was angry.

"You'll find me two criminals for the price of one?"

"You want to know who did it, and I think I can find them." *Don't look at Allen, don't crack, you got this.* "I have some leads. You let me prove my innocence, and I'll find you two killers."

I knew Greaves was not a gambling woman, nor was she one to put personal issues before procedure. But she was human, she knew I could go where she couldn't, and she wanted the man who'd killed Masters more than she wanted the Vierling Killer. She was silent for some time, weighing her options.

"And if you can't find someone to take the fall for you?" she finally asked.

"Then take me in. I'll be here in five days either way. You can cuff me and drag me away, seize my assets, I won't care." Time to roll the dice. "Even my car."

That made her raise her eyebrow, intrigued. There was a risk that her lackeys might squeal on her for disobeying protocol and giving a man with my track record the chance to run. But the carrot I was dangling was too good to pass up. I knew it and she knew it. I wasn't a gambler, either, but desperate times …

"Two days," she said. "Midnight, December twenty-sixth."

"Two days? Are you kidding me?"

"I want you here, and the metal man, in two days. I want it to see you get put away for overstepping your bounds. Unless you pull off a miracle, that is."

"Are we done?"

She ordered the agents to pack up and leave. Before she reached the door, she came up within a few inches of me.

"Don't try to run from the city, or hide, or kill me," she said softly. "I will send the entire Plate after you if you do anything stupid. You have forty-eight hours. Make an effort to clean up your name, for once in your life. Oh, and have a merry Christmas."

She left.

The moment the door closed, Allen grabbed its head and began to moan. It didn't speak until we heard Greaves get into the elevator.

"Oh no, this is bad, this is very bad!"

"Relax, I have a plan." I made my way to the kitchen and got to work boiling some water.

"How are you not panicking!" Allen asked, hysterical.

"I've dealt with worse, Al. We can do this. The timeline will just make us try that much harder."

"We are out of leads! With both Vierlings being duds … wait, did yours have only one trigger?"

"Yes."

"Do you think someone could have stolen the Vierling in France, smuggled it here, modified it, and used it to kill some mobsters?"

I put my hands on my hips. "If the France Vierling had been stolen, it would have been front-page news across Europe, and here, too."

"Oh, then we're screwed." It was surprising to hear Allen use that kind of language. "We have no more leads, no more witnesses, no more anything! We are at a loss! And your promise to find Masters's killer … Well, you know what I think about that!" Yeah, I'd had a feeling Allen had figured out who did that. "How do you hope to catch this Vierling Killer person?"

"Easy." I watched the coffee drizzle down into my cup, then grabbed the mug to sip the hot liquid. *Ah, perfect.* "We wait."

"For what?"

"For the killer to strike again."

Allen shot up, almost flipping over my table in the process. "Elias, you're insane! We need to find something, anything, before you get thrown in prison! I don't want you dying behind bars for something you didn't do! And why are you so relaxed?"

I sipped my coffee. Lord, I needed it. I was swapping out my alcoholism for a caffeine addiction. "Two reasons. One, you're freaking out, and having had multiple partners, I know that when one of us freaks out, the other needs to keep their cool. I'm losing my mind right now, but if I panic, it'll make things worse for both of us."

Allen sat down, its eyes still darting around in a panic, but at least it was trying to control itself. It really was worried about me, wasn't it? It hadn't even noticed the present in my hands when I walked in.

"And two, the killer knows the noose is tightening. We just need to find them."

"Okay. Suspects again," Allen said, with forced composure. "Schafer?"

"Dangerous, resourceful, intelligent, good motive … but not stupid enough to do her own dirty work. You said her weapon was a dead end?"

"Never been used," Allen confirmed.

"Cross that one off."

"Simone?"

"Resourceful in a different way, easy access to a weapon — one that wasn't used recently, but still. Personality doesn't fit, though, no evidence that she was attacked, no motive."

"Someone working for the Iron Hands?" Allen asked.

"Perfect motive, discreet, and the Eye has all the money in the world and a few hundred custom weapons at her disposal. But it's too convenient."

"The perpetrator's blood at the last crime scene rules out the Rabbit."

"True," I said. "Plus, most suspicion for Mob activity falls on Maranzano, seeing as the Iron Hands have a complex identity. We're missing something or someone."

"Agreed." Allen nodded.

"And there's that mystery man I've been seeing all too often. Could he be working together with the Rabbit under the Eye?"

"If there is a third crime scene, he may show up again."

"I'll be ready," I said. I finished the coffee and put the cup in the sink next to the other five. *Jesus, I need to clean up my act.* "So either we wait for one of the three to show their hand, or we find a fourth suspect whom we've overlooked."

"Which will require waiting, as well," Allen concluded.

"Stay here, get some rest, and we'll deal with this in the morning." If we survived that long. The Eye had probably bugged this place long ago. She might cut our throats in our sleep for disobeying her once more. I grabbed the present and started to head to my room. Tomorrow would probably be a better day to give it to Allen.

"Are you sure about this, Roche?"

I turned back. Allen was looking at me like I had all the answers. Funny thing was, lately I'd expected it to have them all. I was stuck between three places: the Mob wanting me dead, the Iron Hands wanting me to be someone that I'd never wanted to be, and the FBI wanting me behind bars for a crime I didn't commit and for another they didn't know that I'd done. Normally, I could have dealt with this using my Diamondback, but the last thing Allen needed was to see me come unhinged. It was suffocating, being in this position with my brain turned on. No blood, no screams, no gunpowder — just human stupidity run amok.

"No, Allen, I'm not."

CHAPTER 18

"YOU WON'T GET AWAY WITH THIS. We'll kill you! We'll burn you alive for this!"

"Funny you should mention that."

I lit a match, and he watched it like his life depended on it. It did, which was the funny part.

The smell of kerosene burned my nose, though it was probably worse for him, seeing as his clothes were soaked in it. Idiot should have known what I was going to do when I'd started spraying the stuff around.

The girls had been evacuated from the house, the three men upstairs were dead, and the basement was trashed. Automatic parts were strewn everywhere. For organized criminals, they were very sloppy. All that was left was to put the nail in this coffin.

"You know what will happen," he whispered. "The Eye isn't one to take things lightly."

"I'm aware. But neither am I."

I flicked the match out of my fingers and made my way to the stairs. Out of the corner of my eye, I saw him burst into flames. He kept screaming long after I had locked the front door after me. The building would take some time to burn. By the time anyone got here, the Auto parts would be slag and he would be bones.

It was a dirty job, but someone had to do it. I was just glad that this time, I'd been able to kill two birds with one stone.

CHAPTER 19

ONCE AGAIN, I WAS BACK IN THE PAST, back in the nightmare of that fateful day. This time, the dream started with me approaching the building. Little West 12th and Washington, the place from which the Morello Mob ran nearly everything. Paddy threw me a lever-action from the car, and the rest of the cruisers unloaded, cops approaching the front door. We were doing what the 5th was known for: replacing warrants with bullets.

The two Mob guards at the front of the warehouse were down seconds after we pulled up. Paddy kicked open the door and made the first push inside, bullets flying toward us as the platoon of officers entered after him. I was beside the door, trying to calm myself, knowing what would happen once I went in there.

The last of the officers filed in, and then I entered. I bumped into someone coming out the door and nearly fell on my ass. It wasn't an officer or a Bruno — Simone was standing there in her green dress, blocking my way.

"*You're not as dark and brooding as I thought you were.*"

I pushed her out of the way. Entering the building, I used the shotgun as it was intended, taking out the guards above me on the warehouse catwalks. The main floor was clear, and we ascended to the upper offices.

Simone was at the top of the stairs, the other cops walking through her, but when I tried to get by she was solid as a tree.

"*You're a man of violence, Roche, but you aren't the kind of man to glorify it.*"

"Get out of my fucking head!"

I fired a shell at her, but she vanished like smoke. Nothing in my way now.

I was outside Morello's office. I dropped my lever-action and kicked the door open, pulling out my Diamondback and pointing it at him. I didn't give him the chance to push out his usual spiel and quickly put a bullet in his shoulder. He slumped down behind the desk. I walked around it, looking for him, but bumped into Simone again.

"*You kill because you have to, right?*"

"Shut up!"

I looked down at Morello, but someone pushed me away. When I looked back up, it wasn't Simone standing there anymore.

It was me.

It was strange, looking at myself. Surreal. He — I — spoke again.

"*You only kill the way you do because you have to, right?*"

I pulled back the hammer and pointed the Diamondback at Morello, still looking at myself. Any moment now the dead Mob boss would morph into Allen or James or Sinclair or someone else beyond the barrel. I couldn't care less anymore.

"You don't understand," I said to myself.

"*If I don't understand, who will?*"

He was right. I was right. It seemed everyone besides me, even my own head, was right.

"*Do you really think keeping her in power saves lives? Or is that just what you tell yourself?*"

"*You think every problem can be beaten to death and buried.*"

"*At least James isn't around to see this.*"

I put the barrel to my own head. Let's see what happened this time.

"*You can't change what happened. One day you need to own up to it.*"

"Fuck off, me."

━━━━━

The gunshot sounded very similar to Allen's voice, and my eyes snapped open, brought back to the waking world unexpectedly. Allen was standing over me in an uncomfortably close proximity.

"Yes?" I croaked.

"I would say that I have good news, but it would be in poor taste."

I shoved myself upright. I was wearing nothing but my drawers and an undershirt, nothing close to the picture of the perfect male body.

"Another one?" I asked.

"Let's hope the third time is the charm."

I looked at my clock. Ten in the morning, Christmas Eve. Well, I'd woken up, but I was still stuck in this mess. Time to get myself and Allen out of it.

"Then get out of my room and let me change."

"Of course."

———

It wasn't pretty. A cozy two-floor building in Hell's Kitchen had been reduced to little more than ashes. The fire engine was staffed by a handful of men and women in purely supervisory roles; lightly dressed Blue-eyes wielded the firehoses and axes. The machines scoured the area, making sure embers didn't surge into flames once again. Outside the perimeter of firefighters were patrol cars and cops comforting hysterical women and bruised men who said they'd been forced out of the building by a gunman in black.

I had expected him to strike again soon, but not this quickly.

This was the 7th's territory, which meant the crazy Russian Viessman was on scene, keeping an eye on everything and everyone. His long silver hair was easy to spot against the backdrop of black concrete. Bastard had been on scene for all three of the crimes. I might have suspected him if I hadn't known him. And if I'd even suggested it, I wouldn't have left here alive.

Allen and I made our way over to him. "What's the situation, Yev?"

The commissioner kept silent, while the dark-skinned officer beside him responded. "Reports of a fire were called in around eight this morning. The fire department came by to get it under control and called us two hours later after checking out the immediate rubble. There is evidence to suggest this was an underground brothel, given the beds, unburnt ledgers, and the presence of, well, women and paying customers, who have already given statements."

"Who does it belong to?" I asked.

"Maranzano, no doubt. No other Mob deals in sex and drugs like they do. But we did find something else in the basement, if you'd care to follow me."

We did as he said, Viessman leading us into the wreckage of the fire. The floorboards were melted, and the smell was assaulting to the senses. I had to breathe through Simone's handkerchief to keep myself from passing out. Allen didn't take too kindly to the scent, either.

The basement door had burned away, leaving nothing but the hinges on the frame to indicate a separation between it and the main landing. The blackened concrete stairs were covered in hoses and tarps, and several Blue-eyes were still down here, making sure to blast any embers with water. Besides the molten wood and plastic, a slag of metal coated the floor. Some discernable shapes popped out from the sea of black and silver. Before us, in the centre of the room, was a pile of bones and half-melted flesh.

I gagged. "Who the hell is this?"

"We believe it is Joey Rossi, one of Maranzano's business partners in West Manhattan." Viessman's officer continued, "This place was not only part of a sex trafficking ring, but also the base of a smuggling operation onto the mainland. Most of the men here were paying customers, and they were beaten for their tardiness in leaving the building. Three men who worked under Rossi were shot, bringing the total body count to four. The bullets used were —"

"Were they 8x50 Lebel?" Allen interrupted.

"Yes." The officer looked surprised, and Viessman grumbled to himself. "How did you know?"

My turn to speak. "This is our man. The one at the Edison and in the Upper East Side. No doubt you heard about Shen, Yev?" The commissioner grunted in affirmation. "This was the Vierling Killer."

"Vierling?" the officer asked, but we ignored him.

"The problem now is that this building is little more than a fireplace. No evidence will have survived that fire. Even if he did get sloppy, he's covered his tracks."

"But the way they set the fire could tell as much as what the fire burned," Allen said.

"So, he used kerosene, pretty easy to get, probably stockpiled here since this was an Automatic smuggling safe house. It doesn't take a genius to light fires, but it did take someone with considerable speed and strength to get through all those men and kill the guards. What did the men who were beaten say?"

The officer pulled out a notepad. "Um … someone in dark, baggy clothes, who moved quick, hit hard, even without a gun in his hands. One said he saw the assailant take on three guys at the same time, kicked the shit out of all of them."

"Military training, just like you said, Al," I commented. "Even if one of those two Vierling rifles was used, neither Simone nor Schafer has that sort of experience to fight hand-to-hand."

Viessman grumbled, "*Nyet.*"

His officer spoke. "The precincts are working together to get to the bottom of this. Apparently, Elise Schafer has a record of being trained by military personnel, though for what purpose, we're not sure."

"And Simone Morane?" I asked, snapping Allen to attention.

"Her father is a general. If he'd wanted those records gone, he could have ordered it with the snap of his fingers," the officer said. "We did some digging on everyone, including you."

"And am I innocent?" I asked.

"Meh," Viessman said.

"But these are all hunches," I grumbled, rubbing the back of my neck. My teeth still hurt from yesterday. "I was really hoping for some actual evidence, but … Shit, we're back to where we were." I pulled out a dart and lit it. The machines in the basement with us gave me the stink-eye, but I ignored them. Wasn't like they could do anything. "I don't got much choice now. I'm going to go see her."

"I don't think that's the wisest move, Elias," Allen began. Viessman and his officer gave us space. "Like you said, she doesn't want you to investigate this further. If she is as dangerous as you say, I can only imagine the consequences she might inflict."

"You see any other way, Allen? All we have to go off are cartridges and the killer's ability to fight. We have nothing else." I took another drag, calming down. "Hold down the fort, try to find something, anything, and I'll narrow down our search. Can you do that for me?"

"Elias, I think —"

"Can you?"

"I can," it said, straightening up. "Just don't get killed."

I nodded, and we stood there for a moment. For once, I felt we had a mutual understanding, a connection that made us empathize with one another. Allen was seeing the things I had to do to keep it and myself safe, and I was seeing that it was doing its damnedest to help me in the right way. We were each going to go off to do what we were supposed to do, what we were good at, though neither of us wanted to do it. Not with so much on the line.

"Nothing in this city can kill me, Al." I smiled. "I proved that years ago."

Allen turned to begin searching the basement for evidence. "I hope so."

═══════

Emerging from the basement into the smoky air outside, I remembered to do what I'd said I would earlier and look over the crowd to see if that same guy I'd noticed previously was here. There were twenty or so people around, most of them firefighters, and three or four officers from the 7th skulking about. Everything looked well and fine, and a quick search of the cruisers yielded nothing substantial or implicating. As well, the firefighters were all unfamiliar, many perturbed when I asked to see their faces more than once.

I was beginning to lose hope when I spotted the man in question near the mouth of an alley beside the burned building. I called out to him, attracting attention, but he disappeared down the alley. I ran after him, my Diamondback instinctively drawn.

The alley went straight for about fifty feet before splitting off into a T-junction. The disappearing figure turned left, and I sprinted to catch up. That part of the alleyway terminated in a line of trash bins and a chain-link fence. The man was standing there, his back to me. I took that as a signal to cautiously approach, my Diamondback levelled and my free hand reaching to grab his shoulder and turn him around.

I froze. I hadn't recognized his face from a distance, but now, standing inches away from me, his identity was very clear. One Mr. Edgar Masters, former Black Hat, the FBI agent I'd "apprehended" on my previous case with Allen, and current corpse. I was sure I'd done enough damage to kill him. I pulled back and pushed my weapon into his sternum.

"Surprised?" he asked with condescension.

"You're dead."

"Correct."

"So, what, am I supposed to believe *you've* been killing people?" I chuckled, and so did he.

"In a manner of speaking, yes. Not directly, and not alone. Is your head breaking yet?"

I pulled back the hammer on my revolver. "Not just yet."

"Soon enough it will, though. After all, you climbed out of the cave, now you have to tell everyone else they're watching candlelight."

"Shut up."

"Now you have to tell them that their reality is nothing but walking shadows. But they will grasp that and keep themselves bound to ignorance. And even you, a free man, are still bound to some sort of ignorance to dull the pain of the truth. Your idea of justice — that's your personal painkiller, right? The same thing you clung to the last time we spoke."

"I said shut up!"

"You're chasing ghosts again, Roche. Be careful that you don't become one," Masters said.

"Detective?"

Viessman's translator came up behind me, looking concerned. He must have followed me when I ran to the alley.

"Yeah?"

"Are you okay?"

"I'm fine."

"Who were you talking to?"

I turned to see that the apparition was gone, and I was pressing my revolver against the chain-link fence. I slid the weapon back into my holster and disengaged the hammer.

"Myself."

CHAPTER 20

ONLY MEN WITH DEATH SENTENCES came looking for her here.

I walked up to the centre of Bow Bridge, looking over the side to see the Plate reflecting off the water. The bridge's colour scheme matched the dead trees and snow-covered grass, making it seem like part of the earth itself. As I'd expected, Central Park was empty; no one was a fan of this place, and Bow Bridge was as far north as anyone would come in the park. I looked south and west. The wind was fleeting, the silence of the world comforting.

Then the wind died down, and the world grew too quiet. Dead. She was here.

I didn't move. If I turned around or left my spot on the bridge, I was dead. Some people learned that the hard way. On clear days, you could see some of her previous employees at the bottom of the lake.

"Hello, darling," I said.

"Elias," she responded. "I heard through the grapevine that you wanted to speak to me."

"That's right. I know you wanted me to stop investigating this assassin or whatever he is, but that ain't in my nature. If you wanted a lackey to nod and obey every word you said, you wouldn't have hired me. So I need to know, did you hire him? Who's causing all this shit? Or is it the Rabbit? I can't believe it just came out of retirement for no reason, especially not during a spate of killings like this. You know I don't like being out of the loop. I need to cross you off my list."

She sighed. Without seeing her body language, I wasn't sure how she felt.

"I need you to find the Vierling Killer."

How did she know we'd been calling him the Vierling Killer? "You threatened my life for investigating, and now all of a sudden you want me on this? Is this some sort of joke?"

"The killer did help us substantially in dealing with the Maranzano Mob. But their use has come to an end since this job in Hell's Kitchen. We need them dead."

"Now you have a sense of fair play? What does some whorehouse of Maranzano's mean to you? Why not let him clean up your shit while you sit back and reap the rewards?"

"That whorehouse wasn't Maranzano's, it was ours."

I almost spun around. "What?"

"Rossi was on our payroll. You think all of Maranzano's boys work for him? Rossi sold us his soul over a year ago, and we'd been using his place as a springboard to sell to the mainland. That storehouse in the basement was full of *our* parts, some of them high-end. The moment the killer torched the place, they didn't just ruin the sex trade there, they ruined one of our best underground shipping hubs. And now Maranzano knows that it was mine, because he never would have dared put a smuggling safe house in Hell's. He's an old-school naval shipment kind of mobster." I heard the spark of her lighter as she lit a cigar and puffed on it a few times before speaking again. The ashes fell into the water and drifted south to my side of the bridge.

"And when were you planning on telling me any of this?"

"You don't need to know the intricacies of the Iron Hands' operations."

"Bullshit! I am *the* Iron Hand! I'm your goddamn mascot! What if I had gone in there on a hunch and shot up the place? What if it had been me who put Rossi's head on a pike? Letting me in on more of these secrets might prevent stuff like this from happening!"

"It's a need-to-know basis." I heard her exhale slowly and tap the cigar against the concrete railing.

"If you want me working for you, *I* need to know!" I yelled, facing the water below. "What if this wasn't intentional? What if he hit your place by accident?"

"There are no accidents in this world. If they kill my people, they get put in the ground."

"Why not recruit him like you did me? You could use him to your advantage, turn him from some random guerilla into something more dangerous than me."

"Elias, look at me."

Was this a trick? I froze, not willing to turn, not wanting to make any hasty decisions.

"Now," she said.

"I don't want to get shot."

"You won't."

I turned to look at her. She leaned against the railing, cigar in her fingers, a black veil over her face. Even in the sunlight, the fabric was completely opaque. I still had no idea what she looked like.

Come on, Allen taught you enough, look for height, foot size, weight, build. She was tallish. Shorter than me, about five-eleven, tall for a woman. Foot size: no clue. She was thin, but not gaunt. Her slacks were tight, but her jacket was baggy. I estimated a hundred and twenty pounds, if that.

Goddamn, I'm not good at this.

"This situation is going to cause a war if we can't play this off," she said. "This Vierling Killer has done enough damage. I want them dead. I need my merciless, relentless, unquestioning Iron Hand once more. There will be no redemption, no more hiring packages — just you and the Rabbit."

I pulled out my own lighter, twiddling it with my thumbs, flicking the flame on and off, resisting the urge to smoke.

"Something the matter?" she asked.

"I'm tired."

"Of what?"

"This. All of this. I'm tired of this city-wide tension, these lies I'm not in the loop about, the Rabbit and everyone else in the city either running scared from me or putting a gun in my face. I gave you this city on a silver platter. Now there's nothing left to hunt in it but ghosts and thunder."

"If you came here for another reason, spill it."

"I came here for the investigation, but this doubt has been nagging at me for some time. I want out."

She didn't laugh, didn't sigh, just stood there. "Elias ..."

"I know you need me or want me or whatever the hell I am to you, but things are different now."

"They're always different, always changing. Loyalties shift, money changes hands, people die, others are recruited. This game changes all the time, and only now do you have gripes with it? You can't keep doing this. This conversation is almost a monthly routine."

"I'm serious."

"No, you're not. I've let you go multiple times, and every time, within the week, you come running back. You left the first time because you were tired of the senseless killing, but came right back when you ran out of money. In '32 you wanted to be a 'real' cop, yet after three days of trying to be one, you came back when you remembered that the law and justice are two very different things. This cycle repeats itself over and over. For a man with such impulses, you've had a severe lack of conviction for ... what, two or more years now?"

Did I ask that often? I couldn't even remember all those times. *What is wrong with me?*

"Things are different," I stated.

"As you've said. Because of Allen?"

"I just don't want it to get hurt. Or Robins, or Sinclair. The Masters case opened my eyes to a lot that

I've been missing. I've found it very, very hard to work for you these past few weeks. I mean, come on, I took a barbed knuckle in the side for you."

She leaned back and groaned. "You wouldn't have, if you hadn't been so sloppy."

"You sound like Nightingale." I lit a dart. I was craving the embrace of tobacco too much. "If I was really your Iron Hand, I wouldn't have asked to leave so many times. You know it, I know it, and I'm tired of pretending that I'm still the man I used to be."

"Then stop pretending. I tried reminding you."

"By making me use the goddamn hammer again?" I threw the cigarette over the side of the bridge. No need for tobacco when adrenalin would do the job. "I gave that to you so you could bury it, throw it over the side of the Plate, anything! I don't need a reminder of what I used to be, what I used to do! I'm not like that anymore, and your trying to coerce me into it won't do either of us any favours."

"You *do* need to remember who you used to be!" She was agitated and stepping toward me. Not too many people could make me flinch, but she was one of them.

"I was a goddamn monster."

"You were and still are the biggest asset both I *and* the police have ever had." She moved closer still, her voice no longer telling me facts, but spitting them at me instead. "I made you what you are today, Elias, do not forget that! Are you so ungrateful that you'd throw away everything I've done to transform a worthless ex-cop into a verified force of nature? You were once the most dangerous thing on two legs, more powerful than any agent on the Plate. Now you're a washed-up has-been who's going to give himself up to the FBI. What is wrong with you?"

There's gotta be a bug in my apartment. "I'm nothing like I used to be."

"Evidently so." She threw the cigar into the water. Her tone wasn't so much angry now as disappointed. "I didn't kill Hartley or McIntyre or whoever else the Vierling Killer has put in the dirt. You want out? Fine, but you'll be back by New Year's. Whether you're some radio star or vigilante or nameless cop or whatever else you want to be, just know what kind of threat this killer is to the stability and delicate balance you have set for this city. I want them found, and I want them dead. And if you want out, this is your last assignment. I can't force a horse to drink from the stream, but I can tire it out so that it begs for water. Are we clear?"

"Absolutely," I responded.

"I don't know what Masters said that changed you so much, but I suggest you try to figure things out, then come back to us." Her voice was soft. She wasn't demanding anymore, but showing me a sliver of sympathy. It was weird. "If it *was* about Masters. If it's about Allen, that's another story."

"It ain't Allen. The robot is just a vehicle for my doubts, not the source."

"We need you. The city needs you. Robins, Shen, all those cops, all those people ... The Iron Hands might be a cartel, but we want stability as much as the police do. But if you cut those ties, we'll be back to where we were in the Morello and Luciano days. I want you to take some time off and really think about where you fit into all this."

"All right." I turned around to look at the water and bit down on another dart. "But I don't want a target on my head the moment I leave the big house."

"Trust me, you won't be going there."

A few moments later, the wind blew once more, carrying voices in the distance; I glanced toward their source. When I turned back to the Eye, there was nothing there but her shoeprints in the snow. She hadn't said goodbye. I looked around for a moment, then kneeled beside the prints and made some rudimentary measurements.

"Hm ... big feet for a human," I said to myself.

I stood and pulled my lighter out once more, and the engraved eye stared back at me as I lit my dart. I shoved the device back into my pocket.

＝＝＝

"Nothing?"

"Nothing," Allen said glumly, reclining in the passenger seat of the Talbot. "Like you said, everything incriminating burned up in the fire. How about your investigation?"

"The Eye didn't order the hit," I said, concentrating on the road. "Funny thing, though: those Automatic parts were hers. Maranzano's man was working for her, and she smuggled her parts out of his safe house."

"What do you think will happen?"

I sighed. "The Five Families started skirmishes over less. Sal is one of those old bastards, so he's the same way. A war in the Lower City is the last thing we need. She wants me to take the helm in preventing it."

"And will you?"

I turned onto 6th Avenue, slamming on the horn as some jackass cut in front of me. "No." Allen looked at me, stunned. "I think I'm retiring from this business. From working for her, I mean."

"Is that wise?"

"I guess we'll see. The only reason I kept working for her was to keep the people I care about safe. She thinks I'll be back ... I don't know. I guess we'll see."

Allen turned away from me, looking out the window. I had a feeling it was smiling. Maybe it did have a positive influence on me.

We drove into the executive parking lot of GE. Allen had already talked to Schafer and examined her Vierling, but I wanted to take a turn putting the squeeze on to get something, anything, useful out of her. Maybe we'd missed something. Maybe another round of questions would crack this nut. The security guards outside immediately recognized my vehicle and urged me to leave. Allen talked them down — or, at least, distracted them while I made my way across the snow-covered lawn, through the workers' entrance, and into the main foyer. The floor was clean, but I swore I could still see a few stains from my bloody nose the last time I'd been here, about a month ago. I swaggered up to the receptionist, who was on the phone.

"One second, I need to —" She looked up, and her face went blank. "Oh no, not you again."

"Relax. Elise Schafer is expecting me."

"She had better be." The woman picked up a phone and dialed. "Miss Schafer, a certain gentleman is here to see you … Understood." She dropped the phone. "She told me to ask you not to cause a ruckus, or I'll have them drag you out of here."

I turned to where she was gesturing and saw two new security guards, one with his hand on his baton, the other talking into his wireless radio.

"Great."

＝＝＝＝＝

Schafer was more jaded than usual, wearing a casual business suit, gloves, and an expression of irritation. She didn't seem in the mood to shake my hand. Allen was still outside, either arguing with security or driving around, biding its time.

"Roche," Schafer said, her voice a monotone.

"Schafer." I smirked. She didn't. "I have a sensitive question to ask you. I'd prefer it if we could step somewhere private to keep things from getting out of hand."

"Out of hand?" She looked enraged by this. "Do not try to manhandle me, Roche. You're not going to pull a fast one by dragging me to some dark corner and making threats about my life and reputation. I've done this little song and dance before."

"Not with me, you haven't."

"You've got a lot of nerve. Let me remind you that you're on General Electrics property, and extraterritoriality is in effect. I could have those men there toss you in a cell and throw away the key, and no one would be able to get to you."

She was starting to piss me off. Every Upper City asshole was the same. "Whatever."

"No, not whatever! You think because you're the star of some radio show that you can call the shots? You're nothing, Roche, nothing! I doubt those stories about you are even real. If you have a question, ask it right here, or it isn't worth asking."

Goddamn it. Always an uphill battle with these people. "Are you aware of a crime that occurred in the Upper East Side?"

"Some rowdy Mafia bastards shooting up other Mafia bastards?" she retorted irritably.

"Do you know where that happened?"

"In the Lower City. Does it matter?" She groaned. "Why are you wasting my time with such trivial questions?"

Time to bite the bullet. "I'm trying to find the Vierling Killer."

"Who?"

"The asshole who shot up the Edison Hotel, among other things. You have the gun and the motive, but not much else, it seems."

I'd never thought I'd see the day that Schafer laughed, but she did, and she continued for some time. It was an amused laugh, like she was watching a comedic play. "You're serious? You're accusing me of murder?"

"I'm not accusing, I'm asking if you did it."

"No, no, I didn't. Even if I had, I'd have said no. Who would ask such a stupid question of someone like me?

You need a hard lesson in how the Upper City works, making accusations like that."

"I think you need a hard lesson on who's who down here in the Lower City. Agent Masters didn't do his research, and he ain't around anymore."

The laughing stopped. "Excuse me?"

I moved closer to her — not quickly, and not too close, but enough to get a response. She stood her ground, unflinching, though she did take on a more aggressive stance. It wasn't the stance a soldier or cop would take; her footing was off. No, she didn't have combat training. I guessed she'd enrolled in the military for the stress and confrontation training. In any case, I wasn't willing to get thrown into a cell for testing her further.

"You see those two guards over there?" I began. "They —"

"What, are you going to shoot up this place and make a ruckus just so we'll think you're a big deal? You're a child, Roche, a child with a toy gun you think gets you anything you want. Am I correct in that analysis?"

I didn't respond. I wasn't really sure how I could.

"Now if you'll excuse me," she continued, "I need to get back to some real business, not just put on a song and dance for you. We've unfortunately made some poor investments, and we need to plug the hole in our profits before our situation becomes as dire as yours."

She began walking back to the elevators.

"I know someone else who made some poor investments recently," I called after her. "She's not too happy about things, either." Schafer stopped. Whether or not she was in cahoots with the Iron Hands, she could see that I knew more than I appeared to. "It seems I was correct: you aren't the killer. Even so, you're in a much worse situation than if you were."

"What are you implying?"

"I might be implying two things." I looked her over. "You seem keen on keeping your arm hidden. Is there a reason for that?"

She almost snarled. "Are you about done, Roche? Or do I need to have security beat some respect into you?"

Her facade was cracking. Not much, but enough for us to see eye to eye. I couldn't tell if she was scared or angry or surprised. Either she was working for the same woman I did, or the two of them were closer than they appeared. Something to worry about later.

"Thank you for your time, Miss Schafer."

She wasn't a coward, I knew that much. That would make my life difficult if I ever needed to come back here. Well, more difficult than it already was.

Outside, Allen was still chatting with security. Spotting me, it got inside the vehicle. The guards called to the building as we backed away in the car, but it wasn't like they could do much off of GE property.

"She ain't the killer," I told Allen.

"How do you know?"

"Something tells me she and I have similar allies, although that doesn't mean we're friends. She's clean, unfortunately."

"Who's left?"

"We should try talking to Simone again."

"What about the man you kept seeing?"

"He's …" I paused. "A non-issue."

"There's something I forgot to tell you," Allen said. "When I was at the library, a man made contact with me. He was desperate to meet with you. I think he left you a phone message a while back. I don't know what it's in regards to, and honestly it's possible that he's mentally unstable. But as we have little else to go on right now …"

"Let's not take any chances," I said. "There's too much shit happening now to pick and choose which leads to follow. Find his address, and let's get this done. After that, we'll figure something out."

CHAPTER 21

WE FOUND OURSELVES at the home of one Reginald Edwin Curio, famed novelist and pain in my ass. On checking my phone recorder, I discovered that he had been leaving messages asking to meet for weeks now. Allen said the guy was off his rocker, but harmless. *Let's see just how harmless he is.*

The light coming from under the door meant he was home. He had a nice little house, one of the few shanty bungalows left within city limits, sitting on the corner of Grand Avenue and Allen Street. I'd pointed out the street name to Allen, who'd responded with a smirk. It was developing a funny bone. I liked that.

The neighbourhood was quiet this time of day, with most people either at work or shopping for the holidays. The bulbs were still on above us, but they'd be switched off in the next hour or so.

"Roche, I feel this is unnecessary." Allen was standing awkwardly in a breaching position to the left of the door. I stood on the right, next to the hinges.

"You want to get to the bottom of this, don't you?" It didn't answer. I put fresh rounds into my Diamondback one at a time. "Besides, this bastard could be trying to lure me into a trap, testing to see if I'm that naive. I don't even know who works for the Eye these days. Now, kick the door."

"Roche ..."

Allen was looking over my shoulder. An all too familiar woman in a white fur coat was walking toward the house. Simone. We both froze, though for different reasons. Allen was staring like a boy at the playground. Simone looked at us and glanced at Curio's door, half frowning.

"I really hope I don't find a body in there." She was only half joking.

"We haven't even kicked the door down. Even if we had, he'd be fine. How the hell do you know this nutjob?" I asked.

"He's an external editor for WAR Radio, and he's very good at his job. You should see some of the transcripts he puts out. Pulitzer-worthy."

"We did want to talk to you, too, actually," I said.

"Coincidence, it seems, smiles upon us both." Simone grinned. "I'm having a little Christmas get-together later tonight, and I wanted to invite you two. Curio will be there, as well as my father and some friends from the station. No GE paper-pushers, I swear."

I looked at Allen, who was practically chomping at the bit. What the hell, I was in a good mood today. "Sure."

"Oh wow, I was expecting to have to do some verbal gymnastics to convince you. Fantastic. Eleven tonight. You know where I live, fifth floor. I should go in and invite Curio."

On cue, the front door opened. All the conversation outside must have attracted the man's attention. He was shocked to see the three of us standing mere inches away. He looked relieved when he saw Simone, and when he recognized me, he lit up like a Christmas tree.

"Ah, Elias Roche! The N—"

"Don't say it, or you get a bullet in the head," I warned.

"The famous Elias Roche, yes, no other names," he stammered, extending a hand to me. I noticed a pack of cigarettes in his breast pocket and reached out to grab one, ignoring the hand. "I've been trying to contact you," he continued. "I spoke to your partner a few nights ago. I didn't think you'd get back to me so promptly."

I chuckled. "Well, necessity led us here. Or, rather, suspicion." Curio nodded, pretending to understand. "I suppose I'll see you tonight," I said to him. "We can talk then."

He was confused and, seeing that I was about to leave, opened his mouth to say something, but Simone breezed into the house, pulling him along with her.

"Don't be late," she said, flashing me and Allen a final smile.

"Never am."

I returned to the Talbot with Allen.

I ran the engine for a few minutes to get heat flowing into the cab. Allen kept tapping its fingers on its knees, jittery with excitement. What was going on with the damn machine? A month ago it had been all hard codes and regulations; now it was bouncing off the walls like a child. I reminded myself that it was new to this whole world, all these experiences.

"What time is it, Al?" I asked.

"It is … six at night."

"I say we grab some chow and head back to my place."

"Do you 'know a guy' who can sort us out for food?"

"No." I paused. "Okay, yeah, I do."

I smiled, almost laughing to myself. Son of a bitch was getting quick, I had to admit.

———

Back at my apartment, it was already dark enough to need the lights on. Eva Greaves's boot prints were still on my carpet, making my lip curl in annoyance. I ignored them for the moment, heading to my room to grab the wrapped package from my bedside table. I returned and handed it to Allen.

"Where did that come from?" it asked, perplexed.

"You'd be surprised what you miss when you're panicking. I brought it in while you were being interrogated by Greaves. You didn't even see it this morning." I went to throw my coat on the rack. "Open it up."

"But it's Christmas Eve. I'm not too familiar with these rituals, but don't people usually open presents on Christmas Day?"

"I'm Italian, I grew up opening presents on Christmas Eve. After all, baby Jesus was born at night, yeah?"

"I didn't know that, either," it said, almost guiltily. "I can't accept this, Elias. I don't deserve a present. Besides, what on earth would you get me? I can't be an easy person to buy for."

"I know. I thought of something useful. Open the goddamn thing, come on!" I grinned.

Having the possibility of being thrown in prison for life looming over my head was making me appreciative of moments like this.

Allen ripped the paper off to get to the box within. He placed it on the counter and lifted off the top. The Hi-Power pistol I had gotten from Moses sat on a small cushion, along with a few magazines of .40 Luger. Allen lifted it out, careful to investigate it without gripping it too tight.

"It's new. A prototype, apparently. Fresh from the presses. It's smaller than Robins's 1911 and has tungsten-tipped rounds for dealing with Automatics or armour. I just thought, you know, if you're going to be a real cop, you need a piece, and I'd rather you had something more your style. If you need more ammo, I can call some favours in, and —"

The air was squeezed out of me, leaving me unable to speak. Allen had wrapped its arms around me, giving me an uncomfortable yet heartwarming hug. I looked around to make sure no one could see us — I was in my apartment, who could see us? — and patted it on the back. It backed up after a few seconds, a smile plastered across its robotic face, and looked at the weapon again.

"This is the first gift I've ever gotten. Elias, I appreciate this. How can I ever repay you?"

"It's a present, Allen, you don't repay gifts. And I know you didn't get me anything. Just get me back next year, deal?"

"Yes," Allen said, retrieving Robins's 1911 and placing it in my hand before refitting the Browning into the holster and taking up the spare magazines. I'd have to return Robins's gun in the next few days. He wasn't a fan of lending things out; I was surprised Allen had had his pistol for this long.

"Elias, why did you opt to question Curio and Miss Morane at the party, instead of earlier today?"

I was caught off guard by the question. "I have another two days of freedom before I'm going to be dragged away to the slammer. I think we can take some time for the little things. Speaking of which, I won't have much time to read and relax while I'm breaking rocks with a pickaxe in prison. Mind if I go do that?"

Allen nodded. "By all means. I'll hold down the fort, as it were."

"Good man. Keep an ear out for Maranzano's boys, will you? Last thing we need is a surprise."

"Of course, Elias."

Now it was time for a nice hot shower and some time alone. I needed to catch up on the few years of rest I might be about to lose.

CHAPTER 22

WHILE ROCHE WAS TAKING A much-needed rest, Allen was at a loss for how to pass the time before the party. He tried reading, but his mind was pulled away from the pages and into itself, engrossed in his infatuation. It was an agonizing new sensation, consuming almost to the point of madness. He felt a tinge of irritation that no one at Camp Theta had warned him that emotions such as this would appear — a severe oversight for everyone involved.

He sat on Roche's couch and eventually gravitated toward the radio. If he had time, he might as well listen to the radio program that Roche had inspired. It was just after seven at night, prime broadcasting hour, when people were just getting back from their day jobs and sitting down to eat or relax.

He waited for the tubes to heat up, then spun the dial to tune in. The front plate of the radio jiggled a bit as he turned the dial. Strange, given Roche rarely used the radio, if at all. He stopped the dial at 980 AM, and crackling voices filled the room. The first voice was a young female playing a character who was much older than she sounded.

"What makes you so sure, sir? I can't fathom what has become of my husband. Please, find him — or the body, if you must."

"I won't find a body, ma'am." The voice of the Nightcaller was deep and gravelly, much more dramatic than Roche's own voice. There was the sound of a lighter clicking and sparking. *"You have no idea who your husband really is."*

"What are you talking about? My husband is an angel. He works at a soup kitchen, feeds the hungry, visits the orphanage, takes care of me as well as he can!"

"He isn't all rose petals and sunshine, darling. Your husband is one of the biggest, baddest fellows on these mean streets. He's merciless, kidnapping people from the street and doing God knows what with them. We call him Mr. Snatch, and I know where he is."

"Oh, please, Mr. Nightcaller, you must save him! Even from himself!"

Allen rolled his eyes, on the verge of laughter. This was entertainment? Roche would have an aneurism hearing this.

"There isn't any saving him from himself, ma'am. I'm here to dispense justice, not save a marriage." The click of a hammer, the holstering of a gun, and footsteps on a creaking floor. *"I'll be back in a half hour. You can do me a favour while I'm gone."*

"Yes, anything!"

"Find yourself a new place to live. I'm sure your husband's life insurance will cover the rent." A door slammed, footsteps went down a set of stairs, a car door opened and closed. *"She's up in arms in there, had no idea her husband was Mr. Snatch. We don't need to do anything else here. You sure you know where to find this guy, Karl?"*

"Indubitably, Mr. Nightcaller."

"I don't sound like that," Allen said to himself, almost writhing in embarrassment at the exaggerated flanging of the voice.

"Good, drive us there. I got a present for our perp," the fake Roche continued.

"And what might that gift be, sir?"

A gun was pulled and a hammer cocked. *"A .38 to the head. Hit it!"*

Tires screeched, and soft jazz music started, followed by an announcer's voice.

"The Nightcaller Tales *will return after a word from our sponsors."*

Allen turned the radio off, sitting in stunned silence for a moment. And then, laughter.

For the first time ever, uproarious laughter overtook him. He doubled over on the couch. It was so cheesy, so bad, so far from the truth that it was almost a caricature of what he and Roche did every night. His laughter was loud enough to rouse Roche out of his room with an expression halfway between concern and curiosity.

"Allen … you good?" he asked.

"Oh, oh, Elias! I'm a chauffeur!" Allen kept cackling. "And you, you're a cheesy soap actor!"

"Read something funny in the paper?"

He sat up, putting his head in his hands, trying to catch his breath. "Elias, that show — never listen to it — you'd break the radio."

"Oh, Christ." Roche cringed but cracked a smile, too. "It took my fame to get you to laugh and enjoy yourself. Damn, this is the best surprise I've had in a while."

"Agreed." Allen gave his partner a thumbs-up. "I'm fine. I might listen to some more. I wonder who else is in the show."

"Knowing Robins, he'd want to butt in there." Roche turned. "I'm heading out to grab some toiletries. Need anything?"

"I'm fine."

Roche walked out, locking the door. Brimming with curiosity, Allen turned the radio back on. The bulbs heated up faster than last time and the sound came crackling through once more.

"*This is the place,*" Roche's gruff voice actor said. "*This is going to be an uphill battle, just like the War. I'm counting on you to have my back if anything goes tits-up. Understood?*"

"*Affirmative, sir!*" the robotic voice responded monotonously. "*I will apprehend any suspects who attempt to flee the premises.*"

"*Keep them alive for me, but remember: we aren't bringing them to the station.*"

Footsteps, the scrape of metal against concrete. A sudden onslaught of faint static, then a moment of silence. Allen peered at the radio, wondering if it was busted, but at first glance it appeared to be running fine.

Footsteps again, these ones clearer than before, now growing louder and louder. Allen was at the edge of his seat. Soft breathing, the flick of a lighter and the searing of a cigarette tip.

"*Who are you?*" This sounded like a different voice actor than before. Allen looked at the radio, confused.

"*I'm not Mr. Snatch, I can tell you that.*" A female voice, not the same one as before. "*But there's someone there I need to speak to.*"

"*The Blue-eye outside?*"

"*That isn't a Blue-eye, and he isn't outside.*"

The lock on the apartment door clicked, and the door swung open. Light shone in from the hallway. Allen's proverbial skin crawled.

"*Come out, Allen. We need to talk.*"

The radio signal went dead, static predominating once again. Allen grabbed the gun at his side, pulling the slide to load a round and gripping it in both hands. The safety was off, and his finger was inside the trigger guard.

He stacked up against the open door, peering through to the hallway but seeing only a long row of doors on either side, with dim lights every few feet. Through the windows at each end of the hall, he could see a showering of snow coating the building and the streets below. To the left of Roche's door there were two more apartments. On the other side there were well over a dozen before the elevator, then more after it.

Allen stepped out, closing the door behind him, his gun drawn and pointed ahead. He crept along the hall, his footsteps almost silent, his ears tuning to pick up anything out of the ordinary. The elevators were quiet, and there was no noise from any of the other apartments. The floor didn't even creak as he stepped.

Above him, the lights oscillated on and off, browning out for a few moments at a time. With the sun gone and the snow falling, they were the only source of light; without them, it would have been pitch-black. The lamps at the far end of the hall went out, followed by the one directly above Roche's door. Allen pushed farther into the hall to keep up with the failing lights, not wanting to be caught in the dark. Before long, he stood under the last flickering lamp. His finger pressed against the firm trigger.

"Who's there?" Allen called, no longer afraid of offending the neighbours. "Show yourself! Come out! If you jump at me, we'll both regret it."

The light above Roche's door came on again, illuminating two burly-looking Grifter models, their hands clasped behind their backs, their red eyes glowing. The lights by the elevators came on and another two Grifters appeared. The apartment door closest to Allen opened, held by a fifth Grifter, who beckoned him inside. The gun in the machine's hand made Allen rethink his position. He fitted the Browning back into its holster, his body tense as he walked inside.

The apartment had been cleared so that much of the central living space was empty. A stack of boxes was shuffled to one side. The only furniture was two chairs facing one another, the one nearest Allen a rickety folding chair lit by industrial lamps at its right and left, the far chair cushioned with red fabric and occupied.

The Grifter gestured for Allen to take a seat, which he did. The strong lights directed in his face ensured that he couldn't clearly see the mysterious occupant sitting opposite, nor much of anything else in the apartment. The figure puffed out a ring of smoke, holding the cigar in the fingers of their right hand. The metal of its augmentation gleamed.

"Mr. Allen Erzly. Or should I say Constable Erzly?" She sighed in something like self-satisfaction. Her voice was hard and piercing, but not unpleasant. "So kind of you to join me."

"Hello," Allen said uneasily. "Can I help you with something?"

"You can. I'm sorry for the dramatic entrance, but I do have a penchant for them. Besides, we didn't want to alarm you and risk getting shot at. I'm sure you know who we are. You're smart for a machine, after all, and Elias has made a point of keeping us as far apart as possible."

"You're the leader of the Iron Hands cartel," Allen said. "You're in charge of everything from planning hits to smuggling parts out of the city. They call you the Eye of New York. I'd thought you were a myth, but it seems that you're more real than many would care to admit."

"I do enjoy people who pay attention to what goes on around them, and you are no exception. On the contrary, you're a testament to engineering and research in the Automatics field. You might even be an improvement on most humans. I'm sure you're aware of Elias's place in my organization."

"I am," Allen replied. "He acts as your enforcer. Only … you use him mainly for intimidation tactics. I haven't seen him do much enforcement outside of spooking Maranzano one time. In reality, I believe he now acts as a buffer between you and the Lower City. And a liaison, if you will, between the police and yourself. Judging by the mannerisms of one particular sergeant at the 5th Precinct, he — and therefore, all the police — must be aware of the relationship, as well. Roche's actions aren't the safest, nor the most legal, but they are logical."

"Well done. Again, a testament. Your description is accurate, though Elias's role as an enforcer was used to great effect a long while ago. Ask him about it sometime."

"I'd rather not, ma'am."

"Oh, I think you should."

Allen began to get impatient with her cryptic speech. "Is there a reason you brought me here, ma'am?"

The Eye got up from her chair, stretching her legs and moving to the small kitchenette to pour herself some fresh coffee. As Allen followed her with his eyes, he spotted more shadowy goons standing guard.

"Constable, are you happy working for the City of New York?"

"I would say so, yes. It does have its challenges, but I think I'm making a positive difference in this city, chipping away at the corruption. May I ask you a question?"

"Of course."

"Are you happy being such a blight on this city and its people?"

She returned with the coffee, taking her time to answer. "Blight is a strong word. I prefer disciplinarian. We assert control, steer people in certain directions, but only take action when our instructions are resisted."

"Using Roche," Allen stated.

"Yes, using Elias. Is that not what the police did when they employed him?"

"The police have better ways of handling such things. They don't kill people for no reason, or extort Automatics who are just trying to survive."

"That's right, the police have *never* once shot an unarmed person without reason, besides their race or social standing. I'm sure the Native Americans in the Midwest can corroborate that. Hell, I'm sure Commissioners Robins and Shen can corroborate it, as well." She sipped her coffee. "At least we have the decency only to kill people who are threatening us. And surely this Second Prohibition has caused worse damage than our price hikes. After all, we allow Blue-eyes to buy from us, unlike the government, which prohibits Blue-eyes from being employed in most businesses. And the people — that's another story. American exceptionalism died many years ago, and with it the American Dream. The only remnants of either are floating above us, and the Upper City folks keep gobbling up all they can find, leaving us — you and I both — with little more than scraps."

"GE is making great leaps in technology despite the Depression, something you should know, being so well connected. Who's to say this technology won't help the people, improve everyone's lives, maybe even save this country from itself?"

"Erzly, I want you to imagine, if you will, a world that you aren't a part of. Imagine a world in which humans are alone: Automatics were never developed, the

Plate was never built, but the Mafia exists just as it does now. In this freakishly different world, would the stock market still have crashed? Would the Depression still have happened? Would people be starving? Would the police be powerless against the Mob? Would the Grotto be the Wild West that it is here?"

"I can't say with certainty, ma'am," Allen said quietly, seeing where she was going.

"I say yes. Everything would be the same. Everything. If I wasn't here, who knows who would be? Constable, technology doesn't matter, because technology may change, but it doesn't run the world — people do. And people don't change."

"Why am I here?" Allen asked again, growing irritable. Maybe Roche was rubbing off on him. That, and he'd heard parts of this conversation before.

"Recently, we've had some openings in our organization, and we are in need of manpower. Not direct manpower, but bodies nonetheless."

"You're offering me a job?"

"I'm offering you a position of power and wealth and benefit that you wouldn't otherwise have. Elias Roche has shown to be more of a liability lately, and I can't have that. You can't, either, I sense. I am asking you to keep an eye on him."

"I already do." Allen's patience was worn thin, and her sales pitch wasn't helping.

"More than that, though, I want you to go about your regular day and just listen, look, record everything you can in that little noggin. And when we meet again, tell me everything. Easy, right? You can make a pretty penny doing it, too. All the cash you could ever want to keep that little place on Madison Street nice and prim and proper for years to come."

"I believe this meeting is adjourned." Allen stood up, but one of the figures in the shadows pushed him back down. The Eye waved her hand, and the figure released him, but stayed nearby to make sure he didn't get back up.

"Do not make a mistake, Constable. Once you leave, this deal is off. I'm offering you a once in a lifetime opportunity. You need to think hard about where you stand — with the people of New York or with Elias Roche. You cannot have both."

Allen scoffed, feeling confident for the first time in a while. "I think you're the one who's mistaken. I side with Roche *and* the people of New York. What you stand for is nothing but control and fear, and I could never condone that. Thank you for the offer, but I politely decline."

The Eye finished her coffee and took out a new cigar. One of her shadow men came out from the darkness to light it. The glow of the flame revealed parts of her face, specifically her deep-blue eyes and fair skin. She wasn't done with Allen yet.

"Our mutual friend has gotten himself into a bit of a pickle, hmm?"

"Indeed."

"You may not want to work for me, but you must admit that it would be a tragedy for him to be carted off the island to prison. How many people are *in* prison because of him? How many had friends killed by him? I don't need to tell you that prison would be a death sentence for him."

"Why do you even keep him around?" Allen asked. "He isn't as crazed or violent as people say he once was, and the only thing he's really done for you is to sort out some territory issues with Maranzano. Why keep him if he's more a liability than an asset?"

"Elias Roche might be nothing more than a has-been, but his name and his reputation still carry weight and inspire fear. He's a legend in this city, thanks to his actions and, now, that radio show. I need his legacy, to meld his fear with our infamy. It's an investment." She blew out smoke. "His mere presence in the city keeps groups both big and small from trying anything too risky. Maranzano has been brave recently, but we'll correct that. I'll give you a more personal example: besides your little foray chasing down the agent who tried to cut into our business, how much action have you seen in the Lower City? Before Roche, how many criminals did you lock up, or take down at gunpoint? How many raids did you have to perform while training with the 5th Precinct? I'd guess only a handful, if any. Correct?"

Allen remained motionless, but did give a little nod after thinking it over.

"Exactly." She smiled behind her shadows. "Back to our little issue with Roche being incarcerated for life …"

"Do you plan on rectifying that?" Allen hated to admit it, but he felt some spark of hope in her words.

"I do have a plan to save him, and to kill two birds with one stone, so to speak. After all, it's rare to get Greaves in a spot that's easy to target."

"And you're telling me this because?"

"Because if you were to make our target a bit clearer, we would be in your debt."

Allen didn't like the sound of this plan and shook his head. "I must decline again. Roche has made his decision, and I respect it. If you wish to free him by your own hand, please do so, but I won't be part of something that threatens the head of the FBI."

The Eye rolled her head back in frustration, but let it go. "Very well. You can see yourself out."

Allen stood, undeterred by the figures in the dark. He walked to the door and paused with his hand on the handle.

"You hijacked the signal to the radio. Clever trick."

"I have a lot of tricks up my sleeve."

"I wonder, how did you know which part of the program I was listening to? I'm no engineer, but I can guess that because Roche doesn't use the radio often, he wouldn't notice the front plate pushing out more than usual and lacking a few screws, perhaps to hide something inside too big to fit in properly. Something to make the radio work two ways, I imagine?" She didn't answer, and Allen smiled. "I had a feeling. Thank you for the confirmation."

"You should be on a side that appreciates your skills, Allen." She sounded a little more urgent this time. "Don't misjudge this offer."

"I haven't. Goodbye, ma'am." And he walked through, shutting the door behind him to stand in the dim light of the hallway.

The lights had been restored, and the goons from earlier had dispersed, leaving him seemingly alone, though he had a feeling he was still being watched. He lumbered back to Roche's apartment and closed the door behind him to sit on the couch and await Roche.

═══

Roche soon returned to the apartment carrying a small paper bag, along with an open box of eggnog. Allen sat rigid on the couch, watching Roche's eyes drift from him to the bramble of wires on the ground next to the radio. The front was torn off, and the large rectangular device Allen had extracted sat on the glass table. Roche sucked down a mouthful of eggnog before speaking to the machine.

"You must not have liked the rest of that program."

"The Iron Hands rigged the radio with a transceiver to listen in on you even when the radio wasn't on."

"Shit." Roche sighed and grabbed the device from the table, taking a seat on the couch to inspect the mechanism. "How'd you figure it out?"

"I had a meeting with her."

"You … goddamn it!" Roche screwed his face up as if he were in pain. "What did she want?"

"She wanted me to spy on you, to let her know everything that you were doing and what we were investigating, and to keep you from being a 'liability.' I declined."

"Why did you do that?" Allen furrowed his brow at Roche. "Allen, they already spy on me all the time, you should have taken the deal! Made some money, maybe gotten yourself on the inside."

"Elias, I would never sell out for profit, and I definitely wouldn't harm you."

"You could have lied. You could have fed them misinformation, given us an edge. Plus you would have gotten paid for it."

Allen looked down at the ground. He had thought about everything except what a human might. Roche's plan would have been better.

"Well, fuck it, right?" Roche continued. "Less she knows, the better. And thanks for finding the transceiver."

"She knows your habits, and knows you never use your radio. Be careful what you do absentmindedly. She might be using it to her advantage."

"Noted, Al." Roche got up from the couch and went to the kitchen. "Get some rest before the party, we might be up late."

Allen kept running his conversation with the Eye over and over again in his head. She was clever, resourceful, and, above all, intelligent. He could see why, with his guard lowered, Roche might have aligned himself with them. He hated to admit that she had a point, but it was true that things were calmer now, if economically poorer and morally bankrupt. No Mob wars every few months, no shops being blown up and civilians killed for no reason. Most of his police work was paperwork and patrols. Rarely, if ever, was there an actual shootout he had to run into or a perpetrator they had to chase across the city. There was an aura of oppression, but it was better than an aura of dread. If he had to pick a lesser evil …

"Hey, Al." Roche snapped his fingers. "You good?"

Allen shook his head. "I'll be fine, Elias."

"Good man. Give me a few, then we'll get you looking good for the occasion. I'm sure I have some spare stuff that'll fit you. Tall and thin, yeah?"

CHAPTER 23

ALLEN LOOKED HIMSELF UP and down in the mirror, virtually sweating as he inspected his suit for any imperfections. He had one of Roche's finer blazers on and had borrowed one of his vests. Now he was struggling to choose between two ties, holding one, then the other against his neck. Roche was on the other side of his room putting on the green tie he said he had been gifted by Sinclair. He was wearing the same suit he'd worn to the gala. It looked like an outfit he was born to wear. Allen sometimes doubted that Roche was in the right profession.

"Having trouble, metal man?" Roche called out, as he finished fixing his own attire.

"I'm not sure which tie would go best with the rest of my outfit. I know the problem is banal, but still …"

Roche approached and took both ties from Allen. "Black or red … maybe neither. Go with something that compliments you, makes you stand out. This is the type of stuff society doesn't teach you."

"Then who does?"

"Usually a dad. My dad taught me all about suits and ties and how to look good for anyone." He dropped the ties on the bed and looked over Allen's suit. "Oh, no, don't ever do that," he said, pointing at the blazer buttons. Allen had done up all three.

"What? I thought if clothing had buttons, you used them."

"It's different with suits. You always do the middle button, never the bottom one." Roche undid the top and bottom buttons and reset the blazer on Allen's shoulders. "Much better. You look good in a fitted suit. Well, it's more fitted than your usual one."

"What about the top button?" Allen asked.

"Only when you meet the Queen," Roche responded, looking into his closet.

"What queen? I don't think I'll ever meet a queen."

"Exactly." He threw Allen a different tie, matte blue in colour. "It'll work with your eyes. Like I said, it makes you stand out. Want to look good for Simone, don't you?"

Allen gripped the tie and blushed — figuratively — while Roche grinned.

"Excuse me?"

"Come on, Allen, it's obvious. Weird that I never saw it before, but I never thought to look for those feelings in you. Anyone else clue in to your little crush?"

"Well, I asked for advice from Paddy and Toby, but they were ... less helpful."

"Seriously? You asked them for advice before me? Bit rude. I thought we were partners."

"We are, but I've felt we were more professional partners than friends." Allen rubbed the back of his neck in embarrassment, but Roche took it well.

"That's fair, I haven't been the most open with you. I do consider you a friend, Al. I'll work on that. Being open ain't my forte, but I can try. You need to relax, though. You're as stiff as a board and half as useful."

Allen noted the shared idiom of the 5th Precinct's officers. "Yes, Elias. I appreciate your helping me with this, but ... don't you have some personal stake in it?"

"Personal stake? You're making less and less sense these days." Roche exited the apartment, Allen following.

"Well, you had a date with Miss Morane."

"Interview. It wasn't a date."

"And she always seems very keen to speak to you, even to be in your presence. She said that you're a good figure for the radio program because people — her included — find you attractive."

Reaching the elevator, Roche gave him an inquisitive look. "Well, that's something to ponder, ain't it?" he began. "But anyway, that's her view of it, and I think you're skewed into looking at things from her angle. I ain't interested."

"Truly?"

Now Roche's eyebrow went up. "Is there a reason I wouldn't be truthful?"

"I just thought, seeing as I feel that way, you might, too. Beautiful woman, tall and attractive, pleasant to talk to ... If she could entrance a machine like me, it's obvious human men would be attracted to her, too."

"Well, Allen, I ain't like most people, as you know

from having worked with me for a while. You've got to admit that, yeah?"

"You're correct in that regard."

They exited the elevator, Allen going to the car and Roche stopping in the lobby to make small talk with Yuri, who had just finished bringing his hot dog cart inside. Allen couldn't hear their conversation through the glass doors, but when he saw Yuri lunging at Roche to embrace him, he suspected the old Russian might have been invited along, too. Yuri almost skipped out of the lobby to the car, and Roche indicated that Allen should get in the back. The machine complied, crawling into the small cramped spot behind the two main seats. The old Russian fellow sat in the passenger seat.

"Mr. Roche, very nice thing to do. But I'm not good for party, very bad clothes and smell." Yuri gestured to himself. "And not dressed for occasion."

"Trust me, Yuri, I know people. Leave everything to me."

———

Roche spent the better part of an hour gathering everything he needed for the party, driving across the city to the contacts he'd once had as a professional enforcer, but who now saw him as an old, misguided friend. The entire ride felt off, with Allen feeling distracted, though Yuri's jovial attitude did help to offset this.

"Doing all right, Al?"

"As all right as I can be. I have a lot on my mind."

"I can feel that. Does it have to do with your conversation earlier tonight?"

"It does."

Roche nodded. "Yuri, ears closed." The Russian obeyed and put his grimy fingers in his ears, humming a tune to drown out their conversation. "Care to tell me?"

"A long time ago you told me about lesser evils, about taking necessary actions to prevent worse ones from happening. About shades of red."

"It was only a month ago, but, yes, I remember."

"I was naive then, I was … overly idealistic, I suppose, about what keeping the peace meant. I don't agree with the methods employed, who they're employed by, or the direct results of such actions, but I can see the larger picture and what it's led to."

"See, now, if you'd said this a month ago …" Roche sighed and slammed his head back against the seat's headrest. "Goddamn it, Al, don't buy into it."

"There's nothing to buy into. This past month, while following you around or working with the other constables at the station, not once did I use my weapon, or get in a high-speed pursuit, or lock up anyone more vicious than a substance abuser or a violent drunk. I'd half expected police work to involve taking down cartels and Mafias and raiding speakeasies every other day, but it's been nothing like that. At least not until that impromptu visit to Maranzano's Kompound. Regardless, it's because of you —"

"Here we go," Roche groaned.

"It's because of you that there is some degree of peace in this city, and that Maranzano hasn't been planting car bombs or gunning people down in the street.

By no means — no means, let me be clear — do I agree with *anything* you've done in my midst. But what you've done before now has helped in some way to keep this city from tearing itself apart."

Roche was practically biting his fist during Allen's speech. "And here I was about to say I regret chasing down Masters and killing him."

Allen squinted at Roche. "You regret it?"

"Does peace really matter if it comes at the cost we've paid for it? With the Mafia and some shadow organization running the show from behind smoke and mirrors? If Masters had kept going, he might actually have pulled it off and undermined the Hands' control over the Lower City. And we might have a leg to stand on now." Roche gripped the wheel harder. "Hardly peace if a simple trip to Maranzano's starts to unravel it."

"All I'm saying is that it might not be a smart move to just up and leave the Iron Hands. You're helping to keep things from boiling over. A skirmish here or there is preferable to the rise and fall of Mafias every other month, as in the '20s."

"And a crime-free Manhattan is preferable to any of this. Sometimes I almost hope we don't find this Vierling Killer, so he can keep ripping them and Maranzano a new asshole. Maybe it'll give the 5th the leeway to actually make a difference, like they used to."

"Can you imagine the danger that would pose to the people of this city? You're talking about starting a full-scale crime war! Elias —"

"Look, you can work me through the logical loopholes and everything after the party. We're nearly there. Cool it."

Roche waved his hand, and Yuri pulled his fingers from his ears and finished his song. "Have a fun time, Yuri?"

"*Da*, 'God Save the Czar'! Catchy song, yes?"

"Yeah, rolls right off the tongue."

———

Arriving at Simone's apartment building in Lincoln Square, the trio could see half a dozen vehicles parked in front. Whether they belonged to party attendees or other tenants of the building was anyone's guess. After calling up and being buzzed in, they ascended the steps, following the sounds to their destination. Roche climbed the stairs holding a bottle of 1915 Chardonnay in his right hand and a suit in a garment bag in his left. Yuri was still in his dirty clothing, and Allen carried a small bouquet of flowers. By the time they arrived at the fifth floor, he was panicking inside, his body vibrating in anticipation.

They were greeted at the door by Simone, wearing a green dress. Allen was awestruck by her appearance. Roche was handing her the bottle of wine when Yuri pushed past them and made straight for the nearest table with food on it, sampling everything he could.

"Friend of yours?" Simone said, jabbing a thumb at Yuri and grinning.

"Yes, a very good friend. He's going to need to use your shower," Roche said. He held up the garment bag. "And somewhere to change."

"Let him go hog wild. A friend of yours is a friend of mine. Speaking of which, there are some other friends of yours here."

The apartment was huge compared to Allen's or even Roche's. The front door opened into a short hallway, with one side leading to a full kitchen and living area and the other to a number of closed doors. The kitchen had an island, floor-to-ceiling windows, and chrome appliances that outshone even Allen's dome. The living area was populated by dark wooden furniture with white upholstery and quite a crowd. There were some familiar faces.

Roche walked inside, toward the gathering. Allen was still rooted in the doorway, his eyes wide, entranced by Simone.

"You all right, Constable?"

"Yes, of course," Allen said, jostling himself from his stupor and extending the flowers to her. "For you."

"Ah, thank you, Allen," she said, smiling. "You didn't have to."

"You look phenomenal."

"I don't think I've ever had an Automatic compliment me before. This is a new experience. Care to explain yourself?"

"I'm no regular Automatic, ma'am. I can explain more over some of that wine."

Simone led the way to the kitchen, looking perplexed but intrigued.

Stumbling into the crowd, I found a few people I knew: Sinclair was there, along with Robins and Reynolds, the desk jockey. I was surprised to see Reynolds; it always seemed like the former two were the only ones running the station. They greeted me with less than sober cheers as I wandered over. Sinclair handed me a drink.

"What the hell are you all doing here?" I said. "This is a party for RCA, not the 5th."

"Name the last time the 5th got out and had a good time," Robins said, making a good point, like always. "Anyway, Simone didn't invite us, our friend here did. Roche, meet Sebastian Morane. Sorry, General Sebastian Morane. The liquor makes me unprofessional."

The elderly man, who had been sitting in a comfy chair, stood erect and jutted his hand out. He was shorter than most of the others there, with a full head of hair, but his creased skin and wrinkles told of his age. Military history was rooted deep in him, and everything he did had the precision of a rifle. I put on a straight face and shook his hand, giving him more respect than I usually gave Robins.

"Sir. An honour to meet you."

"Likewise." General Morane's voice was raspy from years of smoking and weak from age. "You served, did you not?"

"Yes, sir. Second Battalion Manual Corps, Cleanup Crew."

"Trenchwarmers, eh?" Morane grinned. "Let me guess, nothing until Strasbourg? How'd you fare in that skirmish?"

"Three bullets across the stomach. One perforated my lower intestine. Almost died." I pointed to my gut where the bullets had hit.

"Cardinals fix that up? I would imagine so, since you're not in a wheelchair."

"Those women knew how to fix any wound. No one here can do what they did."

"They could pull a man apart and stitch him back together, and he'd probably run like he was fresh from the womb." The general laughed. "I met your superior here back in the day, when he was running with the Second Bat, as well. He ran a Manual named Black Beauty. Fitting, right?"

"Hey," Robins said, half joking, half serious. "Different world — don't you be saying that shit."

"Ah, cool it, Jeffrey. You can take it, you're part of the old guard." Morane turned back to me. "They don't make us like they used to. Jeff reminds me of ol' President Hughes: a tough bastard, and one hell of a leader. Not like this hack Coolidge. Son of a bitch thinks he can save the world with his tax cuts. Huh. GE lapdog if ever I saw one."

I hesitated. "Roosevelt."

"Huh?"

"Roosevelt is the current president."

"Same difference. Who's your friend over there?"

"Yuri Semetsky. He's been working the streets for a long time. I thought he could use some fun. He'll come over when he gets cleaned up … speaking of which."

I excused myself and went to grab Yuri, pushing him away from the food.

"Come on, let's get you in some nicer clothes. Shower, now."

════════

"So you're not an Automatic, even though you have the same frame, and have, like, pseudo-organs?"

"Right."

"So you're somewhat alive?"

"Correct."

"Jeez." Simone sipped on her wine, leaning on the island. "And why are you and the others, like, on the down low?"

"As it's been explained to me, if people found out and felt threatened by us, it might cause issues both for us and for Automatics. So it's best for us to stay under the radar and not give away our true nature until the time is right."

"But the people who made you didn't let you go, there wouldn't even be a risk of people finding out. So why did they let you leave?"

Allen put a thumb on his chin, pondering the question. "I suppose maybe they felt they couldn't keep us locked up. I couldn't really give you an answer, but, even so, they weren't the ones who told us to stay out of the spotlight. The man who sent me off did say as much, though. Commissioner Robins also advised me not to tell anyone willy-nilly. He even kept me away from the station for months until he felt I was ready to meet Roche. And when Roche found out, he seconded the advice."

"That's so interesting. I mean, the police aren't even supposed to recruit Blue-eyes for the Force. Same with the military, according to my father, since they only recruit Green-eyes, and really only for ordinance transportation. Speaking of which." Simone looked behind her and pointed at the old man lighting a cigar with Robins. "That's my father, General Morane. Just to make sure you're in the loop."

"Understood. And no, the police aren't supposed to, but the 5th is an exceptional precinct with exceptional people."

"Like Roche?"

"Like Roche, yes." Allen tried the wine himself and found it wasn't to his liking, but he kept up appearances. "Your father ... he's retired, but he still seems to be serving, in a way. His manner is striking compared to the other veterans."

"Military officers are different than foot soldiers. The GIs get to go home afterward, but for Dad, it was a career. He's been in the military for so long, it's like he was born into it. I'm just lucky I wasn't. I'd be a colonel by now if I was. I prefer journalism. Just as much death and dismemberment, but much less chance of getting shot."

"And I suppose you have a grudge against the military."

"Oh? What makes you say that?"

"The way you speak about it, and about your father. He must not have been the most attentive with you growing up." Allen shut his mouth a few seconds too late. Simone froze, staring at him, speechless. "I'm sorry for the intrusion, it's just habit. I noticed there was some distance, and —"

"I think that's enough."

"Yes. I'm sorry," Allen said again, making his exit from the kitchen.

═══════════

Yuri emerged from the bathroom in the suit, his olive skin now stripped of grime and given a new sheen from the water. His unkempt hair was parted and combed, and his beard had the unnatural ability to straighten itself out without help. I went up to fix his collar and tie.

"Roche, very good clothes!" Yuri said. "I owe you my life, anything you need."

"Nonsense, Yuri. You're a friend. Keep the suit and everything else. I'll go out and get you some new clothes sometime, because those in there are going to get thrown out."

"*Da*, very old," he laughed, turning to enter the bathroom again and stare disbelievingly at his reflection in the mirror. "How I thought I would look in America. Very weird."

"Hardly anyone makes it here. If you're not on top exploiting everyone else, you're one of the ones being exploited. Anyone can get rich, but it requires breaking hearts and skulls. You were never meant to wear a suit here, Yuri."

"I used to wear suit, when I traded in building. Very large, sent much money back to wife and children in Russia, they very happy. I tell them I would make much for them to come here." The old man looked down at his callused hands. "Now I can't get home, all money in Russia, and I have not seen family in long time."

"You either get rich and go back, or you die here. Fucked, ain't it? Corporate America rotted and spread it to everyone else. Well, almost everyone else," I said. "Yuri, we'll figure something out. Go have fun, talk to people. Forget about things tonight."

Yuri turned, giving me another hug before walking off to join the gathering. Passing by the kitchen, I spotted Simone alone with her wine and saw that Allen had rejoined the group. It glanced over at me, looking guilty. I started to head over, but was intercepted by Reginald Curio.

"Roche!" he announced, making me jump.

"Curio, just the man I wanted to talk to. Care to explain why you've been so keen to get in touch with me?" I asked.

"I want to write about you."

"Nothing to write about."

"There's plenty to write about! For one, I know you hate that name. You would never call yourself what you do in the radio program."

"The guy in the show actually calls himself the Nightcaller? Christ, those are some unimaginative hacks running that show." I tried to catch Allen's eye in the crowd, but my partner was preoccupied. "So you know I don't say that shit, and I'm sure you know I'm a brutal son of a bitch, but if that's all you know about me, what is it you want to write about?"

He recomposed himself before answering. "You're no hero, Roche. That's something people need to be told."

"Sure."

"There is no plain good or evil; it all melds together into an indistinguishable grey blob in this city. Normalcy is something people both love and hate — monotonous jobs with scraps for pay, the rich staying rich, the poor staying poor. The divide is more noticeable than ever, and that's the way things are going to stay, unless people like you decide to change all that."

"How?"

"In this new media age, we run on chaos and complacency. People hate the position they're in, but the shlock they put on the radio keeps them in line, dreaming that they, too, could be the Nightcaller. It keeps them rooted in their homes, in front of the radio whenever they aren't trying to feed their families. Are you even getting royalties from RCA?"

I chuckled. "What do you think?"

"I don't think, I know. You see, GE knows they can get away with it because they're an omnipresent cancer. People are afraid to step out of line because the higher-ups or the Mob might take care of them. This chaos that's been happening, this brewing war that everyone can feel in the air, this is good. This is going to turn the city upside down. We need this. Nothing will change until these streets are rife with bullets and bodies. GE needs to remember who's going to build their towers and run their conveyor belts if they're not employing Automatics. And the Mob — whoa, the Mob needs to be taught a lesson in dignity, in respect, in … goddamn keeping their noses in their own business!"

"And will you be on the streets fighting, as well?"

"Hell no. I'll be safe at home, writing."

I started to laugh. "Everyone's a hypocrite."

"You got that right."

"Speaking of fighting in the streets and chaos and whatnot: been to the Upper East Side recently?"

"Recently enough, I guess. I'm not a fan of the place, too clean, or pretending to be."

"Right, right ..." I picked at my teeth, keeping my eye on everyone else at this little get-together. "Heard of any crimes up there?"

"A fire or something, whatever was in the paper. Oh, and an explosion yesterday, I think? It all blends together after a point; the writing is pedestrian enough to fill a textbook."

"Heard about Edison Hotel a fortnight ago?"

"A bomb went off in the penthouse. Nasty stuff, huh?"

He didn't look like he was lying. He didn't look nervous, either, only mildly entertained by my company. His answers gave me some sort of relief. I didn't see the need to take him outside and beat anything else out of him.

"Regarding the writing thing ... I'll think about it, how about that?"

"That's all I need," Curio said excitedly.

"Good, now ... just fuck off for a bit."

I pushed him out of the way and headed to the kitchen, ready to talk to someone with a less bleak outlook.

Simone's head snapped up as I entered. "You okay?" I asked. "You don't seem to be having much fun at your own party."

"Ah, I'm fine. It's nothing." She sipped her wine. "Your partner is ... presumptuous."

"It's good at its job, both on and off duty. An unfortunate quality, but I'm ironing it out."

"Yeah."

I could sense the tension in her and felt terrible for Allen. What had it said to her? Poor thing didn't have a full grasp of social boundaries yet. I couldn't fault it, though. After all, it picked people apart, and I blew them apart — different, but the same.

"So, I wanted to talk to you again."

"All right." She straightened up, brightening.

"About the murders in the Upper East Side …"

"When you got cut up and shot at?"

"No, that was a different one. Well, kind of the same one, but … it's complicated."

Simone nodded. "I was there for a bit — you remember — but I didn't really get any information besides what you and Commissioner Shen said. There were rumours about another bomb going off."

"I'm going in the slammer in two days if I can't find the real killer. The FBI have pinned it all on me."

"Oh my God …" Simone walked around the island toward me, looking utterly shocked. "But surely they don't have any evidence."

"You remember our little jaunt into the Met a few nights ago? Seems the security cameras spotted me … but not you. Got any kind of explanation for that?"

"I … well, I've snuck in there a few times. I know where all the blind spots are. I tried to guide you through them as best I could. Maybe you slipped into range and a camera spotted you. I'm sorry, I had no idea I'd lead you into a corner like that."

Plausible. Still, I wanted to get a look at that footage.

"They've got the security footage, and they have their assumptions, and that's how they work, just going with a gut feeling and thinking it'll fix everything. I'm not the most innocent guy, so I'm sure in their eyes, it's the perfect resolution. What with every lead being a dead end, I guess I'll have to get used to prison food."

"I'm sure you'll find a way out of this, Elias."

"I don't think so. Prison isn't so bad … three meals a day, six hours of sleep, monotony, and the promise of safety if you aren't a prick. Lord knows the inmates in there will all know me. Not sure if that'll make me a target or a threat. Probably both. At least my usual troubles have been easier to deal with, what with this looming overhead."

"I'm sorry this is happening to you." She placed a hand on my arm, her expression heavy with concern. "Anything you need, you tell me."

"So, what did you hear from Shen that day?"

"Just that there was a crime on 72nd and 3rd. Four dead, if I recall correctly."

I froze for a second before reminding myself to act natural. The gears in my brain were spinning.

"Shen said that?"

"I think it was in his statement."

I knew damn well that Shen hadn't had any idea how many bodies there were. The 11th hadn't investigated the scene. That had been the whole point of the killer's intimidation tactics.

"I'll be right back," I said. "Don't do anything I wouldn't."

Allen was sitting near the 5th veterans, only half-heartedly taking part in conversation. He was still mortified about what had happened with Simone, how he'd ruined the moment they'd shared when he confided in her.

"Yuri, come here!" Sinclair called. The Russian, now besuited and cleaned up, was still pigging out on appetizers. "You were in the War, eh?"

"*Da*, I was, Eastern Front, you on west."

"Robins over there used to be head of a squad of Manuals."

"Man-u-al?" Yuri asked, walking over to join them.

"The big robot things — you know, big guns, buzz-saws, six-foot combat knives?"

"Ah, the *Svyatogor*, the great giants from the west. You drove them, Mr. Robins?"

The commissioner turned from his conversation with General Morane. "I did. They called me the Winger. Got some nasty wounds, but they've healed well. Where did you fight on the Eastern Front? Poland? Hungary?"

"I fight as Cossack in Czar's great guard."

"You were a Cossack?" Sinclair grabbed another glass of whatever they were serving and took a drag of tobacco. "Goddamn, that must have been rough. You rode horses?"

Yuri nodded. "We fight for Czar. Was 1916, deep snow, the Austrians bring out large, hulking beast, smell of fire and diesel, burn the nostrils. They big and tough, but the *Svyatogor* from America are smaller, quieter, run on electricity. They crawl in snow. Czar and men hide in snow for three days for ambush. The hulks did not know what hit them!"

"What did you do on a horse that the Manuals couldn't?" Sinclair asked.

"*Svyatogor* strong, but too slow, even though faster than Austrian hulk. We ride out against the machines, use rope and chain to tie them down, make them fall, and pull them apart with bare hands. Many Cossack die running up to destroy, but not I! I say to them, 'Yuri Semetsky will outlive you all!'"

All the veterans laughed along with him. In spite of his moroseness, Allen observed this bonding over war stories with interest.

"Where you fight, Mr. Robins?" Yuri asked.

"I was in Strasbourg, Passchendaele, even Gallipoli for a spell," Robins answered. He put a hand on Sinclair's back. "This guy was with Roche in the Cleanup Crew for the entire war, making sure those big things worked damn well."

"Aye, they did, but they could have done more," General Morane interrupted. "Cleanup Crew boys sat on their backsides and let the Manuals do all the work. They should have been mobilized earlier."

"Excuse me?" Paddy piped up. All the liquor in him was weakening his inhibitions. "Last I checked, that war would have been lost without the Manuals. We kept them from breaking after we found out Ford was sabotaging them."

"More men on the field is more men firing at those Kraut bastards, am I right, Robins?" the general said. The commissioner didn't respond.

"Those Krauts helped us win the War, asshole! Next you're going to call them traitors, too?" Paddy said.

"They're all nothing but traitors," Morane retorted. "They'd do the same to us if Austro-Hungary ever got the upper hand."

The bickering continued. Robins said nothing but looked uncomfortable with the brewing storm.

Allen's focus drifted as he tried to block out the argument. He wandered away from the group and came across Curio.

"Do you work closely with Miss Morane?" Allen asked, after they'd exchanged greetings.

"Decently close," Curio said. "I mean, WAR ain't a big station physically, but we're churning out shlock all day every day for the news. They hire me to write and edit, two things no one there can do."

"Is she ... good at what she does?"

"Good? You must not know her well. She's more than good. She's ruthless. I've seen her barrel through traffic to get to crime scenes, flip off officers, trespass, all to get that story so she can impress. I mean, this whole Nightcaller thing? She tracked police reports for years — *years* — to find out who he was. She went to precincts that were condemned, stole files, everything under the sun. And RCA struck gold with it. Any of that comes out, they'll defend her tooth and nail. Girl knows how to get the job done, let me say."

"Interesting," Allen said.

"You ever serve in the military, Constable ...?"

"Allen Erzly."

"Yeah, you look familiar."

"My frame is inspired by the old models first re-leased during the War."

"Ah!" Curio exclaimed. "That makes sense. I was knee-deep there. I wrote my first poem while stuck in the western trenches: 'Ballad of the Boots.' I was starved for creative titles at the time, which is terrible since I won the Pulitzer for it in '18. Now that terrible title is cemented in history. How embarrassing. That reminds me of another piece of writing I did ..."

Now Allen tuned Curio out, as well, looking over the crowd and spotting Simone and Roche engaged in deep conversation. He felt a pang of envy in his stom-ach and clamped down his steel teeth to keep himself from doing anything impulsive. As he watched, Simone flipped her hair, briefly revealing the back of her dress and the tops of her shoulders.

Allen's eyes went wide.

On the back of her left shoulder, barely visible to anyone but him, was the edge of a brown and purple bruise. Given its colour, he guessed it was a few days old. Roche walked away, and Simone looked up and met Allen's gaze. He pulled back into the crowd and waited to tell Roche.

═══════

Having taken a moment in the bathroom to wash my face and re-collect myself, I headed back to the party, but paused upon noticing the bedroom door was ajar. Unfortunately for Simone, old habits died hard for Elias Roche. My brain was running on all cylinders since catching her slip-up. I needed to confirm my new theory. The old Roche might have caused an immediate ruckus, but working with Allen had rubbed off on me. I'd stop and think and confirm before rushing to a conclusion.

I checked that everyone was in the living area before making my approach to the bedroom, gently pushing the door open, and sliding inside. There was an armoire, a closet, a small bed, two nightstands, and a radio. Framed photos sat on all of the flat surfaces. Looking over my shoulder once again to confirm I was in the clear, I picked up and inspected one frame at a time.

The first was an old picture of Simone and General Morane. She, like the city, must have been in her early 20s. She looked happy. Her father's expression was passive. The celebration scene in the background showed the simple delights of a bygone decade.

The next was a group photo in front of WAR Radio, featuring Simone along with radio operators, writers, journalists, and some of the brass from RCA. It reminded me of my photo of the men in my platoon. Out of the five hundred or more men from Cornell that I'd gone overseas with, less than a tenth of them made it home, and I cherished the picture as she must cherish this one.

The picture by her bedside table was very different and much older than the others. It showed a small family of five: mother, father, two brothers, and a young girl no older than thirteen or so. Looking at it closely, I was able to confirm two things: this was not the United States, given the Tudoresque style of the house the family stood in front of, and that father was not General Morane. It raised more questions than answers.

The creak of the floor near the bedroom door alerted me. I looked up sharply and sighed in relief when Allen poked its head around the door.

"Goddamn, Al, be quiet! Get in here." I yanked Allen in by the wrist and closed the door just enough to keep people from hearing or seeing us.

"I have critical information for you," it said in a harsh whisper.

"Same here. How good are you at profiling people?"

"Pardon?"

"You know, analyzing shared traits and facial features and all that. Can you do that? If so, tell me — that girl in the picture, is that Simone?"

Allen grabbed the picture with both hands, bringing it near a lamp and holding it within inches of its face. A few seconds later, it turned to me. "The eyes, the creases by her nose, the lips ... I'd say with near certainty that that is Simone Morane."

"Then who are those people?" Allen looked at the photo again, then back at me, astonished. "Come on, spit it out!" I said.

"Don't you recognize him?" It pointed at the father.

"This is not the time for games, Allen, just say it!"

"That's André Mercier."

CHAPTER 24

AS THE PARTY DIED DOWN, we made every excuse in the book to stick around. Allen paced around the living room, looking for weapons, escape points, anything Simone might use to her advantage if things didn't go our way. Meanwhile, I tried to keep her occupied to prevent her from suspecting anything was amiss. Her concern over my impending arrest helped cover my impatience, but even so, I almost blew it more than once.

The first to leave the party were the 5th's boys, Sinclair in a sour mood for having to deal with General Morane, and Robins interested as to why we were staying. I told him I'd go through it all later. Recognizing my tone of voice, he hurried away all the more quickly. Yuri caught a ride with them, having been invited to stay the night at Sinclair's.

Next was the general, kissing his "daughter" on the cheek, giving me a formal goodbye, and ignoring Allen at every opportunity. Simone took care in directing him to the door and reading him the riot act to make sure he kept to himself while outside. A very protective daughter.

Finally, Simone's cronies made their way home at almost two in the morning, drunk and happy, singing songs with gibberish lyrics and flat notes. I had told Simone that I needed to speak to her about a private matter. That piqued her interest, though she'd soon learn she shouldn't have fallen for it.

Allen was at the far end of the room, helping to clean up, and I stood by the door as Simone closed it after her colleagues. Allen had done me the service of heading down to the car earlier in the night to grab the cuffs I kept in the car. They were now hanging out of my back pocket.

Simone turned to me with a smile. "So, Detective," she whispered. "Do I have the honour of being privy to your secrets?"

"Kitchen." I nodded in that direction and let her go before me.

"I have to say, you're a hard man to impress. By all accounts, if I didn't know better, I'd say you —"

Her face broke when the cuff wrapped around her left wrist. The other cuff I quickly snapped to the fridge door handle. Déjà vu.

I backed up just as Allen appeared in the doorway. Simone looked frightened for a second, then infuriated.

"Elias Roche, what the hell are you doing?" she screamed. "Get this off me or I swear you'll regret ever setting foot in this apartment!"

My Diamondback came out, flicked to double-action, and I drew the hammer. She stopped when the barrel was pressed against her forehead.

"You lied to me," I said.

"Excuse me? What possible reason do you have for saying that shit and putting a gun to my head?"

"You aren't Simone Morane, you are Simone Mercier, the Vierling Killer, and the asshole who was going to have me put in prison."

"Are you insane? You are a troubled and slow man to think such a thing, Roche. What evidence do you have?"

"The fact that any other civilian would be pissing themself right now, but you're still talking. After all, you acted pretty scared when Maranzano did the same thing."

Her face went blank.

I continued, "The crime scene at 72nd and 3rd. No civilian would have known there were four bodies. Not even Commissioner Shen knew. We never released a statement, and Viessman's people don't talk."

Allen handed me the photo it had nabbed earlier, and I raised it to her face.

"André Mercier. And this is you with, we presume, the rest of your family. Not smart to leave it lying around your apartment, was it?"

"I didn't expect a pervert to walk into my bedroom to snoop," she said through gritted teeth. I could see that Allen was getting spooked.

"You lied to me. Your little slip-up and your bruise — the one Allen dealt you — gave you away. You had me fooled when you showed me your arms — there were no cuts."

"You'd be surprised what Syneal and makeup can do for a wound."

I frowned. "Care to explain everything before I put a hole in your head?"

"You wouldn't."

"He would," Allen piped up. Simone's eyes snapped up to meet its gaze. "We both know he would have killed you that night if I hadn't tried to stop him, letting you catch him off guard."

"A punch right to my fresh stitches." I felt my side tingle and the wound stretch with each breath. "Why? Money? Infamy? Some great conspiracy to destroy the Maranzano Mob?"

"My father," she spat, staring at my gun with malicious intent.

"Your 'father' seems to be doing fine, especially if he lives up on the Plate."

"He's suffering. He's in his seventies, and while he may look fine, he's not all there. Some days he forgets my name. One day it'll be my face. He was pushed out of Upper City, and now he lives in the Upper East Side."

"Your father is …" I faltered, trying to make sense of it. "He's registered as a resident on the Plate, everyone says as much. They're saying he might be made secretary of defense someday. Why would they lie?"

"So that the government doesn't look bad shoving some old bastard in the Lower City with a pitiful retirement fund. They wait for him to pass before they fill the slot. It's all for appearances."

"But why keep him registered in the Upper City? Surely they could just move him off the island to a nice retirement home."

"The last thing the Upper City wants is for people to think they'll toss you off for the slightest indiscretion. But he's a liability now. The moment he stumbled saying his own name, they set him up down here and made sure to keep all the paperwork the same."

"I'm sorry to hear that, but how is that a motive? That sounds like an Upper City problem, not a Mafia problem," I said.

"The Mafia is exploiting him. Threatening him. I know how Maranzano found out where he lives: Hartley tipped him off, seeing as he was never a fan of my father. Do you know what I've done to try to get him to safety?"

"So that's why you wanted to transfer to the Upper City," Allen interrupted. "I eavesdropped on your conversation with Schafer. I thought it was odd that you wanted to go up there —"

"Shut the capek up before I beat it to death with this fridge." She looked at me, ignoring Allen. In response, it went unnaturally silent. "My father is all I have left. Blood or no blood, he is family. Maranzano has been exploiting both him and the people of New York, and he needs to be put in his place."

Something didn't add up.

"But what does threatening your father accomplish?" I asked. "What do they have to gain from roughing him up?"

"Money."

"They make more in a minute than your father could ever provide from his own bank account," I retorted. "And that last place you hit wasn't even Maranzano's."

"Of course I know that! The Iron Hands are just as bad, if not worse."

"How did you know Rossi was part of the Hands?"

"A girl has her ways." She squinted at me. Hard to tell what she was hiding.

"So what started out as a poorly founded personal issue transformed into vigilantism?"

"Call it whatever you like, but I'm making good headway dealing with them."

"You're starting a war," Allen interjected. "Violence is ramping up in the Lower City. According to the 5th, Maranzano and the Hands have clashed more this week than they have in years. If this continues, the Lower City will become a war zone, and the only way it ends is when one group annihilates the other."

"Fine, let them kill each other!" Simone spat back. "The sooner this city is rid of those blights, the sooner the people can focus on the root of their problems."

"You have no qualms condemning innocent people to death?"

"They're only condemned to death if they choose a side."

"Your actions will force them to choose a side!"

It was like looking at myself all over again. To my right was a younger version of me, full of hope and pride, believing she could be the one to fix everything and save the world with the business end of her gun. And to my left was another me, one who accepted that oppression was better than death, that peace was something to strive for, no matter the quality of the peace granted. No, no, I wouldn't do this again. Otherwise, I'd be back at square one, with another person trying to prove a point, and me hunting them down once again. It was high time I started thinking. And doing the right thing.

I reset the hammer and put the Diamondback under my arm. Simone looked shocked, Allen doubly so.

"The Eye sent me after you because you're now a threat," I whispered to myself. "We need a threat, now more than ever."

"What?" she asked

Allen stared at me in disbelief. "Roche, you can't be serious."

"This is the only way."

"No, it is not!" it said, raising its voice. I'd never seen this side of it before. "Elias, she is a danger to everyone! She's brewing a war between the two largest Mobs in America, and you want to let her *continue*? There's no telling how great the casualties will be."

"I know that —"

"No, you don't! You have the foresight of a blind man! Her actions alone will cause havoc, and we'll be the ones who have to clean it up! The people don't deserve the wrath that you and she and the Eye will bring upon them! I won't allow this!"

"Well, good thing you ain't the one making the decision." I slid the key into the cuff around Simone's left wrist and unlocked it.

"Roche!" Allen yelled, making me turn just as the latch came undone. Before I could speak, I was cut off by a slap in the face.

Fuck ... that was hard.

"You're lucky I don't punch you in that wound again, asshole! Don't you ever do that to me again!" she screamed, pushing me away from her. She looked at Allen. "And that thing is lucky I don't want to break my fist on its head."

Allen didn't speak. It only glared at me. It looked like it was actually angry.

"Ow ..." I rubbed my cheek. *That's not going to look good tomorrow.* "I'm sorry. You see what kind of pressure I'm under."

"Which is why I don't trust you. Why let me go?"

"Because you can do what we can't. You can sow some discord and make the Mobs suffer, give this city a chance to be free of their influence. It's a long shot, but it's better than working for her and getting my friends killed. You are objective, unaffiliated with anyone who presides over this hellhole."

"Not entirely objective, but ..." Her shoulders relaxed a little, though she still didn't trust us, especially not Allen, who was beside itself. She looked at it. "That pistol-whip hurt, capek."

"It was meant to," Allen said. Its hand was on the grip of its gun, the one I'd gifted it.

"Al," I said, "stand down."

It didn't like that. It complied, but with reluctance.

Simone spoke to me but kept her eyes fixed on Allen. "What's next? Going to stalk me to make sure I do everything according plan? Maybe try to sneak a knife in my throat while I —"

"The gun," I interrupted.

"What?"

"The Vierling. Which one have you been using, and how?" She blinked. "Show me."

She sighed, rolling her eyes, and moved past me, heading for the front door of her apartment. Allen and I followed in hot pursuit.

═══════

She led us down to the basement, entering with the use of a key. It was a laundry room full of currently empty washing machines and an uneasy stillness. She stepped over to a large cabinet of cleaning supplies and nodded at it. Allen took the initiative, sliding it aside. There was a conspicuous vertical crack in the wall large enough to fit a hand through. Allen yanked at it, discovering that a large portion of the wall was set on a hinge; it swung outward to reveal a hidden second room. While it did all this, Simone locked the door to the laundry room so no one could get in — and no one could get out.

"I'd better not get shot down here," I said.

"If you're smart, you won't," she responded.

The room was messy, but functional, containing everything from tables to racks to filing cabinets. Near the entrance hung the outfit we'd caught her in so many days ago: goggles, hood, heavy coat. The filing cabinets contained pictures and documents. Strewn about were black-and-white photos of the Edison Hotel, 72nd and

3rd, and Rossi's little whorehouse. An image of her next target sat in plain view: Chelsea Piers, the Eye's new playhouse and the perfect place to set a bomb off to ignite an actual, honest-to-God war.

And there at the far end of the room, on a worktable covered in tools and materials, was the item of the day: Mercier Vierling number four, Renaud, the lost masterpiece. Not as immaculate as the one I had seen in the museum, no engravings, and the trigger mechanisms were so different it was like a completely different gun. Three triggers, four barrels, the bottom one longer and rifled to fire 15mm Von Whisper shells instead of the common 12-gauge shell. Speaking of which, there were half a dozen shells on the table nearby, along with several stripper clips of Lebel cartridges beside an ammo press.

"Like the place? Put it together myself after getting here a few months back," she said.

"A few months? How long have you been operating?"

"Back in May was my first real jump into the fray. You think I started at Edison? The only reason you got on my tail is because the stiffs belonged to GE. Every other corpse I've made was from the Maranzano Mob, and since they drop like flies, no one noticed when they died in fours. People do suddenly take notice when the higher-ups are threatened, though, funnily enough."

"Jesus, and the Mob is only starting to feel it now?"

"It took some effort to root out the big players. Now the killings are quick, but before now, I had to get up close and personal. I brought some of them back here, tortured them for hours, days even, to get what I needed. That's how I found out about Hartley and my father. I've been working my way up the chain, taking out key players, but it seems Maranzano is paranoid — not a bad trait to have, with me on his tail. It'll take time to get him."

"Christ …" Impressive. Barbaric, but impressive. "Where did you get the money for all this?"

She paused, lowering her voice. "A girl has her ways …"

She still wasn't telling me everything. How did a girl like her finance quality clothes, an apartment in Lincoln Square, and resources like this? How did a girl in the Lower City get Von Whisper cartridges without going through the cartels? I didn't think she'd let on to me, but there was something there. Perhaps she wasn't working alone …

"I'm guessing this hasn't been your first foray into combat," I said.

"Correct," she affirmed.

"Your father lived in Reims, near Verdun. You weren't here when the War broke out, were you?"

Simone didn't face me. Watching her lean wearily against the workbench, I could tell this wasn't an easy thing to talk about. "I was fourteen when the War began, seventeen when it ended."

"You served?"

"Not exactly. I wasn't recruited, if that's what you mean. After everything began and the country started to conscript, my father and brothers joined up, and when the trench was pushed near Reims, my mother and I decided to do our part, too. But by the end … I lost everywone, everything. My mother first, then my brothers, one by one. My father died a month before the surrender. *A month.*

"I did get you, Roche, when you talked at the restaurant about your service, how you were unable to go back to a normal life. I understood then, and I still do now. I never had the chance for a normal life after my childhood. I was fucked up, and there was no going back. I spent more time around American and British and Canadian soldiers than with my own family. Morane — Dad, I mean — felt something like pity for me, so after I lost my father, he offered to bring me to America and give me a life far away from the hell of France. How could I say no? I was seventeen and an orphan. I had no other options unless I wanted to scrub shitters for the rest of my life. So of course I accepted his offer."

"Did he have any idea that you were capable of ... this?" I motioned toward the table full of equipment.

"Thankfully, no," she said. "I'm not proud of what I did to survive, nor of what I do now, but it's necessary. My enemies are nothing to me when I have a knife in my hand and bullets in my rifle. Afterward is a different story, but, in the moment, you have to close yourself off to their suffering if you want to live."

I never did that. Perhaps I was weak; that explained why I had almost died several times, while she seemed to be bulletproof. I sat down in a rickety chair. Allen was silent, unable to pull itself from the conversation.

"I told you about my first kill. Tell me about yours," I said, to break the silence.

She still didn't turn to face me. "An old German bastard manning a machine gun. The French hated machine-gunners. They'd let every other German boy live, but the best Germans with the most stripes manned those guns. I was young, small, and I could sneak through shelled-out trenches to get to the German line. You shot your first man, I stabbed mine. How did you feel after your first kill?"

"I threw up," I said, almost laughing. "I vomited all over myself and my gun. Paddy hasn't let it go ever since. How did you feel?"

"Not a goddamn thing." She turned to me now. I wished she hadn't. "But now ... now I can't sleep, now it takes ten coffees to get through a day, because I wake up in the night screaming. I felt nothing back then, but it caught up with me, fast." She looked at Allen, her brow furrowed. "How about you, capek?"

Allen didn't respond.

"I don't think it wants to talk about it ..." I began.

"Well, I do. Killed a man yet? Got blood on your hands? Not an Automatic, huh? Bullshit. To think I gave either of you the time of day."

"Don't patronize me," Allen spat back.

I put my hand on Simone to pull her away and was met with a knife to my throat. She had grabbed it off the worktable. She was quick.

"Don't you fucking touch me," she said.

"Understood." I pulled away, and she lowered the knife slowly. "You framed me, didn't you? At the Met."

"Framed you? No. I skirted around the cameras, sure, but I didn't think they'd go hunting for you over that. I thought you'd be immune due to your reputation, but it seems not. I didn't mean to get you charged for my actions."

"So you knew where all the cameras were?"

"Some, not all of them."

The conversation was cut short by a crackling noise. I knew that sound. There was a police scanner in here. She was listening in on police radio chatter. No wonder she always knew what was happening and where.

"*Call the 5th, get R here. Firefight in Midtown … 3rd Precinct officers on scene, requesting backup. Maranzano's people are on the move.*"

Simone turned to me. "Looks like you're needed." I glanced back at the radio, raising my eyebrows. "I had to track you somehow," she said.

"How did you get the scanner?" I asked.

"Don't you have a call to answer?"

I nodded and got up slowly. Allen and I headed for the door.

"I'm coming with you," Simone said.

"Absolutely not. If you want to make the most of your freedom, stay here, maybe move apartments, but do not come with us."

"It's my fault you've been incriminated. I owe you for my negligence, and I'm coming with you, like it or not. Besides, with that injury of yours, do you really think you could take *me* in a fair fight, let alone Maranzano's thugs?"

I gripped my side and took a minute to consider the options.

"Stay in the back and follow my orders," I said.

"Roche, if you want her to live, she's not leaving this building," Allen cried.

Simone grabbed the rifle, cracked the breech open, and loaded three rounds and one shell. She tossed it to me, ignoring Allen.

"Wait for me in the car. I need to change into something more appropriate. Don't you dare leave without me."

"Will you be quick?" I asked.

"Shut up and get in your car."

CHAPTER 25

I PARKED THE TALBOT BEHIND a small blockade of police cars on 50th. Four cruisers were lined up bumper to bumper, blocking the street, and eight officers were crouched behind the vehicles, holding .38s. Allen and I made our way to the blockade, ducking behind one of the cruisers for cover, while Simone kept her distance. I hoped she wouldn't decide to turn the gun on us to keep her secret safe.

I approached the nearest officer. "What's the news?"

The rookie jumped at the sound of my voice. "Sir, please, we need you to back up, this is an ongoing crisis." He had a faint French accent. Figured, being from the 3rd.

"I'm the guy you called for."

"Oh!" He was awestruck. Goddamn it, this radio program was turning me into some sort of urban legend. "Sir, a group of Maranzano's thugs just raided a clothing store, and they have hostages."

"That doesn't seem that big of a deal. Why the blockade?"

"Look up and see who owns the shop."

Great, just what I wanted to hear.

The street on either side of the shop was blocked off. A total of nine cruisers sealed the area off from the rest of the city. The shop was busted, with broken glass everywhere and a body or two shot up with holes lying just outside the front door. Between all the cop cars, soldiers stood in the middle of the street, wielding advanced Frag Rifles and wearing heavy body armour printed with a logo on the shoulder and back: the letter *G* surrounded by a ring of eighteen dots and one single dot above the ring. The Gould Corporation.

"They must have robbed a shop owned by Gould's boys," I relayed to Allen. "This is going to turn into a bloodbath real quick. If we even look like we're thinking about jumping over these cars, we're getting shot."

"Why not send the girl over?" Allen suggested. "I doubt she'd have a problem dealing with hostages the way she does mobsters."

I turned to it. "What the hell is wrong with you?"

"You know very well."

"You're as helpful as a hole in the head," I said, more to myself.

I looked up. There was no way into the alley behind this shop unless we wanted to cross down to the nearest perpendicular road. That would leave a large gap of time during which anything could happen. The rooftops? The nearest building had a fire escape at the front and was only two stories tall; the bottom was a shop, the top a living space, just like Jaeger's place in SoHo.

We walked back to the car. Simone was waiting impatiently, rifle in hand, wearing a padded black suit. She had goggles hanging from her neck, a bandana wrapped under her chin and around her scalp, and her hair was stuffed down into the neck of her collar.

"Allen, get up to the rooftops, cross to the building in question, and find a way inside. Keep a low profile." I looked at Simone. "You, too. Another way."

"You want me to run around up there at this time of night?" Simone asked dryly.

"I imagine you've done worse," I said. She shrugged. "I'm taking the long way. We need to hit them from two different angles. But whatever you do, keep Maranzano's boys in your sights, and don't get spotted."

"And Gould's?" asked Simone.

"That goes without saying, but I think they're less interested in us and more interested in getting this place cleared out."

I knew Allen didn't want to follow my orders. Even Simone looked uncomfortable.

"Can you keep me from getting caught when the dust settles?" she asked.

"I can try."

"Can you also keep your partner from putting me in the dirt?"

I peered at Allen, who was staring daggers at me. "I can try," I repeated.

"All right."

I made my way east, looking for the nearest alley-way, leaving Allen and Simone to tighten the noose their own ways. I hoped they wouldn't make any corpses before I got into position.

———

My poor health and my stitches let themselves be known during my journey. In the five minutes I spent circling the block, my run turned into a limp jog. *Jesus, when I get to prison, I'm going to work on my cardio.* I used to run for miles through the trenches and after perps. Now I was a sack of potatoes.

The back of the shop was ruined: the door was blasted off its hinges and the open entranceway was now blocked by a rickety shelving unit. That must have been how Maranzano's boys had gotten inside, and they'd covered their exits well. No doubt moving that shelf would create some serious noise and make me easy pickings.

I approached the entrance and looked through the shelves into the storeroom. It was a small area for storing maintenance tools and whatnot, only a few square feet in size. The room terminated in an archway leading into the main backroom, which connected to the storefront via a now busted wooden door about thirty feet ahead. There was an iron safe in one of the corners of this smaller area. It had been blown open and the contents cleaned out.

Near the door leading to the storefront sat six hostages, bound at the wrists and pushed together in one corner. The Bruno looking after them was holding a Thompson. The other mobsters were at the front of the shop, making sure Gould's boys didn't get too trigger happy and try to flush them out.

The distance between me and the guard was more than thirty feet. Getting past this shelf and killing him quietly would give me more leeway than shooting him, but I wasn't sure that was possible. Where the hell were Allen and Simone? They should be inside by now.

Fuck it. Time to get messy again. I pulled the hammer back, the click inaudible to the hitman due to the noise in the storefront. The gunshot was difficult to ignore, though. The hostages screamed, and several Frag Rifle flechettes flew through the wall, confusing Brunos and hostages alike in the midst of the standoff.

I threw down the shelf to get inside and ran through the small room into the main storage area. I dropped my guard for only a moment, but I should have known there would be more than one person looking after the hostages. I caught a glimpse of the baseball bat just before it slammed into my forehead. I sailed backward, landing on my back. My Diamondback fell from my grasp. When my crossed eyes righted themselves, they were looking at the business end of a Colt.

I was getting sloppy. I wasn't thinking. No wonder the Eye said I was a liability. I'd be dead within the week.

Turned out the upstairs area was connected to the store by a set of stairs conveniently located at the back of this storeroom; Allen busted through, Browning handgun pointed at the guy with his gun to my head.

"NYPD, you're under —"

It was cut off by another hitman from the storefront running in and clobbering it in the head with brass knuckles. Allen slammed into the wall, stripped of its weaponry. The hitman kept beating it in the head, leaving dents as it tried to defend itself. My blood boiled. *No one fucks with my partner.*

I grabbed the gun that was still in my face, pushing it up as the trigger was pulled. A hot casing hit my fingers, and the slide pushed forward to load a second round, jamming due to the chamber being busier than it should have been. Yanking the gun from the Bruno's hand, I received a punch in the head as a result. An attempt to get up led to a second punch, leaving me spinning where I lay.

Well, shit, didn't expect my life to end quite like this. I didn't even get a montage.

The man above me suddenly screamed. When my vision steadied itself again, I saw him against the nearest wall, clutching his throat where a chef's knife was protruding. The guy pummelling Allen was dispatched similarly as a black-clad figure inserted a fluting knife into his spine, paralyzing and killing him. Simone had left her rifle upstairs in favour of a set of kitchen knives she must have grabbed from a block. She was down two blades, but she had a few more to play with in her left hand.

Three men ran into the storeroom from the far door, surveyed the carnage, and rushed us. Automatic fire sprayed from one mobster holding a Thompson. His friends stayed behind him as bullets peppered the ground toward Simone.

I remembered from chasing her back on 81st Street that she was fast. Now, I couldn't even follow the blur as she rolled and came up inches from the gunman. A boning knife entered his eye socket and after a few seconds of screaming, he went silent and limp. The other two mobsters were dispatched next, one taking a cleaver to the calf and a bread knife to the throat, blood spraying across the wall, and the other forced to the ground when the same bread knife was plunged into his neck.

"Holy shit," was all I managed to say.

I turned sharply as an unaccounted-for mobster came around the corner from the storefront and put a gun to the back of Simone's head.

"Drop the knife, bitch!" he screamed.

"Drop the gun and you might live," she responded.

"Are you dumb? Drop the knife, you got —"

I grabbed the pistol I'd jammed, pulling back the slide to clear out the chamber and firing at him. The bullets didn't hit him, but the supressing fire pulled his focus away from Simone. She spun around, grabbed his pistol with her right hand, and forced both it and its wielder to the ground. He was stuck looking into her eyes. Her last weapon was a paring knife.

"Men are all the same. In one ear" — she finished the job by jabbing the blade into the side of his head — "and out the other."

His screams subsided moments later as he bled out on top of his dead friends.

Allen and I were in shock over what we'd just witnessed. My skin was crawling from the last kill. Simone was ruthless, she was terrifying. She was worse than I was. Allen looked sick. It had seen me dispatch people with guns before, but this was something else.

I pushed myself up and helped Allen. Its head was severely damaged; some of the plates on the left side of its face were unable to move, making it look like it had experienced a stroke. We recovered our weapons before approaching Simone — slowly.

The hostages were still screaming. Allen freed them and told them to get out through the back door. All six were happy to follow orders and run. Then the three of us were alone. Simone hadn't moved after the final kill. She was still kneeling there, panting, unwilling to look at us.

"You good?" I asked.

"I hate this feeling, this adrenalin. It makes me feel like conflict is the only place I can exist without losing my mind." She stood up finally, recomposed. "You know that feeling, too?"

I did, Lord knows I did, every time I pulled my gun out. That was how I'd been able to stay sane working for the Eye for so long. But now wasn't the time to be dissecting ourselves.

"Answer me, Roche."

"Can we just …" I gestured to the back door. "Get your shit and run. Gould's boys will be here any second."

She grunted and pushed past me, knocking me off balance by hitting my shoulder with hers. Allen and I looked at one another. I wasn't so sure letting her go had been a good idea.

Maybe she — like me — should have been left chained to that fridge.

═══════

I walked out of the storefront with my hands up. Gould's boys nearly shot me, but, thankfully, the cops recognized me. They defused the situation as the task force from the Plate swept the store. The police swept in next, clearing the area, finding the hostages in the alley, and questioning them. They told investigators that a woman in black had butchered the men with knives. When they asked me, I told the investigators that I had used the knives, and the hostages might have been confused in the moment. I was so glad when they bought it.

Allen and I went back to the car once they let us go. Simone was waiting at the mouth of an alleyway nearby. Allen was careful to keep its distance, and even I was nervous being within five feet of her.

"You never answered my question," she began.

"Simone ..."

"Do you know that feeling?"

"I used to. I used to know it all the goddamn time. I felt like I had focus when I was fighting. I felt composed or at peace or at least able to drown out that sinking feeling I always have," I said. "But all I feel now is an apathetic numbness to it all. To combat and the Mob and the FBI, to everything. Is that what you wanted to hear?"

She pulled back slightly; she could tell she'd struck a nerve.

"I'm tired, Simone. I'm trying to get out of this game of Mob politics because I'm not what I used to be. I've been going through the motions so I don't get a bullet in the head, so my friends don't get their fingers chopped off or their homes blown apart. I'm surviving. It's what I do. It's what I've been doing ever since I sold my soul to the Eye. I'm trying to keep people alive … or at least, I was."

She let a silence hang in the air. Not long, but long enough for me to check my breathing and calm myself.

"I don't trust you," she said.

"I know. I don't trust me, either." I laughed, trying to alleviate the tension. "I don't know what I'm doing anymore. Half of me agrees with you, the other half agrees with Allen. But that's why *you* need to do something about this. No matter how badly I want to change things, I can't do anything with the Eye watching over me."

"So I'm on my own?"

"I didn't say that. We just have to be smart about this. We can't leave a power vacuum like the one I created to get the Eye where she is now. If we do, someone worse might pop up. Another Five Families? Who knows what the result would be?"

"Let's get there first. This time, one in the hand is not better than two in the bush."

We'd have to see. We'd have to rip up the Iron Hands first, and that would be a crusade all its own.

"And if I'm set to hunt you down while you go about dismantling two cartels? What then?" I asked.

"You'll have to catch me first," she said with a smile.

She departed down the alleyway soon after, letting Allen and me return to the Talbot. Its eyes never left the mouth of the alley. The moment we got inside, I drove as fast as I could from the scene, wanting to distance us from everything that had occurred.

"You've let her go free to destroy this city and condemned yourself to a lifetime in prison," Allen said after a lengthy silence.

"Like I said, she can do more than we can."

"That doesn't change the fact that we have no idea what kind of destruction this will cause."

"Allen …"

"And where will I go?" It turned to me, its voice wavering. "What'll I do when you're locked up? You're the only thing keeping me away from a shredder, as Greaves so eloquently put it."

"Al, there are other —"

"There is no one else, Elias!" It looked like it might cry, if it could. "This goes beyond her actions destabilizing the peace — this is about you. Without you, I'm a Blue-eye working for a precinct already under the microscope. I won't last long."

I couldn't look it in the eye. "I'm sorry. That's how things are, Al. That's how they have to be. I'll deal with it."

It turned its body to look out the window, a gesture to show me that it was pissed.

"Let's get that face of yours fixed," I said.

"I'm fine."

"Then at least be there when Greaves puts me in cuffs. Will you do that?"

Allen sighed, taking a few agonizing seconds to decide, then it nodded. "Yeah."

CHAPTER 26

ALLEN REFUSED TO GET ITS FACE FIXED, no matter what I said or did. It asked to be dropped off at home until the deadline. I obliged, but felt gross about it. There was a rift between us, and I wasn't sure if I could ever fix it.

Even so, the time alone gave me space to reflect, to really consider my options. *I'm fucked if I run, fucked if I go to the slammer, fucked if I rejoin the Iron Hands.* But now this city was truly out of my hands, if it had ever really been in them before. Well, if I was going out, I should make amends while I could.

I drove to Central Park and once more walked to the Bow Bridge. It was about five in the morning. The sun hadn't yet reached the horizon, and the darkness made Central Park foreboding and dangerous. I could see the homeless folk, desperate and violent, and they could see me. They knew not to get close.

Once more, silence descended. She always was quick.

"Elias."

"Darling."

"You can turn around."

I did so, seeing only her silhouette in the darkness. The lights around the bridge had been snuffed out, allowing her to be here without a veil. She held a cigar, as was her habit.

"Changed your mind?" she asked.

"Something like that. I've had a day or so to reflect. A lot has happened. I've been … lying to myself."

"Oh?"

"I'll never be free from what I was or what I've done. I can't hide what I am. All these names — Nightcaller, Iron Hand — they're just different words to describe the same shit, but I'm none of them anymore. I'm in this life for good, so I might as well be here for the right reason. I'm not the same enforcer you hired four years ago."

"But will you continue to be my Iron Hand?" she asked, sounding confused.

"No," I said. "I'm not your Iron Hand. I don't know what I am or what I want to be. Give me some time to take stock of things, to really decide what it is that I am to you, to everyone in this city. I'm done fighting for the wrong reasons."

The Eye threw her cigar on the ground and stamped on it. "Interesting. Do you think this sudden change of heart will save you from the FBI?"

"No, but you will."

"How's that?"

"I need that security footage from when I broke into the Metropolitan. I have a feeling I wasn't the only one caught on camera."

"We retrieved that soon after I saved your sorry ass. And you are correct, the girl was seen alongside you."

Blind spots, my ass. "I thought as much. Broadcast that to my place at the right time. You'll know when. I'm sure you still have a few bugs in there." I couldn't see her smiling, but I knew she was.

"You have a plan? Been a while since I've seen you with a plan."

I scowled. "If my plan doesn't work … don't touch Allen. Ever. That is my only other demand."

"You mean request."

"No. Demand."

She snickered. "I don't know what's gotten into you, Elias, but I do believe you are a different man."

"You're goddamn right."

"I still can't decide — are you a liability or an asset?"

"I'll get back to you on that. Don't take it as a formal resignation yet, but give me a week."

She hesitated for a moment. "You'll be back."

I turned and walked away, not looking back behind me.

That went better than expected.

———

Back at my apartment, I sent out two calls: one to Allen to get it over here, the other to the FBI to tell Greaves I had both her killers. I didn't, obviously, but speaking to

Simone had made a part of my brain itch, that part that told me things didn't add up. I needed Allen with me, maybe just for emotional support. I had a hunch, and my track record hadn't been terribly bad as of late.

It was barely three in the morning, December 25. I sat on my couch, finishing up my book, trying to make each and every sentence stretch out in an effort to force time to slow down. My foot kept bouncing up and down, and the words failed to stick in my brain as I reread sentences over and over and over again. Until either Allen or the FBI arrived, I was accompanied by someone else.

"Never thought I'd see the day you turn yourself in," Masters said.

"You knew me for a week at most, asshole."

"Maybe. But you know you aren't talking to the real Masters, are you?"

I grunted in affirmation. "How long are you going to hang around?"

"I guess we'll see. Ever chased a ghost before?"

"Shut up."

"Of course you have. James was a ghost for years. And before him was Eddy, right? Looks like I'm just the newest iteration."

Down the hall, the elevator dinged as it arrived on my floor. I ran over to the TV and flipped it on. Static faded in slowly on the screen as the tubes warmed.

I breathed a sigh of relief upon seeing Allen walk through the door without knocking. Good. We'd have a moment to talk.

Its face was still pretty dented: half of the plates from its left cheek to its brow were busted up, making the right side of its face carry all the emotive weight. "Detective," it said softly.

"Allen."

"How are you?"

I sighed and dropped my shoulders. "Stressed. Numb. Just gross, really. I don't know what I'm doing or why. I know you're pissed at me for earlier, but it wasn't my action to take."

"I feel like you want to tell me something," it said.

"That's my line," I chuckled. "I wish I could tell you. Maybe another day. But right now, I need you to trust me. Can you do that one last time?"

Allen nodded. "I can."

The door opened again. This time, half a dozen agents entered, hands folded, jackets open for easy access to their guns. Greaves entered last, her outfit and hair immaculate, but her face betraying her exhaustion. She must have sprinted to get over here.

"I don't see two killers here," she stated.

"On the contrary," I said. "I see two. One more of an indirect killer, but two nonetheless."

She raised an eyebrow and walked across the room to look out the floor-to-ceiling windows. "Talking about yourself and the machine?"

"No, about you and me."

She didn't turn. "What are you insinuating?"

"You didn't expect me to catch the Vierling Killer, did you? You knew she was going to be hard to catch."

"Indeed, she's a quick one."

"Seems she's the only one, though." I lit a cigarette. "After all, you don't seem surprised to hear that it's a woman. You also, conveniently, didn't see her in the Met's security footage a day ago."

Greaves wasn't moving. The Black Hats weren't, either, but the quick glances they exchanged told me they didn't know as much as she did.

"Who would have the money to sponsor their own enforcer, and the resources to refurbish a weapon as unique as the Vierling? To put her up in one of the most expensive neighbourhoods outside the Upper East Side? Who would have the political power not only to push a general off the Plate, but to hide her own involvement in it while threatening him in order to keep her enforcer complacent? After all, a man like General Morane, whose mind is slipping, could easily have an 'accident' if your little patsy ever slipped up or threatened to run off."

Greaves didn't respond. Neither did her entourage.

"On top of that, who would be stupid enough to identify an Iron Hands safe house and send someone to burn it? Rossi was barely a blip on the map when it came to Maranzano's organization, which means your girl would have no real reason to chase him. Unless, that is, she was informed of Rossi's significance in another well-known criminal cartel."

I dropped my cigarette on the carpet. It wouldn't be the only blemish in my apartment today.

"If I've hit the nail on the head, tell me to stop," I said.

"I'm impressed, Roche. At your ability to leap to conclusions," Greaves said. "You don't have any evidence to back up these claims."

Right on cue, the Eye delivered on her promise.

The TV flickered as the signal was hijacked, and grainy, black-and-white security footage from the museum's rudimentary cameras came into focus. At first I was the only one visible in the museum, but eventually the angles showed me and Simone together. She had succeeded in escaping some of the cameras, but the ones near the Vierling had clearly captured her, as well as me.

"I don't see only one trespasser. Do you?"

I smirked. Allen was looking back and forth between the TV and Greaves. She, meanwhile, was altogether too calm, still looking out the window. No one said anything or moved. I could tell she was pissed. I could tell I was right.

Looks like I'm getting back into the swing of investigating.

"Get the cuffs on him, by any means necessary," Greaves said.

Some of the Black Hats reached for their guns. I widened my stance and placed my hand over my own, pushing Allen behind me with my free hand.

"You boys think you can draw faster than I can shoot?" I asked, my focus darting between the seven possible targets in my apartment. "Other cops have tried. Other cops have failed."

Greaves put up her hand to stay her agents. She looked at me, composed. "You said there were two killers in here, Roche. You made a case for me. Are you going to make one for yourself?"

"After I confirm one other hunch," I said, flexing my fingers over my Diamondback. "This wasn't your first time trying to dismantle the Iron Hands, was it? Masters hid his plans from everyone ... except you." Her eyes narrowed. *Yup, there we go.* "I gotta say, it felt really good when I fucked him up —"

She grabbed the pistol from one agent's belt. Allen leaped onto me, pushing us both behind the wall separating my living room from my kitchen.

"Get him, goddamn it!" Greaves screamed. The other G-Men jumped into action.

"You're insane!" Allen whisper-shouted at me.

"No, just decisive. Finally," I said, untangling myself from it as we shielded behind my kitchen cupboards.

One of the agents rounded the corner closest to the windows. Two bullets made him stumble back, the thermite rounds passing through him and weakening the glass enough to make him fall through.

"You okay fighting for your life?" I asked Allen.

In answer, it pulled out its Christmas present and chambered a bullet.

The crack of long-range ammunition told me that Allen's assistance might not be necessary. Another window broke, another G-Man slumped over the kitchen sink, blood pouring from a hole in his neck. Another fell behind the counter, slamming into the carpet. A third screamed, yelling about his leg being hit.

Allen and I made a break for the front door, a hail of bullets passing over us as we ran. I heard glass cracking again. Looking back, I could just make out a glimmer of chrome beyond the window, on the opposite rooftop.

There was heat. I went deaf, and everything turned black.

CHAPTER 27

I HAD TO FOLLOW ROCHE, had to know what he was planning.

His route took him to Central Park, which made staying hidden a challenge. I could see him wandering over the Bow Bridge, the other side of which was obscured from my view by bare tree branches. He spoke to someone, and it wasn't a wild guess as to who. I could hear everything from my hiding spot. It seemed he was under more pressure than I'd realized.

If I wanted to talk to her myself, I'd have to come here later.

Hours after Roche had left, as the day was waning, I made my own way to the Bow Bridge. It could be suicide, my setting up this meeting. But just letting things play out would be worse.

I did as Roche had and looked southward, waiting. An unnatural silence descended, my cue to turn. The Eye was leaning against the railing of the bridge, flanked by a legion of Red-eyes. We were both disguised, pretending to be someone else — she cloaked in darkness and her veil, me in my regular garb.

"Yes?" she asked impatiently.

"I'm here to make you an offer." I had an old Automatic voice box that scrambled my speech enough to hide my identity without making me unintelligible. It had come in handy more times than I cared to admit.

The Eye laughed. She was beside herself, laughing like I was doing a comedy routine. She wiped her eyes and exhaled.

"An offer? For me?"

"Yes."

"How generous! I hope what you're offering is your life, because that's all you have to bargain with. My people and my business have been put at risk by you, and I do not take that lightly. What on earth could you give me to make up for that?"

"I can give you Elias Roche."

"We already have a plan to rescue him. It'll be put into action soon. I assure you, we do not need your help."

"You do. After he's freed, then what? The supposed Vierling Killer is on the loose, along with the real one? Any more people I kill — Maranzano's or yours — he'll be blamed for it. And if he's associated with you, that'll make his life harder and, therefore, yours, too. It's all connected, all dominoes that can be knocked over where they are now, or redirected elsewhere. If you free him and kill Greaves, the city will find out who you are. If I free him …" I paused.

"I'm listening."

"What better way to save him than to have the actual Vierling Killer do it? His name is cleared, you get your enforcer back, I'm still wanted, and everyone's happy. He keeps doing jobs for you, and you keep paying him, without the need to move him from safe house to safe house every few days."

She rubbed her chin. "What do you offer in return?"

"Roche, like I said."

"Sweeten the deal."

"Fair enough. I melted a few parts of yours in Hell's, didn't I?"

"Indeed, you did. Burning down that safehouse put me back quite a lot …"

"I'm sure I can find a way to compensate you, monetarily or otherwise. And I won't touch another of your operations."

"Ever?"

"For three months. Then I'm fair game again. Kill me if you catch me."

The Eye grinned, still rubbing her chin, laughing to herself. "Anything else?"

"We both know who really sanctioned those hits on Maranzano's people and your safe house. She'll be at the meeting with Roche. I can take care of her."

The Eye laughed. "I like you! You should be working for me."

"We both know that would be a terrible idea."

"Truly. You have a deal. American Apartments, Bowery and Bayard, in one hour. Don't be late."

"I won't."

═══

I watched the meeting from the opposite rooftop. I had four barrels, but too many targets. Greaves was looking out the window, Roche and Allen stood in the centre of the living room, and there were six other FBI agents inside: two by the window, two by the far wall, one near the radio, another out of view. Damn it.

Greaves turned, speaking to Roche. His not putting up a fight must have surprised her.

Allen — had it just looked at me? Damnit, it had. It could see me. It had good eyes.

Greaves pulled a gun, and bullets began to fly. Time to call it.

Front trigger, left barrel: Greaves.

Glass shattered, but my bullet just missed her. She ran deeper into the apartment, behind the TV. *Goddamn it.*

Agent to the right of Greaves: back trigger, right barrel.

Down and out. Hit two that time, one in the neck, another in the chest. Good shot by me.

Middle trigger, centre barrel: he moved too early. Got his knee. That was fine.

I turned the barrel assembly 180 degrees and aimed. Last two were the guy nearest the windows and Greaves, backing away, trying to get into cover.

I yanked the trigger, only then seeing Roche and Allen making a beeline for the door, Greaves jumping behind a couch while firing on them.

The trigger was already pulled.

"Shit."

CHAPTER 28

I WOKE UP, MY BODY FREEZING. I felt like someone had used my head as a kickball and my body as a punching bag. I was afraid to open my eyes.

When I did, I saw Lower Manhattan from thirty stories up. I had to blink a few times to make sure that, yes, I was seeing things right. Much of my upper body was hanging out of my window frame. There were glass shards stuck in my chest. My body felt heavy, ringing like my deaf ears.

Allen was out cold, but its iron grip still held on to my ankle, preventing me from falling. My left arm was close to the radiator pipe near my window. I gripped it, using it as leverage to wrench my top half back into the apartment. Turning over, my hearing began to return: glass cracking under my weight, my own groans, the sounds of the street below. And sirens, too.

The FBI agents' bodies were strewn about the place, though some, I knew, had been thrown through my now broken windows. Greaves was nowhere to be seen, though the trail of blood from my overturned couch to the door might be hers. She was lucky my apartment was a Control Point.

I roused Allen, waiting for its blue bulbs to turn on, blinking as it recovered.

I pulled my right arm inside and tried to get up … but I couldn't. My legs were fine. So were my arms.

But not my hand. My right hand wasn't there. Just a bloody stump with white bone sticking out.

My hand.

My hand.

"My hand," I finally said.

Then it began to hit me.

"Fuck, fuck! My hand!"

Allen saw me panicking and got up. It grabbed me, lifted me over its shoulder, and ran into the hall. There were neighbours milling around, trying to see what the commotion was about, but Allen didn't slow down, bulldozing right through them.

We were outside the building when the shock got to me. Ambulances and cruisers were out front. The last thing I remembered was a pool of blood at Allen's feet. My blood.

"Someone!" Allen was yelling. "Someone, help! Help me, goddamn it!"

EPILOGUE

SURGERY HAD BEEN QUICK, but recovery was something else. It was December 31, and I was still in the hospital. Thankfully, I had capable people taking care of me.

"*Fraulein*, get out of my way!"

Capable enough.

Allen, after getting his face — yes, *his* face — fixed by Jaeger, had brought over our favourite Tinkerman to give my arm a new lease on life. He also gifted me some street clothes. He had gone back to my place after the whole ruckus, and he told me my apartment looked like a war zone. Figured.

Nightingale was looking me over, making sure the doctors didn't leave me with a staph infection out of negligence. I had just enough money to pay for the best public care available, but even so, I preferred Nightingale be here. The personal connection set my mind at ease.

"How does it feel?" She was attentive and irritated at how Jaeger treated me more like a machine than a person, or so she'd muttered.

I looked at my stump, now adorned with some extra features. My ulna was intact, but my radius had been shattered by the detonation, so much of it had been replaced. There was a nice lengthwise scar running from my wrist to just below my elbow, with bolts and stitches visible in the skin. The tip of my arm where my wrist should have been was capped with a titanium pit; the socket in the bottom connected to my nerve endings. The hand they had outfitted me with was top of the line: silicon fingertip pads, full reticulated movement, and greater flexibility than I'd had in my old human appendage. The only problem was that I couldn't feel it.

"Try to give us a fist, Elias."

I did so. The metal joints worked, soundless and fluid, and curled the hand into a fist. It was weird. I made the movements, same as I had before, and expected to feel my fingertips against my palm and my skin stretching. Instead, I felt a weird tugging at my wrist from the muscles pulling at the titanium cup.

"Good." Nightingale smiled and checked the IV drip over my bed. "Any pain or discomfort? Beyond what we've already discussed."

"Yeah, my fingertips."

She picked up my left hand and moved my fingers. "That could be due to some shrapnel, or maybe nerve damage. That should rectify itself in a few —"

"My other fingertips."

She released my left hand and sighed. "I'm afraid that's going to be around for some time, Elias. Phantom pain is common in amputees. You're lucky you've got something to replace what you lost."

"Yeah."

She withdrew, and Jaeger took over. The crazy German looked even more strung out than before. His business must be booming, what with the Iron Hands and the Maranzano Mafia throwing Automatics to their deaths left and right. But, out of the kindness of his heart — and a hearty tip — he'd decided to take care of me for the day.

"Now, it will take time to get used to the new hand," he began. "Might be some stinging or shocks, possibly loss of control due to muscle spasms. No need to be concerned, it will go away with time. Try to stick with your left hand for delicate tasks, however."

I nodded. "Of course."

"No pain? No other tugging?"

"I'm good, Karl."

"Just be careful. This is top of the line stuff from Desoutter, there is literally nothing better. Their warranty program is good, but even so, new hands are expensive, almost as much as an entire Automatic. And be sure to clean the plugs for the first few months. We don't need you developing Rustrot."

"What the hell is that?"

"Trust me, you don't want to know." Jaeger tipped his hat and left the room. "Rudi, where the hell did you go?" he called out. "I swear, if you've disappeared again ..." The rest was muffled as he walked away.

Allen had been hanging back respectfully, but now he approached me, concern on his face.

"You okay, Al?" I asked.

"I'm fine, Roche. How do you feel?"

"Just peachy," I chuckled. "Looks like we're turning into one another. Next thing you know I'll be getting blue bulbs put in my head."

"Don't talk like that," Allen said.

"It's just a hand, Al, don't worry. I've lost more before and still kept going."

Nightingale pulled the IV from my arm, capped the vein, and had me apply pressure. There was a knock at the door. Allen went to answer it. His expression transformed to one of suspicion, but he moved aside regardless. Simone Morane stepped in, looking pale.

"Night, thank you for everything," I said to the doc.

"You're very welcome, Elias," she responded, brushing past Simone on her way out.

Allen stayed where he was as Simone approached the bed, though he followed her with his eyes the entire time. She had a bunch of flowers. Where had she gotten those at this time of year?

"How do you feel?" She was acting like I was on death's door. I almost could have been, and she'd've been the one to put me there.

"Could be better."

"Elias, I'm so sorry for this. I never meant ... I pulled the trigger just as you and Allen were trying to get out. I didn't —"

"Some forewarning might have been helpful. We could have avoided all this if you'd told us your plans!"

Allen's voice was hard and growing louder. He was angry. I hadn't known he could get this angry.

"Warning you would have compromised the situation," Simone said.

"And *this* hasn't? Do you understand what a missing hand means for him?"

"Allen, calm down." I put up my right hand, waving him down. It was still weird to move it without feeling it. "I do understand what you did, Simone, but you put yourself in plenty more danger by going against your former employer."

Allen put his hands on his hips and groaned. "The *capek* will wait outside until you two are ready." He stormed out of the room, being sure to give Simone as wide a berth and as dirty a look as possible. *Yikes.*

"It was bound to happen eventually," she began after Allen had left. "I did have to make a deal with a few devils to get my father to safety, but at least I know he won't just disappear one day. It puts my mind somewhat at ease. Greaves will be gunning for me and me alone. And I'm glad you're okay, too."

"Oh, she was upset to find out I survived that explosion. Well, more nervous than upset." I snickered, rolled to face my bedside table, and showed her an envelope from the FBI. "Now she's trying to buy my silence."

"Really?"

"A fresh scrub of my files at the FBI, plus my name removed from certain secret lists … It's enticing, but I don't think she knows that I'm not the one with all the evidence. I'm going to milk it for all it's worth, though."

Simone laughed. "You really enjoy flirting with the edge, even from a hospital bed."

I shrugged. "It's in my nature."

She gave a half-hearted smile. "What are you going to do now?"

"My apartment is trashed, as is the one above it, so two people are out of a home. Allen and I discussed sharing his place. Not a bad idea, considering it's better than the street. I might refurbish the old place once they fix the supports, maybe rent it out, make some side cash."

"You own it?"

"Sort of. It's a long story."

Awkward silence surrounded us.

"Shall we?" I asked.

"Yeah, let's go."

She helped me up from the bed. Walking around with more weight attached to my wrist than before was jarring; it made my shoulders sit unevenly. The hand was nimble, but it was surprisingly heavy. Outside my room, Allen followed us to reception, not attempting to hide his animosity toward Simone.

I put my hands on the counter and asked for the bill. When the paper was slid toward me, the number made my chest hurt. The well of money the Eye had provided was now closed off, and after factoring in my lost apartment safety deposit and this hospital bill, I didn't have much left. Meanwhile, Allen had spent the last bit of his money on Jaeger's services. The poor bastard was running on a trickle of cash. And so was I.

"Oh, sir, my mistake," the receptionist said, pulling the paper back and looking it over. "It seems your stay has already been paid for."

"What? By who?"

She rummaged around her desk for a moment. "They chose to remain anonymous, but ... it left this for you."

It. The Rabbit.

She handed me a small envelope. I was getting more mail now than I'd gotten over the past few years. A small folded note. Formal cursive in the centre of the page. It wasn't signed.

Now you can truly be my Iron Hand.

I crumpled the note and threw it in the trash. I wasn't that name anymore, and that name was no longer me. I looked at my hand, making a fist again, unable to feel it. The hand that wasn't there.

"Who was it from?" Allen asked.

"Just ... no one."

"No one, mm-hmm."

"Later, Allen."

We made our way to the hospital entrance. Before Allen and I could leave to find my car, Simone stopped me.

"Do you mind if I give you a ride home? We need to talk."

"I don't think that's a good idea," Allen interjected. "For all I know, you'll finish the job and drop his corpse off on my doorstep."

I agreed with Allen, but I had my own things to say to her.

"I'll see you there, Al." He grimaced at me. "I'll be fine! If I do die, you'll know who to look for."

"Yeah, it'd be poetic justice ..." His voice trailed off as he left.

═══

Despite having said she wanted to talk, she didn't speak until we stopped in front of Allen's place. I placed a cigarette between my new fingers and lit it, as always noting the eye engraved on my lighter.

"Elias, about what happened ..."

"Don't worry about it." The smoke tasted bitter. More bitter than usual, that was.

"Allen is right, a missing hand is catastrophic —"

"Hey, a bit of positivity while I'm in earshot?" I forced a laugh to ease the tension. "I made a decision and I believe it was the correct one. At least, I have no reason to doubt it."

"I never thanked you for ... well, saving my skin. From the FBI, from the Mobs, from everyone. I owe you."

"You don't owe me nothing, Morane. Er, Mercier ... whichever you prefer."

"At least let me make it up to you."

"How do you plan on doing that?"

I wasn't sure what to expect until her lips met mine.

She pulled away, and I sat in stunned silence. She was soft, vulnerable, and I was ... unsure how to process this.

"It's all I can really give you," she said.

"Uh, yeah."

She looked at me. "Was that wrong?"

"I mean, confusing ..." I said.

"I just thought ... I don't know. I'm not one for admitting my feelings to people, but with you, it felt natural. It felt right. Of all the people I've ever met, dated, killed ... you're the only person I've really connected with. No one else understands what I've been through."

"Any war vet would —"

"No, not any war vet. And you aren't just a war vet. I can tell that you lost something or someone just as I did. The fact that you know that kind of loss, that pain, that rage that builds inside and takes root forever ... You understand me. But ... you don't share that need to be understood, it seems."

"Simone, I'm not one for opening up to anyone, either, not even to myself. I'm sorry I can't be the one to give you comfort or solace. The War wasn't what changed me. It stopped me from going back to my old life, but that's not what made me jump at the chance to work for the Iron Hands. I lost people — someone in particular — and that changed me. We do understand each other, but not in a way where we can be something."

"I see." She nodded, looking away. It felt disgusting to crush her like this, but it was better than giving her false hope.

"But ..." I started. This was going to be hard to explain. "Allen does, or did, have some sort of attraction to you."

"Allen?" She almost laughed. "Really? Doesn't seem to anymore."

"No argument there. It's unconventional, I know. And it seems to be causing a rift between him and me ... I guess he thinks I saved you for some other reason than I've said. I just thought you should know. He's a good guy."

"You mean 'it'?"

"No. *He.*"

She smirked. "Getting soft, huh? I mean, I don't have a problem with Automatics, but I'm not an Autophile, or whatever they call them. I just don't get that, by the way, attraction between machines and humans. I mean, who on earth would fall in love with a machine?"

She looked back at me, my expression, and I didn't need to answer. A rush of guilt made her put a hand over her mouth.

"Oh," she said.

"Yeah."

"I didn't mean anything by it."

"I know."

"Was it ..." She was struggling with the issue. She took a breath, recomposing herself. "I mean, it couldn't have been too long ago. Was she nice? Special?"

Time to bite the bullet.

"Yeah, he was."

And there it was. Everything clicked in her head: her eyes widened, and she flushed with embarrassment. "Oh, my God. Sorry!" She covered her mouth again as though the exclamation had escaped her mouth by mistake. "I never meant to ... when I ..."

"Simone, stop. You couldn't have known."

"Does Allen know?"

"I don't know. He's good at picking up on some things, but ... the only people who definitely know are Robins and my parents, that's it. Not even Sinclair. I don't even want to imagine what he'd say if he ever found out."

Simone looked shaken, blinking rapidly. "I never would have conceived it."

"It's fine, that's the usual reaction. I've been pretending to be someone else for a long time. I think I should be true to myself for once. I think I've earned that."

She sighed, taking some more breaths.

"Hey," I said, grinning, "there is a way for you to repay me for saving your ass. My birthday is in a few days. I wouldn't mind a letter or something on the sixth."

"Maybe," she said, more comfortable.

I gave her a wink and exited the car. I started to ascend the concrete stairs to the entrance when a voice jarred me.

"IT'S ALMOST BEEN A WEEK," it said, from out of view. "YOU PLAN ON GIVING HER AN ANSWER SOON?"

"I still have a day, capek," I said without turning. I was too tired to deal with it. Or with her.

═══════

Allen's place was the first apartment on the ground floor. It was small. Very small. But I could make it work for the time being. He was cutting open mail with his paper knife and he looked up to greet me as I entered. I spotted something I hadn't expected to see on his little dining room table: a brass box about the size of a cigarette holder. He noticed me leering at it and swiped it quickly, stuffing it into a pocket.

"Have a good *talk* on the way here?" he asked.

I groaned. "Al, it ain't like that."

"You say that far too often these days." He stabbed at one of the letters, cutting clean through the centre. "Why did you really save her?"

"I told you why."

"For some reason, I don't believe you."

"Regardless of what you believe, it's the truth. I don't know what it would take to make you believe me. Of course I have feelings for people sometimes, just not her." I built up my backbone and didn't beat around the bush for once. "You ain't the only one who's ever been betrayed. Or the only one to experience shit. If you're insinuating something, you'd best just say it."

Allen looked a little less mad, but I could still feel tension emanating from him.

"You've been referring to me as 'he' for a week or so now," he said, ignoring my previous prompt.

"Yeah."

"Do I remind you of your car or something now?"

I chuckled. "No, no ..."

"Did something about my saving your ass trigger the part of your brain that treats machines with decency?"

I coughed and looked at the ground. What was I supposed to say? That these days, he reminded me of my scrapped partner? He was smart enough to deduce things; he could go back through all our past interactions and cut through the subtext. Would he think our friendship up to this point had been disingenuous?

"People refer to Automatics as objects because they don't want to see them as people," I began. "Until now, I wanted to see everyone as an object because it was easier to cope with loss if what got destroyed was a piece of property, not a person. I wanted to distance myself from everything that reminded me of that person — including you — to avoid feeling pain. But I shouldn't anymore. It's complicated."

"Everything with you is complicated." Allen returned to opening letters, but with a normal amount of force this time. "You going to talk to the Eye soon? You only have a day left."

"Great, now I got two of you hounding me."

He looked up from the letter he was holding. "What do you mean?"

I didn't sense any more hostility, but unease lingered between us.

"Nothing."

"You do know letting this go could cause irreparable damage, right? Simone will rip this city apart," he stated. "She'll destroy this uneasy peace you've built. And if you up and leave, the Hands will resort to other, less humane methods to reassert their dominance. Just being employed by them, letting them trade on your name, could mitigate the damage."

"I have a day, Allen," I repeated. "And if what I built is a constant state of fear and oppression, then … it might be better to let it burn."

Midway through opening a letter, Allen stabbed the letter opener into the table in frustration.

"Do you know what you're doing, Elias?"

I looked back at him. He was a changed man, machine, whatever. I shrugged.

"No, I don't."

ABOUT THE AUTHOR

BRENDEN CARLSON is a chemist and D&D dungeon master with a love for hard science fiction, tabletop role-playing games, and art house movies. A postmodernist by circumstance, he has a master's degree in organic chemistry, focusing on the catalysis of isocyanides with other unpronounceable compounds. Combining his love of history and classic sci-fi authors, he began his writing career with the Walking Shadows science fiction series. He lives in Hamilton, Ontario.

Victor Lessard Thrillers
by Martin Michaud
(QUEBEC THRILLER, POLICE
PROCEDURAL)
Never Forget
Without Blood
Coming soon: *The Devil's Choir*

The Day She Died
by S.M. Freedman
(DOMESTIC THRILLER, PSYCHOLOGICAL)

Amanda Doucette Mysteries
by Barbara Fradkin
(FEMALE SLEUTH, WILDERNESS)
Fire in the Stars
The Trickster's Lullaby
Prisoners of Hope
The Ancient Dead

The Candace Starr Series
by C.S. O'Cinneide
(NOIR, HITWOMAN, DARK HUMOUR)
The Starr Sting Scale
Starr Sign

Stonechild & Rouleau Mysteries
by Brenda Chapman
(INDIGENOUS SLEUTH, KINGSTON,
POLICE PROCEDURAL)
Cold Mourning
Butterfly Kills
Tumbled Graves
Shallow End
Bleeding Darkness
Turning Secrets
Closing Time

Tell Me My Name
by Erin Ruddy
(DOMESTIC THRILLER, DARK SECRETS)

The Walking Shadows
by Brenden Carlson
(ALTERNATE HISTORY, ROBOTS)
Night Call
Midnight

Creature X Mysteries
by J.J. Dupuis
(CRYPTOZOOLOGY, FEMALE SLEUTH)
Roanoke Ridge
Lake Crescent

Birder Murder Mysteries
by Steve Burrows
(BIRDING, BRITISH COASTAL TOWN)
A Siege of Bitterns
A Pitying of Doves
A Cast of Falcons
A Shimmer of Hummingbirds
A Tiding of Magpies
A Dance of Cranes

B.C. Blues Crime
by R.M. Greenaway
(BRITISH COLUMBIA, POLICE
PROCEDURAL)
Cold Girl
Undertow
Creep
Flights and Falls
River of Lies
Five Ways to Disappear

Jenny Willson Mysteries
by Dave Butler
(NATIONAL PARKS, ANIMAL PROTECTION)
Full Curl
No Place for Wolverines
In Rhino We Trust

Jack Palace Series
by A.G. Pasquella
(NOIR, TORONTO, MOB)
Yard Dog
Carve the Heart
Season of Smoke

The Falls Mysteries
by J.E. Barnard
(RURAL ALBERTA, FEMALE SLEUTH)
When the Flood Falls
Where the Ice Falls
Why the Rock Falls

ABOUT THE AUTHOR

BLAKE GIROUX PHOTOGRAPHY

BRENDEN CARLSON is a chemist and D&D dungeon master with a love for hard science fiction, tabletop role-playing games, and art house movies. A postmodernist by circumstance, he has a master's degree in organic chemistry, focusing on the catalysis of isocyanides with other unpronounceable compounds. Combining his love of history and classic sci-fi authors, he began his writing career with the Walking Shadows science fiction series. He lives in Hamilton, Ontario.

Victor Lessard Thrillers
by Martin Michaud
(QUEBEC THRILLER, POLICE
PROCEDURAL)
Never Forget
Without Blood
Coming soon: *The Devil's Choir*

The Day She Died
by S.M. Freedman
(DOMESTIC THRILLER, PSYCHOLOGICAL)

Amanda Doucette Mysteries
by Barbara Fradkin
(FEMALE SLEUTH, WILDERNESS)
Fire in the Stars
The Trickster's Lullaby
Prisoners of Hope
The Ancient Dead

The Candace Starr Series
by C.S. O'Cinneide
(NOIR, HITWOMAN, DARK HUMOUR)
The Starr Sting Scale
Starr Sign

Stonechild & Rouleau Mysteries
by Brenda Chapman
(INDIGENOUS SLEUTH, KINGSTON,
POLICE PROCEDURAL)
Cold Mourning
Butterfly Kills
Tumbled Graves
Shallow End
Bleeding Darkness
Turning Secrets
Closing Time

Tell Me My Name
by Erin Ruddy
(DOMESTIC THRILLER, DARK SECRETS)

The Walking Shadows
by Brenden Carlson
(ALTERNATE HISTORY, ROBOTS)
Night Call
Midnight

Creature X Mysteries
by J.J. Dupuis
(CRYPTOZOOLOGY, FEMALE SLEUTH)
Roanoke Ridge
Lake Crescent

Birder Murder Mysteries
by Steve Burrows
(BIRDING, BRITISH COASTAL TOWN)
A Siege of Bitterns
A Pitying of Doves
A Cast of Falcons
A Shimmer of Hummingbirds
A Tiding of Magpies
A Dance of Cranes

B.C. Blues Crime
by R.M. Greenaway
(BRITISH COLUMBIA, POLICE
PROCEDURAL)
Cold Girl
Undertow
Creep
Flights and Falls
River of Lies
Five Ways to Disappear

Jenny Willson Mysteries
by Dave Butler
(NATIONAL PARKS, ANIMAL PROTECTION)
Full Curl
No Place for Wolverines
In Rhino We Trust

Jack Palace Series
by A.G. Pasquella
(NOIR, TORONTO, MOB)
Yard Dog
Carve the Heart
Season of Smoke

The Falls Mysteries
by J.E. Barnard
(RURAL ALBERTA, FEMALE SLEUTH)
When the Flood Falls
Where the Ice Falls
Why the Rock Falls